be with me

ALSO BY
JESSICA CUNSOLO

She's With Me

Stay With Me

Still With Me

be with me

JESSICA CUNSOLO

wattpad books

wattpad books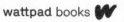

An imprint of Wattpad WEBTOON Book Group

Published in Canada by Wattpad WEBTOON Book Group, a division of Wattpad Corp.

36 Wellington Street E., Suite 200

Toronto, ON M5E 1C7 Canada

www.wattpad.com

First Wattpad Books edition: January 2023

ISBN 978-1-99025-970-8 (Trade paperback original)
ISBN 978-1-99025-971-5 (eBook edition)

Library and Archives Canada Cataloguing in Publication information is available upon request.

Printed and bound in Canada

1 3 5 7 9 10 8 6 4 2

Cover design by Mumtaz Mustafa

Images © Pekic via Getty Images

To those of us who sometimes feel lonely.

prologue

No one warns you how much blood there will be when you stab someone in the neck. But unless an artery was hit or today is the exception, there is a gory, horror-movie amount of blood seeping out of Stan Roven's neck. It's splattered all over me, my white work uniform, the mattress, the carpet.

My younger sister, Gia, gazes up at me from where she's cowering against the headboard, bruises already forming on her tan skin.

"Siena," she gasps, wiping at the splash of blood on her face with a shaky hand. "He . . . I . . ."

"It's okay," I shush her, approaching the slumped body

on the bed. He's lying facedown on the mattress Gia and I share, his neck hanging over the edge, causing the blood to drip onto the carpet.

Gia wraps her arms around her legs, hugging them to herself and trying to hold together the torn edges of her shirt. There's barely any blood on her. "Is he . . . ?"

"Dead," I confirm. Living in this sleazy building on the wrong side of Los Angeles means we always tried to be careful, especially with the number of strangers regularly traipsing through our apartment, so we kept a large kitchen knife in the bedside drawer for emergencies, though we never really thought we'd have to use it. Now that same knife is sticking out of Stan's neck.

Gia shudders, her tiny body seeming even smaller than usual. "He just . . . burst in here from the party. I tried fighting him off, I swear."

"It's all right, Gia. Everything's going to be fine." I think I'm in shock. I don't feel scared or panicked or petrified. I feel numb. Numb mixed with hatred for Stan Roven and what he was trying to do to Gia—a fifteen-year-old girl barely a quarter his size—before I walked in. Outside the walls of our measly ten-by-ten bedroom, Aunt Julie's party rages on. It's a wonder none of our neighbors ever call the cops on us, but they're probably here too, probably just as high as our aunt.

"What do we do?" Gia whispers, still staring at Stan's pale face like he might start swinging at her.

"Stan?" Aunt Julie's voice is right outside our bedroom door. "Where did you go?"

Gia's panicked eyes meet mine, and I know I have to keep Aunt Julie away from this room, at least long enough to give me time to think.

I grab a cardigan that's escaped the gore and put it on over my shirt, wrapping the ends tight against myself before slipping into the hallway.

"Siena!" Aunt Julie exclaims, a baggie of cocaine dropping to the floor. "You scared me. Have you seen Stan?"

Yes. He's dead on my bed with a knife sticking out of his throat.

At my blank look, she sighs with impatience. "Did he leave? Did you insult him? You know he was about to give me my big break! The one I've been waiting for forever!" She plucks the baggie she dropped from the floor and gives it a little shake as if to make sure it's all still there. "I'll finally be famous for something other than being Florence Bowen's sister . . . what's that on your chin?"

I furiously wipe what I'm sure is blood away. "Nothing," I say, wrapping the cardigan tighter around me. I just need to get her out of here. I'm not sure what I'll do next, but dealing with Gia is my first priority, and I'll figure out the rest later.

Her bloodshot eyes go from my face to the white carpet on the floor. "What's that?" she asks, pointing at the deep-red liquid seeping from under the door.

"Nothing!" I exclaim quickly, but she pushes past me into the room before I can stop her, and gasps at the sight.

Gia freezes where she is trying to sop up the blood on the carpet, and Aunt Julie's face turns white. She stumbles until her back hits the wall, and she grasps at it as if trying to stay upright.

"No," she says, shaking her head rapidly. "What—this can't be real." She blinks rapidly, trying to clear off whatever drug-induced fog is wrapped around her brain.

Gia jumps up and I scramble to her side, wrapping my arm around her and pulling her close.

Gia's voice trembles as she speaks. "Aunt Julie . . . he was—"

"Save it." Aunt Julie holds up her hand. She refuses to look at the body sprawled on the bed. "As your mother's sister, I thought I had seen it all, but this . . . Florence never did anything like *this*."

Tears form in Gia's eyes, and she clings to me harder.

"But . . . Siena was . . ." Gia can barely get the words out as tears stream down her face. "It was . . ."

"Self-defense," I finish for her.

Aunt Julie holds her arms out toward us, like she's preparing for us to pounce at her. Keeping her back against the wall, she slides toward the door. "I'm calling the police," she says, sniffling and rubbing her nose with the back of her hand. "I did your mother a favor when she dumped you here so she could flounce around LA doing God knows what, but this is too much. I can't do it anymore. I don't care if you're able to track Florence down for long enough to convince her to take you back or not, but you're not welcome here anymore."

My heart drops. She's kicking us out? She's the only family we have left since Mom dumped us here five years ago. I'll deal with the consequences regarding Stan, but Gia has nowhere to go.

"Aunt Julie, please—"

She cuts me off. "No, Siena." She stands in the hallway now, still refusing to turn her back to us. Behind her, the party continues, everyone too drunk or high to care about what happened to Stan or their host. Aunt Julie points at me as she retreats. "You may have your father's last name, but you're your mother's daughter through and through, even *worse* than her." And then she's gone.

Gia bursts into tears and crushes my rib cage with her grip. "I'm scared," she blubbers. "I can't—I can't lose you. I can't survive in—"

"Hey, it's okay," I shush her, tucking her hair behind her ear. My voice is strong and confident despite the frantic beating of my heart. "We're going to be okay. I'm going to take care of you, just like I always do, okay?"

She nods and shivers between quiet sobs, releasing her grip just long enough for me to slide a sweater over her torn shirt.

I don't know how long we stand there, with me

whispering reassurances in Gia's ear as she clings to me. Long enough for Aunt Julie to clear the apartment of people and drugs. Long enough for her to call the cops. Long enough for them to arrest me for killing Stan Roven.

one

The modern two-story house in the middle of the suburbs couldn't be any more different from the drab gray cement walls of the detention center where I spent the last three weeks. I stare at it from the sidewalk, a backpack containing my favorite belongings dangling from my shoulder. The house looks like it's straight out of a movie, the place where the pretty girl next door would live, and where she'd fall in love with the hunky football player who never noticed her. There are flowers lining the walkway, recently mowed grass, and an actual welcome mat, although it doesn't make me feel welcome.

The house belongs to my dad. The same dad who forgot to pick me up from the airport. I don't know why I'm surprised; he's forgotten about my existence ever since he walked out on us when I could barely walk. But for some reason, despite knowing almost nothing about the man except that he was alive somewhere, I thought he'd show up. I also thought he'd answer my call, but he let me down there too, so I had to Uber here.

After Aunt Julie washed her hands of us, I spent countless nights wondering if Gia and I would be split up in foster care. So when the lawyers told me Dario Amato was taking us in, I was shocked. Hell, I thought the odds of Mom coming back from wherever she's off galivanting were higher. The man hasn't sent me so much as a birthday card in fourteen years, and he's opening his house to us? I don't know why he's stepping up to be a father, now of all times, but I don't care. Anywhere Gia and I can be together is good enough for me.

I stare at the pretty house that's so at odds with where I pictured my father living. I don't want to go in yet; I can't bring myself to move toward the front door. The thought of stepping inside the house nauseates me. I just need some fresh air; ever since being released, I can never get enough fresh air.

After leaving us, Dario moved back to King City, the town where he grew up, the town where he met Mom. It's *so* quiet here. I can literally hear the birds chirping, and a neighbor a street over mowing his lawn. How long has it been since I've just had *quiet*? Not on our block in LA, where there always seemed to be shouting, sirens, and other activity throughout the day and night, not in the detention center, and definitely not inside our apartment, since Aunt Julie loved having people over. The silence makes me uneasy.

It's going to be better here. It has to be better here.

Gia's in there somewhere. I haven't seen her since they hauled us off in different police cars, but the lawyer told me she was released almost immediately and sent to live with our dad. This has been the longest I've gone without seeing her, and the monitored phone calls I've had with her just weren't the same as *being* with her, especially after what happened.

My phone vibrates in my back pocket, and I pull it out to see a missed call from an unknown number.

"Hey!" a voice calls, taking me so off guard that I drop my phone on the sidewalk.

A girl around my age is standing on the neighbor's driveway. Even with dark circles under her eyes, she's so well put together and perfect looking. Her long hair is dyed a dark auburn and curled in loose waves. She's even dressed impeccably, like she's getting ready for a runway show at five on a Friday night.

"I saw you from my window." She points at the second floor of her house. "You've been standing there for a while. You must be Gia's sister, Siena. She talks about you a lot; I feel like I already know you."

I edge closer to her, placing her from Gia's phone calls. "Are you Lily? Lily Liu?"

She smiles and crosses the grass separating us to stand with me. I don't know how she does it, considering she's in red stilettos, but she traverses over the uneven grass and gravel with such grace it seems like her feet aren't even hurting and her ankles aren't at risk of twisting.

She must realize my train of thought because she waves me off. "It *doesn't* come naturally, trust me. Lots of practicing in heels at summer modeling camp. It got a lot better once I grew out of my awkward braces and gangly limbs stage."

Modeling camp makes sense. Gia told me Lily wants to be famous, and once her parents found out where Gia was from, they grilled her about every famous person they could think of, as if everyone from LA knows all the celebrities.

Lily eyes me, and I've never felt more disheveled and unkempt than right now under her scrutiny. "You don't look much like Gia. You're poutier and not as tan. And your hair is pink."

My face must turn as pink as my hair. "Only the ends," I say, holding my hair up as if she can't already see it. "Gia was bored one day, so she dyed my hair pink and then did hers to match."

She did a good job too. The pink blends into the blonde, so it doesn't look like there's a straight line of pink going across the bottom half of my hair. It's growing out now, and the pink is super faded.

Lily's lips purse. "Gia doesn't have hair. Or she does, but it's shaved short in a pixie cut."

I didn't know Gia shaved her hair.

My phone, still on the ground, vibrates, and I grab it, groaning when it's clear the screen is shattered. But after dusting it off, I breathe a sigh of relief when the screen lights up, showing I have another missed call from the same number. The phone works, but the top fourth of the screen remains black. Annoying and inconvenient, yes, but still usable.

"Are you starting school with us in two days?" Lily asks. She's pretty chatty considering this is the first time she's met me, and after hours of isolation and travel, I can't decide if I find her friendliness welcome or annoying.

"Yes. I'm going to be a senior at King City High." The same high school my parents went to way back in the day.

Lily's face lights up. "No way! Me too! Listen, there's a party tonight. Warren is throwing it as a 'goodbye summer' thing. You need to come! I can introduce you to my friends so you know people when you start on Monday."

"I don't know . . ." I mumble.

"Siena?" a voice calls. A woman in her late thirties rounds the garage and comes into view. "Siena!" she repeats, coming right up to me. "I thought I heard you out here. I called you a few times to ask when your plane landed, but you're already here! Your dad told me you were coming in today, but not what time."

I blink at this woman I've never met before. She must

be Stella, my father's younger sister. I never knew I had another aunt—a *zia*, to be exact—but Gia said she's nice enough.

She reaches out as if she's going to throw her arms around me but then hesitates. She reaches out again as if to shake my hand but then stops herself. She settles on patting me on the shoulder, and I force myself to remain still.

"Um, hi . . . Zia Stella," I say, the words sounding weird even to me. "I just took an Uber here."

She frowns and finally drops her hand from my shoulder. "Next time call me. You have my number, right?"

Technically I do now since she called me, so I nod. I wonder if it's just as weird for her to suddenly have two teenage nieces. Gia says she comes around to Dario's a lot to check in even though she works weird hours as an ER doctor, and that she doesn't have any kids.

"Hey Stella," Lily says, surprising me. I forgot she was here. "I was just inviting Siena to a small get-together tonight with my friends. Don't worry, it's nothing crazy; you know my parents would never let me go anywhere that could get out of hand. Is it okay if she comes?"

Zia Stella's eyes light up. "Of course it's okay! Thank you for extending the invitation, Lily. It'll be good for you to meet some new people, Siena."

"Shouldn't I ask Dario . . . ?" I start, but Zia Stella waves me off.

"Oh, no bother," she says, her tone turning apologetic. "He's at a friend's house watching some game. He won't be back until late, so I'm sure he won't mind if you go out."

Her words shouldn't bother me, but they sit heavily on my chest. He *knew* I was landing today, Zia Stella even confirmed it, and he couldn't even *pretend* to want to meet his daughter for the first time in years?

The garage to Lily's house opens and a woman calls out to her, followed by some shouting in Chinese. Lily winces and turns to her house. "I'm coming!" she shouts before turning back to me. "Sorry, I have to get to a dress fitting. It's just a small shoot, but my agent told Mom this one could be the one that kick-starts my career, so she's been riding my butt about it." She pats under her eyes to get rid of the nonexistent mascara smudges.

"It's all right," I say to Lily as a BMW backs out of her garage, and Zia Stella steps closer to say hi to Lily's mom.

Lily grabs the phone from my hand. "Let me put my number in your phone. Oh shit. You need a new phone. What's your passcode? I'll add myself to your contacts."

I'm too stunned to do anything other than give her my passcode and watch her enter her contact information. I take the phone back from her and text her my name like she asks.

"Siena Amato," she recites from my text, presumably saving my number when she taps the screen. "I'll text you when I'm heading out tonight. Be ready around eight thirty. But anyway, I've got to go." She surprises me when she leans in and wraps her arms around me. I'm about to return the hug but freeze when she says into my ear, "I know you're

Florence's daughter, and I know what happened in LA. I overheard Gia talking to your aunt about it." My blood runs cold in my veins. "But don't worry," she continues, "I won't tell anyone you killed a guy; it sounds like he deserved it."

She pulls away from me, and my arms hang uselessly at my sides as I stare at her. I can't read her face, can't tell what she's thinking.

"So happy you're here." She smiles, then struts over to her car. I can do nothing but watch her go, rooted to the spot as my heart pounds.

"That was nice of her," Zia Stella says as she rejoins me, completely oblivious to the tension in my body. "It will be nice for you to make some friends."

I focus on a pebble on the sidewalk, too distracted by Lily's declaration to pay attention to Zia Stella's words. "Right."

"I'm going to order pizza for dinner," Zia Stella says, breaking the awkward silence. "What do you want on it?"

"Anything's fine," I force out.

I don't bother telling her I don't feel like eating anyway. How can I when my stomach's in knots, and my throat feels like I've swallowed rocks?

I don't want to be known for what happened with Stan, and I don't want to be known as the daughter of Florence Bowen, a B-list actress who's in the media more for scandals and arrests than her movies. I just want to be normal, want people to see me as Siena Amato, not part of the media circus that followed my arrest. The media only really cared *because* I'm Florence's daughter, and any scandal relating to her is prime clickbait. The only good thing about being seventeen is that everything the media said was "speculation" and from unnamed sources and couldn't be proven since I'm a minor and the courts can't release my name. However, it doesn't help that the "unnamed source" was undoubtedly Aunt Julie, happy to share how fucked up her niece is, how I'm just like my mom. No doubt she's waiting until I turn eighteen to get her name in the papers and claim her fifteen minutes of fame. I wouldn't be surprised if she wrote a book about me and Mom. She tried to write one about Mom before but didn't have the patience to sit and write more than a few incoherent chapters. Now that there's renewed interest in Florence Bowen, she might stop snorting cocaine long enough to pull it together. But I don't want that legacy to follow me here, and I don't want that for Gia either.

"Zia Stella," a voice calls, followed by the front door slamming. "I thought you said we were going to be late . . ." The words trail off as Gia comes into view, freezing as she sees me.

It's only been weeks, but it feels like forever since I've seen her. Her hair really is different—it's a classic pixie cut now, with the sides shaved and short, sideswept bangs, and it looks so good on her heart-shaped face.

She stands there, staring at me for a moment, before she breaks into a sprint and launches herself into my arms. Her tiny frame throws me off balance for a moment before I steady us and return the tight hug.

"You're back!" she exclaims, "I thought Zia Stella was leaving for the airport later?"

"There was a communication mix-up," I say because Zia Stella is here, and I don't want to bad-mouth her brother right in front of her.

Gia pulls back and gently twists a strand of my hair in her fingers. "Well, I'm so happy you're here. I've missed you."

She glances up at me with her big brown doe eyes, and all the things left unsaid pass between us. I know it's been hard for Gia, and I can't imagine what she's been going through without me here to talk to, without anyone really to talk to since her girlfriend broke up with her, citing long distance, though Gia was brief when telling me about it over the phone.

"I missed you too," I say, scanning her. If it's possible, it looks like she's even smaller than the last time I saw her. I hold her an arm's length away. "Have you been eating?" Gia's never been much of a cook, so if I didn't make something for us at Aunt Julie's, she'd eat cereal and Pop-Tarts for every meal.

I glance at Zia Stella, but she smiles reassuringly at me as Gia answers, "Yes. And we're ordering pizza for dinner when I get back."

"Get back? I just got here, where are you going?"

Zia Stella answers for her. "Gia's weekly therapy session was rescheduled to today, but we only agreed because we thought you'd be flying in later."

"Oh, no, that's all right," I amend quickly. "You just reminded me that I'll probably need to check in with Anusha anyway."

Zia Stella nods and checks her watch. "But Gia is right, we are going to be late. Siena, why don't we help you get settled inside so you can get ready for your little party with Lily? But we can all sit together for dinner when we get back so we can catch up." She gestures for me to give her my backpack, but I hesitate. She continues, "I hope you like your room. I decorated it the way I think you'll like based on what Gia's told me. Your dad basically gave me free rein to do whatever I wanted, so I may have gone a little overboard."

"Wait, party?" Gia asks, looking between the two of us excitedly. "You were here for like two seconds, and you're already invited to a party? Is it Warren's? It's supposed to be awesome, can I come?"

Since when does Gia get excited over a party? "Um, no, no party for either of us," I tell her, looking back at the house I'm going to be alone in for the next hour or so, and my throat feels like it's closing.

I was only in the detention center for three weeks while custody was being sorted and the case was analyzed, but it felt like an *eternity* before I was acquitted on a "self-defense of others" clause. It helped that there was a record of other girls—young girls, like Gia—who came forward with charges against Stan Roven. It strengthened my case and made me feel less terrible, less guilty about what happened.

For a while there, I really thought I'd be stuck in prison for the rest of my life. It terrified me, but for Gia, I didn't regret it. When I got out and breathed in the fresh air, I swore to myself I would steer clear of any and all things that might land me there again. I wouldn't litter; I wouldn't speed if I ever got my license; hell, I wouldn't even jaywalk. Anything to avoid getting arrested and hauled off to jail, I'll do. I never *ever* want to set foot in a police station or jail again. I never want to be trapped without fresh air ever again.

I finally hand my bag to Zia Stella. "Actually, is it okay if I go for a walk before dinner?" I ask, already stepping away from her.

"Yes, of course, you don't need to ask! I'll bring your stuff in," she says quickly. "Gia, let's go grab our things so we can head out." Zia Stella reaches out to me like she's going to hug me then freezes like before. This time, she settles for a stiff pat on the top of my head like I'm a golden retriever, then peels Gia off me when she gives me one last hug.

I watch them walk into the house for just a second before turning and aimlessly wandering down the street.

Zia Stella's being all awkward and weird around me. Is she acting like that because she has no idea how to behave around a niece she's never met before? But she seems normal with Gia. Maybe she's scared of me? Is that what I can look forward to for the rest of my life when people find out what happened? How will the kids at school react when they find out what happened and who I am? *Lily* knows, which means it probably won't be long until everyone knows. Being Florence Bowen's daughter isn't easy, but it's even worse when you're living in the town she grew up in, the town that remembers her.

I shake my head as I walk. I can't think about that right now. I just want to walk and enjoy the cool breeze and smell of the pines.

I don't know how long I walk, but eventually I find a trail leading into a forest. I'm not exactly dressed for a hike or particularly fond of hiking, but I follow the trail anyway.

I have no idea where I am or how long I've been out here, but it's getting dark. Storm clouds are moving in, and I swear the mosquitos have been treating me like an all-you-can-eat buffet. My legs are tired, my breathing is labored, and my Converse aren't offering my feet the same support that real running shoes would've. And to make things worse I've been picking random directions when the trail splits into two, so now I'm really turned around. I don't even know what time it is because the top of my phone screen is black.

There's a break in the trail, so I push through the thick trees, ignoring the branches scraping my skin, and finally emerge on a dirt road.

There's nothing around except the road and more pine trees and the steady chirping of cicadas. The sun is setting behind the dark clouds, and a fat raindrop hits my nose, making me flinch.

I wonder if Dario has thought about me, if he knows

I've arrived, if he wants to get to know me, like I stupidly was kind of excited to meet him. I even put on *makeup* for him before getting on the plane, because for some reason it was important to me to make a good impression. But if he couldn't even be bothered to be home when I got there, then he's not setting the bar high in terms of what I can expect from him. I try not to be sad about that. There hasn't been a single adult in my life who has ever cared—or tried—to have a relationship with me and Gia, so it's nothing new, but this was supposed to be my fresh start, and I hadn't been able to help being naively excited.

I continue walking in the middle of the deserted, muddy road as I open the GPS on my phone to figure out where I am. The drizzle has turned into a real rainstorm, and I'm completely drenched. My hair hangs in clumps in front of my face. My white tank top sticks to my skin, and my jean shorts are stiff and incredibly uncomfortable. I try to shield my phone from the downpour, but it's pointless. I can't see anything, and my phone isn't reacting to my touch as I try to type in the app.

Thunder rumbles overhead right as my foot slips out from under me. My arms cartwheel and my phone flies from my hand as I land hard on my back, just barely avoiding slamming my head.

I groan and lie there, not bothering to get up as my head pounds and my back aches. If this isn't an omen about how my new life in King City is going to go, I don't know what is.

The rain continues to beat down on me, and thunder booms. I close my eyes and will the rain to wash away all my sadness, to be my relief like it used to be.

You can't be sad when you dance in the rain, Mom would say, before stripping off our shoes and twirling us around in the rain. *It makes you feel free.* It's one of the better memories I have of her. But the rain trick isn't working right now. Maybe it's because I'm not dancing, but I can't bring myself to move.

The thunder mixes with the pounding in my head. It gets louder and more constant, and my eyes pop open.

That's not thunder.

I sit up as headlights speed in my direction. The driver must notice me at the same time I notice them, because the tires skid on the wet road, sending the car sliding toward me.

I'm unable to move, unable to breathe, unable to do anything other than watch the impending accident. It's so fast. The front end of the car races toward me, but it swerves off the road, *just* missing me. It slams into a skinny tree, snapping it, and coming to a stop.

My heart beats loudly in my ears as I realize I was milliseconds away from becoming roadkill.

The driver's door opens, and a person gets out. I can't see him clearly through the rain, but as he gets closer to me, I let out a little gasp.

He's *beautiful.*

He's around my age, probably, and is tall, so tall that

he'll easily tower over me. There's a frown on his face and concern in his blue eyes as his lips move. They move again, and I stare, not hearing anything over my frantic heartbeat. His short brown hair is soaked and matted to his forehead, and his black T-shirt instantly molds to his body as the rain continues to beat down on him.

He crouches in front of me, bringing him to eye level, before placing a rough hand on my shoulder and giving me a shake. Heat seeps through my body from where he touches me.

"Hey!" His deep voice breaks through to me. "Are you all right? Have you been hit? Is anything broken? I can call an ambulance."

He lets go of me to pull out his phone, but I stop him. "No, I don't need an ambulance. I'm all right."

He blinks at me, running his eyes over me like he doesn't believe me before scanning my face. "You're all right?"

"Yeah. You didn't hit me."

A few seconds pass. "Did somebody else?"

"No."

A few more seconds. "Do you have a concussion?"

I shake my head. "I was on a hike."

His eyebrows draw together. "Are you *sure* you don't have a concussion?"

"Positive. I swear it."

He stares deep into my eyes before examining the sides of my head. I flinch when he shines the flashlight from his phone into my eyes, but he must decide I don't have a concussion because he straightens and puts his phone away. "So why the *fuck* are you *lying in the middle of the road*?" he shouts over the rain. "I almost *hit you*!"

Finally, I stand. I'm muddy and soaked through. He must think I'm crazy. And a mess. A crazy mess. As I blink up at him, still perfect looking even though he's soaked, I suddenly wish he thought I were a hot mess instead of a crazy mess. For some reason, the thought makes me laugh.

"Are you seriously laughing right now?" he exclaims, then points to his car, where the tree is bent at an odd angle over the hood. It's running—the headlights and windshield wipers are still on. It's black and sleek, and it looks expensive. "I literally could've run over you! Look at my car! I'm lucky it was a small tree, and it didn't destroy my car! Or injure me!"

"I'm sorry," I say. "The rain was refreshing." Kind of.

His eyes widen, and I realize I sound crazy. Maybe I *do* have a concussion, but I don't think I hit my head *that* hard.

He glances behind him in the direction he came. There are sirens in the distance, but I don't know when he could've called an ambulance because I swear I stopped him.

"Get in the car," he demands, rushing back to it.

"What?"

He grabs hold of the broken tree and snaps it the rest of the way like it's nothing, then tosses it aside.

"You need a special invitation or something? Let's go!" he shouts as the sirens get closer.

I don't move. "You want me to get in the car with you? I'll get everything muddy."

He jogs back to me and gives me another once-over. My hair is knotted and dirty; my now-ruined tank top is so soaked it reveals the pink bra underneath, the same one I was wearing when I was arrested. I'm shivering under his gaze, or maybe it's the cold or the near-death experience, I can't tell. And I notice that for some reason, I'm only wearing one shoe. I wiggle my toes and feel the mud squishing through my once-white sock. I wonder if my mascara is running down my face or if the rain has washed it completely off.

Even though he's also soaked, he looks like he's the lead in a steamy romance movie, with his broad shoulders, the shirt plastered to his chest, water sliding off his smooth tan skin and—oh my goodness, are those abs?

I force my eyes back to his.

"Yes," he says, and for a second, I almost die because I think I asked about his abs out loud, but he says about his car, "Just try not to touch everything." He grabs my shoe from the ground and somehow manages to find my phone. He doesn't look back at me. "Let's go!"

The sirens are even louder now, and I can see lights flashing through the trees in the distance.

My feet are rooted to the ground as he shuts his door. The engine revs, but he doesn't move the car. The driver's-side window rolls down.

"NOW!" he snaps. I don't know what's gotten into him and what the rush is, and I don't know why he wants *me* in his car with him, but he's got my right shoe and my phone, so I jog over to the passenger door. He opens it for me from the inside, and I sink into the black leather seat.

I don't even have the door entirely closed before he shifts into Reverse. I jerk in my seat when he switches into gear and sends us speeding down the dark road.

"Seriously?!" I exclaim, rubbing the back of my head. He doesn't answer. He's rigid despite his relaxed position behind the wheel, and stares straight ahead, his eyes occasionally flicking to the rearview mirror. The sirens sound like they're right behind us. Flashing red and blue lights illuminate the inside of the car, and I glance at the passenger-side mirror to see multiple police cars trailing us in the rain.

I can feel the blood drain from my face. *Police.* If I never have to deal with them again it'll still be too soon. I delicately press the button to lower the window a few inches even though it's raining outside.

"I think they want you to pull over," I force out, but he just shifts into a higher gear.

I'm pushed back into the seat as he speeds down the road, and I immediately ignore his "don't touch everything" rule to slap on my seat belt.

"What the hell!" I exclaim, finally cluing into what's going on. *So stupid, Siena.* "Why are you running from the cops?!"

"*I'm* not running from them," he says, taking a corner faster than should be possible. "*We're* avoiding getting arrested. There's a difference."

We?! There is no *we*! I'm an innocent bystander! All I

wanted to do was lie in the rain and contemplate how much my life sucks, and now I'm an *accomplice*! My stomach drops. I was just released from police custody *hours* ago, and now I'm going to be sent right back.

"Pull over!" I order, gripping the seat for dear life with both hands.

He glances in his rearview mirror. "We're trying to avoid arrest, remember?"

Again with the "we" stuff. There is no we. There's a him, and there's a me, which means there's no we, especially when it's followed by "'re trying to avoid arrest."

Oh God. Great going, Siena. You willingly got in the car with a psycho! A *wanted* psycho. Why is he on the run from the cops—or avoiding arrest, as he put it? Did he rob someone? Stab someone? Oh shit, am I in the car with a murderer? No one even knows where I am!

I don't drive so I know nothing about cars, but even I know that at this point he's run out of higher gears, and we're taking turns at full speed. I have never been in anything on four wheels that moved this fast before, and I do not like it. In fact, I hate it, especially since I don't know the guy driving or his abilities, or why we're running from the cops. *Double* especially because I am not going back to prison. Ever. For anything.

"Let me out!" I demand, trying to put as much authority in my voice as I can, but the look he sends me tells me he's not planning on doing that.

He takes another turn at breakneck speed, and I swear

I see the psycho smile when I shriek.

"I had such a good lead before you decided to lie in the middle of a deserted road and blow it," he huffs. "Hopefully it's too dark and rainy to properly see what kind of car I drive. I still have a good lead. I'll lose them."

If they've been chasing him, don't they already know what kind of car he drives? Despite not wanting to let go of the seat, I turn around to look out the back window. He's right. He's losing them already, and they may be too far back to properly see his car. Their lights are only vaguely visible now, blurred by the pouring rain.

But why is he running from them in the first place? I turn back in my seat and consider my options: 1. Do nothing, hopefully not get arrested or murdered, 2. Try to fight him for the steering wheel, hopefully not crash and die, or 3. Jump out of the moving car, hopefully not die. I don't like any of these options, especially since all of them involve a chance of dying. I can't even call someone; my water-damaged phone sits uselessly in the cupholder between us. And I'm still only wearing one shoe!

But of all those options, there's one I'm scared of most, and that's getting arrested. So, I grip the seat harder. "Lose them," I demand.

"I'm already on it, sweetheart," he shoots back.

"Well, lose them *better!*" The lights are still visible in the distance.

"Would you like to drive?" he asks.

"I don't know how——" I'm cut off by my own scream as

he jerks the wheel and pulls a lever beside him, throwing me into the door. He smiles as the car drifts around the corner. I knew it! He's loving this! Why did I get into the car with the one guy who's going to ruin my chances of staying out of trouble?

He drifts around a few more corners, and I close my eyes, not wanting to see what happens. I told him to lose them, and it looks like he's doing just that. I only hope he can control the car. The back end keeps sliding around, and I don't even know if he's kept it on the road this whole time.

The car jerks as it straightens out again, and I finally open my eyes to see the trees fly by in one big blur. My breathing is hard and fast, and my fingers hurt from how hard they're gripping the seat.

He glances over at me and does a double take like he's forgotten I'm sitting here, then slows down a bit and takes some turns at a slightly more normal speed, but my heart is still beating out of my chest. The flashing lights are long gone, and even I know he's lost our tail.

After a few minutes of silence, I force words out of my dry throat. "Pull over, please." We haven't seen a single car, and I have no idea where we are, or if we're even still in King.

"We might not have enough distance between us yet."

"I don't care." I do care, but I need air. I need my legs on solid ground, and I need to get away from the boy who almost got me arrested less than twenty-four hours after I was released.

He studies me for longer than his eyes should be off the road, before giving an aggravated sigh and pulling over. There's nothing around us, just trees and abandoned roads and dark, stormy skies. I stumble out of the car as soon as it comes to a complete stop and gulp in deep breaths.

I'm alive.

He rounds the car and stands in front of me, unbothered by the rain, which is finally easing.

"Are you all right?" he asks.

"Am I *all right*?" I repeat, straightening to my full height, though it's no match for his. "Are you for real? You just kidnapped me then went all *Tokyo Drift* while running from the cops and making me an *accomplice*! No! No, I'm not all right!"

"You're being a little dramatic," he says calmly.

"I have every right to be as dramatic as I want!" I throw out my arms as if to emphasize said dramatics. "Why the hell did you rope me into this?"

He's still so eerily calm, but it's even more intimidating than if he raised his voice. "Well, did you want me to leave you there to get arrested?"

I'm taken aback. "Why would I have gotten arrested? I was minding my own business."

He shakes his head as if praying for patience, like *I'm* the one who involved *him* in a high-speed chase worthy of the Channel 5 news-copter. "They didn't know you're a weirdo who lies in the middle of the road in the rain for fun. You're a teenager in the middle of nowhere and near the Tracks. They would've assumed that you were running on foot and part of it."

I wipe the rain from my face and stare at him. "I don't understand half of what you said. The Tracks?"

He sighs and looks back in the direction we came from. "I'll explain in the car. We still need to get out of here."

I back away from him. Fool me once, shame on you, but twice? Nuh-uh. I'm not getting in his car again. Teachers used to warn not to get in strangers' cars if they offered you candy, and I went and did it just because he's *handsome* and *asked me to*. But I'm not falling for it again.

"Not until you explain what just happened."

A muscle in his jaw jumps, and I refuse to think about how sculpted it is, how regal it makes him look. "We were street racing. It was a smaller group, but there must have been over fifty cars there watching or participating, and even more people. Most people will slip away undetected in the chaos, but we're screwed if they find two teenagers here, in the middle of nowhere, close to the Tracks, where they just busted a bunch of kids for drag racing. So can we leave now?"

He was drag racing? Or watching? Definitely participating, especially if he was driving like that, like he knew what he was doing and loved every minute of it. But I'm not going anywhere with him. Even if I do believe his story, my heart is still working overtime, and my breathing is still too shallow.

"No," I say, even though I walk back to his car. I grab my ruined shoe and phone.

"What?" he asks, following me with his eyes.

"Where are we?" I ask, wrapping my arms around myself to stop from shivering. "How do I get to Pinewood Street, if you know where that is?"

He stares at me. He's been doing that a lot, and I can't decide how I feel about his intense gaze on me. He has to be my age, but something about him makes him seem older, more mature.

He wipes the moisture from his forehead as the rain becomes a light spit. "It's about a twenty- or thirty-minute drive that way." He points in the direction he came.

A twenty- or thirty-minute drive is probably about an hour's walk. That'll give me time to compose myself before entering my dad's house and pretending that everything's okay. Pretending I wasn't lying in the middle of the road in the rain, pretending I wasn't involved in a police chase, pretending I'm happy. Though, now that I think about it, I haven't felt that empty ache since meeting the handsome boy in front of me. I haven't even thought about all the problems I'm facing right now. He was a good distraction, even though I was terrified the entire time, maybe *because* I was terrified the entire time. That fact softens my anger toward him, but I cling to my resolve. I am keeping my nose clean, and I do not get involved in illegal activities or shenanigans. I want nothing to do with it, or him.

The shoe in my hand is completely muddy and soaked, but I still try to put it on. The boy watches me silently, and I realize I must be a pitiful sight, hopping around trying uselessly to put on a muddy shoe. I slip and catch myself multiple times before completely losing my balance and toppling to the ground. Eventually I give up and hold the shoe as I try to wipe my phone clean. His eyes follow my every move, silently assessing me. I can feel his gaze burning into me. It warms me up.

"What are you doing?" he finally asks.

I straighten my spine, trying to compose myself as much as I can. "I'm leaving."

He raises an eyebrow. "Leaving?"

"Yeah."

He gestures at the abandoned terrain around us. "And where are you going?"

I lift my chin. "I told you. Pinewood Street."

Without waiting for him to answer, I turn and walk in the general direction he pointed to before. I don't know what I'll do when I get to the fork in the road, but I need to do *something*, need to distract myself before I do something stupid like get back in his car.

"You're going to *walk*?" he asks, easily catching up and keeping pace beside me.

I don't look at him. "Yup."

"That's like a two-hour walk."

Damn. My estimate was off. I guess it's a twenty- or thirty-minute drive if *he's* driving. "Well, it's a good thing I've started then, isn't it?"

He huffs in annoyance. "Don't be stubborn. You can't walk."

Now I stop to turn and look at him. "And you can't just rope people into your illegal activities!"

"I was doing you a favor."

I laugh humorlessly. Almost getting me arrested was not a favor.

"Besides," he adds, "you were the one lying in the middle of the road in the rain like a lunatic for fun!"

"It wasn't for fun! I told you the rain was refreshing!"

He steps closer. I could reach out and touch him with ease. The rain has all but stopped now, so there's nothing between us, nothing shielding me from the force of his gaze. My heart beats for an entirely different reason than when he almost ran me over or when I was in the speeding car.

He opens his mouth to say something, then closes it. His eyes scan my face for a moment before he steps away from me. "Fine. Have it your way. Walk back."

"I will!" I retort, turning and walking into the night.

"Good!"

"Good!" I repeat, refusing to look back at him.

"Fine!"

"Fine!"

"Don't get eaten by bears or wolves!" he calls, and that makes me stumble before catching myself. He can't be serious. Can he? We *are* in the middle of nowhere, surrounded by nothing but trees and darkness. I never had to worry about bears or wolves in LA.

I decide he's bluffing and continue walking. My sock squelches in the puddles with every step I take and my thighs are chafing from my wet jean shorts, but at least there's a fire in my belly that keeps me warm, along with the glare I feel on the back of my head. It keeps me going, keeps my steps steady, at least until I pick a random direction at the crossroads and know I'm hidden from his view by the trees.

Great. *Now what, Siena?* I really need to think things through more. I attempt to wring out my freezing shirt and hair, but it's hard with one hand and mud everywhere. I probably only tangle my hair more. A twig snaps in the forest beside me, making me jump, but I don't see anything. Maybe this wasn't the best idea.

I hear swearing, then feet pounding on asphalt. The handsome boy comes into view and halts at the crossroads, looking around before spotting me. He jogs to catch up, and he's not even out of breath despite apparently running the whole way here. I turn to continue walking, hating that part of me is comforted by his presence.

"You are *so* frustrating," he fumes, falling into step beside me.

"What are you doing?" I ask.

"What does it look like?" he seethes. "I'm walking with you."

I almost trip over my own feet. "What? Why?"

He refuses to meet my eyes, and I'm glad, because he looks extremely annoyed. At me. At himself. At the world. "Because you're refusing to get in the car, and I can't just let you walk alone. Also, here." He tosses something soft at me.

I catch it and hold it out. It's a black hoodie with a King City High logo on the front. It's dry and warm, and I am not. "Your teeth are chattering so badly it's annoying," he says by way of explanation.

He's walking with me knowing we'll probably run into the police or scary wildlife, leaving his car behind for a two-hour walk, and *still* had the foresight and kindness to bring me his sweater, even though he's in a soaked T-shirt. My throat squeezes. "I'm going to get it all muddy."

He spares me a glance. "I know."

I stare up at him as we walk. Now that it's drying, his hair looks more dirty blond than brown. He has a nice profile. I was once told I had a nice profile and never understood what it meant until now. I have the sudden urge to trace the straight slope of his nose and sharp cut of his jaw with my fingers.

"Do you stare at everyone you claim kidnapped you, or just me?" His voice makes me jump. I didn't realize how long I'd been staring at him.

"Well, I've only been kidnapped by you, and a middle-aged woman named Alice who spent tons of money to look like my mother, so just you."

I feel his gaze hot on my face but refuse to look at him. I don't know why that slipped out; I haven't thought about Alice in years. I also just admitted that I liked looking at him.

I pause long enough to drop my shoe and put my phone in my back pocket so I can pull on the hoodie. The hoodie completely engulfs me, but it's warm and smells comforting, like cedarwood and spice. Despite his apparent distaste for me, he's still here, walking with me in the middle of nowhere in the dark, letting me dirty his sweatshirt even though he would probably like it for himself. For the first time in years, I don't feel lonely. My eyes sting, and I look down, clenching my teeth.

He doesn't say anything. Doesn't rush me to keep moving or persuade me to go back to the car. Just stands there with me, his presence impossible to ignore.

With a shaky inhale, I reach for my shoe and turn around, walking back in the direction we came from.

"Are you already lost?" he asks, easily reaching my side with his long strides.

"No. You win. Let's drive."

I expect him to gloat, to rub it in, but he doesn't. He just slows his stride to match mine and keeps his eyes forward.

"So, do you believe that I helped you avoid being arrested?" he asks after a while.

I wrap my arms around myself. "I believe that you believe you helped me avoid being arrested," I answer as the car comes into view. "But I am *not* paying for whatever damage that tree caused to your car when you swerved to avoid hitting me. That's the price of my forgiveness."

I don't think there was any damage to his car anyway. Maybe a dent or scratched paint. I would've offered to pay for it before he dragged me into his illegal antics, even though I can't afford the new phone I'll apparently need. I need to look for a job ASAP.

He snorts a laugh. "Who said I wanted your forgiveness?"

I cut my eyes to him. "I did. And congratulations, you've almost earned it."

He shakes his head as we reach the car and opens the passenger door for me. I don't fool myself into thinking it's chivalry, merely the fact that I'm still muddy and he doesn't want me touching everything. He shuts the door and I watch as he rounds the front of the car.

I'm wearing his King City High hoodie, so that must mean he goes there. I wonder if I'll run into him at school. Will he pretend he doesn't know me, the weird girl who lies in the middle of the road in the rain "for fun"?

He gets in beside me and closes the door, and suddenly I'm all too aware of *him*. In this small space, he's everywhere. He smells like cedarwood and fresh rain. Or maybe the cedarwood is from the car or from the sweater. I wonder what he smells like when not obscured by rain and my muddy hair. The car itself is neat and clean, not a single wrapper or water bottle littering the floor. The engine roars to life, and as I buckle my seat belt he pulls onto the road, the song on the radio a soft hum between us.

"You're going the wrong way," I tell him.

He lifts an eyebrow. "You don't even know where you are."

He has me on that. But he said Pinewood Street was behind us.

"I'm going the long way around," he explains.

The long way around. More time spent in the car with

him, surrounded by his scent, his intense eyes, his oddly comforting presence.

The rain has completely cleared. If it weren't for the fact that the two of us are completely drenched, it would be like it hadn't happened. I lean against the headrest and something pokes me, so I feel the back of my head and pull a twig out of the tangles. Despite the no-touching rule, I open the window a bit more to throw it out. The twig flies away in the wind. If only my problems could disappear that easily.

two

We sit in silence for a while, and I don't mind. It's weirdly comfortable, not awkward, and now that he's not driving like he's trying to set a speed record, the lull of the car's motion is relaxing.

A new song plays, and I eye the dashboard to figure out how I can change the station. As I wonder if that constitutes "touching everything," the boy beside me groans and selects a different station before I can.

He shoots me a glance. "I hate that song."

"Me too. I don't mind Siren of the Heart, but I can't stand that one song."

"'Always Be There'? It's their biggest song."

He's right, it is their biggest song, which means it's on the radio the most. It was the song that was playing years ago in the car when Mom dropped us off at Aunt Julie's and never came back. Ironic how a song about always being there for the person you love was playing as my mother decided she was tired of being there for her kids. I've hated it ever since; it always brings me back to that moment in the backseat of Mom's broken-down ten-year-old Mustang, knowing deep down that she was deserting us but not brave enough to call her out on it.

I'm not going to tell the boy in the driver's seat that, though, so instead I nod and say, "Yeah, that's why I hate it, it's way too overplayed."

He chuckles. "Tell me about it. My oldest brother's girlfriend used to play this song all day every day, it drove me insane. Plus, Thea can't sing for shit, so that was extra fun. Now I can't hear this song without cringing."

"That sounds . . . sweet though." I wish my memory of this song was cute like that.

"Sweet? Wait until you hear it on repeat 24/7 with what sounds like a screeching chalkboard singing, then get back to me on how sweet it is."

I laugh. "Well, you're being awfully harsh when you probably aren't the greatest singer out there either."

There's a challenge in his smirk. "As a matter of fact, I'm the best singer around. Could probably get a record deal if I really wanted."

"Is that so?"

"It is."

I shift in my seat to face him better. We have a long drive ahead of us; I might as well be entertained. "All right, now I need to hear this angel voice you apparently have."

"Your words, not mine," he says.

"Come on, let's hear it," I say, more for the principle of it than actually caring about his singing voice. I turn up the volume on the radio as high as it can go. It's playing Taylor Swift's "Lover." He gives me an eye roll despite the quirk in his lip, and just to be extra annoying, I sing at the top of my lungs.

He says something but I can't hear over the music and my own singing. It helps that the stereo in the car is so loud I can barely hear my own voice. I roll down the window more, letting wind whip into the car, and feel a settling in my chest. Maybe it's because I can't remember the last time I let loose singing like this, or maybe it's because the wind is freeing, or maybe it's because there's a stranger sitting beside me who can't possibly judge me any more than he already has after today's events, but I feel *good*.

When he doesn't sing, I go even louder, and finally, finally, he relents and joins in, barely hitting the notes.

When the song ends, he lowers the radio to a reasonable volume and clears his throat. "Remember how I told you Thea sounds like a screeching chalkboard? I think you're a close second."

"I do *not* sound like that!" I exclaim, but I can't do it

with a straight face, because he has a point. "And you're no better. Record deal my ass."

"I don't know all the words! Plus, I have a deep voice, I can't hit those high notes."

A trill of a phone cuts off my response, but he doesn't move to get it.

"Aren't you going to answer that?" he asks me.

"Why would I answer your phone?" I ask, before realizing that the sound is coming from under me. It's *my* phone! I didn't think it would still work. I lift from the seat enough to grab my phone from my back pocket and rub off any remaining mud on my jean shorts. I missed the call, but the screen shows I have a few missed calls, one from Zia Stella, and two from Lily, as well as some unopened texts.

Did I miss dinner? My stomach growls in answer. I most definitely missed dinner.

"What time is it?" I ask.

He points to the dash where I read the time. 10:00 p.m. Wow, where did the time go?

I open the text from Zia Stella first: The pizza is here. Will you be home soon?

I wonder how long she waited for me. I send Zia Stella a quick text back, apologizing for missing dinner and telling her I'll be there soon.

I open the texts from Lily next: I'm outside.

Then five minutes later: Gia told me you're not coming. There's another party Sunday, you're coming to that! Nonnegotiable!

I feel bad making Lily wait for me, but I'd be lying if I didn't acknowledge my relief at not having to go to a party. Plus, I never actually agreed to go.

Another text comes in from Lily: Gia is here, I think alone, and she's completely hammered.

What?! Gia went to a party and is *drunk*? She's never been drunk before! She's only fifteen! Was she looking for me?

I call Gia, but it goes straight to voicemail. I try to call Lily, but the rings sound weird, and I can't tell if she answers.

I shake my phone and groan. I'm not sure if the phone is ruined because of the rain and mud, or if I have no signal, because the top of the screen is black and that's where the signal bars are located.

"Use mine," a voice says, making me jump in my seat. I forgot the boy was here—I even forgot I was in the car with him.

"Thanks," I say as I take the phone he's holding out. He has signal. I copy Lily's number and dial it into his phone.

"Hello?" she answers curiously, yelling over the music and sounds of people talking and squealing.

"Hi, it's Siena," I say.

"Whose phone are you calling me from?"

I open my mouth to answer, then realize I don't know the name of the guy sitting beside me, the guy whose sweatshirt I'm wearing and whose calming scent I'm breathing in.

"Where's Gia?" I ask instead. "Are you sure it was her?"

"Yes, I'm sure it was her. When I knocked on your door

she answered. We were making small talk, and she asked me where the party was."

Gia's not a partier. Did she think I had gone instead of hanging out with her my first day back?

"Are you with her now?" I ask.

"No. I don't know who she's here with," Lily replies. "But she's *plastered*. She can barely walk straight. She was doing a keg stand. Considering her size, I'm surprised she's not hurling already."

What the hell is she *thinking*? Gia hates beer—she says it tastes like puke and old man sweat and hurts her stomach. So why would she think drinking a shit-ton of it upside down was a good idea?

"Do you know if she left with anyone?" I ask, panic squeezing my throat.

Lily hesitates. "I don't know, I'm sorry, but I think you should come and look for her."

That's my little sister. I'm supposed to protect her, take care of her, keep her away from older kids who are getting her drunk and who knows what else. I'm failing. *What if she gets in a car with someone?*

Something is wrong, I know it is. This is not like Gia. This is the same girl that not even two months ago would lock herself in our room anytime there was a party going on in the apartment. But I can't do anything, not from here. I hate this feeling of helplessness, just like I did when I was locked away, leaving Gia to figure everything out by herself.

"Can you see if you can find her?" I ask Lily, but there's

no response. The loudness from the party is gone too. "Hello? Lily? Hello?" I pull away from the phone to see the call failed and the signal lines are gone. *Shit.*

"You okay?" The boy asks, making me jump again.

His eyes bore into mine, still so intense, still so damn *calm* while my stomach is in knots.

"What's your name?" I ask, handing his phone back.

"Jason."

I don't want to rope him into helping me, but I don't have a working phone so I can't call an Uber. And I'm already in his car. And I'm desperate. I wasn't there for the last three weeks for Gia, but I'm here now.

"No, Jason. I'm not okay. Do you know where Warren lives? He's throwing a party tonight."

His eyebrows draw together. "Yes, I do."

"Great," I say. "I'm going to need you to drive me there. How far are we?"

His eyes rake over me. "You want to go to a party now?"

I realize I'm a mess. I realize I'll be making my debut in front of my classmates looking like a swamp monster and that's not exactly the impression I want to make, but I don't care.

"I moved to King today, and my fifteen-year-old sister decided to go to Warren's party by herself after hearing our neighbor talking about it, and said neighbor just informed me that Gia is so drunk she can't even walk. So yeah, I need to go to that party."

Jason nods once and makes a sudden left turn. "We'll

be there in ten. Five if there's no one on the road."

The car speeds up, and for the first time tonight, I'm *glad* I'm sitting in the car with a dude who drag races for fun and is apparently good at it. I even want him to go faster. If we weren't nearing town, I'd tell him to pull whatever damn stunt he needs to to get me there in record time.

"Can you just . . . not get pulled over?" I ask.

"I didn't avoid arrest just to get a speeding ticket," he says. "We'll be fine."

His reassurances should make me feel better, but he can't control a speed trap. Maybe I should tell him to slow down. My leg bounces in the seat, and I only just stop myself from biting my nails because of how dirty they are.

Jason eyes my bouncing leg and the hand precariously close to my mouth.

"Put it in rice," he says.

"Huh?" I look back at him. He has one hand on the steering wheel, the other on the stick shift.

"Your phone," he says, pointing to the useless piece of glass and plastic on my lap. "It might work fine and it was just the shit signal, but if it is water damage, submerging it in rice usually works. It's worth a shot."

"Right. Guess I'll have to try that."

I don't want to talk. I want to focus on Gia. On what she's doing, on where she is, on who she's with. I curl my fingers into my palms so I don't bite my mud-stained nails.

"What's your name?" Jason asks suddenly, clearly not taking the hint that I don't want to talk.

"Siena."

He speeds up at a yellow light and makes it before it turns red. "Are you starting at King City High on Monday?"

Why is he asking me this now?

"Yes. I'm a senior."

"Me too," he says, making a quick turn. We enter a neighborhood with mansions lining the streets and perfectly landscaped yards. They remind me of the ones in Malibu and Beverly Hills that Gia and I would bike around and make up stories about as if we lived there. Except these houses are surrounded by pine trees, not palm, that look like they've been here for hundreds of years. "Bit of advice?" He continues, "Maybe don't make lying down in strange places a habit. The halls are packed, you can't just lie there."

I stare at him incredulously. Here I was, thinking we were getting along after that Taylor Swift singing fest. "I don't do that!"

He's unconvinced. "Right . . ." He eyes my leg again.

"I don't! I was having a shit day, and I went on a hike and got lost and slipped and decided to just . . . lie there. I thought it was an abandoned road. I didn't know you would come speeding down it!"

"I was going the speed limit," he deadpans.

"You were not!"

"I was. You don't speed on a gravel road. It'll kick up rocks and scratch your paint. Besides, I told you, I already had a lead. I could've done the speed limit all the way into town and wouldn't have seen a single cop."

For some reason I believe him. I don't want to, but there's no way he could've avoided hitting me if he was going as fast as he was while I was in the car.

"For the record," I start, "playing in the rain *is* fun. Do you even know what fun is?"

"My definition of fun and your definition of fun are *very* different."

"Right. You get your kicks from doing illegal shit," I huff. Sure, he's handsome and muscular and I can't stop sniffing his hoodie, but he's into stuff like street racing. I'm steering clear of trouble. I'm distancing myself from what happened in LA and the Florence Bowen legacy.

He scoffs. "Yeah, well, what do you do for fun? Other than lying in the rain? I bet you do homework and organize your pens by color."

I don't know how to answer his question. I can't remember the last time I *had* fun. Between work and home and Gia and school and Mom, I never had spare time for myself. These last three weeks were the first instance in years that I've had nothing *but* spare time for myself. But all I did was stare at the cement ceiling, talk to officials and lawyers and therapists, and worry about Gia, which *isn't* exactly a hobby.

"What do you do for fun?" I shoot back. "I bet you hotwire cars or break into buildings."

"I don't hotwire cars for *fun*."

I stare at him. "You can actually hotwire a car?"

"Of course," he says blandly. "My brother Aiden taught me when I was thirteen."

He's joking, right? Except he's not. He's completely serious. This boy really is trouble and I had to find him as soon as I landed. "What need could you possibly have for knowing how to hotwire a car at thirteen?"

He shrugs. "What need could you possibly have to lie in the rain?"

I want to reach out and shake him. He is so *infuriating*! Is he never going to let that go?

"We're here," Jason says, pulling through open metal gates and speeding up a long driveway to a grand entrance. This house is *huge*, with modern dark-gray bricks and a front door that's easily twice as tall as me. All the lights are on outside, with spotlights moving around the front of the house in presentation mode. There are cars parked all over the place, even on the grass. We drive around a large bubbling water fountain, and I briefly wonder if Warren put soap in the fountain or if someone else did.

Gia's here, somewhere, drunk off her face. She has no one to look out for her, no one who cares if something happens to her. But I care. I'll look after her; it's what I've always done.

We come to a stop, and I hop out. Jason comes around to meet me. "What does she look like? I'll help you search."

My heart stutters, and it takes me a second to recover. "You don't have to—"

"It'll be faster if we're both looking. I'm helping, so we're wasting time," he says, gesturing for me to hurry up with the description.

"Gia's about five-foot-two, brown eyes, brown hair in a short pixie cut . . ."

"Jason!" someone calls out. The guy is coming from the backyard, where the party seems to be. I guess it wasn't raining here or the party went on rain or shine.

"Hey Warren," Jason answers.

Warren closes the distance between us. He's only a bit taller than me but has wide shoulders and smooth dark skin. His head is shaved, and he does a double take when his brown eyes land on me.

"Hey Warren, great party," I say, skirting right past him to enter the heart of the party. Technically I'm not crashing since Lily invited me, but he doesn't know that.

"Jason?" I hear Warren ask.

"Yeah, she's with me . . . I guess," Jason answers. I can't hear anything else over the noise.

The backyard is large and beautifully landscaped. It's perfectly set up for entertaining, with different conversational areas like fire pits, couches, hammocks, and tables, and there are tons of kids. There are kids swimming in the pool while others are playing beer pong on a row of tables. Near a large tree is a keg, where some guys are chanting, "Chug chug chug," as they hold another guy upside down over it, a tube in his mouth as he sucks up the alcohol. The backyard is lit from the house, but also from white string lights wrapped around all the trees. There's an outdoor kitchen area with a large granite counter, covered with food. On the neat interlocking patio near the back door, a guy with large headphones stands behind DJ equipment set up on a table. Some people are dancing in front of him, but there are speakers throughout the backyard, making the music equally loud everywhere.

I'm almost in sensory overload from how much is going on. Though I don't go to many parties, I've never been to one this extravagant. I've never even *heard* of anyone throwing a party like this.

"*Siena?*"

I turn and find Lily. She's just as beautiful as before, and she's standing with a pretty girl a little shorter than her. Lily notices me eyeing them.

"This is Nyah." She gestures to her friend. Nyah's dark hair is twisted in braids that hang down her back, and her makeup is beautiful, perfectly suiting her deep-brown skin.

"What happened to you?" Lily asks, trading glances with Nyah.

Nyah says, "And was that *Jason* you drove here with? He and his brother are *so hot*. They're best friends with my boyfriend."

"Yeah, that's Jason," I reply. "Have you found Gia?"

They shake their heads. "We saw her leaving the pool house," Lily says, pointing at a building that looks like a mini house and is bigger than our old apartment.

"But then we lost her," Nyah finishes.

I try to focus. Where would Gia be? This party, this house, this *backyard*, is huge. But the music throbs directly into my brain, making my temples pound. "How can you guys think over all this music? How have the cops not been called? Where are Warren's parents?"

"My boyfriend told me Warren's parents are in Nigeria visiting family, but they usually don't care if he throws parties anyway," Nyah says.

Lily nods. "And the neighbors are pretty spaced out. But see that house?" She points to a house in the distance. It's obscured by the heavy trees and only discernible by the glowing lights. "That's Principal Anderson's."

"The principal of King City High?" I ask as they lead me through the party, scanning groups of kids for Gia. People give me weird looks, probably wondering why someone as well put together as Lily is hanging out with me.

"Yup," Lily answers. "You never really see her though, except at assemblies."

Does that mean Warren knows the principal personally? I barely even knew what the principal at my old school looked like, never mind where he lived. Our school was so big we were relegated to a series of vice principals that you only saw if you were in trouble. I was never in trouble.

I only met our VP once when Gia was caught cheating on a test. She was suspended, but he wouldn't let her go unless it was with a parent. She texted me from the office where she was forced to wait, and the VP wouldn't let me sign her out and take her home. We sat in the office together for six hours, knowing full well Aunt Julie wasn't coming even though she had been notified about the situation. Two hours after the final bell, the VP gruffly handed me Gia's suspension paperwork and ordered us out of his office. To this day, I don't know what Gia was more pissed about: getting caught cheating, getting suspended, or Aunt Julie not bothering to come pick her up.

"Sorry guys, this is my mom," Nyah says, gesturing at her ringing phone, "I'll be back." She disappears to answer the call, and Lily leads me deeper into the party.

There's a girl puking into a flowerpot beside us and we sidestep, only to have to dodge a practically naked couple snorting something off each other's bodies. Everywhere I look, there's something going on, something Gia shouldn't be around, something she shouldn't be doing, something she hated seeing in LA.

"Why would Gia come here?" I ask, trying to wrap my head around it.

Lily shrugs. "I told her to come."

I stop in my tracks, and she walks for a bit before noticing that I'm not beside her.

"What?" I ask.

She frowns. "I told her to come. Is that a problem?"

"Well, yeah! She's drunk and alone and probably scared and who knows where! She could be passed out somewhere!"

Lily closes the distance between us. "I didn't force her to come here. She asked and I told her to come. But with the way she acts, I'm surprised you're surprised."

"What's that supposed to mean?"

Lily rolls her eyes. "Come on, Gia's not some delicate little flower who's never touched alcohol before."

Gia's taken one shot of tequila in her life, and she spat it out immediately after. "She doesn't like it. She's not a partier."

Lily huffs a sarcastic laugh. "Are we talking about the same Gia?"

I cross my arms tight against my chest despite my body temperature starting to rise. "I think I know my sister better than you."

She raises a condescending eyebrow. "Do you though?"

A big guy with a mullet and his friend in a jersey accidentally bump into me and give me a weird look, which I can't fault them for because I must look like a sewer rat. The tension between me and Lily is palpable, and the guy with the mullet asks, "There a problem here, Lily?"

She doesn't break eye contact from our stare-off when she says, "It's fine, thanks, Thompson."

Thompson and his friend give us one last questioning look before shrugging and walking away.

"Whatever," I say, dropping my gaze. "I don't have time to argue with you about this when I need to find Gia. If you don't want to help, fine."

She looks at something behind me, her eyes going wide, before walking past me without another word. I don't know who or what she was looking at because all I see is a crowd and her retreating back.

If she doesn't want to help, *fine*. At least Jason is helping, so I'm not completely on my own here. For some reason, despite having only just met him, the thought of him helping reassures me. He's always calm, always seems like he has his shit together—even when he's running from the cops. I don't know him, but he seems to have a handle on everything. That quiet confidence . . . that must be what gives me that impression.

I spend the next ten minutes combing through the party. There are so many people here, too many. There can't possibly be this many seniors at King City High. I get a lot of strange looks, but I don't care.

After no sign of Gia, I stop at the side of the house to check my phone for any messages from her, and that's when I hear arguing.

I peek around one of the large pine trees and spot Lily with her arms crossed defensively, and a guy I haven't seen before. She doesn't look like the confident, large-and-in-charge future model with her shit together that I met today. She looks . . . small.

"Just drop it, Brandon," Lily says, trying to push past him, but he grabs her arm.

"No," the guy, Brandon, says. "You need to stop running away from me."

"I don't owe you anything." Lily tries to pull away, but Brandon's hand won't budge.

Despite our little argument, I like Lily, so I move closer to them through the trees. Brandon is bigger than me and looks like he works out; I doubt I could wrap both hands around his bicep. I've never been in a fight before, but maybe if I'm here, Brandon will see he's not alone with Lily and let her go.

"Yes, you do," he says, and Lily struggles harder.

"You're hurting me," she tells him, slapping at his chest, but he doesn't release her.

"Stop being such a stubborn bitch!"

I know men like Brandon. I have years of unwanted experience dealing with entitled men like him. I know how he'll react if I jump in there, guns blazing; I got a black eye when I was twelve to prove it. So instead, I take a deep breath for confidence and stagger between the trees.

"Nyah! Where'd you go? I fell into the mud and totally embarrassed myself in front of Connor!"

Lily and Brandon freeze.

"Oh, hey guys!" I continue, pretending I don't notice the obvious tension. "Thank God I found you, Lily. Look at me! I'm a disaster and fell into the mud in front of *Connor!*" I don't even know if there's a Connor here. Brandon drops Lily's arm, and she takes a step away, rubbing the spot he had been holding. "This is a level nine emergency, I need help."

"Level nine, huh?" she says, hurrying toward me, not looking back at him once. I force myself to nod along, to not give away how creeped out Brandon is making me feel, how no one would hear our screams unless they wandered away from the party.

Lily, like she went to acting camp along with modeling camp, doesn't miss a beat as she says, "That's serious. But don't worry, we can still fix it."

I pretend to be relieved, and a part of me is since

Brandon's letting her go without a fight. "Really?"

"Yes. Come on, Siena." She grabs my hand, and just before I'm turned around, I catch the glare Brandon sends me. It makes shivers run up my spine, and I mentally note to steer clear of him at school.

"You're such a lifesaver," I say, keeping up the charade as we walk. Lily is shorter than me and still in those red heels, but I'm the one being forced to keep up with her pace. "I can't believe I did that!"

"I'm sure Connor doesn't think any less of you," Lily says, her voice confident, like none of that stuff with Brandon just happened.

We round the house and enter the large backyard. Brandon hasn't followed us, and I'm about to drop the act when Lily quietly says, "Thanks, Siena."

Despite knowing I was faking it, Lily still pulls me to the pool house. The door opens just as a group of girls are leaving, and Lily ushers me in and toward the bathroom, closing the door behind us. Only then does she drop my hand, and I realize how hard she was clutching it.

She places her hands against the sink and hangs her head. I stand there for a few moments, unsure of whether to go comfort her or give her space.

Lily sniffles. "God, he *sucks*."

"He does. I'm sorry that happened."

Lily wipes her face with a shaky hand, and I can't believe how well she masked her fear in front of Brandon, how she must have felt in the moment. "I really thought he was going to—" She cuts herself off and gives me a nervous look, like she forgot who she was talking to. "Never mind."

She turns to the mirror, dabbing at her eyes until it's almost impossible to tell she was crying. "Anyway, sorry to bring you into all this," she says, fixing her hair and straightening her shoulders. The Lily Liu everyone sees is back in place, and the vulnerable one I just witnessed has vanished.

"It's all right, I don't mind," I say.

She reaches for the door but pauses. "Thanks for out there, Siena. But please don't tell anyone."

I don't know why she doesn't want anyone to know what a huge dick that guy Brandon is, but I find myself nodding anyway.

"Thanks," she says. "And I know you're starting at King on Monday, so just be careful."

"Careful?"

"Yeah. Careful. Especially around some of the guys," she says.

I study her. That's a generic warning. We always have to be careful around guys, especially if they're anything like Brandon.

"Okay," I say.

"No." Lily steps closer to me, her gaze boring into me. "I mean it."

She's starting to creep me out, so I just nod at her again. Seemingly satisfied, she straightens her faux fur jacket. "Have you found Gia?" I shake my head, and she sighs.

"Maybe she's gone home. I think I'm going to head out anyway. I'll check at your house to see if Gia's there and keep you posted if she shows up."

I don't blame her for wanting to leave, and seeing if Gia's already there is a smart idea too. It's one less person to look for Gia, but at least Jason's helping. He seems to know people; I'm sure he's making more progress than I have. Maybe he even knows if she left with someone.

"Thanks, Lily, I appreciate it."

We exit the pool house, and Lily smiles at a girl who comes up to her. I watch as she works the crowd like she wasn't just crying through an emotional breakdown. I wonder what's worse: feeling alone but not needing to put on a happy face for everyone or having all these friends and people who adore you but feeling the pressure to always be perfect around them.

A sound draws me back into the pool house. I'm standing behind a couch that's in front of a mounted TV that for some reason is turned onto the fish tank channel. This is a pretty big pool house; maybe Gia is passed out in one of the rooms here.

There's a couple making out on the couch, so I ignore them and walk around. There's a kitchen, bathroom, changing area, and room full of pool equipment, but all of them are empty. I head up the stairs; this place clearly doubles as a guesthouse. I knock on the closed doors, and when there are no gross sounds or answers, I poke my head in. There are two bedrooms, and Gia isn't passed out in either of them. This was the last place I could've looked. No one is allowed inside Warren's house, so she can't be there, and she isn't anywhere in the yard. I check my phone to see if she's answered any of my texts or called me back. She hasn't.

Downstairs, the couple is still on the couch, and I'm about to slip past them unnoticed when something makes me pause. I stare at the guy, anger burning in my chest, growing like an unchecked fire.

Jason doesn't owe me anything. He's not my friend. And yet, the betrayal of seeing him here with his tongue down a girl's throat instead of helping me look for Gia like he said he would infuriates me.

"That's just great," I seethe, causing the couple to jump apart. "This is how you help me?" I ask, almost blinded by my indignation. "You could've just dropped me off, I wouldn't have blamed you. But *you* volunteered to help me! You made me think other people were out here helping me! You made me think you *cared*."

Jason stares at me with wide eyes. The girl looks back and forth between us. Did he even bother looking for Gia? Did he jump right in here to have his fun and forget all about me?

Jason exchanges glances with the girl. "Um, do I know you?"

Now I'm seeing red. I knew he was infuriating, but this . . . this is next level.

"You are *such* an asshole," I snap. Jason is nothing to me, just a guy who I spent the last few hours with by chance, but still, I can't help the raw hurt that punches me in the gut. The weight on my chest that seemed to disappear during the time we spent together reappears tenfold, almost suffocating me.

I'm still wearing his stupid hoodie, the one that means nothing to him but brought me so much comfort, and I can't stand it. I can't stand it touching me, bringing me warm memories that I have no right to. With uncoordinated haste, I shove my arms through it and attempt to pull it off. It takes longer than normal, but no one says anything. Once it's off, I throw it at Jason. "Thanks for nothing."

Before he can say anything, I march back out to the party. I have no right to be as upset as I am, I know that, but I don't care. He said he'd help me look for Gia. I felt better knowing he would, and he decided to try to get lucky instead. I'm only upset because he's not helping me, not because he's with a girl. It doesn't matter what he was doing instead of looking. I don't care. It doesn't bother me. Not one bit. He could kiss all the girls he wanted after we found Gia. There's a sting in my heart and I ignore it, pushing down the hurt and instead focusing on anger.

The phone in my back pocket rings, and I fish it out, surprised it's still working. I groan when I see the number. This is not the time, but I can't ignore her calls.

"Hello?"

"Hi Siena," a calm woman's voice replies. Dr. Anusha Khan has been my social worker and assigned counselor through it all. She's nice enough, but she likes talking about my mother, and I hate talking about my mother, so she makes it hard for me to like our chats.

"Hi Anusha," I greet. *Dr. Khan is my father. Call me Anusha*, she'd said at our first meeting. I think it's to get me to think of her as more of a friend and less of a shrink, a little trick to get her patients to open up.

"I'm just calling to see how you're settling in. I tried earlier but my calls weren't going through." Her voice is a little warped from the speaker, but her words are clear.

"Yeah, sorry, I had no signal."

"Why didn't . . . Siena, what is that noise?"

I silently curse and clutch the phone. "Oh nothing. I'm just out."

"Are you at a party?" The disapproval is clear in her voice, and I silently curse again. I need her to like me. I need her to decide I'm okay and move on to checking in on other people. I need her to decide I'm good at Dario's and can stay with Gia.

I contemplate lying to her, but someone runs by me, yelling, "Dude, toss me a beer!" and now I can't tell her the loud music is from a gym or something.

"It's just a small get-together."

I hear her scribbling notes down as she calmly says, "Why are you at a party? I thought you'd be settling in with your dad? Reconnecting."

It's hard to tell what Anusha's thinking. She usually only has a few tones, and they're all slightly different from her normal calm, analyzing one. She has her neutral-interested tone, her neutral-disapproving tone, and her regular neutral tone. It makes it hard to read her and give her the answer I think she wants.

"He wasn't home. I haven't met him yet," I admit, and it sounds pathetic even to me, so I rush to add, "But I met Zia Stella, and she encouraged me to come and make friends, just like you did."

"And is that something you're interested in? Making friends? Only a few days after being acquitted of manslaughter? I thought you wanted a quiet evening?"

I did tell her that. I promised her I'd stay out of trouble. "It's a bonding experience for me and Gia," I lie. "Plus, you're the one who encouraged me to make friends, and that's what I'm doing."

"Hmm," she replies, and I can't tell which neutral-adjacent tone she's using.

"Everything's fine, Anusha. I'm settling in here. I'm going to like King City." I hate King City. I've only been here a few hours and everything's falling to shit and I can't find Gia. But she needs to believe everything's perfect.

A guy holding a red Solo cup saunters up to me and ignores my hand gestures to shoo him away. He looks me up and down, and I try turning away from him for some privacy, but he moves to stay directly in front of me. "I didn't know there was muddy bikini wrestling!" he says, his eyes raking over me, landing on my chest where the pink bra is still clearly outlined. "You definitely won. Can't believe I missed you, I bet it was hot."

"What did he just say?" Anusha's voice is neutral-interested, and I pull the phone away from my ear and plant my hand over the speaker.

"Fuck off," I hiss to the guy, who scowls.

"I was giving you a compliment," he grumbles, and I flip him off as I move away from him, successfully this time.

I place the phone back to my ear. "Maybe I can call you back tomorrow morning, Anusha, you know, after I've actually met my dad." After I've found Gia and gotten her home safely and can make Anusha believe I'm a perfectly well-adjusted kid recently released from prison.

"Hold on a minute, Siena," she says, and I have to keep in my frustrated groan. "Have you decided what you're going to do if people find out what happened? And that you're Florence's daughter? Your aunt told me that she's quite infamous in her hometown."

None of this is new information. All small towns know about the semifamous person that made it out, especially when she's always in the headlines for screwing up.

"No one is going to find out," I tell her, making the promise to myself and the universe. If they find out, I can leave when I turn eighteen. Gia's stuck here for years with Dario, and I don't want to subject her to the looks, stares, and harassment we've gotten elsewhere when people have found out.

"You can't control that, Siena," Anusha says. "But speaking of, has your mother contacted you since I last asked?"

She always ends our sessions with this question, and she

never believes me when I give her the same answer. "Like I said before, I haven't heard from Mom since she dropped Gia and me off with Aunt Julie. It's been years."

"Hmm," It's the neutral-disapproving tone. She scribbles something else down as I sidestep a flying football.

"She's not going to contact me, Anusha."

"You'd tell me if she did, right?" Another question she always asks.

"Yes," I say, falling into our script. It's pointless. Florence wants less to do with us than our dad apparently does.

"All right then, I'll check in on you tomorrow," Anusha says as a group of boys near me start chanting, "Chug, chug, chug!"

"All right, bye, Anusha!" I hang up and groan, tapping the corner of my phone on my forehead a few times. I hope tonight didn't cause a red mark to be put next to my name in Anusha's books.

———

Gia isn't here. At the front of the house, I sit on the wide steps leading to the huge door. Jason's car is right in front of me, still haphazardly parked in the middle of the drive, like he doesn't care about people's ability to get around it, like he's too important. *Like he was in a rush to help me.*

I pull my phone out, and by some miracle, it works enough for me to order an Uber. It's a good thing too, because there's no way I could've asked Jason for a ride home, or called Zia Stella, or *Dario*.

I stare out at the yard. I can't see the front gates from here. The bubbles are almost out of control, completely engulfing the fountain and the grass around it. If possible, there are *more* cars parked around the property than the last time I was out here.

I don't know what to do. I hope Gia's at home already.

A car pulls up and I double-check my phone to see if it's my Uber, but a bunch of kids pile out of it—more kids than there are seat belts.

The last person to get out of the car is laughing at whatever someone is saying, until she looks up and meets my eyes.

"Gia!" I yell, marching up to her.

For a second, she looks guilty before her face morphs into a scowl. Her makeup is smudged, and she wobbles as she stands. She *reeks* of alcohol.

Her phone is in her hand; she's been deliberately ignoring my calls! "What the hell, Gia! You can't just ignore me!"

"Do you know this homeless girl, G?" one of the girls from the car asks.

G? Gia *hates* being called *G.*

"Her name is *Gia*," I say to the girl.

She raises an eyebrow at me and stands beside Gia. She appears to be around Gia's age and is taller than Gia but not as tan and has shoulder-length brown hair.

"It's fine," Gia blurts out, darting toward me unsteadily. "You're embarrassing me!" she slurs at me.

I realize that I probably look even worse than her. I'm

covered in mud, disheveled, and wearing one shoe, but I don't care.

"Me! Embarrassing you? Gia, you're fifteen, and you're absolutely smashed! Keg stands? Seriously?"

Her jaw clenches as she looks away from me. Her "friends" look on from a short distance, leaning on the car. The driver pulls out a cigarette and lights it, and the smell makes it immediately obvious that it's *not* tobacco. Gia trusted this kid to *drive*. She's better than that. I *taught* her better than that.

"We're leaving," I tell her, holding on to her arm when she stumbles. She can barely even stand straight. "And *you*," I say to the driver who is clearly *not* sober, "give me your keys."

"Huh?" he asks, his eyelids heavy.

My anger is so palpable I'm practically shaking. This whole night has been absolute shit, and this is the shit-cherry on the shit–ice cream. "I said *give me your car keys*."

He looks at his friends in confusion. Gia pushes my steadying hand away and wobbles over to a tree before bending over in the shadows and puking.

I storm up to the boy and hold my hand out expectantly. He's lucky he got here in one piece and didn't hurt anyone in his car or another one. Up close he stinks of beer and smoke.

Tentatively, he reaches into his pocket and drops a cluster of keys into my hand.

"You should be ashamed of yourself," I lecture him as

I attempt to undo the car key from the other keys in case one of them is for his house. "You don't drive while high and drunk! And you can't fit seven kids in the back of your Camry!"

He says nothing, just stares at me like he's struggling to keep up with the words coming out of my mouth, and that only frustrates me more.

"Is there a problem here?" a voice asks, and I turn to see Jason and Warren walking over to us. Yeah, *now* Jason pretends to care. His presence only pisses me off more.

"No," all the kids from the car answer. Gia's still puking by the tree. I want to go help her, but I need to deal with this first.

"Yes, there is," I tell them, my spine straight, my hands still fiddling with the stupid key ring. This kid must have twenty additional keys on it. Who needs that many keys? How many doors could he possibly need to open? To Warren, I say, "You let these kids come to your party and drive around drunk and high? And if they get in an accident or hit an innocent person, then what?"

Shadows pass over Warren's face. "No, I do *not* condone this type of behavior. What the hell, Chris?" he asks, then turns to the girl who called Gia "G." "And Brianna, what do you think your brother's going to say when he hears about this?"

She mutters something under her breath and looks down. I'm glad Warren seems responsible enough to scold them, but I still can't believe Gia got in the car with them.

My hands are shaking so badly I can barely even grip the keys.

A hand closes over mine, a hand belonging to the boy I've been trying not to look at this entire time.

"It's all right," he says softly, taking the bundle from me and undoing the car key from the ring in one attempt. He tosses the cluster back to Chris, and it bounces off his chest before he even moves to try to catch it. My hands clench.

Jason turns his attention to the kids, and I can't see his face, but it must be scary because they practically shrink into themselves. "You'll get this back tomorrow morning," he states.

Now that they're being handled and can't hurt anyone, I rush over to help Gia. She's wiping her mouth with the back of her hand when I get there and shoves me away when I reach for her.

"I heard all of that! You're so fucking embarrassing!"

"Embarrassing? Gia, you could have *died* or hurt other people! What's gotten into you? Don't you remember when—"

"God!" She cuts me off. "You're not my mom! Did you really have to go narc to your *boyfriend*?"

My head rears back. What's happened to Gia? She's never talked to me like this before, never defended an incapacitated driver before, and she's certainly never gotten in their car before. Is this what she's been like these past few weeks? Is this how she's been coping since Stan?

"My life has sucked since moving here!" she continues,

refusing to budge. "And now you're trying to make it worse by ruining my social status. You weren't here, Siena!"

Her words are a kick in the gut. "I know, Gia. But I'm here now."

"Too little, too late." She shoves me and almost falls on her face. She might as well have stabbed me. She's going through a lot, I know. I shouldn't have expected her to just pick up and go on her merry way like nothing happened, the way I hoped she would. Just because I was acquitted and wanted everything pushed behind me doesn't mean she does. I wish I was there for her. I wish I could've given her someone to talk to.

She goes to another tree and bends over to finish emptying her stomach. I try to help her, but she weakly gestures me away, so I stand back a few feet, my heart breaking. I take a deep breath and push down the hurt that's rising inside me and threatening to make me spill tears. I can't cry in front of Gia. Right now, we need to get out of here, and then I can lock myself in my room and cry as much as I want.

"Hey," Jason says, and I immediately tense up.

"You don't have to pretend to care now, Jason," I say.

His brows draw together like he doesn't remember what happened fifteen minutes ago. "What?"

"I meant what I said in the pool house," I say, crossing my arms over my chest as if to shield myself from him. He's so achingly handsome, it almost hurts to look at him.

"Pool house? I didn't . . ." He trails off, but then a smile tugs at his lips. It's the first kind of smile I've seen him direct at me, and that small action transforms his whole face. I didn't think I could be any more attracted to him. I was wrong. And I hate it.

"Why are you smiling at me? I'm being serious."

He doesn't say anything, just shakes his head in amusement.

"You *are* an asshole. You know, guys like you think you can do whatever you want and not get called out on it with your perfect hair and your blue eyes and your black shirt and . . ." Wait, wasn't he wearing green in the pool house? I thought he had changed because he was soaked, but he's still wearing the black shirt, and it's still damp.

I turn to look around, and then freeze, because walking around the house from the backyard is *Jason*. I swivel to look at the Jason behind me, *my* Jason, who's not even trying to hide his grin anymore, then back to the imposter walking toward us.

The Jason who's not Jason pauses when he sees me. His eyes go from me, to Jason, back to me. Realization registers in his eyes, and now he's full-out laughing.

"Wh—" I look back and forth between Jason and not-Jason. Now that I think of it, compared to not-Jason, Jason's hair is a bit shorter, less messy; his eyes are a bit deeper, a bit more intense.

It finally clicks in my mind, and I remember something Nyah said earlier. I turn to Jason. "That's your *brother*."

"Yeah. Jackson. We're twins."

"So, in the pool house . . ."

"Did you call my brother an asshole?" He's *immensely* amused, and I can literally feel the blood draining from my face. Of course, it's Jason's twin. I should've known something was off right away. He holds himself differently from Jason, and he's dressed completely differently.

Jackson finally reaches us. He stands beside his brother, and I want to facepalm. The difference between them is minute, but to me it's so clear it's almost laughable that I mixed them up before. It *is* laughable according to Jason and Jackson.

I thought Jason was intimidating, but two of them, standing beside each other like a tall, unfairly good-looking brick wall, makes me take a step back.

Jackson hands me the black hoodie, and my fingers curl around its familiar softness. "I think you meant to throw this in *Jason's* face."

I'm saved from my mortification when a car pulls up and my phone dings. I use the distraction to check it, and see that it's my Uber.

"Sorry for calling you an asshole," I tell Jackson, and then don't wait for a reply as I stride over to Gia. She's leaning on a tree, barely able to keep her eyes open.

"We're leaving," I tell her. She can hate me all she wants, but there's no way I'm leaving her here to continue puking and probably unable to get home.

"I'm not ready to leave," she slurs, and this time I catch her before she stumbles.

"You're getting in the Uber."

I lead her to the car and open the door, where the driver greets me and confirms my name. I settle Gia into the seat and buckle her in, all while she weakly protests. As I shut her door and round the car, I make eye contact with Jason. His eyes bore into mine. I've only seen him look at me this intensely when he thought I'd been thrown out of a moving vehicle earlier this evening. Something stirs in my chest, but I ignore it. I get into my side of the car and confirm the address to the driver.

"Uh . . ." he starts, looking from me to Gia, who's groaning with her head against the seat rest. "You know if she throws up in my car it's a hundred dollars extra, right?"

"She'll be fine," I say, and need it to be true. I don't have that kind of money readily available, and I doubt I can ask Dario for it—I still haven't even met the man.

"All right," he says, then starts driving.

I couldn't wait to see Gia, it's all I thought about in our time apart. I thought she was doing better than me, *hoped* she was thriving away from Aunt Julie and LA. Now the moment is here and I've discovered my worst nightmare is coming true: Gia's not coping with it, not at all, and there's nothing I can do to make it better.

I grip something warm and soft, and only just realize I have Jason's hoodie, and I'm clutching it like a lifeline.

After a few moments of stewing in silence, I can't take it anymore. I know she's going through it, but getting in a car with a drunk driver after what happened to us with

Mom's creepy stalker? She should know better.

"I can't believe you," I scold her. "Don't you remember what happened with Alice?" I point at my arm, where the scar is still visible from the crash. She's got one on her leg.

Gia scoffs. "Alice was arrested for that, I saw it, just like I saw you get arrested." Her head rolls against the headrest to look at me. "But she didn't get arrested for murder."

She doesn't mean that, I know she doesn't. She's drunk and upset and goading me. I take deep breaths like Anusha showed me during our mandatory five-minute meditations before each session, forcing myself not to take the bait.

Instead of answering her, I grit out, "It was so irresponsible of you."

Gia laughs. She actually *laughs*. It's a drunken, lazy laugh, but a laugh nonetheless.

"Why are you laughing?"

"Because I'm about to get real fucking irresponsible," she slurs, then leans over, and pukes all over the Uber's floor mats.

three

Gia spent most of Saturday sleeping off her hangover, and I spent it holed up in my room, unpacking, looking out my front-facing window every so often like a puppy waiting for its owner to come home. I hated myself every time I did it, but I couldn't stop checking to see if a car pulled into the driveway, hoping to catch a glimpse of my father. Now it's Sunday and I still haven't met him, still don't know what he looks like; he didn't come home yesterday.

I used to ask Mom about Dario all the time when I was younger, wondering where he was, when he was coming back, what he looked like when I started to forget. I refused to believe he left and wasn't coming back.

When I was eight years old, my school hosted a daddy-daughter dance. I wrote the invitation myself, decorated it with sparkles and stickers and little hand-drawn pictures of the two of us, asking him to come. Mom said she'd mail it out, and to this day I'll never know if she did, if she even knew where he was. But I sat at that dance in my little pink dress with a perfect view of the door, watching and waiting for my dad to show up, confident he would. When the other girls picked on me for coming alone, I'd stick my chin in the air and tell them, *Just watch and wait to see my daddy. He's coming.*

Despite no longer being that naive little kid who kept getting disappointed, and despite learning time and time again that my father would never show up for me, I can't seem to kill that little girl in the pink dress buried deep inside me. I was her again yesterday, looking around at every man in the airport, hoping it was her dad, and no matter how much I hate it, no matter how much I tell myself I don't care, I'm still that little girl, glancing out my window every time a car drives by. Two days in a row now.

It's especially torturous because I'm sitting on my bed folding laundry and have to stand every time I want to check.

Stupid. Stop being so stupid.

I grab the next thing off the top of the laundry pile, and it's Jason's hoodie. It smells like fresh laundry detergent instead of the cedarwood and spice that I associate him with, and it makes me sad, then angry that I'm sad. It's just a hoodie, and yet I feel like I've lost something.

I laugh and place the sweatshirt over the back of my desk chair. Jason is not the kind of boy I should be thinking about, never mind sniffing his hoodie like a complete weirdo. If I want to live a boring, squeaky-clean life free of drama and arrests and murder charges, I should probably stay away from him. All I want are good grades and a college degree and a white picket fence and maybe a few kids and a dog. I'll be normal; boring. Not a topic for a true crime podcast.

I eye the bedroom Zia Stella set up for me. It used to be Dario's home office that she converted just for me. It's a good size, and with the windows and door wide open, it doesn't feel as stuffy. Cold air breezes in; it'll probably be a problem in the winter, but for now, I can *breathe*.

There's a queen-sized bed with a fluffy baby blue comforter and pillows—at least ten, all different sizes—more pillows than I'll ever need. The walls are painted a lighter shade of baby blue, and there's a corkboard on the wall with baby blue pushpins waiting to be used. Even the small plush carpet covering the hardwood in front of my bed is baby blue. It's like someone told Zia Stella baby blue was my favorite color and she went a little overboard.

But even though a baby blue fairy threw up all over the room, it's nice—normal. It looks like a regular teenage girl's room. I wasn't a regular teenager with Aunt Julie in LA; I couldn't be. If I wasn't cleaning up after her or one of her parties, or holding her hair while she puked, or entertaining the constant parade of people she brought over, I was working or looking after Gia. I couldn't be normal with Mom either, not when we were always dragged along to some movie shoot or the next, or sitting in the car with snacks and coloring books for hours while she went to a networking party. But here, I'm free of Mom, of Aunt Julie, of the memories of that night. And unless I screw it up somehow and get kicked out, I have a real shot at getting my grades up enough to win some scholarships. So, I'll steer clear of Jason, of his drag racing and hotwiring and running from the cops, even if I can't get the memory of his carefree singing, of his eyes burning into me, out of my head.

My phone chimes from the desk, and for some stupid reason my pulse quickens, thinking it's Jason. But he doesn't have my number, and he wouldn't be texting me. I followed his advice though and put my phone in rice. The screen is still cracked, obviously, but it helped with some of the water damage and the staticky speaker.

The text is from Zia Stella: How are you settling in?

I'm about to text my reply when the sound of the garage opening beneath me startles me. I rush to the window in time to see a Mercedes pull into the driveway and disappear into the garage.

For a second that little girl in the pink dress is back, but I stomp her deep, deep down. This is not my dad here to rescue me. It's the man who would have nothing to do with us if not for some legal and moral obligation—the same man who couldn't be bothered to pick me up from the airport, who didn't care to meet me until days after I arrived.

Even with that knowledge, I exit my room, forcing myself to go down the stairs at an even pace, and open the kitchen pantry, examining its contents casually without actually seeing anything. This isn't a big deal, *shouldn't* be a big deal, and yet my heart is still hammering in my chest. I wonder what he looks like now, what he'll think of me, if we share any features.

The door that leads to the garage opens, followed by footsteps into the house, and still I keep my head in the pantry, acting casual.

"Stella, have you seen my—"

I step out from behind the door that was blocking his view of me.

"—oh," he finishes when he realizes I'm not his sister.

"Hi," I say, hating how timid and stupid I sound. I'm supposed to be *mad* at him for forgetting about me at the airport.

He somehow looks different and exactly the same as I remember him. He's tan, like he enjoys spending time outside, and has deep-brown, almost black hair, like Gia's, that's cut short to his head. His eyes are brown like Gia's too, and he's not incredibly tall, but still a head taller than me. Even with the frown lines on his forehead and other slight signs that he's aged since the last time I saw him, he's still a handsome man.

My father—Dario—takes a surprised step back. He

scans my face before his own pales. I stand there, unmoving, as we take each other in.

"Siena . . . you look . . ." he starts, closing his eyes and shaking his head. He clears his throat. "You're here."

"Yeah, since Friday," I say, getting that little jab in.

"Right." He looks around the kitchen. "Have you seen a file folder around here? It's blue. There are a few contracts in there I need."

I open my mouth, then close it. I'm standing in front of him for the first time in years, and the only thing he asks is if I've seen a stupid file folder?

"Um, no," I respond.

With that answer, he turns to leave without another word, and I stand there stupidly for just a second before scrambling after him. "Where are you going?"

"Back to work."

"It's Sunday."

"And I need to get to *work*, Siena."

I don't know why I'm following him when he's made it clear he wants nothing to do with me, but I stay on his heels all the way to the door until he suddenly stops, and I halt just in time to not run him over.

He curses when he turns around and just barely misses me. "What the hell are you doing, Siena?"

That's a great question, because I don't know either.

"Umm . . ."

He sighs and pinches the bridge of his nose. "Is this how it's going to be the whole time?"

"I—"

"Listen, Siena. I took you in because you're my kid, and I have some kind of responsibility here, but that doesn't mean you can come in here and get in my way."

His words freeze me. I was wondering why he took me in, but never expected him to outright explain.

He continues, "I've lived for fourteen years without kids, and it's no skin off my back whether you're here or not. You're a minor, so until you're eighteen you're under my care. But I don't have the patience to sit around and deal with kids and their problems. I didn't then, and I don't now. Act like an adult, don't cause any problems, don't bother me, and we won't have any issues. All right?"

He doesn't wait for me to acknowledge what he's said, instead opening the door to the garage and disappearing when it slams shut behind him.

I stand there, stunned. He just admitted that he wants nothing to do with me. I'm only here because of court-ordered responsibility, and I'm out on my ass when I'm eighteen. The thought sits heavy in my chest. A part of me knew all this already, but to hear it out loud, from my father's mouth, makes it all too real. That's another adult in my life to add to the list of people who want nothing to do with me.

A notification on my phone goes off, and I grab it from my pocket to check. It's a text from Zia Stella again. I'm picking up sushi for dinner, there's a great place on the way home from the hospital. Let me know what to order for you. Ask Gia too.

The phone chimes again, and it's a PDF of the restaurant's menu.

I haven't had a real conversation with Gia since last night, so this is my chance to try. Putting that huge letdown of an encounter behind me, I go upstairs and cross the hall to Gia's door. She's painted it black.

"Gia?" I knock a few times.

"What?"

I open the door and step into Gia's room—the first room she's ever had to herself. It's a lot like my room, except it's much more lived in, and it was a dark-purple fairy that threw up all over it instead of a baby blue one. There are clothes piled up on her dresser and in the corner on the floor, as well as posters of various bands she likes all over the wall. She's sitting on the bed using her brand-new laptop—also dark purple—and watches me as I enter.

"How are you feeling?" I ask, stopping by her desk.

"Fine."

Pinned to her corkboard are pictures of her and her friends from LA. In some of the pictures, there's a smiley face sticker covering the face of one of the girls.

"They were still nice pictures," Gia says, following my gaze. "I didn't want to throw them out just because Nora was in them."

I lean against the desk to study her. Since she cut all her hair off, the heart shape of her face is much more pronounced, and so are her big brown eyes.

"Nora didn't deserve you, Gia."

She shuts her laptop but fiddles with the protective case. "I was staying with her and her mom until Dad agreed to take custody since Aunt Julie wanted nothing to do with me . . ."

I grit my teeth but don't say anything. She's opening up; we're having a civil conversation. This is not the time to cuss out Aunt Julie.

Gia continues, "I was quiet for a few days, but Nora kept asking me to tell her everything that happened, and I couldn't hold it in anymore, so I told her."

I straighten. "You told her *everything*?"

"I told her the same things I told the cops," she says, moving her laptop aside.

I nod and ask cautiously, "Okay, and what happened?"

Gia frowns and picks at the skin around her nails. "She . . . she was . . . I don't know how to describe it. Frightened? Appalled? She said killing him *wasn't the appropriate response*, or some other bullshit like that, and that I should've stopped you."

Gia can't even look at me, and I can barely think straight. Her *girlfriend* knew what Stan was doing to Gia, how he was hurting her and how much worse it would've gotten, and didn't comfort her? And then made her feel guilty about something she can't change?

"Oh, Gia," I sigh, rushing to sit with her on the bed. I wrap my arms around her and she doesn't push me away like she did the other night. "She wasn't there," I say. "She can't comment on what you should or shouldn't have done.

83

Besides, the courts agreed it *was* the appropriate response. Don't dwell on things we can't change."

She looks straight at the wall, her eyes glazing over. "I can't stop seeing it. Him reaching for me. The knife going in. The blood." She touches the spot on her cheek where the bruise had been. There's nothing there now.

I squeeze her tighter to me. I wish she hadn't had to go through any of that. I wish she hadn't had to *see* that. I was only there for the tail end, the brutal part, and I still have nightmares about all the blood. I can't imagine what it's like for Gia.

"I'm sorry you had to go through that, Gia. I'm sorry I couldn't protect you better, but I did the best I could. If I could've done something more or different to protect you, I would've."

Gia shakes her head. "She looked at me like I—like we—were monsters."

"Gia . . ."

She slips out of my grasp and shifts away. "Zia Stella came to get me the next day and Nora told me she wanted to break up."

For a while, neither of us says anything. Gia adored Nora. I can't imagine how reliving her words on repeat have affected Gia after all these weeks.

"Has talking to the counselor been helping?" I ask quietly.

"Kind of."

She looks down at her fingers and picks at her cuticles. My sister has always been happy and bubbly, and this version of her only reminds me that she might never be the same again. Not after what happened. Not after all that blood.

"Are you going to tell me what Friday night was about?" I ask.

"You wouldn't understand."

"I can't understand if you don't tell me."

"It was nothing," she mumbles.

I force my tone to remain even. "It was not *nothing*. You or someone else could've gotten seriously hurt."

"But no one did."

"That's not the point, Gia! Someone very easily could have." It could've been her. And I wasn't there to protect her. "Promise me you'll stay away from those kids. I don't think they're good influences on you."

She jumps up from the bed. "You can't tell me who to hang out with."

I stand too. "Those aren't the kinds of friends you need."

Any openness and vulnerability Gia has shown me completely disappears. The hardened girl from Friday night is back. "Being a new kid is social suicide. Just because you're okay not having any friends doesn't mean I am. Do you know how hard it was that first week in this godforsaken, boring town with nothing to do and no friends? All I had to do was sit here and stare at these hideous purple walls and think about what happened over and over and over again." She stomps toward her corkboard, where she scans the pictures. "I was popular before, and if I have to live in this cold, miserable town, then at least I'll do it being *popular*. So you can't tell me who to hang out with. I will have friends, and it will be Brianna and Chris and the rest of them."

She thinks I don't understand boredom? She thinks I haven't been trapped in a room with hideous walls and had nothing to do but think about what happened repeatedly? About what I could've done differently? About what she was doing? About what was going to happen to me, and if I'd spend the rest of my life staring at those same hideous walls?

I want to say that all to her. Scream it over and over until it sinks in that she's not the only one going through shit. But I don't, because that's not going to help, because I need her to think I have my shit together. So instead, I stare at her profile, forcing myself to do Anusha's deep breathing until I'm calm enough not to shout.

"Fine," I say. She's made up her mind, but hopefully once school starts tomorrow, she'll be too busy to do stupid things with her friends. "Zia Stella is picking up sushi for dinner. What do you want?"

"I'm not eating dinner here. I'm going to Brianna's. I'll probably be home late."

For the first time I notice the backpack and outfit laid out on the end of Gia's bed.

"Why are you bringing a bikini?" I ask. "It's way too cold to go swimming." Or maybe it's fine for locals. Maybe I'm just used to the LA heat.

Gia shoves the bikini into her backpack, and glass clinks as the bag shifts. I yank the front of the bag down, forcing the zipper open to reveal a bottle each of tequila and vodka.

"Seriously, Gia? You're drinking? And where did you get these from?"

Gia snatches the bag back and zips it closed. "From Dad's liquor cabinet."

I'm taken aback. "You're stealing from *Dario*?" Doesn't she realize we have to play nice with him? A person who's a virtual stranger and won't hesitate to throw us out on our asses if we cause him any trouble? He literally admitted that to me not even twenty minutes ago!

"He hasn't noticed. As you can tell, he's never home," Gia says, her back rigid.

I try to move so I can see her face, but she keeps it down toward the bag as she stuffs things in the front pocket. "How long have you been stealing from him? What the hell, Gia, you hate tequila."

"Well, I can't take his expensive Scotch, can I?" Gia shoots back.

"You shouldn't be stealing at all!"

How am I supposed to live out a normal year if Dario kicks us out? How is Gia going to have the kind of stability we've never had with our mom or Aunt Julie if she's actively trying to piss him off? Plus, she really shouldn't be getting that drunk every night. Or ever.

"I can't show up to a party with no alcohol like a loser," she grumbles.

"Since when do you care about drinking or what other people think?"

Gia's phone chimes and she glances at it. "Since now." She barges past me, and I stand there stunned for a moment before my body catches up to my brain, and I chase after her down the hall.

"Where are you going?"

"I told you, a party." She jogs down the stairs. "It's the most exclusive party of the year. Popular kids *only*. I'm lucky Brianna's even invited me."

She pauses at the front door to slip her shoes on.

She can't leave like this and go to who knows where to party with kids who think it's okay to shove seven kids into the back of the car and drink and drive! It isn't safe! Has she been doing this the whole time I wasn't here? Who's been making sure that she's okay? Hell, look at last night; How would she have gotten home? What if that stupid drunk, high kid drove her home? What if they just *left* her there in the trees puking her guts out?

"Gia, you can't—"

"Don't wait up!" And then she's gone. She jumps into a car that is waiting in the driveway, and I watch as they speed down the street.

There's a pounding in my temples, and I pace the

porch. I should be organizing my room right now. Maybe getting my things together before school starts tomorrow. But now I'll never get anything done. I'll be waiting for my kid sister, who I practically raised, to get home safely, with the added bonus of making sure Dario doesn't hear her come in drunk, if he's even home.

Gia's dealing with stuff, and I think that's what scares me most. If this is how she's handling it, what's going to happen when she realizes it's not working and starts spiraling even more out of control?

I stop pacing and make the decision. I shouldn't intervene, but I wasn't there for her then, so I'll be there for her now, whether she wants me to be or not. Besides, there's no harm in finding out where the party is and swinging by.

I run upstairs and call Lily. It goes straight to voicemail, so I send her a text asking her to call me back. If anyone knows about an *exclusive* party, it has to be her.

After an awkward dinner with minimal small talk with Zia Stella—who informs me that Dario left on some business trip to Vegas—I'm back in my room, still with no word from Lily. Maybe she's at that photoshoot she was talking about Friday and can't answer right now, but Nyah must know about a party. I find Lily's Instagram first, then find Nyah's profile from the tagged photos. I send her a message on Instagram, asking if she knows about any exclusive party happening tonight, then sit on my bed and chew my fingernail. It's getting dark and the breeze through the window is cool, so I change from my tank top into Jason's hoodie. For some stupid reason, I sniff it again, expecting something different from the clean detergent scent.

I haven't heard from Gia at all. Swimming and drinking is a bad combination. How many school presentations have we had to sit through explaining just that? I've never had to worry about her like this before.

With still no word from Gia, Lily, or Nyah, I play with the sleeves of Jason's hoodie. He seems popular, so he must know where this party is. But I'm not supposed to be associating with him. I'm not supposed to be seeking him out or messaging him. And I'm especially not supposed to be asking him to bring me to another party. Out of curiosity, I check to see who Nyah's following and find a few Jasons. But when I click on "Jason Parker," I know I've found him.

There aren't a lot of pictures, only a few with him and his twin and a combination of other people. Them with an older, more serious-looking version of them—most likely the older brother he mentioned. Them with an older woman who has a soft smile in front of a fiftieth-birthday cake. Them with the older brother again, who's standing with a pretty brunet and a little girl, no older than five with the same brunet hair, and another guy tagged in the picture as Mason.

Nothing about this Instagram profile matches up with the boy I know. These pictures all seem family oriented. I was imagining pictures of his car, maybe. Or pictures of him at parties, running wild. Not pictures at family barbecues and birthdays.

But I know better. I know that beneath this innocent-looking Instagram feed is trouble, at least trouble for *me*, and that's why I shouldn't message him. I should not, even in these dire circumstances, message him. *Do not message him!*

I message him.

The words are sent before I can think about it, and then I stare at the message in horror, pressing the oversized sleeve that engulfs my hand against my nose and mouth.

It's the same thing I sent to Nyah and Lily, and now I'm thinking that may not have been the best thing to send to Jason.

Hey, it's Siena. Do you know if there's a party tonight? Please call me.

Followed by my phone number.

Maybe I should message him again to clarify that I'm looking for Gia, not awkwardly flirting with him. But at this point, would he even believe it? I groan and flop backward on my bed. Maybe he won't see it. But I need him to see it, and I've messaged him already anyway—what's another one?

I lift my phone to open Instagram again, but it starts ringing, shocking me so badly I drop it onto my face. Scrambling, I sit up and check it; I don't recognize the number.

"Hello?" I answer.

A deep voice greets me, sending a shiver down my spine. "So, you had such a great time at the party Friday you're already looking for more?"

"No. Well yes. I—" I take a deep breath to collect my thoughts, though it all comes out as one sentence. "Gia stole some alcohol from our dad for some exclusive party and I have a really bad feeling about it especially since they're swimming and she's having a rough time and I don't trust her friends and I just want to make sure she's okay."

He's quiet for a moment. There are loud noises in the background. Music. Is he already there?

"I don't know about any parties," he says. Is he lying? Has he had enough of me? But then why would he bother calling me just to lie?

"Do you know who she's with?" he continues.

"Those kids from Friday. I only know the names Brianna and Chris."

Someone in the background calls Jason, and he shouts that he'll be a second. Then his voice is clear again. "Brianna is Brandon's little sister." Brandon, as in the guy who grabbed Lily and made her cry? The one who creeps me out? "Let me make a few calls, I'll get back to you."

And then the line is dead. He just hung up on me!

"Such a jerk," I grumble. But he's a jerk who's helping me and is my only lead right now.

After ten minutes with nothing from Jason, I realize he might have forgotten about me. Which is fine. Totally fine. He was a long shot anyway. I'm not bothered at all.

My phone rings, and I jump to answer it.

"Where on Pinewood Street are you?" Jason greets.

"Um, 147?" It comes out as a question.

"I'll be there in ten."

I spring up from my bed. "What? Why?"

"Because I know where Gia is, and you're going to want to go get her."

four

Jason's words have me running to my closet scanning the boxes from LA that I haven't unpacked yet. "Where is she?"

He sounds like he's talking on Bluetooth, so he must already be driving. "Brandon, the fucking idiot, was screwing with Brianna and told her all the incoming popular sophomores break into the school pool and throw a party the day before school starts. He told her we all did it when we were her age, but that her friends wouldn't have the balls. Apparently, she thought he was serious and took it as a personal challenge."

"Gia's breaking into the school?" I toss boxes around

reading labels. "She could get expelled! Or *arrested*! What is she *thinking*?" She must've known the plan; that's why she had a swimsuit. I can't pretend they just sprang it on her. She's there, fully committed, even after what happened to me, after what I've been through. My blood boils in my veins, but I force myself not to get mad, at least until *after* I find Gia and bring her home. But it's hard. Really hard.

"Brandon's not home but according to his mom, the girls didn't leave that long ago. She doesn't know where they're going. Maybe we can stop them before anything happens."

I can't find the box labeled "shoes." The ones from Friday are still a mess and I haven't needed to find another pair until now.

"You said *we*," I point out.

"Yeah. What part of *I'll be there in ten* don't you understand?"

"Um, the *we* part?" I say, still frantically looking for sneakers. He says *we* a lot. From the very first moment we met, it was always *we*. "*We* are running from the cops." "*We* are walking back to town." "*We* are finding Gia at a party." I'm not used to *we*, not when I've spent my life taking care of myself.

"How else do you expect to get to school? You don't drive."

I don't even remember telling him that.

I find a pair of heels in one of the boxes with my dresses,

but no sneakers. Not even flats or flip-flops. Where are all my shoes? I don't have time for this right now! I grab them anyway since they're my only option and peek out of my bedroom to check that the door to the guest bedroom is closed. Zia Stella's in there. She decided to stay since Dario's away, but she went to bed early after a long day.

Jason continues, "You're not going to walk, since it's a ten-minute drive to school from Pinewood, and that's assuming you even know how to get there. You're not going to ask your dad, because you said Gia stole alcohol from him, and my assumption is that you don't want him to find out. And if I were you, I wouldn't call an Uber, because what's stopping that driver from telling on the kids if they've already broken in? Especially if the driver's a local."

I pause as I creep down the stairs. He's completely right. He's clearly put a lot of thought into this—way more than I would've.

And he's volunteered to help me.

"I'm on your street," he says when I don't say anything.

"You said ten minutes," I reply, sitting on the floor and hastily trying to fasten the strap of my heels.

"I got every green light."

I snort. I've seen him drive. "Likely story. Don't get pulled over before getting here."

"Well, it must be my lucky day, because I'm outside."

Lights illuminate the house through the front window, and as quietly as I can, I open the front door and shut it behind me. I'm sure Zia Stella wouldn't mind me going out, she's practically been pushing me out since I arrived, but I don't want her asking questions about *where* I'm going, and with who.

I hang up on Jason without saying goodbye and wobble out to his car, slipping into the passenger seat. I'm immediately engulfed in that smell of cedarwood and something with warm, spicy notes that heats up my insides.

"Thanks for this," I say in greeting.

"The shoes are certainly a choice," Jason says as he backs out of the driveway.

I tuck my feet to the side as if to hide them from his view. "I couldn't find a single other pair of shoes," I mumble. Maybe I should've stayed in my socks. I did it Friday, what's the difference?

"And I see you've decided to keep my hoodie," he says, glancing at the warm pullover.

My cheeks burn. "I meant to wash it and then give it back, but I got cold . . ."

He raises an eyebrow. "Likely story."

I roll my eyes at him for throwing my earlier words back at me, and the corner of his mouth lifts in a smirk.

I take the opportunity to study his face. His profile is just as nice as I remember it, his nose just as straight, his jaw just as sharp. My daydreams about him haven't done him justice, and I hate that I've been daydreaming about him in the first place. His hair is disheveled, and his arms are bare, with black smudges of . . . is that grease? His black T-shirt is clean.

"Do you always stare at boys whose hoodies you've stolen, or just me?"

I quickly turn from him. "I didn't steal your hoodie. Technically, I returned it—it's not my fault Jackson gave it back to me."

"Right . . ." he says, then notices me eyeing his arms. "I was at work when you called. I obviously didn't have time to shower."

"Work?" For some reason I didn't picture Jason with a job.

"Yeah. You know, a place that pays you for your time and labor so you can afford—"

"I know what work is." I cut him off, and he bites back a smile. "I'm going to have to look for a job soon."

"You know," he starts, "you almost look like a completely different person out of the rain and mud."

"Yeah," I say. "It's almost like I don't make a habit of lying around in the mud."

He chuckles. "Could've fooled me."

"Ha ha," I deadpan. "You need to try it one day and see what you're missing."

"I'll have to take your word on it."

A ringing cuts off the soft music that was playing in the car, and the caller ID on the car's screen says it's "the better-looking twin."

Jason shakes his head. "He likes to steal my phone and change his name every once in a while." He taps Accept. "What? And be nice, you're on Speaker."

"Speaker?" Jackson's voice fills the car. "Who are you with? I thought you didn't finish work for another half hour?"

I swing my head to look at Jason, who shifts uncomfortably in his seat. He left work early? For me? I glance down at my hands and hope my face isn't turning red.

"Why are you calling?" Jason asks, ignoring the question.

"Natalia asked me to pick up some milk for tomorrow morning and I forgot. Can you?"

"Yeah, sure, if the store's still open."

"Cool," Jackson says. "Where are you going?"

"School. It's a long story. Ask Tyler to fill you in."

"Why are you being so weird?" Jackson asks, then pauses. "Are you with the hot, muddy girl from Friday with the big—"

"*Goodbye*, Jackson," Jason interrupts forcefully, then hangs up. To me, he says, "Ignore him."

We stop at a red light. I can't look at Jason, not after learning he left work early for me. He didn't have to do that, and I don't know why he did. We're not friends, and I'm pretty sure he finds me annoying, or at least weird. But here he is, risking himself and helping me make sure Gia doesn't get in trouble, even though I'm nothing to him. I open the window a bit to let in some air. My whole body stiffens when a police car pulls up behind us.

"Um, Jason," I say, facing straight ahead. "There's a cop behind us."

The light turns green and Jason resumes driving. The cop follows. "Yeah, I see him. He's been there since your house."

I still don't look back; I don't want to seem suspicious by constantly turning around. Do they know where we're going? Do they know about Gia and her friends? Are they on their way there now to bust them? Do they recognize Jason's car from Friday? I force my breathing to remain even. I haven't done anything wrong.

Jason eyes my bouncing leg. "If they were going to pull me over or arrest me for Friday, they would've done it already."

He turns and so does the officer. It makes me bite my nails.

"You're acting like you just robbed a bank," Jason says. "Relax. They're going in the same direction as us."

I check the side mirror again and the officers behind us turn while we continue straight. My breath comes easier.

"What's up with you?" Jason asks, his eyes searching my face.

I'm not going to explain to him that I never ever want to be in the back of a police car again. "Cops just . . . make me nervous."

He huffs a sarcastic laugh. "They make everyone nervous. But you're like three seconds away from biting your finger off."

I drop my hand from my mouth. I don't want anyone to know what happened in LA, but then again, he is helping

me, has been helping me since I first got here. And I don't
have to tell him everything.

Before I can think it through, I say, "I was arrested
once."

The car jerks before Jason forces his gaze back to the
road. "You're serious."

It's not a question. "Yes. And it was . . . a terrible
experience. I never ever ever want it to happen again." I
open the window a little more to help the closing of my
throat. "There was a time I never thought I'd breathe fresh
air again."

He's quiet for a moment. Maybe I told him too much.
Maybe I've scared off the only almost-friend I have. But
then he laughs and says, "And Friday you were looking at
me like I was the criminal."

His laughter throws me off for a moment. "You were
actively evading the police!"

"You mean *successfully evading* the police," he counters,
and I can't help but laugh at his cocky smile. I can't believe
I'm laughing at this. I told him I was arrested, and he's not
harassing me for details or judging me. I felt ashamed telling him, telling anyone, about it, but he's making it seem
like it's no big deal.

"You know," he continues, "I totally pegged you for a
jaywalker the moment I saw you. Goes hand in hand with
the lying-in-the-middle-of-the-road thing."

"I *do not* make that a habit!" I exclaim, giving him a
light shove, and when we stop laughing, the memory of

that night comes back to me, making me frown at my lap.

Noticing my sudden sobering, Jason says, "Well, if it makes you feel better, my older brother Aiden was arrested for killing our stepfather when he was seventeen and I was nine."

My jaw drops as I stare at him. That wasn't a joke.

When he notices my shocked expression, he adds, "Oh, he didn't do it. He was released a few hours later."

I'm speechless. His brother was arrested for murdering someone when he was seventeen, and so was I.

When I get my thoughts together, I say, "Wow. I'm sorry to hear about your stepfather. Did they find who did it?"

Jason doesn't answer me, and all his playfulness is gone. "We're here."

I'm too distracted by staring at the *huge* school to question his sudden shift. But he passes right by it, instead turning on the street behind it. He parks by the curb at the entrance to a subdivision behind another car.

"The school's back there. What are you doing?" I ask as Jason undoes his seat belt and exits the car. I scramble to follow.

"It is," he acknowledges, closing his door. He meets me on the sidewalk and walks back the way we came, and I quickly fall in line with him. "There are no cars in the parking lot at the school. If they've already broken in, Principal Anderson is going to check the cameras, and I don't want her to see my car."

We round the corner, and the school comes into view. He gestures at my—his—hoodie. "Put the hood up. Tuck your hair in too. I don't know how advanced the cameras are or if they're particularly good in the dark, but on the chance that they are, the pink hair will give us away."

I hastily do what he says and make sure all my hair is down the back of the oversized hoodie. I didn't think about cameras. I would've charged in there and pounded on the door, yelling Gia's name.

"So, you do a lot of breaking and entering?" I ask Jason, mostly as a joke to distract myself from my nerves, but partly because I'm curious to hear the answer. He barely even blinked at my earlier admission, but maybe it's because of his brother's experience.

He shoves a baseball cap I didn't notice him holding onto his head. I guess I stole his only backup hoodie and that's all he's been left with as a disguise. I should probably give the hoodie back, but not right now. It's cold, and I need it for the cameras. Maybe after we get Gia and we're safely back in the car.

He raises an eyebrow. "Not particularly. You seem to have it in your head that I'm into illegal activities."

I hold up a finger for each point, counting them off. "Well, first, I met you while you were running from the police because you were drag racing, then you told me you can hotwire cars, and now we're breaking into the school. Frankly, you're a terrible influence on me."

"Talk about the pot calling the kettle black." He

chuckles, and though I shouldn't be attracted to him for all the reasons I just listed, I find myself leaning in close to him. I straighten up and wrap my arms around my torso as we walk as if to remind it to stay in place.

"That's it," he promises. "I don't participate in any other illegal things."

"Right. Because all of that is enough illegal activity for you."

"Hey, I never said I regularly hotwire cars, just that I know how. And may I remind you that I was minding my own business at work, and now I'm breaking and entering for you. So actually, I think you're the terrible influence on me."

I attempt to find a comeback, but I can't because he's technically right. Of the two of us, I'm the only one who's been arrested and acquitted of murder.

He laughs, his eyes alight with amusement, as if he enjoys getting under my skin.

"You're going to be my undoing, Siena Amato," Jason says. "I already know it."

My mouth drops open, but I can't find the words, so instead I stare up at him with wide eyes as my mouth flaps open and closed. Eventually, I say, "Well, don't worry. After we find Gia, you won't ever have to talk to me again."

"But then who would make sure you didn't lie in the middle of the road in the rain?"

"*When* are you going to let that go? I th—"

"Shh." He cuts me off. "Do you hear that?"

It's quiet. I don't hear a party or a bunch of kids, just my heels clicking against the asphalt. Maybe they didn't go through with it. I *hope* they didn't go through with it.

But then I hear it. Music. It's faint, but it's there.

"This way," Jason says, leading me to a door at the side of the school. It's propped open, so the music grows louder as I slip inside behind Jason. It's dark, the surroundings illuminated only by emergency lights in the ceiling. There's a huge, official-looking swimming pool in the middle of the room, with bleachers on either side of it. About twelve kids sit on the ones directly in front of us. They're giggling and talking and taking sips from bottles and haven't even noticed Jason and me.

"What the hell is going on in here?" Jason demands in a booming voice that startles even me. The kids holding bottles all hastily hide them behind their backs. No one says anything as we approach, though they seem relieved that it's us and not the police or principal. "Do you even comprehend how much trouble you'd be in if you got caught?"

The kids look back and forth between me and Jason, who's wearing a scowl that gives me shivers. I scan all their faces but don't see Gia. Maybe she left? Maybe she couldn't go through with it after all?

"It's okay, we won't get caught," one of the boys says. "We spray-painted the cameras as soon as we got here and didn't tell anyone outside of who's here right now."

"Great, so you've added vandalism to the breaking and

entering and the underage drinking," I mumble as I scan the room for Gia, praying she's not here.

"All right, everyone out," Jason announces, leaving no room for argument.

The kids groan and collect their bags, and Brianna steps up. "Come on, Jason. We got here literally five minutes ago. Plus, we know you guys did it too."

Jason shakes his head. "Your brother lied to you. We've done stupid things, but never *this* stupid. I'm serious, everyone out. *Now.*"

That sets everyone into action, scattering to grab their things and leave the pool as quickly as possible. The music abruptly shuts off too.

"Brianna!" I rush to her as she angrily grabs her belongings. "Where's Gia?"

She eyes me like she doesn't recognize me. I feel Jason's presence behind me. "Brianna?" he prompts.

She sighs and points to the other side of the room. "She's in the changing room puking. She can't hold her liquor."

I don't wait to hear more, instead sprinting around the pool toward the door marked "changing rooms."

"Gia!" I burst in, going through random doors until I find the bathroom. She's at the sink washing her face.

"Siena?" She straightens from the sink. She doesn't look as bad as Friday, and her words aren't slurred, but she looks a little green. She's wearing shorts and a hoodie that's zipped down just enough to reveal a bikini top. "What are you doing here? How did you find me?"

"It doesn't matter." I rush to her and grab her hand. "We need to get out of here right now."

She yanks her hand out of my grasp. "We just got here."

"What the hell, Gia?" I explode, the anger and frustration in my chest finally giving out. "Are you *trying* to get expelled? Are you trying to get kicked out of Dario's house? Are you trying to end up like me? Because believe me, it wasn't fun being confined to a little room with a tiny little window with someone watching over me, telling me when I could eat, sleep, and shit." Her face pales as I talk, and I feel guilty before I remember that it's my job to make sure she doesn't end up there too.

"It's—it's not that serious . . ." Gia stutters. "We won't get caught, it's—"

"Siena?" calls a voice. It's Jason.

"This is the girls' changing room!" Gia exclaims, though she's completely presentable and there's no one else in the entire school.

Jason appears around the corner holding Gia's backpack. She notices and snatches it back.

"We're leaving. The police are here, they'll be inside any minute now."

"Fuck," Gia and I say at the same time, racing behind Jason as he exits the changing room.

The pool room is clear, but I hear sirens approaching.

"Everyone left, but you guys must have triggered an alarm when someone broke the window to get in here," Jason explains, pivoting to the door we entered from, the one the police are closing in on.

"You guys *broke a window?*" I ask Gia as I try to keep up with Jason's brisk pace in these stupid heels.

"Not us, the guys did it like a minute before we got here," Gia clarifies, putting both her arms through the straps of her backpack. I pull her hood over her head to hide her face. The sirens are loud, and I hear car doors opening and closing.

They're *right here.* My vision blurs. I can't even think how many charges could be laid against us when they bust in here. We'd be expelled and kicked out of Dario's at the bare minimum, that's guaranteed. I can't protect Gia, not this time. And Jason. I roped him into this. He's going to be in trouble because of *me.* The room spins, and I don't realize I've stopped moving until Jason's in front of me, bending down to meet my eyes directly. His are blue, so blue. And clear. They remind me of the beaches back in LA.

"Siena, I need you to keep moving, okay?" he says, his voice so calm, like it always seems to be in times of crisis. It's grounding.

I nod, and he ushers us to a different exit, which brings us out at the back of the school. We're trapped. We can't get to the parking lot because we'll be walking straight toward the police, and in front of us is just an open field of grass that ends in fences. We're screwed.

"Let's go," Jason orders, and we follow his lead as he starts running.

"Where are we going?"

"There." Jason points to the fence at the end of the field. He keeps pace with us even though he could definitely run faster than Gia and me on a good day, never mind when we're in flip-flops and heels respectively.

I barely get a proper foothold on this grass, but I try to keep up as much as I can. About halfway to the fence, Jason stops and groans, dropping to his knees in front of me and fiddling with the straps on my shoes.

"Keep going, Gia," he commands, and she obeys without question.

My heart pounds. "What are you doing?"

"Your stupid shoes are going to get me arrested," he complains, getting the first one unbuckled and whipping it out from under me. I grab on to his sturdy shoulder for support as I'm thrown off balance. I'm too shocked to do anything other than stand there and grip his shoulder and ignore how broad it is.

He undoes the second shoe much faster, and soon he's standing, holding both heels in his hand, while my toes spread in the grass.

"Let's go," he says, grabbing my hand with his free one and pulling me to join Gia at the fence.

"Up and over, Gia," Jason says, cupping his hands together and bending over to give her a boost. Without hesitation, she places her foot in his hand and he throws her over the fence with ease.

"You next, Siena," Jason says as two people with flashlights appear in the field, shouting at us to stay put. My breathing becomes hard, but Jason tosses my heels over the fence.

He bends down and links his hands together like before. Behind him there's more shouting and officers running to us. I can practically feel the cuffs around my wrist, smell the bleachy cleaner and coffee in the police station, hear the ringing of phones then silence as I sit in the interrogation room for hours.

"*Siena!*" Jason hisses, grabbing my leg and placing my bare foot in his hand. "Now!"

My head clears, and when he feels my weight press into his hand, I'm flying through the air. My arms support me as I pull myself up and straddle the wood fence. Jason, with more grace than a guy his size should be allowed to possess, hops over the fence with ease and lands on the grass, all while I'm trying to gain my balance and finally manage to get both feet on the right side of the fence. While I'm contemplating how to get down, a beam of light lands on my face.

"Hey! Freeze right there!" an officer demands.

FUCK!

Large hands grip on my waist, and then I'm landing safely in someone's backyard.

There's shouting on the other side of the fence, but they're still halfway across the field. Lights turn on, and before we see what the owners will do about some kids loitering in their backyard, Jason drops his hold on my waist and instead grabs my hand. Together, we run to the gate at the side of the house. Gia's already there, undoing the latch, and we emerge on the street. Jason points Gia in the direction of the car and she runs in front of us, setting the pace. I run with Jason, my bare feet slapping against the sidewalk, my hand securely in his, really, really glad that Jason had the foresight not to park in the school's parking lot.

We run all the way to the end of the street, only slowing long enough to open the car doors. Jason drops my hand as soon as we stop, and a pang hits my stomach that I can't even begin to understand. He opens the passenger door and moves the front seat so Gia can hop in the back before adjusting it so I can sit in the front. My heart pounds the entire time, not slowing down even as Jason closes my door, effectively putting distance between me and getting arrested. Jason slides into the car and wordlessly hands me my shoes, which I didn't even realize he had picked up from the person's backyard. I had completely forgotten about them, but he didn't.

"I can't believe we just did that!" Gia wheezes, her cheeks flushed and chest heaving for breath like mine. She slumps against the seat. "We just got away with that! I can't believe how lucky we are."

"Not luck," I say, my head lolling against the headrest to look at the driver as I catch my breath. "Jason."

If it weren't for him, I wouldn't have found Gia. If it weren't for his quick thinking, Gia and I, along with all those other kids, would've been sitting ducks. If it weren't for him, I would've been having a panic attack in the middle of a field before getting tackled by a police officer.

I shove the hood down and crack the window to let in some fresh air, to help me *breathe*, as Jason drives down the street and away from the school.

"We're not home free yet," Jason says. "You guys did more than just break in, you damaged school property. They're not going to just let that go."

Gia looks down at her hands. "I didn't know they were going to do that."

Frustration claws at my throat, and I turn in my seat to face her. "You knew they were breaking in, Gia! How did you think they were going to do that? Pick a lock with a bobby pin and credit card like we're on some episode of *Scooby*-fucking-*Doo*?"

"I didn't know, okay! We were having *fun*! You should try it sometime," she bites back, crossing her arms over her chest. "Plus, I was already drunk when we got there, I didn't care what they were doing."

I huff and turn away from her, banging my head against the headrest a few times. We did get lucky this time, lucky because *Jason* was there. But I can't keep asking him to help me. He's not going to be there for me all the time, and he sure as shit can't do anything when the principal checks the cameras and sees Gia and all her drunk friends breaking into the pool before spray-painting the cameras. I need to get Gia to talk to me, *really* talk to me, tell me what's going on and why she feels the need to hang out with kids who are dead set on getting her drunk or causing trouble. I need to get her to see that she's better off without those friends, and to understand that I didn't almost lose everything for nothing.

But then what? Have her be all alone, like you?

I shake the thought away and rub at my temples. It's late, we're tired, and the adrenaline is wearing off. I'll worry about it tomorrow.

"Fuck," Jason says, breaking the silence we've been stewing in.

"What?" I ask, sitting up. We're on Pinewood, and it's calm and dark, with most people having gone to bed already—nothing looks out of the ordinary.

But then I see it.

There's a police car pulling up to Dario's house.

five

"I can keep driving," Jason offers, voice even and calm, the exact opposite of my heartbeat.

We went through all that tonight just for them to show up at my house anyway. For a moment, I consider taking him up on his offer, but then what? They'd find us eventually.

"No," I tell Jason. "Bring us home. Maybe we can talk to them and get off with a warning before they wake Zia Stella."

He nods once and pulls into the driveway as the two officers step out of their car. A quick glance at Gia shows her face white and eyes wide. She looks like she's going to keel over and puke right on the spot.

"I'm really sorry, Jason," I say. Jason helped me and now he's paying for it. If I can protect him, I will. "We'll tell them I called you after we ran, and you didn't know where we were coming from."

Jason parks and undoes his seat belt. "You'll say nothing," he says, turning the full force of his eyes on me. "You're a minor and they can't question you without a parent or guardian. So say nothing, understand?"

His intensity forces me to nod, and he turns the same look on Gia. "You too. Got it?"

"No," I interrupt. "Gia, you go straight inside. I'll handle it."

Her head bobs up and down just as there's a knock on my window. Jason gives me one last look for good measure before I open the door and step out.

"Can I help you, Officer?" I ask with a shaky voice. Jason glares at me as he walks around the car.

What? Did he expect me not to say hi? Or maybe it's because I *sound* guilty. I clear my throat as Jason stands beside me. Gia scurries to the house without a backward glance. I feel better once she's inside.

There are two uniformed police officers, one middle-aged, and one who seems just barely older than me. The younger one shifts from foot to foot and his eyes dart around, but the older one's attention is all on me.

"Are you Siena Amato?" he asks.

"Um, yes?" How did they know who we were from the school? It was too dark; they couldn't have seen our faces. My spine tingles. This all feels wrong.

The older officer nods, his face giving nothing away. "And you just moved here?"

"What is this about?" Jason asks.

"This doesn't concern you, boy," the officer snarls, catching me off guard. I wasn't expecting the hostility, and my pulse quickens. This can't be about the school; there's no way they could've found out who I was and beat us here. So, what is this really about, and why does the young guy look so sweaty and flighty?

Jason confidently steps forward. "If it concerns Siena, it concerns me."

The officer's nostrils flare and his hand moves to something on his belt. With wide eyes, I glance around. We're on a dark, sleepy, suburban street. No one is outside to witness whatever is happening.

The officer steps closer to Jason, who holds his ground despite being the same height as the officer but significantly less armed.

"Now, you listen to me—"

"No, I don't think we will," Jason says, and I stop breathing. Jason continues, "Legally, you can talk to us, but since this seems to be getting hostile and bordering on an interrogation, we'll be leaving."

Jason's hand lands on the small of my back. "Let's go, Siena," Jason commands, and my legs only work because he's guiding me around the officers, toward to the front door. We're so close, just in the middle of the driveway, but it feels so far away. My breathing is ragged, and I'm only focused on the feel of Jason's hand burning through the hoodie, imprinting itself on my skin, and the front door.

Loud steps follow us, and then the officer is standing in front of me, forcing us to stop.

"We're not done here." He scowls, and Jason pulls me back a few feet, away from the officer, away from the safety of the house.

"Officer Liu," comes a timid voice behind me, "maybe we should just go."

"No," Officer Liu tells the younger officer. He approaches us again and ducks down to meet my gaze. His eyes are bloodshot, and his breath smells like coffee. I force myself to stay in place. "I know who you are, Siena Amato. I was good friends with your dad. I knew your mom back when she was a trouble-causing delinquent in high school, partying and getting arrested and sending ex-boyfriends death threats. I know you *murdered* a man in Los Angeles, and you've come here to do the same thing."

I stop breathing, stop blinking, stop thinking, stop *everything*. I just stand there with my mouth open, staring at the officer.

For a few beats there's complete silence, a silence so loud and deafening I think I've stopped hearing too. But then a voice breaks the silence. *Mine.* "We're done here."

I'm too scared to look at Jason, the only kind-of friend

I have, and see the horror written on his face. But I refuse to feel bad about what happened—I refuse to *think* about what happened. He's here harassing me at my father's house, *my* house, for something I was acquitted for, and I'm not going to stand here and take it. I'm going to go inside and shower and forget this whole shit day happened.

I step around Officer Liu, but he moves to block me at the last second, causing me to bump into his shoulder.

"You just assaulted an officer!" he exclaims, pulling handcuffs off his belt.

I shuffle away from him. "What! No, I didn't!"

"Resisting arrest, noncompliance with an officer, and now assault? You saw all that, right, Officer Clark?"

Panic squeezes my throat. "No! I didn't do anything!" I trip over my own feet as I try to back away from him, only to bump into something. I twirl around and the younger officer, Officer Clark, stares at me with wide eyes. It only takes that second for Officer Liu to grab me and roughly haul me to Jason's car, slamming me face-first onto the hood. Jason's shouting something, but I can't make out the words over the ringing in my ears. I only barely register the pain as he cuffs my hands behind my back and pats me down, taking my phone and wallet before forcing me to stand.

"If you're not going to cooperate here, maybe you'll cooperate down at the station while your charges are being processed," Officer Liu fumes as he drags me to the back of the cop car.

Charges? I didn't do anything! How long will I be held there? What's going to happen to me? I'm *not* going back to juvie.

I dig my heels in, but it's hard to do when I'm barefoot on asphalt. Still, I struggle as Officer Liu half drags, half carries me toward the car.

"Hey! Stop that!" Jason commands, stepping between us and the back door of the car that Officer Clark opens.

"Out of the way," Officer Liu growls, shoving me directly into Jason, who steadies me.

Officer Liu doesn't care that Jason's standing in the way and continues forcing me to the car. My biceps sting where he's gripping me, and my feet burn from trying to find purchase on the ground. But still, with my hands cuffed behind my back and the dark interior of the caged police car looming in front of me, I don't go easy.

"Let her go!" Jason demands, catching me again when I'm shoved.

"Officer Clark, remove him," Officer Liu huffs, out of breath from our struggle. Then Jason is gone, and there's nothing standing between me and the car. My panic rises as I'm abruptly shoved inside, and the door is slammed in my face.

I'm trapped. I instinctively move to open the window, but my hands are cuffed. There's no *air* in here. Trying to control my breathing with the windows sealed gives me nothing but stale air, a weird combination of cleaning chemicals, and puke.

This is the first time I've been in the back of a police car without knowing where I'm going and why. I'm here completely blind and alone, and it terrifies me. I can't catch my breath.

There's a thud and the police car lurches. I look through the little metal and plastic dividers separating me from the front seat, shocked to see Jason with the side of his face pressed against the hood of the car. Officer Liu handcuffs him, and Officer Clark confiscates his possessions. Jason doesn't struggle.

"You've really done it now, boy," Officer Liu seethes as he shoves Jason in beside me and slams the door closed.

"Fucking assholes," Jason fumes as he shifts around in the seat, as if trying to get comfortable but knowing he can't with the handcuffs. "Don't say a goddamn word to them at the station. Not about where we were tonight, not about when you moved here, and especially not when he tries to bait you with whatever shit he thinks he knows about your past in LA." He gives up trying to shift around and instead settles on glowering through the windshield at the two officers, who are having an intense conversation outside. "Besides all the other bullshit, they didn't read us our Miranda rights. We'll be out of here before Officer Dipshit can blink."

I'm too shocked to say anything. Jason should *not* be sitting here beside me.

Moving here was supposed to give me a fresh start, away from the painful memories, away from the whispers, but here I am, barely three days later, in the back of a police car with my past haunting me. And even worse, I brought down the one person who's been nice to me.

I thought Jason would be the bad influence on me, but he was right. Only an hour or two ago he told me I would be his undoing; he probably didn't think it would be this fast.

"I'm sorry, Jason," I say, unable to look at him.

"Don't you dare apologize for this shit, it's not your fault," he says with such fierceness that I believe him. I'm just glad Gia's inside and has no part of this. I wonder if she's gone straight to bed or if she woke Zia Stella up. I'm not sure which I'd prefer.

The officers get into the car, and I look through my window at the house one last time, but my breath hitches when I see Gia standing on the porch, staring at us with a horrified expression.

Shit. How long was she standing there? How much did she see?

Like it pains her, she reluctantly starts walking toward us, to do I don't know what. Confront the officers? Make a scene? Either way, there's nothing she can do in this situation that could help. As she takes a hesitant step off the porch, I shake my head at her, causing her to freeze. I continue shaking my head, hoping she'll get the message. I don't want her having any part of this. Everything I've done is to keep her *out* of the back of this cop car.

She stays where she is, watching me with scared eyes

as the officers pull away from the house, leading us to the station. I watch Gia until I physically can't anymore. At least she's been kept out of this. She'll be okay.

The officers talk quietly, but I can't really make out what they're saying through the plastic dividers. Judging by the way they keep throwing annoyed glances over their shoulders at Jason and me even though we're just sitting here quietly, it's probably about us.

"For fuck's sake, Siena," Jason grumbles, looking down at the floor. "Why are you *never* wearing shoes?"

I follow his gaze to my feet, which are muddy and feel sore and scraped on the bottoms. I never bothered putting the heels back on; they're sitting on the passenger-side floor of his car.

Jason uses his foot to slip one of his sneakers off.

"What are you doing?" I ask, using my leg to stop him from taking the other off.

"I'm giving you my shoes. I'm not letting you walk through the station barefoot. Who knows what kind of shit is on that floor."

There's such conviction in his voice I have to swallow the thickness in my throat. Last time I was arrested and sat here in the back of a police car, I was alone. No one was there to look out for me. But now here's Jason, sitting right beside me, offering me his fucking shoes, just like he offered me his hoodie, the one I'm still wearing. I really am the bad influence. *He* should stay away from *me*.

"Jason, those are way too big for me. It's probably more

dangerous for me to wear them than to not."

He curses and glares at the shoes like they've personally offended him. "If I had use of my hands, I'd at least give you my socks."

The thought is touching and does weird things to my chest.

Maybe I'm a terrible fucking person. Maybe I'm selfish and greedy and a bad influence and whatever else people think about me. But right now, I'm glad Jason's sitting beside me, fussing over something as trivial as my shoes; I'm glad I don't have to figure this out myself; I'm glad I'm not alone.

I can't help but shift closer to him until our arms are touching, and the spicy smell of him calms my nerves. "It's all right," I say, softly adding, "Thank you, Jason."

"Don't thank me until we're out of here."

———

All interrogation rooms are the same. The last one I was in was miles away, but it's like I'm back there, looking at the same drab, windowless gray walls and breathing the same stale air. The table is different, this one is wood, not metal, and the chair is heavy, too heavy to lift, probably so it can't be thrown. This room has a two-way mirror, and I wonder if Officer Liu is staring at me from the other side of it, analyzing me, comparing me to Florence, plotting my demise.

He said he was friends with Dad, that he knew him and Mom back in high school. I can only imagine what kind of reputation she had. Small towns always remember the troublemaker, especially if they grow up to star in some cult classic movies and carry their reputation over to Hollywood. I'm not surprised he remembers and dislikes Florence, and he won't be the last person in King to do so either.

I bite my nails, not caring how dirty they are. The cuffs are off, meaning I have free access to them, so I indulge in the bad habit.

I don't know what he wants, and I don't know why I'm here. I wasn't offered a phone call; Aren't I entitled to one? But who would I call? Anusha? I can't let her know I've been arrested, and besides, she can't help. Gia's a child, so she's out too. Aunt Julie wrote me off, Dario's not an option, and Zia Stella would tell Dario, who would kick me out, and Jason . . . Jason's somewhere in his own interrogation room or cell. I wonder if he got his phone call, if he has someone he can call.

The heavy door swings open, making me flinch and drop my hands to my lap. Officer Liu strolls in, a fuzzy pink notebook in his hand. I stare into the hallway, out to freedom, but I don't bother trying to run. I'm in a police station—where could I possibly go?

The door closes and Officer Liu drops into the seat in front of me. He takes his time getting comfortable, shifting around and placing his things on the table. I don't look at him, not even when he incessantly clicks the top of a pen.

He clicks it over and over and over again, and I clench my fingers to stop myself from ripping it from his hands and stabbing him with it. That probably wouldn't help my case to get out of here.

"Siena Amato," Officer Liu finally starts, opening the fuzzy pink notebook that's completely at odds with everything I've observed about him.

He levels me with his stare. In this lighting, his under-eye bags are more pronounced, as are the bloodshot veins in the whites of his eyes. "You were released, what? A few days ago? You couldn't even go a full *week* without killing again?"

Again? My mouth opens and closes. "I—I didn't kill *anyone*! I don't know what you're talking about!"

He slams his hand on the table, and the sound makes me jump. *"Bullshit!"* he yells. "Tell me where my daughter is! Tell me what you did with her!"

His *daughter?*

"Tell me where Lily is!"

Lily? I inhale sharply as it clicks together. *Lily Liu. Officer Liu.* This is my *neighbor*; this is Lily's *father.*

"I don't know! I haven't seen her since Friday. Has something happened?"

He laughs sarcastically and shakes his head. "Has something happened?" he repeats, and his constant changes in mood make me wary—I'm not sure what he'll say or do next. One minute he's calmly having a conversation, and the next he's slamming my head against a car. He clicks the pen. "She hasn't been home since she went to a study group with *you*, which, as it turns out, was a *party*, one that you coerced her into going to, no doubt. It's been over forty-eight hours and no one's heard from her."

There's so much there to unpack, but the main thing that sticks out is that Lily's *missing*.

It all makes sense now: his erratic behavior, his young, jumpy partner, the late night, the lack of parental overview, the breaking of all the protocols. I'm not supposed to be here, and he's doing this all on his own, off the books. I don't know if the thought calms me or makes me more unnerved. On one hand, I'm not on the police's radar, meaning I'm not at risk of actually being arrested, but on the other, an unhinged man who can hide behind the badge is even more dangerous.

Lily lied to him, told him Warren's party was a small study group. Clearly he's learned the truth, but for some reason is still trying to pin her disappearance on me. "She invited me. I didn't *coerce* her into going anywhere."

"Liar!" he shouts, making me flinch. "Lily doesn't go to parties. She knows better, and I won't believe any lies you or anyone else says about her. She's the perfect daughter and student. So, I'll ask again, why did you want her at that party? Where did you take her after?"

My thoughts fly in a million different directions. He doesn't want to hear anything negative about Lily, even if it's the truth. Have people been telling him things he refuses to believe about her, and he's been purposely ignoring it?

Instead of arguing more about something he won't

believe, I say, "I saw her for a few moments there, and she left without me."

His hand slams on the metal table again. "Tell me where she is!"

"I don't know! She hasn't been answering any of my texts."

"Because you've *done* something to her."

"Why would I text her if I knew she couldn't answer?!" I ask, trying to approach this with logic.

He leans in conspiratorially. "To throw us off your track."

Yes, dealing with an unhinged officer is much more dangerous than dealing with the regular system and process. "Do you even hear how crazy you sound? Why would I hurt Lily?"

"Because she knew your secret. She knew what you did. She could ruin your chance at starting over, at living like a normal teenager."

I stare at him for a few moments, *really* stare at him. "How did you know she knew my secret?"

He holds up the pink fuzzy notebook by one cover and lets it dangle open, shaking it a little to emphasize the pages flowing freely. "When she went missing, I read her diary. It detailed what she heard your sister saying to your aunt that day in the backyard. She heard everything through the fence, sound travels clearly in quiet neighborhoods, you know." He sets the notebook back in front of him on the table. "She wrote that she was going to talk to you about it. My wife said she was talking to you Friday, the same day she went missing. Other witnesses from that party said Lily was arguing with a new girl, and they confirmed it was you when I showed them your picture. Some kids said it was an 'intense discussion,' others said it was a full-blown screaming match. You called my daughter a 'fucking crazy bitch.' Did she tell you that she was in on your secret, and you snapped? Is that what happened? *Tell me!*"

I open my mouth, but nothing comes out. I've watched movies before, so I know that this looks bad. They're going to say I had motive, even if it's not true. How did my conversation with Lily go from a stare-off to me calling her a crazy bitch? How fast did that rumor spread? How long did it take for it to be completely blown out of proportion?

Instead of giving in, adding more fuel to the fire that he can use against me, I force myself to remain calm. "How did you know what I want?" I finally ask. "Why do you think I want to start over?"

"Of course that's what you want. Why would you want to walk around the halls at school with everyone knowing what you've done, hearing them all talking about you? You wanted to have your cake and eat it too. Lily threatened that chance, so you solved your problem the only way you knew how, by getting rid of her."

Maybe I should do what Jason advised and shut up now. Anything I say can incriminate me, if I didn't already do that. But Lily's missing, and I know I didn't do anything.

Maybe I can help. If he stops looking at me, he can focus on finding out what *actually* happened.

As calmly and clearly as I can, I say, "I told you, I didn't do anything to Lily. She invited me to a party, and I didn't even *go* with her."

Officer Liu rubs his temples, like I'm the one stressing him out. "Let's pretend I did believe you, and you did arrive separately. Then what?"

I groan. He's so convinced I did something to her he won't even face facts that could help find her. Is this what will happen when everyone else finds out about my past? That's not the life I want, but it's also not the life I want for Gia.

"She left before me, and I left with my sister." Maybe I should've left her out of this. I don't want him to go after her, put her through this kind of questioning. But she is my alibi, and once Officer Liu leaves me alone, he can find Lily. "I have a receipt for my Uber with a timestamp of when Gia and I left the party, including our to and from locations. She even threw up in the Uber, I'm sure the driver will remember us if you contact him. Then we went straight to bed."

Officer Liu laughs, and the sound is cold and hollow. It makes my skin crawl. "Right. You're going to use *Gia* as your alibi? Any moron can discredit her as a legitimate witness."

My nails dig into my skin from how hard I'm clenching my fists. "Why? Because she's young? Because she's my sister?"

He leans in, his words dripping with venom. "Because she's a *drunk*."

"What?" She's not a drunk. She's a teenager who's fallen in with the wrong crowd. Sure, she's been drunk both times I saw her, but she was at parties. Kids drink at parties. And last night she stayed in her room all night. She wasn't drunk. I would've known, though I did go to bed early . . .

Officer Liu scoffs. "The family is always blind to it. Gia likes to lie on a picnic blanket in the backyard and drink all day. Lily wrote about it in her diary, she can see her from her bathroom window."

"You don't know that," I reply. "Did Lily see a bottle? A label? She could be drinking anything! Juice. Water. A smoothie. You can't assume it was alcohol."

"I *know* it was alcohol. There's not one time I've talked to Gia that she's been sober. Hell, I've run into her at night when I'm finishing my shift and she's coming in from God knows where. She's *just* like her mom. You don't think Florence didn't do the same shit when she was Gia's age? Hell, she was arrested for shoplifting at the beginning of her sophomore year; I remember, it was all everyone could talk about, and I won't be surprised if I get called to arrest Gia for the same thing soon." He shakes his head. "I told Gia to stay away from my Lily. She doesn't need people like your sister holding her back."

"There's *nothing* wrong with Gia!" I exclaim, jumping up from my seat. I wish I could leave. I want to leave; I need to leave. But I'm trapped in here, in this stupid gray room with no *air*.

"Sit," Officer Liu commands, "or I'll cuff you to the table."

The thought of him wrestling me to cuff me to the table is enough to make me immediately drop into my seat and grasp my wrists, as if that'd protect me if he went through with it.

We've traded places. Now I'm the unhinged, emotional one, and he's the calm and collected one. He nails me with a cold glare, and I force myself not to bring my fingers to my mouth.

"Last week your aunt asked for my advice," he says. "She said bottles were going missing from Dario's liquor cabinet, even shit ones like banana liqueur that he hasn't touched in *years*. She wanted my advice on how to handle it, didn't want to tell her brother. I guess she got sidetracked by your arrival. I would too if a murderer was coming to live with me."

I look down at my hands in my lap. Gia said our dad hadn't noticed the alcohol going missing, but I guess she didn't account for Zia Stella being over all the time. I had thought she took a little occasionally, a negligible amount. I hadn't realized she was drinking almost every day, or that Zia Stella knew about it.

"Your poor father." His voice drops. "He never wanted kids, never wanted to be with Florence. Why do you think they never got married? He stayed around because of some sense of fatherly duty to you, but he could only take so much of you, of Florence. Why do you think he left?"

Officer Liu sneers. "How long will he put up with taking care of a murderer and an alcoholic, kids he doesn't even know, want, or like? Kids that are just like the woman who made his life hell."

"You know *nothing* about what happened between Mom and Dario," I snarl. "You know nothing about me or my sister."

He leans back in his seat, points at me with his pen and ignores what I've said. "You know where all the trouble begins? With you. You ruined your sister. You're stressing out your aunt. You're going to ruin that boy who's being booked for assaulting a police officer," he says, using the pen to point at the door leading to wherever Jason is being held. "You're just like Florence. Everything she touches turns to shit. She has hurt *everyone* around her, ever since she was a kid."

I hate him. Hate that he's wrongfully arrested me, hate that he's accused me of things that aren't true, but especially hate that he might have a point. I had the same thought in the cop car about Jason: that I'm the bad influence on him. Is it true for others too? Am I the problem? Is Dario distancing himself because he hates me? And Gia . . . if Officer Liu is right and she is drinking, is it because of me? What I did? I did what I had to do to protect her, and I can't take it back, but is she drinking to forget what's happened?

"But I don't care about any of that," Officer Liu continues. "I just want my *daughter*!" He whips the pen at the wall, and it shatters, making me flinch.

"I don't know what happened to Lily!" I exclaim for what feels like the hundredth time, when the door to the room flies open. A man in an expensive-looking suit strides in.

"You're done here. Let's go, Siena."

I don't know who this man is and I don't care. I scramble from my seat to get over to him, to escape this damp room and the unhinged officer.

Officer Liu stands. "Who the hell are you?"

The man isn't concerned by Officer Liu's aggression at all. In fact, he *closes* the distance between them. "I'm Jason and Siena's lawyer. I'm sure you'll be getting to know me quite well when I slap you with lawsuits for the multiple offenses you committed tonight. By the time I'm done with you, you'll be lucky if you escape jail time, never mind keep your badge." The man looks at me, frozen where I stand in the doorway, and repeats, "Let's go, Siena."

I exit the room as quickly as I can but still hear Officer Liu call, "I'll be watching you, Siena!"

I don't pause to acknowledge it, to consider the weight behind his words. Instead, I follow the narrow hallway until coming to a set of doors, where I stop to wait for the lawyer I'm assuming Jason contacted. I don't know how much he's charging, and I don't know why Jason has asked him to take me on as a client, but I can't afford a lawyer, especially not one as expensive looking as the man in front of me.

"Are you all right?" the lawyer asks me. I follow his lead

through the station. No one stops us or yells at us for being here, so I must really be going free.

"I'm fine," I lie. There are windows in the station, and rain has started since I've been trapped in here. My freedom is just in reach, so close I can smell the rain. "Thanks for getting me out of there."

"Don't thank me yet," he says, "thank me once we've sued the station and gotten that asshole fired."

I stop in my tracks. "Will I have to testify?"

He pauses and studies me. He's a slightly tan man with kind eyes, and he has smile lines around his mouth. "If the case gets to court by the time you're eighteen, then it's possible."

"Then no," I say, continuing to freedom as he keeps pace beside me. "I will not be pressing charges, so you won't be suing the station."

"What? Why not?" the lawyer asks. We zig through the police station and around desks and chairs. Even at this time of night the station feels alive with activity.

"Other than the fact that I can't afford a lawyer?" I ask, eyeing the front door. "I don't want to."

"Oh no," he says, "you wouldn't be pay—"

"Siena!" a voice calls. Jason's in the waiting area in front of the door, his twin standing with him.

Jason knows what happened in L.A: he knows I was arrested for killing someone. So why is he still here? Does he not believe that's what happened? Did he forget? Does he want to confront me? The thought of scaring Jason away causes an aching hole in my chest, like I know I'll be missing something, even though I barely know him.

My transition to King has been anything but smooth, but the one person who's sort of been there through it all for me is him. I've come to depend on him, and that's wrong of me. I've always been the person to take care of things, take care of others. No one has ever had my back, except Gia, in her own way, but not the same way I've had hers. I got complacent with Jason here to depend on, and it's gotten him arrested. Officer Liu, as much of a dick as he is, was right about one thing: Jason is here because of me. I hope the fancy lawyer got him off with no charges and no record.

When I'm close enough, I catch Jackson gloating to Jason saying, "I knew it was the hot muddy girl." Jason elbows him then meets me halfway.

When he's close enough, Jason asks, "Are you okay? Did he touch you?" He scans my face, then quickly down my body. He grimaces when he sees my feet.

"I'm fine, let's get out of here."

The lawyer is behind us talking to some officers in suits. The people in charge, maybe?

Jason studies me for a moment like he doesn't believe me, but I can barely look at him. "Jackson," Jason calls, gesturing for him to join us.

"Hey," Jackson greets, then holds out a pair of flip-flops. "I stole these from our mom. I figured Natalia's would fit you better than a pair of ours."

The shoes hang in his outstretched hand between us,

and I stare at them like they might bite me. Jason asked his brother to bring me shoes? With everything going on, my bare feet shouldn't have been his priority. My throat tightens. Behind the twins, the rain pelts down against the glass door.

"It's all right, we're almost outside." I decline the offer, and Jackson's smile wavers.

"Just take the damn shoes, Siena," Jason demands, grabbing the shoes from his brother and shoving them at me until I have no choice but to accept.

"Thanks," I mumble, slipping them on. They're a tad too small for me; but they provide my feet some relief from the hard floor.

"Is my zia here?" I ask him, but Jason's not paying attention to me, he's focused on something behind me, his face hard and jaw clenched.

I turn and follow his gaze. Officer Liu is speaking to some other officers, but they're all watching me. He points, and they all laugh. Was everyone in on it? Did they all know I was arrested and held without a phone call, questioned without an adult? Is this what happens on the night shift when there are fewer people in the station? The cops get to do whatever they want, unchecked?

Officer Liu raises his chin at me, as if to say *I'll be seeing you soon*. I shiver and turn back to Jason, even though I can still feel the officer's stare burning through my back.

"I can't wait for Alan to nail him to the fucking wall," Jason seethes, finally ripping his gaze away from the officer. "Also, Alan got your stuff back."

"Alan?" I ask as Jason hands me my phone and wallet.

I check my phone for messages but it's dead, and I groan. Zia Stella isn't here, so I wonder if no one's notified her or Dario that I'm here, or if they decided they're done with me and didn't bother coming.

Jason gestures to the man in the expensive suit. "The lawyer. Alan. He's going to sue on our behalf."

I shake my head. "I told him I don't want to press charges."

"What do you mean you don't want to press charges?" Jason repeats incredulously.

The rain pelts so hard on the glass door I can hear it over the sounds of the police station. I want to be out there, not in here, not dealing with a court case for who knows how long, with a small town dissecting everything about me, including who my mother is. I want to be a normal kid.

"Because I don't want to," I tell Jason. "If you want to, fine, but leave me out of it."

He turns to say something to his twin, and I walk past them and out into the rain. Jason calls after me, but I keep walking until I create some distance. I stop in the middle of the parking lot, and turn my face up to the rain, feeling the cool wetness wash over my skin. My hair is drenched instantly, and my wet hoodie becomes heavy, but I don't care. I let the rain pelt me while taking deep breaths of that sweet earthy smell.

"Siena!" Jason calls, stopping beside me. I don't open my eyes, just keep my head tilted to the sky for a few more moments of peace.

He doesn't say anything, and if I wasn't annoyingly

aware of him, I'd have thought he left. After a few moments, he says, "What are you doing?"

"Doesn't it just . . . make you feel free?"

"It makes me feel soaked."

I open my eyes to look at him now. He's staring at me. He is soaked, with his hair matted to his forehead and his T-shirt molding to his chest. It's raining so hard the grease stains on his arms have completely washed away, but still, he stands in the rain with me.

"Did he hit your head extra hard when he arrested you?" Jason asks, and I shove him.

"Why do you always think I have a concussion?"

"Why do you always lead me to believe you have a concussion?" he counters, and I shake my head at him, ignoring the smile growing on my lips.

Instead, I tilt my head up to the rain again. I don't know how I'm getting home, and I don't know if I even *have* a home to go back to. Zia Stella's not here, and Gia must have told her what happened if she didn't see the spectacle herself. I don't know where I'll go if she tells Dario and he decides I'm not welcome back.

Jason sighs, and I feel him move a strand of hair off my face. "At least you're not lying in the middle of the road," he mumbles, causing me to bark out a laugh.

I know I can't keep being friends—or whatever *this* is—with him. But for now, in the peaceful rain with his sturdy presence beside me, I'm going to enjoy the moment.

six

Jackson's SUV idles in the driveway next to Jason's car, both twins waiting for me to enter the house. I've been standing in the rain staring at the front door for at least three minutes, and they still refuse to leave until I'm inside. Stupid chivalrous boys. Now I feel obligated to go in and face my fate instead of taking off in the other direction and lying in the middle of a dirt road in the rain. Jason would get a kick out of that, that's for sure.

I glance back at the boys. Jackson gives me a smile and a wave, and Jason raises an eyebrow at me from his own car. He's still soaked. He stood with me in the rain outside the station without complaining until Jackson came out with Alan and offered me a ride home.

They're clearly not going anywhere until I go inside, so I might as well get it over with. I hope Dario doesn't kick me out. Aunt Julie would've. I'll promise him I'll steer clear of any trouble. I won't go anywhere except school and whatever part-time job I can find, and I'll do all the chores. I just need a safe place to stay for me and Gia until I go to college. I can figure out where Gia and I will go after that when the time comes, but for now, I need Dario.

With a deep breath, I wave goodbye to the annoyingly considerate twins and head inside. It's late, and the house is quiet as I slip the borrowed flip-flops off.

"Siena?" a voice calls, and the light in the family room turns on. Gia sits up on the couch, her short hair sticking up in all directions and her makeup smeared halfway down her face. She launches herself at me.

"Siena! I'm so sorry," she sobs, wrapping her arms around me, soaking herself in the process. "I didn't mean for you to get arrested; we were just having fun."

"I'm fine, Gia," I say, patting her back when she hiccups. "What are you doing down here? Where's Zia Stella?"

"I was waiting up for you or Dad or Zia Stella." She releases me and wipes her nose with the back of her hand. "Dad wasn't answering the phone, and Zia Stella left a note on the fridge saying she got called in for an emergency surgery. She isn't reachable by her phone, I tried calling."

Relief floods through me. They didn't not show up

because they're done with me, but because they didn't *know*. And since I wasn't charged and I'm pretty sure I was arrested illegally, they won't tell Dario, so he doesn't need to find out.

Gia sniffles, her words coming out fast and without pause. "I called Aunt Julie for help and she was asking me for details about what happened so I told her the whole story but then she just hung up on me! She didn't answer my other calls either and I don't know any other adults and—"

"Wait, what do you mean you told Aunt Julie?"

She frowns. "I told her about how you and Jason were arrested and how . . . why are you making that face?"

I don't know what face I'm making but I force myself to stop. "I'm not making a face."

"You are," she accuses. "Like you're upset. Or horrified. Or both."

Aunt Julie is the last person we need to tell about any of the things going on here. I bet she'll sell that information to whoever still cares about Florence Bowen's murderous daughter, or at the very least save it for the book she's probably writing. "Let's never tell Aunt Julie anything ever again, okay? In fact, you should delete her number."

Gia frowns. "I know but . . . she's Mom's sister."

"Who washed her hands of us and is trying to use Mom to get famous, Gia." I start up the stairs, my legs heavy. "We're better off without her."

Gia's silent as she trails behind me, before she asks quietly, "Don't you ever miss her?"

"Aunt Julie? No."

"No," Gia says as she follows me into our shared bathroom. "Mom."

I pause from stripping my soaked hoodie off. Do I miss Mom? I miss how she'd put little notes under our pillows for us to find as a middle-of-the-night surprise. I miss how she'd rub our stomachs when they ached until we fell asleep, and always baked cookies in the shape of a heart. I miss how I could tell her anything and not be afraid of being judged, and I miss laughing as we spun around in the rain holding hands. But I don't miss her only being around when it suited her, or her forgetting about us for days while she went on some rich guy's yacht, or how she'd make us run lines with her until 4:00 a.m. on a school night when all we wanted to do was sleep. I especially don't miss the way I felt when I realized she wasn't coming back for us when she left us at Aunt Julie's all those years ago.

My answer is complicated, so instead I deflect. "Do you?"

Gia shrugs as I take Jason's drenched hoodie off and leave it in the tub.

"Sometimes." She frowns at her reflection as I struggle to take off my soaked jeans. "It's hard to remember what she looks like. I know we have pictures, but they don't do her smile justice." Her eyes find me in the mirror. "It's like yours."

I finally get the jeans off and throw them into the tub before facing the mirror with Gia. We stand side by side, two sisters with barely any resemblance. We both have things that make us look like Mom, but me the most. Gia got her heart-shaped face, but I got her green eyes, her full, downturned lips, her blond hair, and the left eyebrow that's a slightly different shape from the right. The media had fun posting side-by-side pictures of me and Mom when she was my age.

"Do you ever think about—"

"No," I interrupt, breaking our eye contact to wring my hair out in the sink.

"You didn't even know what I was going to say!"

"You were going to ask if I ever thought about contacting her, and the answer is no, and that should be your answer too." She'll only be disappointed when she doesn't get the response she wants, or *any* response at all.

Gia pouts. With her makeup smudged and her hair sticking up all over the place, I'm reminded of just how young she really is.

"Gia," I say, more gently this time. I stop wringing my hair to look at her. "Mom *left* us without another word. She doesn't *care* about us. Leaving us to be treated like shit at Aunt Julie's is proof of that. But we're here with Dario— who, let's be honest, probably isn't any better than Mom or Aunt Julie—but at least we're in bedrooms that are our own, with a fully stocked pantry and *laptops* bought just for us. Let's not ruin this, okay?"

I'll have to talk to her about the drinking thing another time. Officer Liu could be full of shit and lying to piss me off. But if Zia Stella really knows about Gia stealing liquor from Dario, we're going to have to fix that and fast. I don't want to take any chances with Gia's future.

"Now wash your makeup off and get in bed so I can shower," I order her.

She does quickly without bringing up Mom again while I wring out my discarded clothes and hang them to dry. As she brushes her teeth, I leave to plug my phone in to charge on my nightstand. It doesn't turn on, and I hope standing in the rain didn't ruin it even more.

Gia's in the hallway when I return.

"Siena . . ." she starts. Her eyes flick everywhere but my face. "I didn't mean for you to get in trouble because of me . . . again."

"I'm not in trouble, Gia," I say softly. "It's all right. But we have to be *good* here, you understand, right? We have nowhere else to go."

Gia nods, her young face looking tired and drawn. "Are you going to tell Zia Stella or Dario what happened tonight?"

"No. And neither are you. We keep tonight a secret, okay?" If Officer Liu decides to tell Dario, then that's another thing, but I doubt he'll admit to arresting me without cause, not to mention all the other illegal shit he did tonight.

"Deal," she says, then heads into her room.

I wonder what I'm going to tell Anusha on our call tomorrow. *How was your first weekend in King, Siena?* she'll ask. And if I were honestly talking about my feelings, I'd say, *Oh good. Just ran from the police twice, was arrested once, made friends with a boy who drag races, and oh yeah, our neighbor is missing and her cop dad thinks I hurt her and will probably make my life miserable. And did I mention Gia apparently has a drinking problem?*

I wonder if I'd catch her so off guard, she'd break her rule of only showing three slightly different neutral faces.

After my shower, I leave my hair to air-dry and quietly pad into my room. As blue as this room is, the thought of being kicked out still sends a pang in my chest. The window is open to let in the cool air, and instead of closing it, I put on warmer pajamas.

My phone turns on and it's a relief. It must've just been super dead before. I have a few messages from two unknown numbers. I click on the first one and decide it must be from Nyah, so I save her name in my phone.

Hey, just saw your message! The police were here, and they told me Lily's missing! That explains why she hasn't been answering me, I thought she was just in one of her "ignore the world" moods. I told them about Friday, and that she left without me. I hope she's okay :(

It's around three in the morning and I want to text her back, but I don't want to wake her. I'll find her at school tomorrow.

I click on the other text.

Everything okay over there?

Jason. It has to be. Just to be sure, I cross-check this text from the number he called me from, and it's him. Sent about five minutes after he dropped me off.

He must be sleeping now. I turn the lamp off and crawl into bed while staring at my phone. I shouldn't have anything to do with Jason, and I'm annoyed at myself for feeling so comforted by him. By his presence. By his calmness. By his eyes—even by his scowl. I *like* having him around and I shouldn't, just like I shouldn't save his number. I should delete this text and my call history and be done with it. I shouldn't have a way to contact him, shouldn't create a contact profile for him, shouldn't save his information.

I save his information.

Since I'm doing things I shouldn't, I decide to text him back. He's probably sleeping already and won't answer until the morning anyway, so there's really no harm.

Phone was dead. Zia Stella and our father aren't home, so we're not telling them. It all worked out.

I exit out of our chat to put my phone down when it vibrates in my hand. *Jason.* Quickly, I open our chat.

Good. See you tomorrow.

See me tomorrow? He wants to see me in school? The thought makes butterflies erupt in my stomach that I want to punch. I cannot be friends with him, and I shouldn't get excited about seeing him in school tomorrow. But maybe he was just saying that in a generic sense, the way you say "see you later" to a person you know you'll probably never see later. It's a way of ending the conversation.

I put my phone back on my nightstand to charge and snuggle into bed.

But then again, he *did* answer right away. Was he waiting up for me? No, he couldn't have been. Maybe he couldn't sleep because of the whole being-arrested thing. He probably had to answer to his mom before getting into bed—maybe his older brother too.

I push Jason Parker from my mind and try not to think about the day. But I do hope Lily is okay. I wonder if I'll get a real police inquiry like Nyah did, not a completely off-the-books illegal one, and until then I have to think of anything that might help them in their search.

I roll over in bed and pull the covers higher to block out the chill in the room. Maybe I'll need a little space heater in the winter, but I'm not sure how cold it gets in King. Hopefully I'll adjust soon enough and I won't mind the chill from the open window.

This bed is huge, and I'm not used to sleeping alone. Usually, Gia sprawls in the middle of the bed and I huddle in the little sliver at the end to not wake her, even though she's an unusually heavy sleeper. But here, I have the whole bed to myself, and it's an odd feeling.

I slip my hand under the pillow to keep it warm when it scratches against something. I freeze, my stomach dropping. I'm almost too scared to move, to check if something's there or if I'm imagining things, my mind recalling distant memories after talking about it with Gia.

Slowly, I move my hand, and again, it scratches against something. My heart thumps as my hand wraps around the object and slowly pulls it out.

It's a folded-up paper—a note.

Instantly, I sit up and turn on my lamp. Nothing in my room seems out of place, the disarming baby blue accessories still exactly where they're supposed to be.

I roll and land on the floor to check under the bed, but nothing's there. Then I race to the closet and swing the door open, but again, there's nothing there, only piles of boxes. I look out my window into the front yard, but there's nothing out of the ordinary there either.

There's no way this is happening right now. It's been years of radio silence and now, when we have the chance of a normal life and of getting our shit together, *now* she shows up? I'd think I was in the middle of a fever dream and imagining all this if it wasn't for the unmistakable feel of the note clutched in my hand.

I do a quick sweep of the entire house and check all the doors, but everything's locked, and the house is empty. Finally, I quietly enter Gia's room. Is this why she suddenly brought up Mom tonight? To see how I'd react if she revealed that Mom's been contacting her?

Her closet and under her bed are the same as mine. I tiptoe to the head of the bed and flip over the spare pillow to reveal nothing but deep-purple sheets. Cautiously, I slip my hand under the other pillow, feeling around for a note like mine. I'm always annoyed by Gia's heavy sleeping when I try to wake her for school or fight her when she's hogging all the blankets, but now I'm grateful.

There's nothing there, and I pull my hand back. Has

she found it already? She would have told me, right? Or maybe not, especially after I *just* ranted about how we need to leave Mom in the past.

But a quick search of her bedside drawer and desk reveals no note, and I don't know where else she'd hide it. She must not have gotten one.

I silently close her door again before shutting myself in my room.

The note in my hand weighs twenty pounds, and I'm too scared to read it. I haven't heard from Mom in years, and she shouldn't be anywhere near us, *we* shouldn't let her anywhere near us, not after what she did. She doesn't deserve me or Gia, and I'm not just going to forget about everything because she left me some stupid note.

Maybe I should rip it to shreds. This note could've been from anyone, and no, Anusha, I haven't *heard* from Mom.

But the curiosity becomes too much. I sit on my bed and unfold the little scrap of paper. The words on the paper are in black ink in a bold, confident scroll. My stomach drops.

I'm so proud of you, sweetheart. Everything will be okay now.

When I was eight years old, Mom was called to the school office. I was there in the seat of shame in the principal's office when she arrived. As she sat, the principal told her that

I was there for punching another student because they were picking on my sister.

Mom was confused. "And why am I being called in?"

The principal—I don't even remember his name now, that's how long ago this was—informed her I was expelled, and Mom was pissed.

In the car, she turned to me and said, "You did the right thing, Siena. You *always* look out for your little sister, just like I'll always look out for you." She delicately stroked my cheek. "Gia's sensitive; things affect her more than they would others, and I love her for that, but you're like me. You're strong, and we take care of those hurting our loved ones, right?"

I nodded, not really understanding. It wasn't until years later, after she left us with Aunt Julie, that I remembered her words, truly thought about them and decided she was a fucking hypocrite. Saying she'd always look out for me? Then why did she ditch us and never look back?

Florence took care of her problems the only way she knew how, by running, and looking down at the note gripped tightly in my hand, I can't help ponder her words.

Everything will be okay now.

What does she mean by that? Everything will be okay because she's here? Because I'm living with Dario instead of Aunt Julie? Because I've been acquitted of Stan's murder? I haven't heard from her in years, and *now* is when she decides to pop back up in my life?

I groan and throw myself backward on my bed, staring

up at the ceiling, which is white instead of baby blue, covered in shadows cast by my bedside lamp. I don't even have any friends to talk to. Lily could've been that friend for me. She lived next door, was kind to me, and knew my secret and didn't seem to care. She could've been my first real friend, and now she's missing.

A light illuminates my room for a moment and a car shuts off. I jump from bed to look outside. It's not our driveway, it's Lily's. Officer Liu steps out of a car—not a police car, I guess they leave those at the station—and drags his hand down his face. He seems tired, and for a second I can sympathize with him—his daughter is missing, and it's been over forty-eight hours with no leads—but then, like he can sense me, his head snaps up to my window and his eyes meet mine. In an instant, his face hardens and his eyes narrow. I'm frozen to the spot. I'm in the safety of my own room but still feel like I'm back in that interrogation room. He holds up the fuzzy pink diary and twists his wrist a few times to shake it, as if telling me that he'll somehow use it to connect me to Lily's disappearance. He's so damn stubborn. I bet someone could tell him Lily's a criminal mastermind, and he still wouldn't believe it even with all the facts right in front of him.

Other headlights illuminate the house, and Dario's Mercedes pulls into the driveway. Officer Liu gives me one last look, then heads inside his own home before Dario gets out. Without him pinning me with his stare, I finally move from the window, turning off the lamp and diving into bed, pretending to be asleep when Dario enters the house.

As I lie there in the dark, controlling my breathing as Dario moves around downstairs, my mind races. I need to find out why Mom is here and what she wants, while keeping her *away* from Gia. I don't want her getting Gia's hopes up that she's come to be a family again. It'll never work; she'll only let us down again. Not only that, but I need to figure out what happened to Lily, not only to get Officer Liu off my back, but to help one of the only sort-of friends I have here in King.

Eventually, pretending to be asleep causes me to actually fall asleep, and I awake to Gia banging on my door, yelling that we have to be at the bus stop in twenty minutes. For a few moments, I lie peacefully in bed, still not fully awake, but then the night's events come rushing back to me. As I sit up, the crumpled note falls from my chest onto the sheets, meaning it *wasn't* just a terrible dream.

I stash the note in my desk drawer under some notebooks and spend most of the twenty minutes sifting through boxes trying to find shoes. After getting ready in record time, I grab my backpack, the same one that made it all the way here from LA with me, and meet Gia downstairs.

She looks perfectly put together, no evidence of being hungover after last night. She sighs impatiently when she spots me and tosses me an apple. "Come on, let's go."

"I've never seen you this excited for school before," I tell her, heading into the kitchen despite her groaning.

"It's the first day at a new school, it's important," she

says, trailing behind me. "Plus, I want to catch Brianna and everyone before class, see if we have any together."

I press my molars together to stop myself from criticizing her choice in friends. I'll give her a break after what happened last night, and now that school started, she might make different friends, or at least calm down with drinking.

"Hey Gia," I say, filling a reusable water bottle at the sink. "I was thinking about what we were talking about last night . . . about Mom."

Her expression turns suspicious. "Okay."

I screw the cap on the bottle and face her. "And I was wondering, you know, why she hasn't contacted us. It's been years."

I watch her face closely, looking for any signs that might give her away. Maybe Mom was here before me; maybe she's already contacted Gia, let her know "everything's going to be okay" before I even got here. But Gia's expression doesn't change much; if anything it turns forlorn.

She shrugs. "I don't know. You said last night it was better she stayed away."

"Right. But what if she—"

Gia huffs. "Siena, we're going to miss the bus, and I don't want to think about Mom on an already high-stress day, okay?"

"Late on the first day?" Dario asks, entering the kitchen and pouring himself a coffee before he adds under his breath, "Figures."

My nostrils flare, and Gia stares at her feet. "We're not

late," I tell him. "We're right on time, and we're leaving."

He takes a sip of his coffee and peers at me before glancing away. He has trouble making direct eye contact with me for long periods of time. I can't decide if it's because he's scared about what happened in LA or doesn't care enough about me to bother, or if it's because I remind him of Mom. Maybe a bit of all three.

"Goodbye," he says dismissively, opening his laptop on the counter without looking to see if we're actually leaving.

Gia's lip quivers, and she rushes to the door. I stand there for a moment, my chest tight, fists clenched, wanting to say something to our dad, wanting to tell him off for being so rude to us, to Gia. But after a few of Anusha's breathing exercises and reminding myself I need to be on his good side, I decide against it, leaving without saying anything else.

I shut the front door and jog to catch up to Gia. She's strolling to the street corner where Zia Stella told us the bus pickup would be. There are a few kids standing there chatting already. I can already tell I'm going to be the oldest kid on the bus.

"I hate the bus; it's so awkward," Gia grumbles, shielding her eyes from the rising sun. Her makeup is perfect, and she's wearing thick eyeliner on her bottom lash line with winged liner on top. The black, as well as the sun, makes her chestnut-brown eyes seem especially warm. "I wish you'd hurry up and get your license so you could drive us to school."

"Yeah, in what car?" I ask.

"Couldn't you have at least asked your boyfriend for a ride? If I can't get a ride home with Chris or something, then ask him to bring us home."

"What boyfriend?" I ask.

She gives me an *are you serious?* look. "Jason."

I hitch my backpack higher on my shoulder. It's a comfortable day today, and I didn't even feel the need to bring a sweater. Jason's hoodie is sitting in my laundry hamper, waiting for me to wash it so I can bring it back to him.

"Jason isn't my boyfriend, Gia."

She's not convinced. "Well, it wouldn't hurt you to have a boyfriend. Or even just a friend that's not me." Her face lights up as someone at the bus stop waves at her. "Erin! Hey!"

She ditches me to rush over to her friend, chatting excitedly as I process the sting of Gia's words. Sure, I don't have any friends, but that never bothered her before. Is she embarrassed by me suddenly? It's clear that my little sister is growing up, but I'll never stop being her big sister, never stop protecting her.

A car drives by, and something draws my eyes to the driver. It's a woman wearing sunglasses, and for a second my body freezes as she looks at me. The car passes too quickly for me to learn anything about it. I shake my arms out, relieving the tension in my shoulders. I'm just on edge after the note, after last night. I can't think every middle-aged woman with blond hair is Mom.

But still, even as I board the bus, spend the ride sitting alone, and enter the school—which looks much different in the daylight—I can't shake the eerie feeling in my chest telling me something is seriously wrong.

seven

The classroom is similar to the one at my previous school, except there are no palm trees outside the window. Even though the window isn't open, I take a seat by it. Looking outside helps calm my nerves, even if the view is nothing spectacular, just a side parking lot and some trees in the distance. English wasn't my strongest subject in the past, but I never had time to do any of the readings. Now I'm determined to get my grades up and get into college; there's more riding on it this time—*like not ending up like Mom.*

The bell rings and everyone takes their seats, including a boy right in front of me. I gasp. *Brandon.* He's as large and intimidating as the last time I saw him, especially when he turns to shoot me an inquisitive look. I look down at my desk until he turns around.

I forgot that Brandon had an argument with Lily. She *cried* because of him, and she felt uncomfortable around him. He grabbed her, and she said he was hurting her—how could I have forgotten that? Maybe if Officer Liu wasn't so dead set on pinning his daughter's disappearance on me, I could've thought more clearly and told him about Lily and Brandon. I drill holes in the back of Brandon's head with my eyes as if I can see into his brain and figure out if he had anything to do with Lily's disappearance.

The teacher stands at the front of the room and introduces himself before going over the class and the books we'll be reading, but I'm only paying attention to Brandon.

He pulls out his laptop and connects his phone to it, then his messages pop up on his screen.

I sigh. Great. I'm going to be stuck behind Brandon all year while he texts in class. He's not even paying any attention to what Mr. Lewis is saying. Instead, he's texting about being annoyed and Lily being a bitch and—wait.

I lean more over my desk, trying to read his text messages over his shoulder. I can't read everything from here, but I see the words *Lily's such a bitch* and *got what she deserved* in the same text message, and the blood in my veins turns to ice.

"Siena Amato?" The teacher calls, and I drop back into my seat from where I was basically hovering over my desk to read Brandon's texts.

Mr. Lewis is holding a sheet of paper in front of him, so I quickly say, "Here," and thankfully, he moves on. A last name starting with *A* means I'm always first on attendance calls, so I listen through the rest of the names until I hear Brandon's name. Brandon Scott. I mentally make a note of his full name so I can tell Officer Liu the next time I see him, or the next time he corners me, whatever comes first.

Mr. Lewis just barely finishes when a woman's voice comes over the loudspeaker, announcing a schoolwide assembly we all need to attend, starting with the juniors and seniors. The freshmen and sophomores will attend during second period. From the surprised voices around me, it's clear this isn't a routine welcome assembly.

Brandon snaps his laptop shut, packing it away, ending any further chances of seeing the rest of his conversation. I follow the rest of the class down the hall and into the gym, taking a seat with my classmates since we're supposed to stay together. Brandon sits at the end of the row with his friends, and I wish I was closer to eavesdrop.

"I've been trying to get your attention since the first bell," a deep voice says as someone drops onto the bleacher beside me. "So, either you have terrible hearing, I got your name wrong, or you're just blatantly ignoring me, which I mean, is all cool with me, I'd just want to know which it is so my ego can take it."

He looks at me expectantly, and then I place him. "Warren," I say. The boy who threw the party Friday night at the giant mansion smiles at me as I continue, "Sorry, I was in my own world."

"Siena, right? We'd been referring to you as 'the hot muddy girl' until Jason overheard and got all pissed, though now that I think about it, I probably shouldn't have told you we've been calling you that."

"Who's *we*?" I ask. Are people talking about me? Why? Because I'm new? Because of who I am? Or because I made a spectacular first impression at his party?

He waves his hand nonchalantly as he looks around. "Oh, you know, just the guys."

The gym is filling up, and even though it's such a large space, it quickly makes me feel claustrophobic. I wonder if I can sit at the bottom of the bleachers, or at least at the end of an aisle, somewhere with a bit more airflow. I shift in my seat and tug at the collar of my shirt, which suddenly feels a bit too high and tight.

Warren's talking but I haven't been paying attention. I glance at him while trying to take inconspicuous deep breaths, when Nyah catches my eye from a few rows behind him. She waves at me and points at her phone, then mine vibrates.

I glance down at my screen to see a text from her.

Did you see the cops in the hallway? I wonder if this is about Lily! Do you think they found her?

If they had, they wouldn't be having this assembly.

"What about Lily?" Warren asks, surprising me. "Sorry, I wasn't reading over your shoulder or anything, but your font is so huge it's kind of hard to miss." I made it bigger so it was easier to read through the cracks in my screen.

"Are you friends with her?" I ask, tucking my phone back into my pocket after giving Nyah a sad shake of my head.

Warren shrugs. "I'm friends with everyone, but Tyler's dating Nyah, and Nyah's best friends with Lily, so yeah, I guess I'd say we're closer than most people since we're always together."

"Have you heard from her since your party?" I ask. It was his house; maybe he's seen something.

He shakes his head. "No. But that's not unusual for Lily. She gets really stressed sometimes and just needs to disconnect. She'll unplug for a while, and we won't hear from her until she's ready."

Nyah said something like that too, but I'm assuming her unplugged times don't include not coming home.

"But I heard the two of you really got into it," he adds, a little sheepish. "Heard you guys took a few swings at each other. What was that all about?"

What? First it was an intense conversation, then it was a screaming match, and now we got in a fistfight? How fast do rumors spread around here? And how much do people embellish them? Is this a small-town thing? King isn't even *that* small!

I'm about to tell Warren we did no such thing when mic feedback interrupts me, causing everyone, including me, to cover their ears to escape the high-pitched whine.

A man hands the mic to a pretty older woman in an expensive-looking pantsuit, and the gymnasium quiets down. There are other people with her, people in suits and dresses, who I think are a part of the school staff, like the vice principals and guidance counselors. But the other people in suits must be detectives, and when they shift, a gleam reflects off the badges on their belts, confirming my suspicions. Then I spot Officer Liu. He's in the back of the group, silently watching the crowd, still gripping Lily's fuzzy pink diary. As his eyes scan the students my breath hitches. I'm in the middle of the bleachers, just another face in a very large crowd, but somehow, as if sensing me, his eyes land right on me.

I freeze as we stare at each other, and his eyes narrow. I can only imagine what he's thinking, and I want to run down there and shake him, tell him he's wasting his time focusing on me when the real person who hurt Lily, or the real reason she disappeared, is out there, waiting to be found.

"Good morning, everyone," the woman in the pantsuit says into the mic, and any last whispering in the crowd dies down. "I've had to gather you all for two very unfortunate reasons."

Warren leans into me and whispers, "That's Principal Anderson. She's my neighbor."

She seems stern, and I hope I never have to talk to her one-on-one.

"First," she continues, "some students decided to break

in and vandalize school property last night."

Shit. I forgot all about the school break-in after everything else that went down. I sink lower in my seat as if that will protect me from her roaming gaze.

"Let me be very clear: we *do not* tolerate this kind of behavior here at King City High. When, and I say *when*, you are caught, there will be severe punishment. If you come forward now, we may decide to be more lenient."

I don't care about any of the other kids, only Gia. Will one of the kids there last night get scared and step forward to sell out my sister? Me? We could get expelled, or possibly even charged. What would Dario do? Or Anusha? If it was up to Gia and me not to say anything, I know the secret would go to our graves, and weirdly I know Jason would do the same, but the other kids? I can't trust them.

I bring my nails to my mouth, but Warren gives me a look. I can just imagine Jason saying *Geez, Siena, can you be any more guilty looking?* I automatically pull my hands away and sit on them.

"Bad habit," I whisper to Warren in response. "Slap them away if you see me biting my nails again."

Warren nods solemnly. "I will protect your mouth from germs and your nails from destruction as if they were my own."

His odd declaration, whispered with a straight face, makes me laugh, and the people around me shoot us a look. I duck lower in my seat, and Warren grins.

Principal Anderson talks about consequences and

responsibility and being contributing members of society, but I'm scanning the bleachers for Jason. He's at risk just as much as Gia and me, since he was there to help me. I don't see him though, and I don't know how Gia and her friends will react because they're in the assembly after us. I wonder if they'll confess right then and there at the sight of all the police and the harsh warning from the principal, or if they'll all silently promise not to say anything.

"And that leads me to the other reason we're here today," Principal Anderson says, and I tune back in. "Your friend, your peer, and a senior here at King City High, Lily Liu, has been missing since Friday."

Beside me, Warren's just as stiff as I am, processing the news. Hushed conversations arise around us. I try to glance down the row to see Brandon's reaction, if this is news to him or not, since he clearly texted someone about Lily getting what she deserved. Was he referring to her disappearance? Did he do something to her? Or was he referring to something else? But his expression doesn't get me any closer to the truth, because he's facing away from me, talking to his friends.

"All right, all right." Principal Anderson gestures for the talking to stop, and when it doesn't, she speaks louder into the mic. "We're asking anyone who has any information at all about Lily to come forward." She points to the man and woman directly beside her. "This is Detective Lopez and Detective Dubois. They'll be here all day, and if you think of something after that, please tell your teacher. Anything you can think of will help, even if you don't think it's significant."

Chatter reignites through the crowd, no one pretending to whisper anymore.

Warren shakes his head. "Missing? Not a social media detox? I hope she's okay." He turns to me. "Did you know?"

I gesture to Officer Liu, who's still standing in the corner, analyzing the crowd like we're all potential suspects. "That cop is her dad, also my neighbor. He . . . talked to me about it last night."

He frowns. "Why did no one come talk to me? She was at my party Friday."

I shrug. "I'm not sure." As of last night, her father refused to believe she even went to parties, never mind lied about going to one on Friday. "Nyah said she was questioned yesterday, so maybe they just started contacting people."

"Yeah, maybe," he says, pulling out his phone and texting.

I tug on the collar of my shirt and shift in my seat. The person on my left has moved closer to me to talk to someone a row behind me, virtually eliminating any free space I had. I scooch closer to Warren to try to get some air. He smells like peppermint, which does nothing to calm my nerves.

Principal Anderson says something to dismiss us, but everyone's still talking, the noise in the gym only adding to the overcrowded feeling.

"I'm going to go talk to the detectives about Lily being

at the party Friday," Warren says, standing up and stuffing his phone into his back pocket. "I didn't see her leave, but maybe they'll have questions I can answer."

I stand with him, waiting for the people on the bleachers in front of me to move so I can get out of here. Everyone's moving slowly, too interested in Principal Anderson's announcements to care about getting back to class. But I care. I want to get out of here, and I want it now. As people stand on the bleachers it only makes the space more crowded, especially as people's bags take up more room on their backs. I'm considering bulldozing through the crowd straight down but doubt I'd be able to move the group of six-foot-plus guys in the row below me.

"... dad say anything?" I catch Warren saying.

"Sorry, what?" I wonder if I can duck under the guy with the mullet—Thompson?—but then there's a couple making out directly under him, and they'd probably notice if I pushed them apart to sneak through.

Something hard slaps my hand, forcing it away from my mouth. "Ow!"

"Sorry," Warren says. "You told me to do that. Did I hurt you?"

I didn't even realize I was biting my nails, but now my fingers feel fidgety. "No, you just took me by surprise. Thanks."

He smiles. "Any time. But did you hear what I asked? About Lily's dad saying any—"

"Siena," a voice calls, and Jason pushes around the group

of kids on my left to stand with us. He takes up a lot of space, forcing me even closer to Warren, and the air around us becomes thin. "Did you see Officer Dickwad is here? Did he say anything to you? Because if he did, I'll . . . You okay?"

"Mmm-hmm." I nod, still trying to triangulate a way off the bleachers. Not a single person has moved; it looks like everyone's too busy chatting with their friends. If anything, there are even *more* people in this particular area because kids are moving from their class seating and finding their friends. Even the teachers are standing in a group on the gym floor talking to each other instead of ushering their students back to class. My English teacher is there too, coffee in hand. When did he get a coffee?

When I look back at Jason, his eyes are narrowed on me, and my body temperature raises several degrees until I start sweating.

He finally turns to the large boy in front of me and taps his shoulder. "Hey, Thompson."

Thompson, which I'm assuming is his last name, turns around, confirming that he is the same guy from the party. "Hey, Parker, who do you think broke into the school?"

"No idea," Jason answers. "But you mind moving? We're trying to get down."

Thompson looks at his friends packed tight beside him. "Move where? Can't really go anywhere."

"Don't care," Jason says, and suddenly his hand is in mine. It's large and warm and I'm very aware that my palm is sweaty, and that makes me sweat more.

"Big step, Siena," Jason orders, stepping over and down the bleacher into Thompson's row, forcing him back. Jason pulls me down with him, and once I clear the bleacher, I'm pressed right up against him in the tight space. He smells like his signature cedarwood and warm spice, and I focus on it instead of the limited air.

"Hey Rob, Hannah," Jason says, tapping on the couple sitting on the bleachers in front of us. They pull apart from their kiss and look up confusedly at Jason. "I'm happy for you guys, really, but . . ."

He starts moving, stepping down the bleacher directly between them, causing them to slide apart from each other. Hannah makes some noise of outrage but doesn't say anything as Jason pulls me down with him. I'm too busy trying to ignore the increasingly tight space around me to care about her glaring daggers at me.

Jason repeats the process directly down the bleachers, stepping through groups of friends without a care for their glares and grumbles, until we're finally standing on the gym floor. Once I'm out of the crowd, the ball in my chest immediately loosens, and I take a deep breath of fresh air. There's still a mix of people's colognes and body sprays, but it's not as stale here, and the collar of my shirt doesn't seem as tight anymore.

"Better?" Jason asks, his blue eyes peering straight into me. My face heats and I realize just how tightly I'm gripping his hand, so I instantly drop it like he burned me.

"Yeah, thanks," I say, unable to look at him.

"I'm going to go talk to Detective Lopez," Warren says from behind me, making me jump. I hadn't noticed that he followed our path down. "Maybe I can help."

He takes off toward the man in the suit, who is talking to Principal Anderson and some other students.

Jason nods toward Officer Liu, who's speaking with a group of students. "So, did he approach you?"

"No. Did you know he's Lily's dad, and my neighbor?" I tell him since I never got the chance to last night. "He told me Lily hasn't come home since Friday. He thought I had something to do with it."

Jason's jaw clenches. "Why did he think you had something to do with it?"

"Apparently people saw Lily and me going at it at Warren's party."

His brows draw together. "He arrested us and interrogated you over a rumor?"

I study him for a moment. For some reason, even though I shouldn't, I trust him. He's done nothing but go out of his way to help me since I met him, and deep in my gut, I know I can tell him the truth.

I pull him farther away from the rest of the students until I'm confident no one can walk by and hear. "He read in Lily's diary about what happened in LA."

"About you murdering a man?" he asks without judgment, simply stating a fact.

I forgot he was there when Officer Liu said that, accusing me of doing the same thing here. Jason's never asked about it, even though I told him I was arrested.

"Yes." I clear my throat. He's staring at me intensely, giving me all his attention, and it makes me lose my train of thought. "I . . . um . . . I did. It was self-defense, and I was acquitted."

Jason nods slowly, never once lifting his eyes from me. I feel like they're peering straight into my soul and stripping me bare. I have no idea what he's thinking; he's always so eerily calm, so in control of his emotions while he processes, and for some reason I feel like crying. I've never had to tell anyone before, and Jason's the only person I know here, really, my only *friend*, and what if he's decided he's had enough of me? That I'm not worth all the hassle?

He opens his mouth and I'm terrified he's going to tell me he wants nothing to do with me, but then he says, "I killed a guy too. You're not that special."

His joke is so out of left field that it breaks the anxious nerves skittering through me, and I laugh. Just like he did when I told him I was arrested, he's managed to make me feel less shitty about admitting a shitty thing.

"You're such an ass," I tease, my breath coming easier. "I'm serious."

"Yeah, so am I," he says, still with a straight face, causing me to grin. I have no idea how he knew to break the tension, but I'm glad.

"Yeah, well, that's why Officer Liu has it in for me," I tell him, my chest a million times lighter. I want to be friends with him, despite our rocky start and the fact that

I'll probably drag him down. He's a great guy and has been nothing but helpful to me, even though I'm just the weird new girl who lies in the middle of the road in the rain. It'll be nice to have someone to talk to, someone other than Gia.

"Lily overheard Gia talking about what happened in LA," I continue, feeling better about telling him—my *friend*, as I've decided—more details, "and told me she knew. She wrote about it in her diary, so Officer Liu thinks that gave me a motive to harm Lily."

"To keep your secret," Jason states, and I nod.

"And it *is* a secret," I stress, "so . . ."

"I would never tell anyone," he promises.

I believe him. Emotions are thick in my throat as I say, "Thanks."

Some students walk by us, and Jason pulls me out of the way. Brandon is one of them, and I stare at him as I ask Jason, "How well do you know Brandon?"

He knew Brianna was his sister. He called him about Friday. Are they friends? I can't picture Jason as friends with Brandon.

Brandon exits the gym and I return my attention to Jason, who shrugs. "I don't know. Well enough, why?"

"Are you friends? Like *good* friends?"

Jason's eyebrows furrow. "I'm friends with everyone, but Jackson knows him better than I do. Why?"

Doesn't sound like they're best friends or even texting buddies. I wonder who Brandon was texting about Lily. That person must know something too.

More students clear out of the gym at Principal Anderson's insistence, and the group talking to Detective Dubois leave as well.

"I've got to go," I tell Jason, seeing my opening. "I'll tell you after."

Before he has a chance to say anything, I weave through the crowd to reach Detective Dubois, stopping her just before she joins a group of chatting guidance counselors.

"Detective?" I ask, and she gives me her full attention. Something about her makes me feel like she hasn't laughed in a very long time and takes everything very seriously. "My name is Siena, I'm neighbors and friends with Lily."

I glance at Officer Liu to see if he'll come stampeding over and demand my arrest, but he's still held up with a group of students.

"Hi Siena," she says, opening a small notepad in her hand. "What can I do for you?"

I look around the gym one more time. Brandon isn't here, and yet I feel nervous, like he's going to tackle me before I get to tell her anything. The students are filing out, making the gym feel more spacious again. Jason is talking with his twin where I left him. He meets my eyes and raises an eyebrow. For some reason, knowing he's still here, watching my back, soothes my nerves and gives me the confidence to say, "I think you should look at Brandon Scott as a person of interest in Lily's disappearance."

She pauses in flipping through her notepad pages.

"Really?" she says, finding a blank page and clicking her pen open. "Why?"

I tell her about what happened at the party, how he grabbed her, their argument, her crying afterward, and about what I saw this morning on his computer. She asks clarifying questions occasionally, but otherwise is silent as she notes down my observations.

When I'm finished, she scans the page once more. "Thanks for this, Siena. It's very helpful. Can I get your information in case we need to ask you some follow-up questions?"

"Yes, of course," I agree, giving her my phone number and address. "I hope you find Lily. Will you let me know if there are any updates in her case?"

Detective Dubois shuts her notepad. "Unfortunately, we're unable to share any specifics regarding the case to non-family members. But if you're able to help us more, or remember anything, please be in touch."

She hands me her card and I take it. I don't have anything more to offer but knowing they're going to look into that asshole Brandon makes me feel better. I already feel guilty enough not saying anything last night, since maybe that could've helped, but at least I've done my part now. I can only hope Lily is found safe, and that the police cross my name off their seemingly very short list of suspects.

eight

The week flies by, and I fall into a steady routine. Officer Liu glares at me every morning when I walk to the bus stop alone, because Gia gets a ride with Chris. Officer Liu's always there, leaning against his car, drinking his coffee, and trying to explode my mind with his eyes as I rush to the bus stop with my head down and goose bumps on my arms the whole time. Alan, the lawyer Jason hired, must have warned him not to talk to me, because I always expect him to step in front of me and initiate a conversation, but he never does.

On Friday, after five full days of trying to settle in at King

City High, I'm at my usual spot outside on the bleachers of the football field, my math book and supplies spread out around me. It's not a popular spot as most people eat in the cafeteria, but there are still some kids like me, sitting on the bleachers enjoying the fresh air while reading or listening to music or writing in a notebook. It's a cool day and I slip my hands into the sleeves of Jason's large hoodie. Most other kids have given up trying to sit outside when it's this cold and gone inside, but not me. I'll sit out here until it starts snowing, and maybe even after that. I spend all day in class staring out the window counting down the minutes until I can get outside, and I'm not going to let some wind drive me away.

As I put the wrapper of my sandwich into my backpack, a body lands beside me.

"There you are," Jason says, setting his own bag down as he gets comfortable. I don't share any classes with him, so I haven't seen him since the first day at the assembly. He's even handsomer than I remember and smells just as good as he always does. He faces me. "I've been—is that my hoodie?"

I glance down at my chest as if the hoodie crawled onto me of its own accord. "I . . . um . . . yes?" It doesn't smell like him anymore, not since I've washed it twice now, but it still reminds me of him, still makes me feel less lonely.

"So you *have* stolen it. It's my favorite one, you know."

My cheeks are hot despite the cold wind. "I'm not stealing it! I brought it to return to you today, but I was sitting out here, and it was so cold and I just happened to have a very warm hoodie in my bag, so . . ."

"So you stole it," he finishes for me, but there's amusement in his voice.

"I'll give it back, I promise." I mean it, but deep down it feels like a lie. I don't want to return it, even though I know I should. It's just a hoodie, but it feels like more to me.

He nods, then says, "Anyway, I've been waiting for you in the cafeteria all week. Nyah says she keeps inviting you to sit with her, but you never come. So today I checked the library and the club classrooms in case you joined one, even asked Gia, who was equal parts mortified when I went up to her table and thrilled when her friends started asking how she knew me."

I smile at that. We've been getting along better since the first day of school. She hasn't been drinking at night, I've been checking the liquor cabinets, so Officer Liu was *wrong*. She's been focused on school and stays in at night doing homework, even though I can hear her on the phone with her new friends. Either way, she seems like her normal self, and that makes me happy.

"I finally realized this should've been the first place I looked," Jason continues, waving his hand in the general direction of the field.

I'm embarrassed that he knows about my need for fresh air, knows *why* I have that need. He knows what happened, that I was arrested for killing someone, but he's still searching me out, still wants to be around me.

"Why were you looking for me?"

He shrugs and rests his feet on the bleacher in front of him. "I don't know. You kept me entertained for like, four days in a row, and then suddenly nothing."

A smile breaks out on my face. "You're saying you miss me. No shoes, lying in the rain, and all."

"I wouldn't go *that* far," he says, though his tone is light and playful. "But I do want to see how you're doing. We haven't been expelled, so I'm guessing no one blabbed about the Friday break-in?"

I shake my head and close the math textbook in front of me. I'll never focus now, not with Jason sitting so close. "No. Gia said everyone swore to secrecy, but there are just too many people involved for me to trust them."

He nods and rubs the back of his neck, making the formfitting sweater he's wearing strain over his biceps. I force my eyes to stay on his face.

"And is Officer Douche giving you any trouble?"

"No."

I also haven't heard anything about Lily. It's been a full week and she's still missing. I've been watching Brandon closely in class, practically breaking my neck trying to read his text messages on his computer in English, but I haven't seen Lily's name come up again. He's also not acting out of the ordinary, at least, what I think his ordinary would be. We share math together too, but I don't sit behind him in that class. He talks with his friends, all dude-bro types like him, and leaves after the bell. I have no idea who he could've been talking to about Lily on Monday, and the need to know what he was saying burns through me with a hot urgency and keeps me up at night. He's involved somehow; I know it.

"But," I continue, "I told the detectives to look into Brandon."

Jason's eyebrow raises, but he doesn't look too surprised. Maybe he's put two and two together from when I asked about Brandon before I talked to the detective.

"Brandon?" Jason repeats. "Why?"

I tell him about the way he grabbed Lily at Warren's party, about how she cried, and about the text messages he was sending on Monday.

Jason's jaw clenches. "Lily's never said anything about Brandon grabbing her before."

"She made me promise not to tell anyone. I would've told Officer Liu while he was interrogating me, but he was so certain that I was involved, it slipped my mind."

He nods, eyes calculating. "So we find out what Brandon was saying, or even who he was texting, then we find out what's happened to Lily, as well as get Officer Dickwad off your back."

We. Again he said *we.* Instead of feeling hesitant or confused that he's in this with me, his declaration makes me feel warm and safe. Jason always knows what to do, always has his shit together. If he's in this with me, then maybe I'll finally start feeling like that too.

"That's easier said than done," I say. "I've been trying to read over his shoulder all week, but I can't properly see everything."

Jason looks out over the field. It's empty, a few birds resting on it in the distance. "If only we could get a look at his phone or something . . ."

That would solve all our problems. We'd know what he was up to and figure out if he's involved with Lily's disappearance like I feel in my gut, or just a total asshole. If we could get his phone . . .

My head snaps to look at Jason at the same time his snaps to look at me. "Are you thinking what I'm thinking?" I ask him, already getting an adrenaline rush.

Jason nods and says, "We should break into his house," at the same time I say, "We should steal his phone."

Jason's eyes widen a fraction before he says, "Right. Let's do your thing first."

I should feel worried that his first instinct is to break into someone's house, but I'm not. It makes me laugh, and I'm not scared of him. After this weekend, something deep inside me knows he'd take care of me if something happened.

The five-minute warning bell goes off, and we both reluctantly stand. The wind is harsher when we're not sitting, and it whips my hair around my face.

"So," I start as we walk down the bleachers, "how do we steal a phone?"

"You're asking me like I have a plan," he says. "I'm a little offended you think I'd know how to steal a phone."

I raise an eyebrow at him as we walk over the field toward the school. "Don't you?"

"Well, yeah, but you're supposed to think better of me."

I laugh along with him. "Right now, your specific set of skills is exactly what we need." As long as we don't get caught. "So, what's your plan?"

"What are you doing tonight?" he asks, throwing me off with the subject change.

"Um, I was going to go into a couple of restaurants and hand out my resume."

He shakes his head. "Not anymore. You're coming to the Tracks with me. We're getting Brandon's phone tonight."

"The what?"

He opens the door for me, and I don't miss the mischievous smirk on his lips. "The Tracks. Don't worry, you'll love it."

"Why do I have a feeling I'm *not* going to love it?"

He just laughs as we enter the hallway. The heat hits me right away and warms up my chilled cheeks and ears. I don't need the hoodie anymore, but I don't want to take it off now. Jason's at my side again as we walk down the crowded hallway. Students are moving to their classrooms, and I already miss the crisp breeze.

"It'll be fine," he says, one lip tilted up in a crooked smile that gives him a dimple. I stare at it, my heart doing weird things in my chest. I've never seen this smile from him before. Grins? Sure. Smiles? Yes, and they're all great. But I decide this crooked smile, the one that showcases his mischievous side and that dimple, is my favorite.

"But I should warn you in advance," he says, and I refocus on his eyes. We're still walking side by side, which is weird because I usually have to bob and weave around students like I'm going through a maze. But somehow, with Jason, we've managed to walk straight down the hall. He continues, "that it's not exactly . . . legal."

My breath hitches. *Not exactly legal* means I could be arrested for being there. Is it worth it?

"Jason, I *really* cannot get in trouble," I finally say. I'm already walking on eggshells at home with Dario. Anusha has regular check-ins with him, and I have no idea what they're saying. For all I know, Anusha could be warning him about all the bad behaviors she's analyzed from me over our sessions and telling him to watch out for them. Or even worse, Dario could be telling her he doesn't want me around, and Anusha is coaching him on dealing with me. Either way, besides the whole *I'm never going back to juvie* thing, I need to be on my best behavior.

We stop in front of my classroom door. Jason doesn't share this class with me, and I realize he was following my lead as we walked. The final bell rings, meaning he's late to his own class, but Jason doesn't leave, and I don't enter the classroom.

He ducks his head to meet my eyes, and I can't mistake the understanding in his. With raw conviction, he says, "I know, and I won't let anything happen to you. I swear it."

There's confidence in his voice, a fierce promise in his eyes. He saw me get arrested last time, saw the fight I put up, knows about my need for fresh air, knows I was held for a while before being acquitted. If I know anything about Jason, it's that he's good at connecting dots, and suddenly I feel very seen. I should feel exposed and scared and stripped bare, but instead I feel relief. Someone knows me, someone *sees* me, in a way that no one has before, and the thought is comforting. It reassures me knowing that there's at least one person in this very vast world who truly *sees* me. And that person is Jason Parker.

Unable to say anything over the emotion in my throat, I nod. I believe him. If anyone can help me avoid getting in trouble while actively doing something that *guarantees* we'll get in trouble, it's Jason.

"Good," he says, straightening to his full height again. "I'll text you later."

———

I have no idea where we're going, so I'm not sure how to dress. Jason only told me to be ready by eight thirty.

I text Nyah for help, leaving out the real reason I'm going tonight. We've been texting a lot even though we don't share any classes, about Lily, but mostly just life in general, and I'm enjoying talking to her.

She replies, You're going to the Tracks?! I've only ever been a few times.

Then a few minutes later, she follows up with: I just told Tyler he has to go and bring me. See you tonight!

Without any guidance, I settle on ripped jeans and a low-cut T-shirt with the Converse I cleaned from the first night here. As I'm heading downstairs to grab a snack, I knock on Gia's closed door. There's rustling, then the door swings open.

"What?" she asks.

I glance around her room. It's messy, like every other time I've been in here, but there are clothes laid out on her bed. Her makeup is done with her signature heavy black eyeliner smoked out on her lower and upper lash line, and when I lean in closer, I smell rum on her breath.

I stiffen. Nothing was taken from Dario's liquor cabinet, I checked after dinner, so I don't know where she would've gotten it from.

"Are you going out tonight?" I ask instead of grilling her.

"Yeah," she says, retreating into the room and studying the outfit options on her bed. Without turning to me, she finishes, "With Lindsey and Grace."

I lean against her desk, casually scanning the mess of papers and notes there. Nothing from Mom.

"No Brianna?" I ask. She seems to do everything with Brianna. *Brandon's sister.* Would she know what Brandon's been saying about Lily? They don't seem especially close, but then again, they don't seem not close.

Gia sullenly throws a pair of pants from her bed onto the floor, dismissing it as an option. "No. She blackmailed her brother into taking her to some cool party or she'd tell their mom about last Friday and say it was his fault." She pouts at the bed. "I'm not invited."

"Cool party? The Tracks?" I ask, surprised.

She drops the shirt in her hands and stares at me. "Even *you* know about it?" Then she scans me like she just realized I'm dressed to go out. She gapes. "Are you *going*?"

I hesitate. "Yes."

She throws her hands in the air. "But *how*?! You don't have any friends!" She pauses when she sees the hurt on my face. "I mean . . . you don't have any friends who would go to the Tracks."

It's a terrible cover-up and she knows it, but I try not to linger on it. "Right, well, I just came to say that I won't be home, and Dario will probably be here in an hour or two, so you can warm up some leftovers if you get hungry."

Gia nods and stares down at her hands, sitting on her bed with a resigned sigh.

I turn to leave but then stop at the doorway. Gia's going to go out and party tonight, with kids I know have a history of not being responsible. She'd rather be at the Tracks with Brianna, for bragging rights as well as to see her friend. I half turn and eye her bed, where there's a rum bottle–shaped lump under the top cover.

She's going to go out tonight no matter what I say, and I'd rather it be with me, where I can watch over her.

I turn back to her. "You want to come?"

She jumps up from the bed. "Really?"

I nod. Jason won't mind, I'm sure of it. She runs at me and throws her arms around me. "Yes! You're the best, Siena!" She drops her arms and looks frantically at all the clothes strewn around her bed. "What am I going to wear? Oh my God, everyone's going to be so jealous when I tell them I went to the Tracks! Do you think leather pants are too much? No, right?"

She runs into her closet and pulls out more things, and I watch with a smile. I did that. I made her happy, and I feel like we're one step closer to bridging the chasm that opened between us while I was away.

I text Jason about our additional guest, and he replies saying it's cool seconds later.

"Jason is going to be here in forty, so be ready by then," I tell her, turning to leave but stopping when she calls out, "Wait!"

She rustles in her closet and pulls out a leather jacket. "Here, wear this." She's very petite so we don't often share clothing, but the gesture is sweet and comforting. I take it and shrug it on. It must be a little big on her because it fits me perfectly.

"Now sit," she says, gesturing to her desk chair. "Let

me fix . . ." Her hand circles my face in a vague movement. "That."

I frown, though inside I'm delighted.

"I put makeup on." I defend my makeup skills, though I don't really care. Gia's always done my makeup for me—she's a hell of a lot better at it than I am—and her fussing over me makes me feel like it's old times again, like everything's going to be okay.

"Yeah, which is fine for a normal school day, not for a date with your boyfriend at the Tracks," Gia jokes, pulling out brushes and palletes and a bronzer I'm sure is too dark for me. But I don't say anything—she's the expert. "You're already hot, let me make you hotter, like old times."

Her words warm my chest—they were exactly what I was thinking. My sister, my little sister who I practically raised, is humming as she applies eyeshadow to my lids with a soft brush. I haven't seen her this happy the whole week I've been here. She's changed in the time I've been away, that's for sure, but she'll always be my little sister, and we'll always find our way back to each other, even if it starts with me bringing her to some party she probably shouldn't be at.

When she moves her hand, I mutter, "He's not my boyfriend."

She dismisses me with a wave. "Yeah, yeah. Now hold still."

Gia finishes my makeup in record time and settles on leather pants and a cropped sweater. She looks good, but the smile on her face looks better. She leaves the inexpertly hidden rum bottle under her sheets when we leave and doesn't even glance back at it.

Jason pulls up at exactly eight thirty, opening the passenger-side door and sliding down the front seat for Gia to slip in the back.

"Hey Jason!" Gia practically sings as she settles in the back.

He raises an eyebrow at me as he adjusts the passenger seat for me. I guess he's just as used to moody Gia as I am. I offer him a shrug in answer.

An SUV pulls up in front of the house, and the driver and person in the passenger seat wave at me.

"Jackson's following us down," Jason tells me, gesturing to his brother, who's driving.

The passenger-side window rolls down, and Warren calls out, "Hey Siena! You look hot! In a not-muddy way." He's joking, and I roll my eyes at him even though I'm amused. Jason glares at him from beside me.

The back window rolls down, and I see Tyler and Nyah. Nyah leans over her boyfriend to yell out the window, "He's not wrong!"

"You look hot too," I tell her. She's wearing bright-pink eyeshadow, and it flashes as she gives me a wink.

"Damn straight," Tyler agrees, making Nyah giggle as she falls back into her seat.

According to Warren, who I sit with in English and chat with when Mr. Lewis tells us to "read to ourselves," Nyah and Tyler are "so in love it's sickening." I think it's sweet that she has someone to unconditionally be there for her.

"All right, all right, let's go," Jason commands, shaking his head at his friends. They laugh as they roll up the windows and I slide into Jason's car. The leather seat is warm, and when he gets in beside me, my window opens a few inches to let in some fresh air. I shoot him a small smile, but he's not even looking at me; he's sliding on his seat belt and shooting daggers at his friends in his rearview mirror, because they are still blocking him from reversing.

The fact that the action was done subconsciously, without waiting for some kind of reward or acknowledgment from me, makes butterflies erupt in my stomach. But then I feel embarrassed for feeling that way and stare down at my hands. He's my *friend*, and that's what friends *do*.

Jackson finally moves, and Jason reverses from the driveway. Gia leans forward in her seat once Jason's on the road, Jackson following close behind.

"So, Jason," she starts, her eyes lit with excitement. "What kind of car is this? It looks like a racing one. Are you racing tonight?"

"It's a Challenger," Jason answers. "My brother gave it to me and got himself a new one last year when he graduated law school, even though he literally just bought this one."

"Wait, racing?" I ask, confused. Why would Gia ask if he's racing tonight . . . ? "The *Tracks*." It finally clicks. "We're going drag racing tonight?"

Gia asks, "Did you not know where we're going?"

"No, Jason told me, but I didn't put it together . . ." I say, turning to Jason. "You're not racing, are you?"

Jason raises an eyebrow at me. He must be remembering the first time we met, when I experienced his skills firsthand. "Not with you in the car, if that's what you're thinking."

"No," I agree, crossing my arms over my chest with a huff. "Never again."

"Wait!" Gia's seat belt clicks off and her face appears between me and Jason. "Siena, you've been racing with him? In his car? You don't even drive! Since when have you gotten so cool? And why were you hiding it from me all this time?"

Her words are so classically Gia, insulting without meaning to be, that I'm only slightly offended. "Gia, seat belt," I order instead of answering her, and she grumbles but complies.

"Can I be in the car with you when you race, Jason?" she pleads, excitement radiating off her. "Everyone would be *so jealous* when I tell them! And the video—"

"No videos," Jason interrupts. "This is not legal, and there are some really bad people there, so stay with us and don't wander off, got it?"

Gia's eyes widen and her head bobs up and down, but she's excited nonetheless. I turn in my seat and try to drill my thoughts into her head, warning her to be on her best behavior. *I am not going back to jail.* She gets the message, because she slides down her seat and nods once at me, face somber.

The last time Jason went to this thing, last Friday to be exact, he was speeding away with the cops hot on his tail. I do not want this night to end like that. We're going to go, get what we need from Brandon's phone, and get out. If Gia wants to have fun and I get brownie points at the same time, then fine, but we're not there to race with Jason.

I'm there for *Lily.* Everyone seems to have forgotten about her. Nyah brings her up every once in a while, and then gets sad, but everyone else in school has gone about their business like she was never even there. Can they all forget a person, their *friend*, so quickly? Did she not matter to them? Lily was well-liked, and if she can go missing and become old news fast, then what would happen with someone like me? The thought makes me feel smaller and even more insignificant than I normally do. They may have forgotten about Lily, but I won't. Not only because Officer Liu thinks I'm the prime suspect, but because I'm going to find out what happened to her, for *her*. Because I care about what happened to her, like I'd want someone to care about what happened to me.

No one cared last time, when I was arrested and sent away, unless it was a media outlet trying to create a story out of Florence Bowen and her daughter, but no one really noticed *me* disappearing. Except Gia, but she had her own stuff going on. I glance at Jason in the driver's seat.

He presses a button on the console that causes my seat to warm up, at the same time that I get a text from Nyah, who sent me a joke about our history teacher. A warm feeling in my stomach starts, and I think maybe this time, it can be different.

nine

The Tracks are nothing fancy, but they're packed. We're in an open field, with twisting roads going around and disappearing out of sight. They're a lot like the small dirt road I got lost on when I first arrived, except we were driving for a lot longer than when Jason brought me home that day, so we must be in a totally different location.

The area is packed, and as I exit the car, the sounds and smells and voices of everyone mingle in the air, making the space feel smaller than it actually is. Jackson parks beside Jason and everyone spills out of the vehicle.

"Didn't this place get busted last week?" Nyah asks as

she comes to stand beside me. She greets me with a playful hip bump, and the familiar action makes me smile.

"About an hour west of here," Jason says, shrugging a jacket on. The wind is stronger here, since we're in an open field with no buildings to soften it, and I'm glad Gia suggested I wear her leather jacket. "Jonesy guaranteed we'd be fine tonight, whatever that means."

I don't bother asking who Jonesy is. I figure there will be a lot of name-dropping tonight, and I'm not going to know any of them. I'll probably never see them again in my life, since hanging out at an illegal drag racing operation that the cops often break up is *not* somewhere I want to be spending my time. So if I'm not introduced to the people here, it won't matter. What *does* matter is finding Brandon, and since Gia said he's bringing Brianna, I know he's here somewhere.

I glance at Gia now, who's busily texting. There are so many people here! It's not just kids from King City High, because even if every single student from school was here, it *still* wouldn't add up to this many people. Besides, Gia seems like she's the youngest person here—in fact, I seem like one of the younger people here. There must be other seniors, but a lot of the people seem older, like college age. I guess they're the people that can afford cars, never mind race them.

People walk by, greeting Jason and the other guys. Warren gets noticed immediately and is pulled away by a group of people. He disappears. No one seems concerned, though, so Warren must be as much of a social butterfly here as he is at school. I'll never know why he chooses to sit with me in English instead of his other friends.

There's a race going on in the background, and many people are standing close to the road, trying to watch the two cars as they speed around turns and disappear. But others are standing around talking on the field, not even watching.

"Hey Jason!" a guy calls out, shaking his hand. "I'm having some issues with my transmission. Think you can take a look?"

"Bring it by the shop on Monday and I'll check it out," he answers, which prompts the guy to launch into a story about the last race he competed in. I drown it out as Gia answers a phone call, instead moving over to Nyah. She's frowning out at the field but smiles when I approach.

"It's weird being here without Lily. Everyone always came up to talk to us because they wanted to get close to her. But now . . ." She gestures around herself, as if to emphasize the lack of people around her. "I feel so alone without Lily. I hope she's okay."

For a second I consider telling her about Brandon, but she already looks so lost, I don't want to pile on. Instead I say, "Me too."

Her smile becomes more genuine. "But I'm glad you're here and that we're friends. I may not seem like it, but I'm really shy, that's why me and Lily worked. She's the social one, I'm the one that tagged along and made friends through her. Without her, it's just me and Tyler, and he's great, but you know boys." She rolls her eyes affectionately at where he's talking with Jackson and a few other guys I recognize from school. One of them makes a dirty gesture and they all laugh.

"Well, thanks for not giving up on me even though I keep turning down your lunch invitations," I say to her. I enjoy texting Nyah throughout the day. I thought she was an extrovert like Lily, so it's interesting to hear that she feels lonely sometimes. "Maybe I'll take you up on it one day this week."

"I'd like that. Actually, why don't we do something this week? We can go shopping for homecoming dresses! Tyler's useless at the mall. I keep telling him green isn't my color and guess what color clothes he always picks out for me is?"

"Green?" I ask at the same time she exclaims, "Green!"

We laugh together, and something about this just feels *right*.

I say, "I haven't given much thought to homecoming, but I'd love to come shopping with you. I promise I won't suggest anything green."

We laugh again, and Nyah says, "Great! I always need another opinion, and I'm an only child so I have no one to ask other than Tyler."

We look over to the boys, where one of them puts Tyler in a headlock and they wrestle playfully.

Nyah shakes her head. "God, I love him. He's my *person*, you know? I'd be so lost without him. Except for his shopping tastes, he just *gets* me. Sometimes he can tell when I've had a bad day and he'll bring me a chocolate macadamia iced coffee and raspberry muffin from a café all the way on the other side of town. He just knows how to cheer me up."

"That's so sweet," I say, wondering what it would be like to have a *person* who gets me, who makes me feel the way Nyah does just looking at Tyler. No one's gone out of their way to cheer me up on a bad day before.

Except Jason, a voice in the back of my mind says. *He got arrested defending you.*

I push the thought away just as Tyler joins us, his short dark hair ruffled from horsing around.

"Have you ever seen Jason race, Siena?" he asks, wrapping his hand around Nyah's. He's a good-looking boy: dark eyes, olive skin, and on the skinny side of lean. Nyah says he plays a lot of soccer in the warmer weather and that's how he stays in shape, and why he doesn't work out with the other guys early in the morning at the school gym. Some girls walking by don't hide the flirty looks sent his way, but he doesn't notice. He only has eyes for Nyah.

She gives him a playful shove. "How would she have seen him race if she's never been here before?"

"Oh, right," he says with a shake of his head. "I remember the first time Jason raced. Got his ass *handed* to him, but he thought he knew everything at fifteen. Now look at him, only a few years later and people already say he's just as good, if not *better* than, his older brother."

More people are showing up, more cars parking haphazardly on the grass. The loud revving of engines occurs once every few minutes, and I'm almost getting used to not looking over to find the source of the noise like everyone else.

"I guess you've known him for a while then?" I ask, keeping my eyes on him and not the loud revving.

"Since we were kids."

And they're still friends now. They must know so much about each other.

Gia finishes her call and tugs on my jacket. "Is that Brianna? Can you see?"

She's standing on her tiptoes trying to look over the crowd, but at five-two, she's really not seeing anything. I'm only two inches taller than her, so I'm not having any better luck identifying her friend. But if that's her, that means Brandon is there, and we can commence Operation Steal the Phone, though I have no idea what the plan actually is.

"Who are you guys looking for?" Nyah asks, glancing in the same direction. She's a bit taller than me, and Tyler is just shy of six feet, and after I tell her, we're all straining our necks trying to look for Brandon and Brianna in the crowd of people.

"I think that's them!" Gia says, pointing in the general

direction we were looking. "Brianna said she's by a blue Audi, and there's one right there."

"What are you all looking at?" Jason's voice comes from extremely close behind me, making me jump.

"Gia thinks she's found her friend Brianna," Nyah chimes in while I work on slowing my heart rate.

Jason nods, something sparking in his eyes. "Well, why don't Siena and I walk you over then?" He looks at me, and I can practically hear him saying *it's go time* out loud, though he'd probably never say those exact words.

"Great!" Gia exclaims, weaving through people without waiting for us.

I turn to Nyah and Tyler. "We'll be ba . . ." I trail off, since they're making out. Warren wasn't kidding when he said they're always on top of each other. I wonder what they're like at lunch in the cafeteria.

"Come on, Siena," Jason says, placing a hand on the small of my back. The heat of it sears through the leather jacket and I force myself to put it out of my mind as he guides me around crowds of people.

"So, what's the plan?" I ask him, keeping Gia in sight.

"You're going to go up to Brandon," he starts.

"Okay, easy part. And then?"

"You're going to flirt with him."

I stare at him, waiting for him to reveal he's joking, but his face is as serious as ever.

"What's the real plan?"

"That is the plan. You have to get him to unlock his

phone and pay attention to his code, and the best way to do that is to get him to ask for your number," he explains, as if it's as easy as pie.

"Okay, of the many flaws in that plan, you're overlooking one big, important one," I say, and he steers me away from some guy who tries to grab my hand and get me to talk to him.

"And what's that?"

"Well, besides the fact that I can't flirt for shit—" because I've literally never done it before "—Brandon creeps me out. I swear warning bells go off in my head every time I look at him. Plus, I don't think he likes me very much. He always glares at me in class."

"That's just his face." Jason waves off my concerns, then his jaw clenches, and his hand presses more firmly against me. "He thinks you're hot. He's very loud about it. You'll be fine."

My brows furrow at that. Brandon's never talked to me, and I've never heard him express any interest in me, so that information is completely out of left field. I guess guys speak differently when they're alone.

"Just be nice to him, and pay attention when he unlocks his phone," he says. Now we're close enough to spot Gia and Brianna, giggling about something a few feet away from Brandon and his friends. "Oh, and this should help." He drops his hand from my back, instead placing it over my shoulders and drawing me close. The entire left side of my body is pressed against his, and my heart rate doubles.

"What are you—" I'm about to step away from him when he stops me by pulling me in closer. I'm embarrassed to admit that I melt into him, and that his arm around me and the heat coming off him make the stupid butterflies in my stomach start up.

As we approach the group, Jason lowers his head to my ear. He's practically nuzzling me, and I have to force myself to keep my breathing even. His cologne, or just *him*, smells so good, I wish I had given him his hoodie back just so it could smell like him again when I wear it. His breath is minty and hot on my ear when he whispers, "He's a jealous guy, likes what he can't have. Play along."

His words are a splash of cold water, and I reprimand my body for reacting to him that way when it's clearly just for show. I feel stupid, but I force myself to remain calm and focus on restoring a normal heart rate. Pressed up against his side, I hope he can't feel how fast it's beating.

He keeps his face turned into mine as if he's whispering in my ear, and one of the guys calls out, "Hey, Jason!"

Jason peers around as if he didn't realize Brandon and his friends were there at all.

"Oh, hey Alex," Jason says nonchalantly, like walking up to them with me against his side is no big deal.

Brandon glares at me, which is nothing new, but I keep my eyes on Alex.

"You racing today?" the guy beside Alex asks as we get closer. Jason drops his arm from my shoulder, and I miss the weight of it instantly. He's somehow managed to position us within the group so that I'm closest to Brandon.

Gia's talking with Brianna a few feet away, and she excitedly points back to Jason's car parked somewhere behind us.

"You're with Parker? Really?" Brandon's voice holds a note of disgust, not even trying to hide it. Jason was right: it's almost comical how jealous Jason's arm over my shoulder made Brandon, especially considering he hasn't spoken two words to me all week.

"Oh, Jason?" I ask, playing it cool. "We're just friends."

"Right." His eyes pin Jason from where he's standing on my other side.

"So," I start, trying to get Brandon to pay attention to me and me only. "Brianna's your sister?"

Stupid. So stupid. If Jason's looking at me, I bet he's staring incredulous holes in the back of my head.

"Uh, yeah," Brandon says. I never realized how big he is, since I've never been this close to him. He must be as tall as Jason, with shoulders just as wide. He's wearing a King City letterman jacket, so he must be into sports. I can use that.

"Which sport do you play? Football?" I ask, and then curse myself for such an awkward transition. The other guys in the group are fully enthralled by whatever Jason is saying, so even though we're standing in a group, I feel like I'm alone with Brandon. It makes the hair on the back of my neck stand up.

"Yes, football," he answers, his chest puffing out a bit.

"The quarterback, but sometimes I like to get in there and get some good hits in."

I nod, pretending to be interested. "Oh wow! Really? Isn't that dangerous?"

That seems to warm him up, a wolfish smile taking over his face. "Not when you're as good as me. Just last week I . . ."

I nod as he talks, pretending to be fully into in his story about how much he can bench. Male pride. This is good. I can do this. Talk about him, find something in common, and take it from there. But what can Brandon and I have in common? We both have sisters, but that's not exactly a flirty topic. I need him to be interested enough in me to ask for my number, but then how am I going to see his code properly to remember it upside down? I need to do it well enough for Lily . . . Lily! Remembering her, a plan forms in my head.

"But how do you keep up with all that training and class? I can barely understand math as it is and I'm not even doing any extracurriculars," I ask, twirling a piece of hair around my finger like the girls at work back in LA did when taking the order of guys they thought were cute.

"Math?" He waves me off with an arrogant confidence. "It's easy. I can do that in my sleep."

I knew he'd say that. He always knows the answer when Mr. Fidiott calls on him, thinking he's not paying any attention. It's really not fair, because he usually *isn't* paying any attention.

"So, you're athletic, strong, *and* smart? You're like the

whole package." I giggle on the outside but inside I'm gagging. I can't believe I just said that, and from the way Jason pauses from whatever story he was telling behind me, he can't either. But Brandon eats it up.

"Yeah, I've been told that before."

I swear he's standing taller than before. He suddenly seems huge, like he takes up much more space now.

"Have you ever thought of tutoring?" I ask, standing closer to him even though my body physically doesn't want to. I'm not sure if what I'm doing qualifies as flirting, but we're getting somewhere and that's the important part.

The corner of his lip turns up and he makes a show of raking his eyes up and down my body. "Maybe if the right person asked. You asking?"

My flirty smile feels pasted on and I hope it looks genuine. I look up at him through my lashes. "Depends. Am I the right person?"

He grins, and I suddenly have a sinking feeling, like I've willingly stepped into a trap. But then I remember the goal *was* to step into his trap, and when he pulls his phone out of his back pocket, I give myself an imaginary victory high five. It's in a black phone case, a large gold "B" on the back, and I pull my eyes away from it.

"We have a test coming up in two weeks," I say to distract him from unlocking the phone himself. "Think we can set up a little study date?"

He licks his lip while eyeing me and it takes a tremendous amount of willpower not to back up into Jason and grab his hand as reassurance that I'm not sticking my arm in a bear trap.

"Yeah," he says, a predatory gaze fixed on me. "We can work something out."

"Great!" I say cheerily, plucking his phone from his hand. When I first met Lily, she asked for my phone passcode with enough confidence that I just *gave* it to her. I need to channel Lily's energy, and I need to do it well enough to get Brandon, a guy who I'm sure doesn't even like me, to do the same. "What's your passcode? I'll put my number in your phone."

He looks at me, stunned for a moment, but I give him my best disarming, innocent smile. At least, I hope that's what it is. It feels like a grimace.

"Uh . . . 6, 2, 6, 4," he answers, and the phone unlocks. I want to do a victory dance. It worked! I wonder if Jason heard anything, but I repeat the numbers in my mind over and over again so as not to forget.

It's a struggle not to just open his message app and find the information I need right this second, but I doubt Brandon will let me scroll through his phone for as long as I need. So instead, I save my number, my *real* number, and hand the phone back to him with a confident smile, not having to fake it this time.

"Great," I say, taking a step back now that I no longer need to convince him to like me. "Can't wait to finally start understanding what's happening in class."

Brandon opens his mouth to say something, but Jason

appears at my side. He was talking with everyone, but he must've still been listening, because his timing to save me is impeccable. "Hey, I've got to go talk to Jonesy before the next race. Come with me?"

"Yeah, sure," I say, sending Brandon an apologetic smile like I wish we could've had more time to talk, while internally I'm celebrating. "Gia! Come on."

She frowns at me, coming over from where she and Brianna were talking to some other girls. "But we just got here," she complains. "Can't I stay here?"

I lower my voice and duck closer to her. "You heard what Jason said in the car."

Brandon is near enough to listen, so I don't go into more detail. She looks like she wants to argue more when Jason says, "Don't worry. We'll come back soon, okay?"

She mulls it over a bit, before finally relenting, telling her friends she'll be back before leading the way to Jason's car.

I wave at Brandon, just so I can keep the charade up long enough to not be suspicious, then walk with Jason around groups of people, keeping Gia in sight.

"That was . . . rough. But it did the job," Jason comments once we're far enough from Brandon and friends.

I elbow him. "I *told* you it was an impossible task. You're lucky I was able to control my facial features, never mind get him to want my number."

Jason laughs. "I told you: you're hot. That was the easy part. I can't believe you asked for his passcode. You remember it?"

He didn't tell me I was hot. He told me *Brandon* thought I was hot. I don't know why I'm stuck on this minor fact, but it completely changes the meaning of his words, and my stomach squeezes.

"Uh, yeah. 6, 2, 6, 4."

"Good," Jason says, his hand landing on my waist long enough to steer me around a rowdy group of guys. Thompson is there. He shotguns a beer before crushing the empty can against his forehead while his friends cheer.

"Parker!" he calls joyfully. "I put three hundred dollars on you, so you better win tonight!"

"You got it," Jason answers, not matching his tone. He pulls me away from them quickly.

"He bet three hundred dollars on you to win a race?" I ask Jason, my mind wrapping around the fact he has that much spare income to gamble away like that. What if he loses? Does he even know how long I'd have to work at my old job to get three hundred dollars? Or maybe he does. Maybe he doesn't care. Maybe he knows Jason will win, or maybe the risk is part of the fun.

I mentally calculate how much money I have in my bank account right now. It's been easier now that we're living with Dario and not Aunt Julie, but the number is not even four digits. I really should send out resumes tomorrow.

"Not all the people come here to race. Most come to watch or gamble."

"That's a lot of pressure on the drivers," I say, thinking about how people must change their feelings about him based on whether or not he wins. "Do people ever get mad at you for losing?"

He shrugs as his friends come into view. "Sometimes. But that's part of the risk of gambling."

"Siena! There you are!" Warren calls, beckoning me over. "The next race is starting; you're going to miss it."

I join him by Jackson's SUV, but Jason disappears. Gia's already ducking inside the vehicle at Nyah's instructions, and her top half reappears through the sunroof.

"Come on, you too," Nyah gestures, and I crawl into the SUV, stepping on the center console to push my head through the sunroof where Gia's legs are dangling. I sit opposite Gia on the roof and scooch over so Nyah can sit with me. It's windy up here, and I wrap Gia's jacket tighter around me. It's hard to see in the distance because it's so dark and there are no streetlights, but the area is illuminated from all the car headlights. Jackson, Warren, and Tyler chat with some people not too far from us.

"There!" Gia points to two cars idling side by side on the empty road. "Brianna said Chris talked the guy into letting him race today! Apparently, he's been trying forever. That's him!"

Sure enough, the car at the makeshift starting line is the same Toyota Camry Gia was squeezed into last Friday. I have no idea if a Toyota Camry is fast, but apparently Chris thinks it's good enough to race. He's going up against a souped-up Honda Civic.

Gia pulls her phone out of her pocket and aims it at the

cars, but I put my hand on hers and lower it. "Jason said no pictures, remember?"

She pouts but reluctantly puts the phone away again, and I know she's thinking about growing her picture board in her purple room, the one filled with memories of her ex-girlfriend and friends that haven't checked in on her for weeks.

Nyah sniffs from beside me.

"Lily used to do that," she says, a wistfulness in her tone. "She'd take pictures, then look at them at the end of the night before deleting them in case her parents saw them."

"Her parents are really strict," Gia adds, watching the race start. "I could hear them arguing with her when the windows were open." She looks at us now. "The other week her mom was upset because Lily had gained weight since her last weigh-in and was worried her agency would drop her."

Nyah nods. "Her parents put a lot of pressure on her."

"Go go go! *No!*" Gia cries, and I turn back to the race to see Chris losing, by a lot. A few more moments and it's over, and Chris lost by an embarrassingly large distance.

"Can we go back now?" Gia asks me, nodding toward where Chris is parking his car.

"Umm." I look around and catch Jason walking back to us. He gestures with his head toward Brandon, which I guess means it's time for Part 2 of our plan.

"Sure, Gia," I agree, and she wastes no time jumping

down from the sunroof. "We'll be back, I guess," I tell Nyah, who smiles and waves Tyler over to keep her company.

I meet up with Jason and say, "Gia wants to console Chris."

We follow Gia to her friend. She's there first when he exits the car, and I lean into Jason. "What now? How are we taking the phone?"

Brandon's coming near us, looking bored and annoyed as he brings Brianna to her friends. He must care about her somewhat if he doesn't want her walking around here alone, even if he does seem put out about it.

"Take his phone from his back pocket during the commotion," Jason says. Brandon is closer now.

"What commotion?"

"Hey! Jason!" an angry voice calls, and when we turn, we see Jackson storming over to us. "You think you can just say that to me and walk away?" he shouts, and Brandon and a few others move closer to watch.

I have no idea what's going on, but Jackson finally reaches us and shoves Jason, forcing me to step away from them.

"I was just telling the truth," Jason seethes, pushing his brother back.

More people are crowding around, watching now, and I stand there with my mouth open. Do I intervene? Do I deescalate? They were best friends literally two seconds ago!

"The *truth* is that you're a selfish asshole who can't take criticism!" Jackson shoots back, shoving his brother again, and then I realize Brandon is thoroughly distracted. I move a few feet until I'm standing behind him, while the two brothers continue shouting and shoving each other. I get as close to him as I dare and prepare my pointer and thumb to pinch his phone out of his pocket, but he'll definitely feel that. I meet Jason's eyes over Brandon's shoulder, and he growls to his brother, "You're just jealous you're not *me*," and shoves him right into Brandon. Brandon stumbles back, bumping into me, and I take the opportunity to swipe his phone. I quickly retreat as I hear Brandon saying something about calming down to the twins, but I keep walking until I'm a safe distance away.

My hands tremble as I punch 6, 2, 6, 4 into Brandon's phone, relieved when it unlocks. I tap on his messages, almost overwhelmed with all the different people he's been talking to. How am I going to figure out which one is the person he was talking to about Lily? I doubt he'd go around telling everyone that Lily got what she deserved, and I'm not sure who his closest friend is. Maybe Jason should've been the one to go through the phone; he'd probably know which chat to open, who Brandon is closest to.

My palms are sweaty, and when an engine revs, I jump and look around, like I've been caught doing something wrong, but Brandon isn't here, and I'm lost between two groups of random people.

I frantically scroll through the list of names and open chats Brandon has, hoping a name will pop out to me. But maybe he erased the messages already . . . I hadn't even considered that as an option.

I'm about to tap on a random name to open that chat, when I freeze. Lily. He has a chat with her, and I tap on it. The last message was sent Friday, in which he reprimands her for ignoring him. It's time-stamped just before I found them together. My stomach clenches seeing he hasn't texted her after that, almost as if he knew she wouldn't answer. I scroll up a bit more and read the messages between the two of them. It's a lot of Brandon trying to get Lily's attention, and her telling him to leave her alone. She texts those words in different ways multiple times to him over the course of multiple days. Leave me alone, Brandon. Stop texting me, Brandon. You can't just show up at my house like that, Brandon.

His responses are always along the same lines. You can't blow me off, Lily. Who do you think you are, Lily? You owe me, Lily.

Dread builds in my stomach. He was obsessed with her. She was blowing him off and clearly felt uncomfortable with him. He didn't want to leave her alone.

I scroll up more, holding my breath, almost scared to find out more, and—

"Siena!"

My head jerks up in time for Brianna and Gia to join me. Brianna was the one who called out to me, and I'm frozen where I am. "Gia said you're dating Jason? I can't wait to see him race, everyone here keeps saying that he's even better than his older brother, though he hasn't raced in years, and I—is that Brandon's phone?"

She's pointing at the phone in my hand, and I quickly lock the screen so she doesn't see that I was snooping.

"What?" Gia asks, narrowing her eyes on me.

Stupid black phone case with the golden "B" on the back. Who has a phone case with their own initials emblazoned across it?

"Is it?" I ask, examining the phone like I've never seen it before. "I don't know, I found it on the ground and was trying to figure out who it belonged to."

"Brandon! Brandon!" Brianna calls while I try to pretend that everything is normal. When he ignores her, she yells, "Hey stupid, you lost your phone."

That gets his attention, and I want to crawl into a hole and die when he joins us. The stolen phone burns in my hand, almost as hot as the suspicious glare he sends my way when he spots it.

"Mom would've killed you if Siena didn't find it," Brianna continues smugly.

Brandon pats his empty back pocket. "I swear I just had it."

"Good thing it was me who found it then," I say, trying to recall that flirty banter from before, but his eyes narrow on me.

"Right," he says, grabbing the phone, and the way he's eyeing me gives me goose bumps. I want to get out of here, but I don't know how to make a casual exit. Luckily, Jackson comes over to save me.

"Hey, come on. Jason was called up early, it's his turn. We're going to miss it!"

Thank God.

"Come on, Gia," I tell her, and when I see her fallen expression, I add, "Come too, Brianna. We can watch from the top of the SUV. We'll see everything."

She doesn't even ask her brother for permission, just hooks her arm in Gia's and lets her lead her to where Jackson's parked.

"See you later, Brandon," I say, not daring to dip my eyes to the phone gripped in his hands. I don't know if I exited out of the conversation with Lily or not. If I didn't, he'll know I had his phone opened to her conversation when he unlocks his phone. Maybe he'll think it was a phone glitch or he tapped on it by accident before tucking it away? I can only hope.

I don't wait for his reply. I meet up with Jackson and speed-walk away from Brandon. Once I no longer feel his glare drilling holes in the back of my head, I can breathe easier.

"What was that about?" Jackson asks, gesturing behind us to Brandon. "He looked like he wanted to eat you and couldn't decide in which way."

I choke on a laugh and gag. "Ew, Jackson."

"What? I didn't make the face, he did."

I shiver, mentally destroying the image he put in my head. But if Jackson is asking that, does that mean Jason didn't tell him? And the fight . . . ?

"Did Jason not tell you what's going on? Was the fight real?"

Jackson laughs. "No, and no. Like three minutes ago he said he needed me to cause a scene and shove him a bit near Brandon."

Jackson's so calm and nonchalant about the whole thing, like that was a perfectly normal request to make.

"And you didn't ask why?" I press.

He shrugs, his hands in the pockets of his jacket. "No. Jason would tell me if he wanted me to know."

I stare at Jackson like I'm trying to unravel a puzzle. The loyalty and trust they have to blindly do whatever the other asks is huge. Gia and I are sisters, but we don't operate that way unless it's an emergency. It must be a twin thing, or maybe just a Jason and Jackson thing.

"Jason's right, you really do like to stare."

His words make me jump, and I look away from him. I hadn't realized I was doing that.

"Tell me the truth." Jackson leans in conspiratorially as we walk, my face burning. "I'm the better-looking twin, right?"

They're identical. Both tall, both broad-shouldered, both with stupidly nice jawlines. But Jason's easier to identify because he seems more grounded, more thoughtful, and logical. Jackson's more carefree.

I say, "That's what Jason's caller ID says when you call, so it must be true."

He laughs as the group comes into view. "You should see what it says now."

He sends me a wink that for some reason would look so out of place on Jason, but suits Jackson perfectly, then asks, "Did you place a bet on Jason yet?"

Me? Bet? With what money? "No. Did you?"

"Yup," Jackson answers. "I put three hundred, and Mason gave me three hundred to bet for him before I left the house today."

Three hundred dollars? And some guy named Mason just blindly gave Jackson that kind of money to bet for him too? They either all have great disposable income or high faith in Jason.

"Who's Mason?" I ask.

"He's . . . hmm . . . how do I explain this? I guess the short answer is that he's our adoptive brother? Natalia adopted me and Jason when we were nine years old. Mason is her son, but he's been best friends with our brother Aiden for as long as I can remember. Mason's in town visiting his dad, and the half sister he shares with our brother Aiden's fiancé, Thea."

That does sound complicated, so I nod, but it reminds me of when I was stalking Jason's Instagram last week. That must have been the guy, woman, and girl he was posing with in one of the photos.

"Everyone keeps mentioning your brother Aiden. Is he the one who taught Jason to race? Did he teach you?"

Jackson nods. "Yeah, Aiden taught us to drive at, like, eleven. Jason picked it up a lot faster than me, and he likes cars a hell of a lot more than me, too, so I never cared about racing. Jason was a natural at it, but Aiden never wanted him to race. Jason would sneak out before he even got his license to come here." He laughs, lost in the memory. "Aiden used to be so pissed when someone would call him and tell him Jason was here, but by the time he got here, he'd end up yelling tips at Jason instead of dragging him back home."

I laugh along with him. I know firsthand how much fun Jason has while driving, so that story fits perfectly with the annoyingly stubborn guy I know.

We reach the group and Jackson playfully slaps Tyler on the shoulder, while Nyah calls to me from where she's sitting through the sunroof with Gia and Brianna.

"He's going to start!" she calls to me, pointing to where I'm assuming Jason is at the starting line. The revving of engines and cheers from the crowd are loud even from here. Fewer people are talking in groups and more have surged closer to the road. I guess a race between Jason and this opponent is a popular event.

I crawl into the car as Jackson hops onto the back of a pickup truck parked beside us with the other guys and the people Warren was talking to. My head pops out of the sunroof just in time to catch Jason's car take off. I don't even bother sitting beside Nyah on the roof; I'm too transfixed to move from where I'm standing to hop up. Jason's leading against the silver Camaro he's facing, but not by much. The cars zoom out of sight as they take a turn fast, too fast, and I hold my breath until they both straighten out again. I thought it wouldn't be as scary watching Jason race compared to being *in* the car with him while he did it, but I was wrong. It's just as gut-wrenching.

The crowd is cheering loudly, louder than they have for any other race, and for some reason, the hairs on the back of my neck stand up. It feels like someone is watching me, but almost everyone here has their eyes glued to the road. I glance around, trying to find the source of my discomfort, and my heart stops entirely when I find it.

My *mother* is here. Or at least, I think that's her. She's standing by herself, about forty feet away from us. She's wearing a gray baseball cap down low on her forehead, blocking her eyes. But it must be her, I'm sure of it.

Gia hasn't noticed or sensed anything out of place. When I look back to where the woman who's probably Mom is, she's walking away.

Before I can think, I duck through the sunroof and scramble out of Jackson's vehicle.

"Where are you going?" Nyah calls to me when I'm on the ground.

"I'll be back!" I shout over my shoulder, my feet already racing toward where I last saw Mom. I catch sight of the woman in the hat and weave through crowds of people to try to keep up, but I'm losing her in the dark. It has to be Mom, I'm sure of it. She had my height, my same slender build, my same downturned lips. As I get older it's almost remarkable how much I'm starting to look like her, so I'd know her in a crowd like I'd know myself. But I need to be sure. I need to make sure it's not my mind seeing things because I've been thinking of her more than usual.

Everyone cheers, with some people cursing and some high-fiving, so I'm assuming the race has finished, but I'm too focused on not losing Florence. I stop and look around, not sure which direction she went, before finally catching sight of her swinging ponytail and charging in that direction.

My heart beats in my ears as she bobs in and out of my sight around groups of spectators. I don't even know what I'd say if it is her. What are you doing here? Why haven't you contacted us? *Do you miss us as much as we miss you?*

The crowd is sparser here, and I'm almost there—she's just an arm's length away—when a hand clamps onto my arm, yanking me to a stop.

I try tugging away from whoever is grabbing me, but I'm forced to watch helplessly as the woman in the baseball hat gets away, my heart sinking.

"What the hell?" I turn to the person with a death grip on my arm and freeze when I'm forced to look up at Brandon.

"Where are you going in such a rush?" he asks, his gaze making me want to shrink back. For the first time I realize I have no idea where I am. I don't know which direction or how far I am from friends. I was blindly following the woman without paying attention, and now that I'm completely alone with Brandon except for people who aren't paying me a second's worth of attention, I really regret it.

"Um, back to my friends?" I say, but it comes out as a

question instead of a confident statement.

His eyes narrow, and I swear he can hear how fast and loud my heart is beating. Lily was afraid of him. She wanted to get *away* from him. In fact, that first day, Lily warned *me* away from him. Now something's happened to her, and I'm alone with the person who is, in my opinion, suspect number one.

"Everyone is *that* way." He gestures with his left hand behind him, because the right is still holding my arm.

"Right. And that's where I'm going." This time I do sound more confident, and try tugging my arm out of his grasp, but it doesn't budge. Instead, he uses his grip to pull me closer, the exact opposite of where I want to go.

He lowers his head to peer straight into my eyes, into my soul, and I become itchy everywhere. His voice is low and menacing when he growls, "Did you go through my phone?"

My voice is caught in my throat. "What? I don't . . ." I try moving back from him, but he won't let me. "Of course I didn't."

I struggle for a few moments but his grip doesn't give, and panic rises through my body. No one knows where I am. No one would notice if I disappeared.

Jason would.

And Gia would too, eventually.

The thought calms me a little, enough to think rationally about how to get out of this situation when blunt force fails, because it *will* fail if it's me against a giant football player. It takes everything in me and all of Aunt Julie's lectures about the different acting techniques that make her a great actress to stop my struggling and look up at Brandon with humorous confusion.

"Wait, did Warren put you up to this?" I laugh, and it sounds real. "He bet me five bucks he'd be able to freak me out before the end of the night." I shake my head and give Brandon a playful pat on his chest with my free hand. "I thought he meant he'd put a spider on my head or something! You're supposed to be on my side!" My smile feels stretched too thin over my teeth, but it throws Brandon off enough to release my arm, his brow furrowing.

I force myself not to rub my pulsing arm, pretending that everything is fine. "You guys are always *so committed* to your pranks." I take a few steps in the direction he gestured to before, the direction where I think my friends are. I don't know if Warren's a prankster or not but I don't care. Brandon stands there, not completely convinced and still with that menacing look on his face, but it's softening from confusion.

I pause where I'm walking, and with my heart still beating too loud, I playfully call out to him, "Well, come on! Aren't you going to walk me back?"

He blinks a few times before letting out a breath, his face relaxing. "Yeah, for sure."

The last thing I want is for Brandon to walk me back, but it sells the whole *I'm too stupid to realize I'm being threatened and we're totally friends* act that's gotten me out of these situations more times than I can count. Sometimes it's too risky to straight-out fight back against someone—sometimes that's what they *want*. So, I've had to disarm them with this little act until I can get away. It sucks. I wish I could just bash a guy's face in every time they grabbed me or hurled crude, sexist remarks my way, but I'd never overpower them, and I don't know how to fight. This technique has worked against the guys who've grabbed me at work or late at night on the bus or even in my own apartment when Aunt Julie threw her parties. It's worked twice on Brandon now, the first time being when I found Lily at the party.

I don't know if Brandon's totally bought the act, and if the way he's glancing at me every once in a while is any indication, he's definitely suspicious of me. But he's not grabbing me, and that's a win in my book. I babble on about random things, pretending to be totally at ease, and eventually we're in a vaguely familiar area. We pass Thompson, and he calls out to Brandon.

"Go, I'll catch up with you later," I tell him, resisting the urge to fist pump with joy when we continue on different paths. My sigh of relief is loud and short-lived when I bump into another body. The person steadies me but immediately releases me.

"What the hell, Siena!" Jason chides, eyes scanning my face. "I've been looking everywhere for you! Sorry I couldn't come to you right after the fight, they called me to race, and I had to go."

"It's all right," I say, feeling calmer with Jason's reassuring presence near me. "Did you win?" My attempt at sounding normal fails. But Brandon's still too close, almost hearing distance. I want to walk around Jason, but he steps in front of me, scrutinizing me.

After a few moments, something clicks behind his eyes, and they darken. "What happened?"

I don't want to tell him about Brandon grabbing me, don't want to get him involved more than I already have. "Nothing," I lie, but he knows it, and his eyes scan the area until they land on Brandon.

"Siena." He enunciates my name slowly, in a low voice that makes me feel like he's not as calm as he's trying to seem. "Tell me what happened." It's a demand, not a question.

"Nothing, everything. Not here, okay? Can we go?"

Without thinking, I grab his hand, and the warmth of it sends a rush of electricity up my arm and straight to my stomach. He doesn't pull away, instead tightening his fingers on mine and even allowing me to lead him back to our friends.

"Are you okay at least?" he asks, his voice softening, which weakens my resolve.

"I'm fine," I promise. "But can we go home now? Do you have another race?" I really do want to leave, and not just because of Brandon. Mom might be here somewhere, and I don't want to risk Gia seeing her. She has enough to worry about already, and I don't think she can handle knowing Mom is in King and hasn't reached out. But maybe it wasn't her; maybe I only saw what I wanted to see, and I can't decide if that makes me feel better or not.

For a moment it seems like he wants to say something, but he only nods. "We can go."

He doesn't push, and I like that about him. He doesn't poke and prod me like Anusha does, doesn't talk over me or dismiss me like Gia does. He just listens, he's *here*.

ten

Dario was up watching television when we got in late last night. He looked at his watch and shook his head in disapproval when he heard Jason's car take off out of the driveway before turning back to the game. I didn't say anything as Gia and I trudged up the stairs, but I was pissed off, nonetheless.

In the morning, it's not him at the stove flipping pancakes, it's Zia Stella.

"Good morning," she greets as I open the large stainless-steel fridge and pour myself a glass of juice. "Your dad told me you were out late last night with a boy?" It's a question, but it's not accusatory like I'm sure Dario intended it to be. She sounds curious, or like she wants to gossip about boys . . . with me.

"It was, like, 1:00 a.m.," I admit, since there's no point in lying about the time since Dario already knew. "But I wasn't *out* with a boy, he was just the one who drove us home."

"Are you sure?" she prods with a coy smile like we're sharing a secret. "Gia mentioned something about you having a boyfriend."

I freeze as I pull out the island stool, then sit as smoothly as I can. "Gia says any guy I talk to is my boyfriend."

"Okay," she says, not fully convinced. She places two pancakes from the griddle onto a plate and slides it in front of me. "But if you want to talk about the boyfriend who's not a boyfriend, I'm all ears."

I stare at her, then the pancakes, then her again. What's going on here? Is this some kind of ploy? Is she trying to get me to admit to something? Or is she trying to butter me up before breaking some kind of bad news? No adult has ever been this nice to me without wanting something or having an ulterior motive.

"Right. Okay." I hesitate, then pick up the fork she laid out for me and douse the pancakes in syrup. They're good pancakes, and she smiles at me as I scarf them down. I don't even know how long it's been since someone else has cooked for me, especially not pancakes from scratch.

"What are your plans for the day?" she asks, pouring more batter onto the griddle.

"I have a phone call with Anusha in . . ." I pull out my phone and set it on the counter to check the time. She frowns at it, and I do too when I remember it's broken, and I can't see the time. I stuff it back into my pocket and glance at the clock on the stove behind her. "Ten minutes," I finish.

"Are you finding your sessions helpful?" she asks, and I shrug.

"I guess." I like Anusha enough, and she's given me some solid advice and taught me some useful breathing techniques, but I'm sure I'd get more out of our sessions with her if I could be honest with her.

"That's better than a 'no' I suppose." She laughs to herself as Gia stumbles into the kitchen, her eyes half closed and short hair sticking up in spikes.

"Good morning, Gia," Zia Stella sings cheerily, flipping pancakes onto a plate and sliding them beside me. Gia drops into the seat and mumbles a greeting to our aunt.

"And what do you have planned today?" Zia Stella asks, fixing a coffee and placing it in front of Gia. She knows how Gia likes her coffee?

Gia pours half the syrup bottle onto her plate and yawns. "Not sure. Can you drive me to Walmart to grab some things?"

"Sure, we can go after breakfast," Zia Stella agrees. "What about after that?"

"I don't know. I think Brianna and Lindsey want to go to the mall."

"Don't you have an essay due Monday?" I ask her.

"Yeah, *Monday*. I have lots of time."

"Have you started yet?"

"No, but it's the first essay of the year, how hard could it possibly be? I'll do it quicky before class."

"But shouldn't you—"

"God, Siena, what's your problem this morning?" she demands, getting defensive. "You were never so up my butt about homework before."

Does Gia really not get it? Does she not see us here in King with a stable life as a possibility to succeed? We never had the chance to get good grades before, but here, we can. We can get scholarships and go to colleges and get good jobs, be anyone and anything we want to be. We have a *chance* here, and I don't want her to blow it because she's caught up in being popular. Maybe Mom isn't here to be a real mom and nag Gia about her schoolwork, and we all know Dario isn't going to do it, because the man could care less about us, so if it has to be me, then fine.

"I also hadn't had my future flash in front of my eyes before," I tell her. "But now that it has, I realize how important it is, and that school needs to come first."

Gia's nostrils flare, and she looks down at her half-eaten plate of pancakes, clearly wanting to argue with me but not outwardly disagreeing. I feel bad for guilting Gia, but she can't blow off school like we've done in the past.

Zia Stella clears her throat. "Well, why don't we finish breakfast, run to Walmart, then work on your essay before you go out with your friends?"

Gia grumbles, but a quick glance at the time informs me that I don't have time to deal with it. I stand with my plate and unfinished juice. "I have my call with Anusha now. Thanks for breakfast, Zia Stella."

"Oh, don't worry about your plate, I've got it!" She takes it from my hands, and I stand there awkwardly.

"Um . . . okay."

She's so . . . nice? Is that the word I'm looking for? I'm not sure what to make of her yet.

In my room I check my phone but there are no missed calls, but I do have a text from Jason. I told him what I saw in Brandon's phone last night before he dropped me off, after Gia got out of the car, and he seemed surprised. He said he never saw Lily and Brandon interacting, but he believed me.

I set the glass of OJ down and open his text.

Bring your resume to Emerald Bar and Grill any time after 5 pm. If you want the serving job, it's yours.

My breath hitches. He got me a job? I told him I needed one in a throwaway line at lunch that I didn't even think he picked up on. Not only did he pick up on it, but he went out of his way to get me a job? My emotions are all over the place and I don't even know how to respond.

I settle on Thanks and send it just before Anusha calls.

The call goes smoothly, and I think Anusha even believes me when I say no to her routine "And have you heard from your mother?" question at the end. It's hard to tell with her regular neutral tone, but I think I pulled it off. I don't know exactly why I lie to her, and I don't even know if I *want* to see Mom. But if I tell Anusha, she'll ask me questions I don't want to answer, make me face feelings I want to ignore. So for now, I stick to my normal answer.

"Knock knock," Gia calls, cracking open my bedroom door and poking her head through.

"Hey," I say, getting up from where I'm sitting on the bed. "I didn't see you come back."

She fully enters the room now, a reusable bag dangling from her hand. "We just got in a few minutes ago." She holds up the bag to show me, as if I can see through the dark-gray material. "I picked up some pink hair dye. I thought . . . you know . . . you'd like a touch-up."

She wants to do my hair? Like we did back in LA before everything happened? A peace offering?

I try not to sound too eager. "Yeah. That'd be great."

Her smile is wide and genuine as I follow her to the bathroom where she's set up, closing the toilet seat lid and sitting to let her work her magic.

I've always let her do whatever she wanted to my hair. The last time she dyed the bottom half of my hair pink, she did hers at the same time to match. As she leans over me to brush and section out my hair, I realize that won't be possible anymore, not unless she shaves off my hair like she did her own.

"So," she starts as she mixes the dye with white conditioner in a little plastic bowl. "Is Jason your boyfriend? You've never had one of those before."

"I've never had *time* for one before," I correct her. "And no, he's not. We're just friends."

"Really? Because you sure do stare at him a lot. Almost as much as he stares at you."

My face turns as pink as the hair dye she's mixing. That makes her person number three to call me out for staring at him. I really need to get a grip and stop doing that. "I do not. And he doesn't either." Though I always feel the heat of his stare when he does, and it makes tingles run all the way down my spine.

"Uh-huh," she says in a disbelieving tone. "Well, for what it's worth, I think he's cool. He's the only reason we didn't get arrested at the school. And he invited you yesterday. And he's an awesome driver. I mean, did you see him win? I've only seen drifting in movies!"

I didn't see him; I was too busy tracking down maybe-Mom.

"Well, I'm glad he's got your stamp of approval, but we're still not dating."

She hmphs as she drapes a towel over my back, under my hair. "You should. He's made you . . . cooler."

I'm about to ask, *I wasn't cool before?* but then realize I'd rather save myself from her glaringly obvious answer. Instead, I say, "How?"

"You know." She rotates her gloved hand at the wrist a few times in a vague gesture. "Less uptight, barring the homework thing this morning. It was either him or . . ." She trails off, and I know we're both thinking *prison*. After that brief silence, she continues, "But it's definitely him. It was cool of you to invite me yesterday."

She starts slathering my hair with the dye, paying attention to how high to go to not make it look like one straight line across. As she works, I realize what this is. It's a thank-you, for bringing her to watch the drag races. My plan to invite her so I could win brownie points *worked*.

"I'm glad you had a good time," I tell her.

"The *best* time. Everyone in the group chat was *so jealous* of Brianna and me when they found out. And Chris confirmed it too, so they know we weren't lying." She bites her lip excitedly. "Everyone's going to be trying to get next to me this week at school to hear details about it."

I never understood popularity, and never realized how much it meant to Gia before now. I always thought it came effortlessly to her, because Gia's the coolest person I know.

"Just remember that it was completely illegal, and to watch what you say and to who," I remind her.

"I'm going over Brianna's tonight and we're going to talk about what we'll say, *after* I start my essay."

I sit up straight at that, and she chides me for moving.

"You're going to Brianna's?" As in, she'll be in the same house as Brandon, the dude who skeeves me out and is obsessed with Lily?

"Yeah. Her brother is going out, so Brianna said we'll get the theater room to ourselves since he won't be around to hog it. Her mom is going to make us spaghetti Bolognese for dinner." And she quickly adds on, "but I highly doubt it'll be as good as yours."

I don't want Gia anywhere near Brandon, but at least he's not around and his parents are home.

"I do make an amazing Bolognese sauce," I concede instead of ordering her to stay home. "But that's nice of Brianna's parents to have you for dinner. Why don't I make some cookies for you to bring over?"

Her face lights up, and I'm glad I suggested it. "Can you? That would be great! Thanks, Siena!"

I swallow the thickness in my throat. Gia's smiles directed at me have been few and far between since I got back, and this one is real and genuine. "Of course, I'll check what ingredients Dario has. Maybe Zia Stella has some stuff here too."

"Think you can make your amaretti cookies? Brianna loves almonds, so I bet she'll love them."

"If we have the ingredients, sure."

"Thanks." Her smile goes shy. "I really like Brianna."

"I think she likes you too." I remember how she stood up to me when she thought I was a stranger bothering Gia at that first party, even if she calls her *G*.

"No but . . . I think I *like* her, like her," Gia confesses, a blush coloring her face. "I know it's stupid to have a crush after only knowing her for a short period, but it feels natural with us."

Gia's dying my hair, spending time with me, smiling at me, and trusting me enough to share her feelings. We used to do this all the time—I heard every detail of her crush and first dates with Nora—but now it feels extra special.

"I don't think it's stupid," I tell her. "Just because you've known someone for a short amount of time doesn't mean you don't know *them*." For a moment an image of Jason flashes in my mind, but I push it out.

Gia lets out a laugh as she moves onto a different section of my hair. "She does this thing where she dips her French fries in ketchup *and* sour cream! Who does that? She got me to try it and it was *awful*, and when I told her she convinced me to . . ." Gia rambles on, sharing stories of her and Brianna and her other friends, and I happily listen, adding a few words of encouragement every now and then.

This is what I've been missing since that moment I was hauled off in the back of a cop car, and the entire time we're together in the bathroom I force myself not to spill tears of joy, or of mourning for the time we've lost.

Once my hair is done and the blond of my roots fades perfectly into the pink of my ends, I wash my hair and Gia blow-dries it out, nodding her approval. Then we head downstairs, and I gather all the ingredients for the amaretti cookies.

Gia's never cared for cooking or baking. I've always done it all, especially since Aunt Julie never remembered to feed us, or stock the pantry or fridge—she had no problem digging into whatever groceries I bought with my own money though. But Gia sits on a stool at the marble island with her laptop to start her essay, watching me and chatting absentmindedly as I mix ingredients and roll out the cookies. She even helps by pushing whole almonds into the top of each cookie before I pop them into the oven.

After we've cleaned up and arranged the cooled cookies on a plate for Gia to bring over, I've forgotten what it was like to be at odds with my little sister. Just before she heads upstairs to get ready for Brianna's, she pauses at the kitchen's threshold, then rushes back to me and wraps me in a tight hug.

"Thanks, Siena," she says, her voice barely above a whisper. "I've missed you."

And then she's gone, and I'm left standing in the kitchen, my heart full and feeling like all is finally right in our world—that maybe things can go back to how they were.

The walk to Emerald Bar and Grill takes half an hour, but I don't mind. It might get harder once the weather becomes too cold to bear, at least for my body, which still hasn't adjusted from the LA heat, but for now the crisp breeze is welcome.

The place is busy for an early Saturday afternoon in September. The lighting is a little dim, and the vibe seems laid-back. The waitresses are in all black yoga pants and tight V-neck T-shirts with the Emerald Bar and Grill logo on the back. It's a weird mix of a family restaurant but also a hangout spot for teenagers and early twentysomethings. I can already tell that it gets busy at nights, especially weekends. There are a few kids from school sitting at one of the tables near the big wooden bar, and Thompson, whose first name I should learn eventually, waves at me as I follow the hostess to the back office.

The manager, Hannah, is in her forties and is no-nonsense in a way that slightly scares me. She ignores the resume in my hand and instead asks if I'm Jason's "girl" Siena, and if I have any experience serving. I don't correct her, and only talk to her for five minutes before she tells me—not asks—that my first shift is Monday night and to bring my information for payment then. She asks my shirt size, digging into the box behind her desk, then completely disregards my request for a medium. Instead, she *literally* throws two T-shirts at my head, and says, "You'll take an extra-small, mostly because I only have this or extra-large right now. But trust me, you'll get better tips this way. If you *really* hate it, we can get you a medium, it'll just take a while. Stupid shirt company ripped me off on my last three orders."

I do need the tips, and I don't want to argue with her and jeopardize this job, so I say nothing and clutch the tiny black shirts. I'm ushered out of the office with a departing call of "Be here for four!" from Hannah.

I officially have a job. I didn't think it would be that easy, but I guess that's due to Jason's string-pulling. I text him a quick I got the job, thanks again as I walk home.

By the time I get home my legs are tired, and Jason

hasn't messaged me back, but at least I've got a source of income at a place where the tips will probably be great.

I'm walking up the driveway when the door to the house beside Dario's opens, and Officer Liu emerges with Detective Dubois. They're deep in conversation, and even from where I stand frozen on my driveway, with a front yard of grass between us, I can tell they're talking about *me*.

"Siena," Detective Dubois says flatly when she spots me. I swear the woman hasn't smiled in the last twenty years, but maybe that comes with the job. She crosses the grass to join me on Dario's driveway, followed by Officer Liu, who stands slightly behind me, and suddenly I feel trapped. I'm outside, the wind in my face and air smelling like freshly cut grass and pine trees, but with Detective Dubois scowling in front of me and Officer Liu blocking my retreat, I feel like a caged animal. I look between the two of them, feeling antsy, wishing like hell I could bite my fingernails but refusing to look nervous and give Officer Liu more reason to be suspicious of me.

"Hi," I force out, gripping the shirts for something to do with my hands. "Have there been any updates on Lily?"

Officer Liu grunts like he can't even bear hearing me say his daughter's name. For a moment, I think that I should've let Jason's lawyer press charges against him on my behalf. Maybe then he wouldn't be allowed this near me, to corner me, to remind me that he has the power to haul me off in the back of his police cruiser if he really wanted to.

I push on. "Have you talked to Brandon?" After what I learned from snooping through his phone, I'm more confident than ever that he's somehow involved, even if I didn't find any real evidence.

"I did today actually," Detective Dubois answers, her poker face even better than Anusha's. "And quite frankly, I'm very disappointed in you, Siena."

Her words shock me, and the only thing stopping me from rearing back is the fact that Officer Liu is there, and I don't want to get any closer to him than I already am.

"Wh-what?" I sputter. Disappointed in me? I didn't do anything except try to help!

"Yes," she answers, voice flat. "For wasting our time and resources on a petty high school vendetta."

I'm so confused I look back at Officer Liu, as if he of all people can offer some clarity. He glares at me like he's trying really hard not to start interrogating me again.

"I don't understand."

Detective Dubois's empty eyes scan my face. "I interviewed Brandon and asked him about the things you told me, only to find out you made up the entire story because of some grudge you and your boyfriend have against him. In fact, he told me you stole his phone last night, in what he thinks was an attempt to frame him to prove your story, and only gave it back because you got caught. His sister, when asked separately, confirmed you were in possession of his phone when she found you."

What? "Frame him? I don't have to frame him for

something he actually *did*! I was there, I saw him grab her, he's *obsessed* with Lily!"

She gives me a doubtful look, like I'm just doubling down on the false accusations. "The evidence proves otherwise. In fact, he said that you were the one being weird with Lily the night she disappeared."

"What? Me?"

"He showed us text messages that were time-stamped the night of the party." She pulls her trusty little notepad from her pocket and reads from it. "His friend, Alex, said, and I quote, *Have you talked to Lily tonight? She just got in a huge fight with some new girl!* And Brandon replied, *No, dude. Some weird muddy chick with pink-and-blond hair has been all over Lily all night. I haven't gotten a second alone with her.* And Alex said, *That's the girl she was fighting.*" She stops reading and closes her notepad, deliberately dropping her gaze to the freshly pink-dyed ends of my hair.

I push my hair behind my shoulders. "That doesn't mean shit!"

"There's video evidence of him at home shortly after that party, his mother took it of him playing with his cat. Plus, all the kids we interviewed said they never saw Lily talking with Brandon, but they did, in fact, see her fighting with you."

I feel like puking. Or pulling my hair out. Or both. "Of course they saw her with me, we're friends!"

"Uh-huh," Detective Dubois says, and I quickly feel the tables turning on me. Her face and tone remain even, though this seems to be turning into an interrogation.

I can't *believe* this. Brandon's managed to spin everything on me when I didn't even do anything besides point the detectives in the right direction. The imaginary walls that arose earlier feel like they're closing in on me, and I force my breathing to stay even.

"Why'd you steal his phone, Siena?" she asks, eyes narrowing. "Was he right? Were you trying to plant evidence?"

I'm so outraged I can't even trust myself to speak. Somehow, Brandon's made it seem like *I'm* the person who should be investigated. And fine, maybe I did steal his phone, but it was to *find* evidence, not plant it. But I can't admit that to them, can't give any more credibility to any part of Brandon's story, not if I want to disprove it.

Detective Dubois must take my silence as confirmation, because she straightens up, tucking her little notepad into her jacket pocket. "He *also* told me that he's concerned about you falling in with the wrong crowd, and he's heard that you were involved in the school vandalism and break-in over a week ago."

I say nothing, flabbergasted by the absurdity of it all, and at Brandon's stupidly clever scheme. Make me look like the bad guy, like he's the victim. The school break-in was literally his idea, led by his sister. But he must know I'd never take my sister down with me and is gambling on that fact to protect his own sister as well.

Detective Dubois continues. "We have informed your principal about your suspected involvement with the break-in. And we were just on our way to tell your guardian about your interference in an official investigation and wasting police time and resources over stupid high school drama with Brandon. If you and your boyfriend have something against him, that's between the three of you. What I absolutely cannot stand is you wasting my time."

And then she turns on me, her back ramrod straight, and marches up to my front door, knocking on it like she wants to break it down herself. I stand in the same spot in the middle of the driveway, staring at her, processing her words.

"She's onto you, you know," Officer Liu says into my ear, making me jump and spin around to face him. Since the last time I saw him, the lines on his face seem deeper, the bags under his eyes darker, the hate in his gaze stronger.

"What?" I back up a few steps, needing distance between us.

He doesn't bother stepping closer to me. He can intimidate me perfectly fine where he is. "She knows who your mother is, knows about her criminal streak, knows what *you've* done before moving here."

Despite the thoughts and emotions rapidly tumbling through me, I manage to spit out, "My records are supposed to be sealed. I'm a minor."

He laughs a spite-filled, hollow laugh. "So? I found out. You think the people working the case just magically forgot? You think other officers or detectives can't make a few calls and talk off the record with their connections at

LAPD? You think you being the spitting image of Florence Bowen would stay hidden forever? Hell, even without that, all you'd have to do is a quick Google search of your name, and anyone can find out all the speculation as to what happened in LA."

Anger boils through me, but at who, I'm not sure. At Mom, for being Florence Bowen. At the media, for being so ruthless when those images of me being arrested started circulating. At Aunt Julie, for spreading the reason I was arrested "unofficially." At Officer Liu, for only seeing me for my past and not what's right in front of his face. At Stan fucking Roven, for putting me in this position in the first place. At myself, for being unable to change the past or do anything about things crumbling right in front of me.

"We're going to nail you for this," Officer Liu vows. "I promise you, I'm going to find out what you did to my Lily, and I'm going to put you back in prison, where you *belong*." Venom drips from his words, and he sneers at me like he'd love nothing more than to squish me under his shoe. "I'm going to make sure you *rot*, then maybe I'll look into that boozed-up little sister of yours. After all, it clearly runs in the family."

My hands are shaking at my sides as my anger and panic continue to rise. I'm not getting locked in a room ever again, and I would do *anything* to prevent it. Moreso, do anything to prevent that from happening to *Gia*. My fingers itch to punch him in the nose, to continue doing it over and over and over like I once saw Mom do to a man in a parking lot when he grabbed me at seven years old. And as my hands clench at my sides, before I can decide what to do or say, my aunt calls my name.

Her voice breaks whatever trance I was in, and I step backward toward her, not breaking my stare-off with Officer Liu. His eyes promise to crush me, to spend every waking moment trying to bring me down and lock me up, while mine promise to destroy everything before I let that happen.

Something shifts in the air. A silent acknowledgment that this isn't just petty verbal sparring. It is now very, very personal, even more than before, and if I wasn't watching my back, and Gia's, before, I definitely am now.

eleven

Zia Stella and Anusha are conspiring together. After Detective Dubois told Zia Stella about my "purposefully misleading her and disrupting a case over petty teenage drama and personal distaste for Brandon," Zia Stella called Anusha, and the two of them are making me apologize to him. Apologize for what, I don't know. "Trying to frame him," Zia Stella had suggested when I asked. I can't believe I thought she was *nice* before, thought she was at least trying to get to know me, that she might have cared.

It's so frustrating. I feel so helpless. No one wants to listen to my side of things, not even Gia, who found out when she went to Brianna's that I "had it out for her brother." That obviously did not go down well considering she has a crush on Brianna, and now I'm public enemy number one in the Scott household. But all three women, Zia Stella, Anusha, and Gia, think I have some personal problem with Brandon and made up stories about him to try to get him in trouble, and their lack of faith in me, in choosing Brandon over me, makes me feel more alone than ever.

Dario doesn't care. When he finds out he scoffs as he pours himself a drink. "Lying, stealing, breaking and entering, vandalism, and manipulating men? Sounds just like Florence." Then he downs his whiskey.

So Sunday morning, with the number Detective Dubois was all too happy to provide, I sit at the table with Zia Stella, and Anusha on Speaker on Zia Stella's phone, and call Brandon. Dario said it was a waste of time, and even though he said it to be malicious, I agree with him. But that doesn't matter to Anusha, who Zia Stella agreed with, so through gritted teeth, I apologize to Brandon for being "mistaken," and that my intention was not to frame him for anything.

I keep it all vague. Technically, I'm not lying to Brandon, or Anusha or Zia Stella. My intention *wasn't* to frame him, it was to find out what happened to Lily, and to help the detectives get to the bottom of Brandon's obsession, which he conveniently turned on me.

"Cool, I accept. See you at school," is all he says before hanging up. I kind of wish he had said more to implicate himself, but he must have known he was on Speaker by hearing Zia Stella's low prompts to me when I hesitated at an actual apology.

Zia Stella and Anusha are not impressed with my half-assed, insincere apology; I could tell by Zia Stella's flat expression and Anusha's neutral-disapproving tone when she asks me how I feel after the call, but that's the best they're going to get out of me, and they accept that.

I spend the rest of the day sulking in my room. I called Jason after the detective left last night to warn him that he might be next on her informing-the-parents spree, since she kept mentioning the involvement of my boyfriend, but he didn't answer, so I left him a voicemail.

He sends me a text around noon saying he was pulling doubles at work yesterday and today but assures me, through a colorfully explicit text, that he's not happy with how Brandon's twisted the narrative. When I text back and tell him about him pinning the school break-in on me, and maybe even him, he replies, Tomorrow morning in homeroom they're going to call you into the office, and you're not going to say a goddamn word. They don't have shit on shit.

He told me not to say anything last time when I was arrested, and I completely didn't listen. Maybe this time I'll take his advice.

When Monday rolls around, I'm sitting in my usual seat behind Brandon. He doesn't acknowledge my existence even though I'm glaring so hard at the back of his head it should spontaneously combust. I'm only interrupted when

I'm called to the office over the classroom intercom during attendance, exactly what Jason predicted.

There are a lot of immature *ohhhhh*s as I stand and pack my stuff, but not from Brandon. There's a smirk on his face, and when he catches me glowering at him, he sends me a victorious wink. I want nothing more than to bash him in the back of the head with my binder as I pass by his desk, but that'll just get me in more trouble.

A text from Jason comes in. Did they call you into the office yet?

He was thinking about me. Yes. Going there now.

Even though he's in class, his reply is instant. Say nothing. Admit to nothing. Remember: they've got shit on shit.

I've barely been in King City for two full weeks and I'm already on my second interrogation. I thought once I boarded that plane from LA, I'd be done with interrogations forever.

They make me sit in the seat of shame in front of the secretary and all the windows leading to the hallway for longer than necessary, considering *they* called *me* here, but it's all a scare tactic. Have me sit, think about why I'm here, get me all nice and nervous for when Principal Anderson grills me. But I already know why I'm here, and I'm following Jason's advice this time. My phone vibrates while I sit there but the secretary keeps shooting me stern glances and pointing at the "no phones" sign, so I keep it in my pocket and ignore the vibrating. She doesn't answer any of my questions either about how much longer it's going to be, and I realize I'm supposed to sit here quietly like I'm in detention or something.

After forty minutes, there's a tapping on the glass window behind me. Jason's there, standing in the hallway instead of being in class. The secretary glares at him too, but he's not in the office so she can't exactly yell at him or passive-aggressively point to a nonexistent sign that says: "don't knock on the window."

Jason says something but I can't hear him, and at my blank face, he pulls out his phone, types something, then holds his phone up to the window so I can see what he wrote.

Forgot about the no phone rule and Sergeant Secretary.

It makes me giggle, earning a dramatic throat-clearing from *Sergeant Secretary.* No noise either. Got it.

Jason pulls his phone back and types something again before showing it to me.

Are you all right?

I nod yes.

He clears it and holds up a new message. Have you seen her yet?

I shake my head.

He gives me a stern look, and I can imagine what he's thinking without him even needing to type it. *They don't know shit about shit.*

He doesn't type that though, instead the new message says: You'll be okay. Eat with us at lunch today, okay?

Jason's got me a job Saturday, and he's skipping class

to check on me. Maybe I'll stop by before going outside to enjoy the dwindling summer.

I nod.

He gives me one last meaningful look, one so intense I feel it all the way to my toes, then his jaw clenches and he takes off down the hall. I can't see him anymore, so I turn back in my seat, and Sergeant Secretary is glaring at me so hard her eyes look like they're popping out of her head.

"Siena?" a woman, I think the principal's secretary, calls, and I stand. They *know* I'm here, they literally requested my presence, so I don't know why she's pretending she doesn't know who I am. When I nod, she says, "Come with me."

I follow her through an office filled with various secretaries, and my friend the sergeant gives me one last glare of distaste for good measure before I pass her and am led into an office. It's not huge, but it's not small either. Principal Anderson sits behind a large desk. She's wearing a navy blue blazer, and her face is set in a frown.

The woman who led me here closes the door as she exits, leaving us alone. There's a large window overlooking the side of the school where the trees are, and I accept the view as consolation for the interrogation I'm about to receive.

"Sit," she orders, pointing to the chair in front of her desk. I sink into it, dropping my backpack on the floor between my feet.

"Siena Amato," she says, leaning forward to analyze me. "Do you know why you're here?"

Yes, I do. But am I supposed to know that? Is that

admitting guilt if I say it's for the break-in even though Detective Dubois warned me? Or do I play stupid and have her fill me in?

In the end, I decide to listen to Jason and literally say nothing, like I should've done at the police station.

My blank stare annoys Principal Anderson, and her nostrils flare. "You were involved in the vandalism and breaking in of the school pool the day before school started."

That was incredibly forward, and a confident accusation if I've ever heard one. She's definitely a person who's never been told no in her life, never not gotten exactly what she wanted, and it shows.

"No, I wasn't," I lie, managing to keep my voice even.

"Yes, you were," she repeats, her tone strong, making it seem like she already *has* undeniable proof and is certain I was involved, and this little song and dance is just to get me to confess.

For a second, her confidence makes me waver. I *was* there, and there could be video evidence somewhere. But then again, if they had proof, I wouldn't be sitting in this office alone. At the very least, I'd be here with Jason and Gia. But since they're not here, I take it that Jason's right, and they don't have shit on shit.

"No, I wasn't," I repeat like a five-year-old.

"You were there. We have proof. If you come clean now and tell us who else was with you, we won't press any charges."

But I'd still be expelled *and* have betrayed my sister and one of my only friends.

So instead of panicking like she wants me to, I calmly ask, "What proof?"

She says nothing, so I continue, "I wasn't there, and I don't know why you think I was. So I'd love to see this proof you have so I can explain how you have the wrong person, and I can go back to class, which I've missed almost an hour of now."

She leans back in her chair, watching me like a person watches their opponent at a chess game, trying to figure out their next move. I channel my best Anusha neutral face, giving nothing away, not letting her see a single sign of what I'm really feeling. If she felt my heart, she'd know it was pounding a mile a minute, but as far as she can tell, I'm cool and collected.

"You're new here; moved a few days before school started, right?" Her tone softens. "You were just trying to fit in, trying to make friends, trying to impress them, and it escalated and now you're in trouble." She puts her hand on her heart like she's genuinely concerned about me. "I want to help you, truly, I do. And I don't want to have your start at King City High cut so short over this. So, you can tell me what happened that night. I give you my word that if you tell us who else was involved, you won't be penalized in any way."

It's almost sincere. She's probably gotten a lot of confessions out of people this way. Maybe if I were someone else, if I didn't have others to protect, it would work. Instead, I double down on my denial.

"I wish I could help you, but I can't tell you what happened since I wasn't there. If you tell me what proof you think you have, I can help clarify."

Her jaw clenches and her nostrils flare again. That must be her tell. Meanwhile I've had a perfect poker face this entire time, good enough to rival Anusha's.

She's struggling to read me and doesn't know another angle to attack this from, because she grudgingly admits, "There have been . . . whispers." She watches my face carefully. "People have been saying you're involved. A *lot* of people. So many that we couldn't ignore it as baseless."

If I wasn't so pissed off at Brandon for planting that idea in her head, I'd smile. She has nothing. *Shit on shit.*

"You've pulled me out of class and accused me of a serious crime over *rumors?*" I ask incredulously.

"Even whispers in a high school hallway have merit and are based on truths."

"There are rumors that Dominic Laurent bottles his farts and sells them to the gym teachers. That have merit too?"

She says nothing.

"There are also rumors that Matias Cruz sneaks into the kitchen in the cafeteria and puts toenail clippings in the mashed potatoes. There are also rumors that Sasha Madina lives on a haunted yacht she got by—"

"All right, all right." She cuts me off, clearly agitated. "You've made your point."

I don't know where my sudden boldness has come

from. I've never talked to a superior like this before. Maybe it's because I'm so pissed off about how this whole situation went down, maybe I'm just tired of being painted as the criminal without any proof, or maybe it's the reassurance of knowing that while no one may believe me, Jason does, and he has my back.

"So can I go now?" I ask.

Her molars mash together. She thought she'd get me to sing, to give up all my friends and everyone involved just to save my own ass. Well, clearly she has no idea who she's dealing with. Even if she *had* proof, I'd confess to going at it alone before selling out Gia or Jason.

She thinks carefully before she finally says, "*Some* rumors are ridiculous. Some are based on the truth. I'm confident this one is, and when we inevitably find proof that you're involved, the consequences will be ten times worse than they would've been if you had confessed right now."

My heart pounds, but I sit perfectly still with my perfectly blank face.

She places her elbows on her desk and leans forward. "There are also rumors that you and another student, Jason Parker, are bothering an A student and devoted athlete, Brandon Scott."

Fucking Brandon.

"I'd just like to take this opportunity to *remind* you that we have a zero-tolerance bullying and harassment policy."

My fists clench in my lap, and I practically force words

out through gritted teeth. "Jason and I aren't bothering Brandon."

The corner of her lip pulls up slightly, satisfied she's finally managed to crack my poker face. Damn it.

"See that it stays that way." She leans back and picks up some papers on her desk. Without looking at me, she says, "You're dismissed."

I let myself stew for two full seconds before I grab my backpack and haul ass out of that office. I won in there; I know I did. But for some reason, I feel like she's got a leg up on me, like she knows that she'll be seeing me again real soon, and next time, she'll have the upper hand.

All I wanted when I moved here was to stay out of trouble, stay under the radar, get good grades, and be normal. But now I'm apparently not only on Detective Dubois's shitlist and person number one on Officer Liu's list of suspects, I'm also on Principal Anderson's radar.

Fantastic.

twelve

The week goes by without any other incidents, and I've fallen into a new routine: glare at Brandon and try to read his computer over his shoulder while in class. Eat lunch with Jason, Jackson, Nyah, Tyler, and sometimes Warren, then spend the last twenty minutes of the period outside on the bleachers with Jason, who always insists on coming with me even when the weather is miserable. Avoid Principal Anderson in the halls. Try to get Gia to acknowledge me in the halls. Glare at Brandon in math class. Run to catch the bus on time after school, get changed at home, then speed-walk to work.

The routine was going strong by the last class on Friday, but then Brandon corners me during the last five minutes of math. This is *not* part of the routine. Usually, he packs up and leaves with his friends, ignoring my existence, and I glare at him the entire time. But not today. Today, he shuts his laptop, which for some reason he has out in math, and turns around in his seat just before the final bell.

"Hey," he says, and I eye him warily as I shove my books in my bag.

"Hi."

"Did you get that last part about the logarithmic function and its inverse applied to the Richter scale?"

I blink at him. I thought we were talking about y's and x's.

He laughs. "I'll take that as a no."

"Right . . ."

I don't know what his game is here. We have a routine going, he and I, and he's violating it by having a conversation with me.

When I don't volunteer anything else, he sighs and scrubs his hand over the back of his neck. "Look, I feel bad about how everything went down."

Does he mean portraying me as an unstable stalker who makes up stories and organized the school break-in? I say nothing, and he continues, "I just . . . I don't know. It got a little out of hand, is all."

That's a terrible apology, if that's even what it is. Only slightly worse than the forced one I gave him. But he seems genuine, if a little uncomfortable, and I don't know what to make of it. He has to have an angle, I'm sure of it.

"Okay," I start, waiting for him to tell me where he's going with this. People around us are packing their things and chatting, waiting for the final bell to ring and let us out of school, but no one comes over to interrupt us, not even Brandon's friends.

"We have a math test on Monday, and I did offer to help you sometime before . . . you know . . ."

I blink at him. He's being sincere, but there's still something *off*, something that unnerves me, that tells me it's not safe to trust him. Maybe it's his eyes, the way he's studying me, like he's waiting for me to play right into his hands.

He lets out a breathy chuckle. "You're gonna make me do all the work here, huh?"

The bell rings and I stand up, along with everyone else in class. Brandon rushes to block my path in the aisle.

"Come over tomorrow. I'll help you prep for the test on Monday."

Everyone has cleared out now, leaving just me and Brandon, and the teacher, who's packing up his things and texting like we're not here.

I don't *want* to spend any alone time with Brandon, especially not at his *house*. But I really don't understand what's been happening in math and he always knows the answers. And more than that, he's invited me to his house, where he keeps all his things, where I can snoop and find out if he's really involved with what happened to Lily. If the police aren't going to do it, I will.

So despite every cell in my body telling me to shove him out of my way and walk on like I never heard his offer, I smile graciously and say, "Sounds great. Text me your address."

———

I don't tell anyone that I'm going to Brandon's. I go homecoming dress shopping with Nyah Saturday morning, but the opportunity never comes up. Warren invites me to a small hangout he's throwing at night too, and I turn him down without telling him the reason why. I don't know how long I'll be at Brandon's but I don't feel like going to a party anyway. Jason messages me from work asking if I'm going to Warren's, and I tell him I can't.

I know why I don't tell the others—I don't want them knowing anything to get their hopes up or raise more suspicion about Brandon if it's unfounded—but I'm not entirely sure why I don't tell Jason. He knows everything—in fact, he's the only person I've shared almost *everything* with, including most of what happened in LA. If I'd tell anyone about what I was doing today, it would be him. But I don't tell him. I mention it to Zia Stella though, when she asks if I want to order takeout for dinner. I don't know why I tell her; I'm still a little pissed off that she forced me to apologize to Brandon without listening to my side of the story. Maybe I tell her because I want her to see I'm . . . friends . . . with Brandon, or at least close enough to go over his house. Or maybe I tell her because I just want someone to know, and I still kind of like her.

When I finish my short shift at work around 7:00 p.m., I'm exhausted. I got about one hour of training my first day on Monday, before I was thrown into my own section because we were so short-staffed. I managed, though, and was scheduled for shifts every day after school. Normally, I'm so tired by the time I get home at midnight that I pass out immediately. I forgot just how *hectic* it is to waitress, even on a slow weekday, but by Thursday night, I had a nice shoebox containing neat little stacks of cash from tips starting, and I'd like to fill it by Christmas. So, I show up to my shifts and smile and run around in my too-tight uniform shirt until my feet ache and am just grateful I'm making money.

It's drizzling when I get out, so I call an Uber instead of walking thirty minutes to Brandon's house. I send a text to Nyah repeating that I can't come to Warren's small bonfire party, then my phone dies. I clutch it in frustration and curse the stupid cracked screen that prevents me from seeing the top quarter. I never know what time it is or what battery percentage it's at. At least it died after I ordered the Uber, and I can borrow a charger from Brandon to order one to get home; his house to mine is an hour's walk, and I don't want to do that after running around all day.

His house is nice, a little bigger than Dario's, and when

Brandon opens the door in gray sweatpants and a T-shirt and leads me down the hall, it quickly becomes apparent that we're home alone. I don't even see his cat.

"Where is everyone?" I ask, trying to sound casual as I follow him up the stairs.

He waves me off nonchalantly. "My parents had a dinner party. And Brianna's at one of her friend's houses or something, who knows."

He leads me into his bedroom, and I pause at the threshold. I'm already on high alert when talking to Brandon with people around, never mind alone in his bedroom.

He raises an eyebrow at me, then must really notice me for the first time, because his eyes scan me, from my face, which is covered in the minimal makeup I know how to do, then dip and take in my too-small black T-shirt with a V-neck that doesn't exactly hide anything, and my yoga pants. I cross my arms over my chest, wishing like hell I had brought a sweater.

"Make yourself at home," he gestures, arms spread, before throwing himself onto his bed.

If I were going to snoop, his room would be place number one, and he's willingly invited me into it. I steel myself and cross into his space, setting my backpack down on the floor by his bed.

It's not a large room. His walls are painted a deep blue, and his bed is made, or at least, the gray comforter is thrown up to cover the sheets. There are shelves filled with various trophies, and as I scan them, I spot a couple of them that are actually academic awards. There's nothing out of the ordinary; it looks like a normal boy room—not that I've ever personally been in one.

"Do you have a phone charger?" I ask him. "My phone died."

I regret adding that last part the second it leaves my mouth. Now he knows I don't have a phone.

"Sure," he says, then joins me where I'm standing *without* giving me a charger. "Got that one just last season. MVP." His chest puffs out a bit as he points to the trophy. He continues to point to various other trophies and tells me how he got each one. He even launches into a full-blown story about how he had to tackle a certain number of people for the unofficial trophy his friends on the team bought him to celebrate. I feign interest and nod every now and then, if only because him talking about himself means less time spent ogling my chest. When he pauses after story number ten, I take my chance and ask, "Hey, can I get some water?"

He pauses for a moment, "Uh, yeah. Sure. Be right back."

As soon as he disappears, I frantically look around, trying to think about *where* he would hide something. Anything. There's no desk, and it's not like there's a bright flashing sign with the words "Incriminating Evidence Here!" pointing anywhere.

It quickly dawns on me that this was a *stupid* idea and won't really get me anywhere.

I'm still frantically looking around when I hear Brandon

pounding up the stairs and yank the zipper of my backpack down to grab my textbook. I sit at the end of his bed with the book just before Brandon returns.

"Here you go." He tosses me a chilled water bottle and I catch it, taking a sip to moisten my dry throat.

Stupid, stupid, stupid. I shouldn't be here; it's not going to accomplish anything unless Lily is going to jump out of his closet popping a confetti cannon. I should've told Jason and let him talk me out of it. He would've told me it was a dumb idea. Maybe that's why I didn't tell him, because I wanted to come investigate myself and knew he'd be the calm voice of reason. But right now, I wish he was here, even though technically, Brandon hasn't *done* anything to me to make me feel unsafe—I just do around him. It's an instinctual self-preservation alarm that goes off in my body whenever I'm near him. I want to go home, but I can't even fake an emergency text because he knows my phone is *dead*.

He sits beside me at the edge of his bed as I set the water bottle down.

"So," I start, flipping through the pages of the textbook. I can't really snoop for Lily, but if we stay focused on math I can get out of here ASAP. "I was looking at the question about the Richter scale and I get that we have to apply the logarithmic equation but—"

He pulls the textbook from my hand and sets it on the bed behind him. "Let's take a break from math."

"But we haven't even started—"

The full sentence isn't even out of my mouth before he

leans over and kisses me. *KISSES ME!* His wet lips press hard against mine and his hands grip the back of my head, holding me to him.

I try to pull back, but I can't. His tongue runs over the seam of my lips, and panic overtakes me. I push at him, but he pulls me closer to him, and one hand leaves my head to grope my chest. I quickly grab the heavy textbook he threw aside and knock him over the head with it. He releases me and jumps up immediately.

"OW! What the fuck was that?"

I stand too, outraged, my chest heaving, tears threatening to spill. "What the fuck was that? I'm the one who should be asking what the fuck that was!"

I drop the textbook and wipe my mouth with the back of my hand. I can still feel him there, still taste him, still feel the panic at being kissed and held against my will. My breathing is ragged and I'm shaking all over. Not only did I *not* want that, but Brandon, of all fucking people, just took my first kiss.

Brandon's rubbing the back of his head. "That was a fucking *kiss*. You didn't have to bash me over the fucking head."

"Yes! Yes, I did! You did *not* have my consent!"

I shove my textbook in my bag, but my fingers are shaking so badly I can't properly zip it up.

"Like hell I didn't!" he exclaims, marching to me and wrapping his hand around my bicep, roughly yanking me up.

I try to pull from his grasp, but it tightens. "You've been giving me all the signals since we first met! You've been eyeing me for weeks. You're sitting here in that tight little shirt showing off your tits and asking me for *math help*? It's the first unit, it's basically a refresher from last year! You're practically begging me to fuck you."

His words scramble my brain. I'm so outraged about this whole situation, about everything he said, that I can't even form proper words. I want to yell at him until my throat is raw. I want to shove him until he releases me. I want to scrub myself clean until I forget about his touch. But I don't do any of that, I just sputter, "That's . . . we're . . . I'm not into you like that!"

He laughs and pulls me to him. How could he still want me after I bashed him in the head? But he does, I can feel his arousal through his sweatpants. "Of course you are. Everyone is."

I struggle violently against him and finally break free of his grip. "Well, *I'm* not!" I scoop my bag up, not even caring that it's only half zipped, but he blocks my path to the exit.

He's angry, but I don't know why. I'm the one who was grabbed, who was groped, who was basically told I'd been *asking for it*.

"Who the hell do you think you are?" he demands, his face turning red. "You walk around the halls at school like you're too good for anyone, like you think you're too hot to interact with us filthy peasants. What? Because your mom is some shitty C-list actress, you think you're above us? You don't even eat lunch in the fucking cafeteria!" He storms closer to me and my heart beats harder as he leans down and sneers, "You're not too good for me. You'd be lucky if I let you suck my cock."

His words are spiteful, and I use my bag to shove him away from me. I slip around him and sprint down the stairs.

"Where the hell do you think you're going?" he calls after me, but I don't stop. I keep going straight to the front door. I've never felt the need for *air* like I do right now, not even when I was arrested. I want to get outside, *need* to get outside, and away from Brandon. It's getting impossible to breathe while I'm locked inside the house alone with him, while he's saying all these vile things about me.

I don't stop when I get to the front door to put on my shoes. I just grab them and fumble with the door handle until it finally opens, and I stride outside into the rain. I'm drenched in seconds, but I don't care. The cool wetness is preferable to the memory of Brandon's touch, or the words that cling to my skin.

"Fine! Be that way, you frigid tease!" Brandon calls from the door. "You'll get what's coming to you."

I hear rather than see the door slam since I refuse to turn around, instead focusing on calming my heaving breath as I storm down his driveway and onto the road. Even with the distance between us and the concentrated effort I'm using to try to follow Anusha's breathing techniques, I still can't manage to catch my breath. I'm just so *angry*. Angry at Brandon for touching me, for kissing me, for grabbing me, for treating me like he has a claim to my body, like he can do whatever he wants with it. Angry at the words he said, at how he's interpreted me and my actions over the course of these last few weeks, about the assumptions he's made and the entitlement feels.

I'm also angry at myself, which only makes me angrier at myself because I *shouldn't* be angry at myself. I did nothing wrong. Should I have gone to his house? No. But that doesn't mean he has the automatic right to maul me. But I'm not just angry at myself for going to his house; I'm also angry that I didn't kick him in the fucking balls, that I allowed him to grab me like that repeatedly, that I allowed that kiss to go on for as long as it did. The more I think about what I should've said, what I should've done, the more outraged and upset I feel.

I don't realize that I'm heaving with unshed tears until I make it to a main road and have to stop and look around. I have no idea where the fuck I am and have no phone to call anyone or check GPS and I *didn't kick Brandon in the fucking balls* and I just don't know what to do with this pain clawing at my chest.

I force myself to move, somewhere, anywhere. I don't know where I'm going but I feel the aching need to put distance between me and him, even though he's miles in the opposite direction now. The sun has completely gone down and the rain pounds at me and mixes with the tears on my face. Cars zoom past me on the dark road, and there's no sidewalk, so I make sure I'm way over on the gravel shoulder.

I *hate* Brandon. I hate him so much, more than I've ever hated anyone. I hate what he's done, hate that he's made me feel this way.

My hair is heavy and soaked and the half-opened bag slung over my shoulder is collecting water and weighing me down. I don't even feel the shoes clutched in my hand.

I want to go home, but in my heart, I know I don't mean Dario's. I don't truly know where home *is*, and that makes my chest ache more. I want my mom. I want to curl into her and cry it out like I used to when I was little, as she'd whisper soothing words in my ear and brush my hair back, but I don't know where she is either, and I haven't known for a very long time. I wish Gia could be the one who takes care of *me* for once, but that's not the way we work. As much as I love her, I know I'm the one who has to be strong, and I don't want that right now. I just want someone who doesn't need me to be strong, who I don't need to defend myself to, who understands me, who makes me feel like I'm not so alone.

I trudge along on the gravel shoulder with no clear direction in mind. A car drives past me then pulls up on the shoulder ahead of me, and instinct makes me move over more, closer to the grass. But it's muddier here, and I slip. My bag and shoes go flying, and I land on the ground hard. I lie there, stunned, my sore back a dull pain in comparison to the sting in my chest.

A car door slams, and I hear the splash of puddles as someone runs to me through the rain.

"Siena?" a deep voice calls, and I'd laugh if I wasn't so stunned and miserable.

Jason comes into view, looking down at me as cars speed past him. "*Siena?* What the hell are you doing?"

I stare up at him through the raindrops soaking my lashes. He looks blurry, but I don't know if that's from the rain or my tears. I must look like a mess, even worse than the first time he found me like this. I don't sit up.

"We've gotta stop meeting like this," I attempt to joke, but it comes out flat, and my voice is too hoarse to land the teasing tone that I don't even feel.

"Jesus Christ, Siena." He crouches down close to my face to block the rain from falling on it. "What happened? Are you all right? And for fuck's sakes, why are you *never* wearing shoes?"

My muddy, destroyed socks are the least of my worries, but I can tell he won't like that answer.

"Didn't have time to put 'em on," I mumble, feeling stupid but still not moving to get up.

He studies my face. I don't know what he sees, don't know if the rain has washed all my makeup off or if I look like a raccoon or if he can tell I've been crying.

"Tell me what's going on," he demands, but I just gaze up at him. I still can't wrap my mind around everything that happened tonight, everything that's been happening.

"Do you ever just get tired of having to keep it all together?" I finally ask him, because that's how I feel now. Tired. Of being strong, of trying to seem like my shit's together, of walking on eggshells at home, of skirting around meaningful stuff with Anusha, of the hot and cold with Gia, of Officer Liu scrutinizing me every time I walk up my driveway, of trying to pretend I don't miss my mom, of Dario hating me without giving me a chance, of being judged before anyone knows my true intentions, my true heart.

After a moment of studying me, Jason asks, "Wanna talk about it?"

The question coming from Jason's mouth is almost as laughable as it is shocking. The only person who wants to talk to me about my problems is Anusha, and that's because she's being *paid* to. No one's ever asked me to talk about my feelings, about how I'm doing, because they genuinely care. But Jason did, while he's getting pelted by rain and crouching in the mud at the side of the road and probably running late to wherever he's going.

And the ironic thing is, I *don't* want to talk about it. I don't want to think about it all anymore. I'm tired of the constant worry running through my brain. I just want a few minutes of peace where I can pretend to be normal and stop thinking about the things bothering me. And so, I tell him that.

He nods, slowly, like he's trying to process, and then before I know what he's doing, he plops down in the mud beside me, on the side closer to the road.

"What are you doing?" I ask, horrified as he lies down completely, ruining his nice deep-blue cashmere sweater and getting mud all over his hair.

He's illuminated by the distant streetlights and moon-light. He turns his head to look at me. "You keep going on and on about how great lying in the mud in the rain in the middle of the road is. Least I can do is try it."

I've never said that, and he knows it. He doesn't mean it and I know it.

My lips pull up in the corner, and when he sees that, his do too.

"What are you really doing?" I ask.

Jason sighs and looks back up at the sky, not minding the steady onslaught of rain. His eyes close.

"I don't know what's going on, to be honest I rarely ever do when it comes to you. But I'm here, and I'll be here for as long as you need."

My heart pounds and I look away from him, closing my eyes just like he did, feeling the rain slide down my face. It's not an uncomfortable feeling, but it's not exactly anyone's first choice for things to do on a Saturday night. But he's here, lying in the mud with me, because he can tell I just needed someone to *be here*.

We lie there for a few moments, not saying anything, and I'm comforted by his presence. The ball in my chest loosens, and I'm able to do Anusha's breathing exercise until my lungs don't feel so tight and my shoulders relax.

"What do you want to do after graduation?" he asks.

I keep my eyes closed and my head turned up to the rain. "I don't know," I answer honestly. It seems so far away, especially when I'm so focused on just getting through each day. "Go to college, but for what? I'm not sure. Something that can get me a job, can help me make money, enough so that I can take care of myself, of Gia." I'm not sure what miracle degree and job that will be, especially with my dismal junior year grades, but I'm working on pulling them up this year, and I'll sort out the rest later. "What about you?"

"I haven't decided either. I like working with my hands, getting under the hood of a car, figuring out what the problem is." He shifts, getting more comfortable, and even without looking I can tell he's moved slightly closer to me. Cars drive by every once in a while, but we're so far from the road, and they move over to give Jason's car, parked ahead of us with the hazards on, wide enough berth that the sound of them passing in the rain doesn't drown out his voice. "Natalia and Aiden think I should study to become a mechanical engineer; I have the grades for it. But Jackson thinks I'd be miserable if I ended up at a desk job with a boss breathing down my neck."

I laugh at the thought of Jason in a cubicle with a tie, bent over furled papers, saying *yes sir, of course sir* to the guy signing his paycheck. I can't picture Jason taking orders from anyone.

I look at him, studying his profile unabashedly now that he can't call me out for staring. "I'm pretty sure there are some kinds of mechanical engineers that get to be out in the field and not stuck in the office all day."

He turns to me, his eyes open, a smile on his lips. "Still

got an office somewhere. Still have a boss."

"That's true," I agree. "So what other options are you thinking?"

He sighs, closing his eyes again as he raises his face to the rain. "I'm not sure. I'm playing with the idea of getting my business degree, but also love working at the shop and tinkering with cars."

"Why not do both? Get your degree and experience with cars and open a mechanic shop?"

He purses his lips. "You think I'd be good at that?"

I think about all the people at the track who clamored to get a moment to talk with him about their car, if they could bring it in to see him, but about other things too. Not only is he good at talking to people, but he knows what he's doing when it comes to cars, and he's not even certified yet. "Of course you would. I bet if you left your shop right now and opened a new one, half the customers would follow you."

His smile spreads, and despite the cold rain still falling, I feel warm all over.

We're quiet for a few moments, just smiling at each other in the mud. I should feel ridiculous, should feel guilty for not getting up and acting like everything was okay when he first arrived, but I don't feel ridiculous, and I don't regret it. For some reason, Jason's the only person who I don't have to pretend like I have all my shit together with . . . who I can be myself with.

"This isn't so bad," he admits, his arms spreading out

wider, his pinky finger just barely grazing mine. "Lying in the mud in the rain. At least we're not in the middle of the road."

I laugh. "You know both times you've found me like this, I wasn't lying here by choice."

"But you like the rain."

Rain makes me feel grounded, reminds me that while my problems may feel endless, they're miniscule in comparison to the vastness of the universe. Plus, it's kind of hard to think of your problems when you're out in nature, breathing the fresh air, feeling the cool rain on your skin, and smelling that fresh grass and pine and soil scent in the air. Something about it settles my heart and calms all the nerves in my body, makes me feel more connected to myself, to nature.

"I do. But I've always preferred dancing in it. My mom always said it's hard to be upset when you dance in the rain. But I haven't done it in years now, since . . . since I last saw her."

Jason sits up. "Then let's do it."

I glance up at him, achingly beautiful despite being soaked through. In fact, it makes him even more beautiful, all wet with clingy clothes and earnest eyes. "What?"

"Let's dance. In the rain."

I laugh at him. "You're crazy."

"I'm not. Since I've met you, you've gone on and on about how much fun dancing in the rain is. So, show me."

I sit up, trying to discern if he's joking but seeing nothing but heartfelt sincerity. "You're serious?"

"As I'll ever be." He peels off his shoes and socks, his feet sinking in the mud as he plants them. "Come on." He wraps his hands around both of mine and pulls me to stand with him.

I laugh as I fall off balance and into his broad chest, where he steadies me. For some reason I feel nervous. "But there's no music."

"Have you ever needed music to dance in the rain before?" he asks, somehow already knowing the answer as he twirls me into short, muddy grass, my socks squelching.

"Jason . . ." I hesitate, not even sure why.

He pulls me into him again, my arms automatically wrapping around his neck for balance. I'm so close I have to tilt my head all the way back to properly see him. Even though he's soaked and muddy and should logically be cold, I can feel the heat of him as he pulls me closer, his hands on my waist. I can feel him everywhere, and I suddenly have a hard time remembering to breathe.

His eyes, blue as the ocean back home in LA, stare into my own. "Come on, Siena. Just be with me in the moment. We can return to our shitty lives and worry about everything going on tomorrow. But right here, right now, be here, with me."

I suddenly feel like I'm drowning in his eyes, but I don't want rescuing. Without breaking eye contact—I physically couldn't even if I wanted to—I grip Jason's shoulder for support and reach down, slipping off my ruined socks and throwing them somewhere without paying any attention to where they land. My feet sink into the ground, mud seeping between my toes as my grip returns to Jason's shoulder.

"Now what?" I whisper.

Jason's hand leaves my waist to gently push my hair behind my ear.

"Now," he says, "we let everything go."

With my hands in his, he spins us around, and I have no choice but to follow. Our arms are held out, and we spin in circles, going faster and faster until I can't help but throw my head back and trust his opposing weight pulling on my hands to stop us from falling. I giggle at the absurdity of it; me and Jason, barefoot and spinning in the rain, and it's *fun*.

He lets me go but catches me before dizziness takes me down. We hop in puddles, splashing and making a mess. We kick and spin and slide around. At one point, Jason slips and his feet end up over his head as he tumbles, but he just laughs it off, and I laugh too. I don't remember ever laughing this hard.

When he gets up, he hoists me into his arms, bridal style, and I squeal as he spins us around.

He's smiling. I don't think I've ever seen him smile so much or so broadly before, and it's beautiful. It lights up his whole face, and the way he's wearing it while looking at me, while making me laugh and while touching me and holding me close and spinning me around, makes *me* feel beautiful, makes me feel like the luckiest person in the world, makes me feel like I'll never ever smile like this or be as happy as I am in this very moment again.

The rain is still coming down, and eventually Jason slips, and we go crashing down together. The fall doesn't hurt me, since Jason keeps me clutched to his chest the whole time, and I land on him.

"Are you okay?" I gasp through my laughter as I try to catch my breath.

His chest is rising and falling deeply as he does the same. "I'm perfect," he says, gazing up at me in a way that hits me in the stomach.

Despite smelling like rain and earth and mud, he still smells *so* good. His hands feel at home on my waist, and his chest is solid under my hands. My lips are so close to his, and when his eyes flash down to look at mine, my breath hitches.

"Siena," he starts, his voice low and gravelly as his hands tighten their grip.

My heart's beating so hard he can probably feel it from where my chest is pressed against him, and before he can say whatever it is that's making him look at me like that, I roll off him.

"That was fun," I say, meaning it. I don't know how much time we spent playing in the rain, but for those few moments, my mind really was here, in the present, having fun with Jason, and not thinking of anything else.

He sits up slowly, planting his forearms on his bent knees. He's looking at me so intensely it makes me shiver.

"Come on, you're freezing," he says, misreading my body's reaction to him. But I don't correct him; I let him pull me against him and wrap an arm around my shoulder. His body emits heat, and I realize maybe I *am* cold as I curl into his warmth.

We walk to his car together, through the rain, our feet trudging through the mud. We stop to collect our things, which are strewn everywhere. He finds my backpack and gathers the contents that have spilled out of it. The school-issued textbook is absolutely wrecked, as is my math notebook with the frantic notes I take during class, but he still places them in the soaked backpack with care and zips it up.

He swings the backpack onto his shoulder and places his arm back around me, our shoes dangling in our hands.

"Where were you going?" I ask as we approach his car, the hazards flashing in the night. "I mean, before you stopped for me."

"Warren's party."

I suddenly remember how nicely he's dressed and feel guilty. "I'm sorry for ruining your night."

"Are you kidding me?" he asks, pulling me tighter against him, and I melt into him more. "There's nowhere I'd rather be."

My breath catches. "But—"

"Nowhere," he repeats sternly, drilling the words into my brain as he stares into my eyes, and I snap my mouth shut.

"Besides," he says, less intense this time, "Warren throws a party once a week, I didn't miss out on anything."

We reach his car, and he opens the door for me. I hesitate. "I'm going to get your car all muddy."

"Yeah, well, just try not to touch everything," he says wryly, and I bite back a smile as I get in.

The black leather seat becomes slippery and muddy right away, and I make a mental note to offer to help him clean it. I hear the trunk slam closed, and then Jason is in the driver's seat. He presses some buttons and turns the air vents toward me, and once the heat starts flowing, I realize just how cold I actually am. I didn't notice, not while I was steaming with fury leaving Brandon's, and not while I was having fun with Jason. My hands are shaking, so I hold them up to the vents, trying to get the heat back in my fingers.

"Here," Jason says, handing me a pair of flip-flops he must've gotten from his trunk.

I take them, slightly confused. They're different flip-flops than I borrowed from Natalia, his mom, the night we were arrested.

"You just had these in your trunk?" I ask, looking them over for the size. There's a sticker at the bottom with the price on it that Jason must not have known was there, but they're in my exact size; Natalia's were a tad too small for me.

"No, I put them there."

I drop them to the floor and slip them on. They fit perfectly. "Why?"

He gives me a look like it's a question I should already

know the answer to. "Because you always seem to lose your shoes. I got a couple of pairs and put them in the back, just in case." He glances down at his own bare feet. "Didn't think I'd need a pair for myself though. You're a terrible influence." He laughs at the last part, not fully meaning it.

But I just stare at him in wonder. Jason Parker, popular boy and race car driver extraordinaire, went out and bought not one, but multiple pairs of shoes, in what he noticed to be my size, because he knows I lose my shoes and it drives him crazy when I cut up my feet?

His laugh dies down when he notices my expression, and there's a heat in his gaze. "Do you always stare at boys who stupidly admit they keep shoes for you in their car?"

I don't even care that I've been caught staring. There's a lump in my throat; I'm overwhelmed with emotions, so much that I ignore the "try not to touch everything" rule again and lean over the center console to throw my arms around him. It's an awkward hug because of the way we're sitting in the car, but it's full of meaning. I hold him tight as he wraps his arms around me as best he can. He went out and did something thoughtful for me, something I wouldn't have done for myself, and it means a lot to me, more than he'll ever know. In fact, everything he did for me tonight, when he was supposed to be at a party, means more to me than he'll ever know.

"Thank you, Jason," I tell him, hoping he doesn't hear the way my voice cracks.

He pulls back slightly to look at me, the corner of his

lips pulled up in an amused smile. He must be thinking it's a weird reaction over *shoes*, but he doesn't say that. Instead, he pushes my stiff wet hair out of my face and says, "Any time, Siena. Any time."

thirteen

Ever since Gia found out I went to Brandon's for a "study date," she's been all too happy to hang out with me, conveniently getting over the fact that she was upset with me for "trying to frame Brandon." I guess Brianna either didn't know or didn't tell Gia how my "study date" with Brandon ended, and since I never want to think about what happened again, I don't tell her either. I just let her think Brandon and I are friends while we spend Sunday together. She paints my toes whatever color she decides, and we binge-watch movies together. Zia Stella even joins us on the couch for the third rom-com in a row with sushi for dinner, and I'm in such a good mood that I don't even care when Dario sighs in annoyance when he passes us, mumbling something to Zia Stella about going to his friend's to watch some game. It's nice, and I enjoy spending time with Gia, seeing her laugh and tease me when Jason's name pops up on my phone.

He messages me occasionally throughout the day when he can since he's at work, and Gia makes kissy faces at me every time my phone vibrates. He turned down my offer to help him clean the car, saying he and Jackson already took care of it, but I still feel bad. He promised everything came out, and it looks good as new.

Gia's sisterly mood transfers to Monday morning too. She drags herself out of bed early and decides she wants to get ready with me in my room. When she sees that my getting ready consists of a few swipes of mascara and a coat of lip gloss—which is mostly for work after school and not school itself anyway—she decides that's not good enough. She gives me a thick line of black eyeliner on my top lids that makes my eyes look deep and sultry, and after I veto a full face of foundation for fear of sweating it all off at work, she only covers a few zits I have on my forehead with concealer and setting powder.

I'm not sure if she's here because she's just in a good mood and wants me to look good because I'm her sister, or if it has something to do with Brandon, but I don't complain either way. We've migrated to the bathroom for better lighting according to Gia, and I'm curling my hair at Gia's insistence it'll get me more tips, while she does her own makeup. It's a weird Monday morning, since we've never done something like this before by choice—usually we're both running late and fighting for the bathroom while running around each other—but getting ready together *on purpose* is nice.

She's chatting idly about some party she was invited to in two weeks and is already planning what outfit to wear. I nod and make generic sounds to indicate that I'm listening, but she's happy driving the conversation, at least until she says where the party is.

"Limelight?" I ask, holding the iron to my head for one last curl. "That sounds like a club name."

She doesn't look away from the mirror, where she's using a fluffy brush to dust something over her skin. "Because it is."

I set the iron down and face her. "A club? Like a nightclub?"

"Yeah," she says.

"Like a twenty-one-plus club?"

She shoots me an annoyed look. "Yes, Siena. That's what a club is, with music and a DJ and a dance floor."

"I know that, Gia. I mean how are *you* going there?"

Her eyebrows draw together like she can't believe I'm this dense. "With a fake ID, obviously."

"A fake—Gia!"

"What?"

"You can't go to a nightclub! You're *fifteen*!"

She rolls her eyes at me and gathers her makeup brushes scattered all over the sink. "Don't be so uptight, Siena. Everyone gets a fake ID."

She skirts past me, and I hastily unplug the curling iron and follow her to her room. "Yeah, when they're in *college* maybe. Not when they're fifteen!"

"Everyone's going to get one, not just me," she says, dumping her makeup bag on her desk. "Brianna knows someone—"

"I don't care!" I snap. "I don't care that everyone's going, and I don't care who Brianna knows! You're not going to a nightclub, Gia, and that's final."

"You can't tell me where I can and can't go!"

"Yes, I can!"

Her face scrunches up in rage and her hands clench. "No, you can't! You're not Mom!"

She said that to me the first night I saw her drunk at Warren's party too, and it stings this time too, for multiple reasons. "Obviously I'm not Mom, Gia. But look around you. Is she here? No. So that means it's my job to take care of you, and I'm saying you're not going."

"It's Dad's job to take care of me," she shoots back.

I cross my arms against my chest. Really? She wants to play this game? Wants to conveniently forget who puts money in her bank account? Who kept her fed and taken care of all these years? Because it certainly wasn't Aunt Julie, and it definitely wasn't Mom.

"Dad doesn't care if I go to the club," Gia continues.

"He doesn't care if I drink or if I come in late or if I do my homework. Why are you the only one up my ass about everything?"

"Because I'm the only one that *cares*, Gia!" I snap. "You think Dario cares if you end up in a ditch somewhere? If you call him crying from prison? You think he cares if you throw your life away? He didn't care when he left us, and he doesn't care now. Once you're eighteen, you think he's going to let you stay here? He can barely even *look* at us, never mind stomach being in the same room with us for longer than a few minutes. You think once his legal obligation to us is done he's going to care where you end up?" My breath is ragged, and her face is red. Maybe I'm being too harsh, but I can't prepare her for life by letting her stay ignorant to reality. "The answer is no. As long as it's not with him, he won't care, which means we're going to be on our own, and the sooner you realize we need to get our shit together *now* to prepare for the future, the better."

"Well, I'm not eighteen for years! I can have fun now and worry about it later!"

"Not if something happens to you! Look at Lily, we still don't know where she is!" The frustration claws at my chest, and even though I don't want to throw this at her, I can't stop myself from saying, "You need to get it together and stop doing illegal shit, Gia, especially after what I've been through. It wasn't fun being locked in a cage, never seeing the sun, hearing people scream all night. You need to grow up a little."

Gia looks like she wants to stomp her foot and throw a tantrum. But she grabs her backpack and swings it over her shoulder.

"I wish it was you who disappeared instead of Lily!" she shrieks, storming past me, nearly knocking my shoulder as she goes. "At least she let me have fun!"

Her words are a knife to the heart. She didn't mean that, she couldn't have meant that, and yet, it hurts all the same. I'm left standing in her room, staring at myself in her full-length mirror, with my made-up face and curled hair that are completely at odds with my ugly expression of grief.

I want Gia to be my friend, want her to talk to me about these kinds of things, but I can't be both her mom and her sister. I can't be her friend while ordering her not to do stupid shit like go to a nightclub; it's causing an imbalance in our relationship. I scowl deeper at my reflection, the one that looks so much like Mom, the mom who should *be here*. I shouldn't have to play mom to Gia, and I resent my mother just a little bit more.

I'm still upset about Gia as I walk through the hall at school. She waited for her friends to pick her up at the end of the driveway without another word to me. I was so pissed off that Officer Liu's morning glare from his porch didn't even faze me as I stomped all the way to the bus stop.

"Hey, Siena!" Nyah calls, catching up to me in the hall. "You weren't answering your phone this morning."

"Hey," I greet, trying to let go of the residual anger from this morning before accidentally letting it out on Nyah. "Sorry, it's been a hectic morning."

"I'll say." She hooks her arm in mine as we walk toward my locker. More people than usual look at me, and I'm not sure if it's because I'm wearing more makeup than normal or if they're still not used to me being new.

"Why?" I ask.

She leans in and lowers her voice conspiratorially. "You know. Because of Brandon?"

What did he do this time?

She continues in her normal tone, "You could've told me, you know I wouldn't have judged you. I mean, I am a bit confused about why *Brandon* of all people because he kind of creeps me out, but I'm still totally not judging you."

At my confused expression, her eyes widen. "Oh no. Did you not know he was telling people?"

We stop in front of my locker, and I withdraw my arm from hers. The way she's talking is starting to make me nervous. Is Brandon telling people about what happened Saturday? But why would he do that? He'd come across as a total asshole.

I hesitate, but ask anyway because I need to know, "What is he saying?"

Nyah bites her lip. "Oh shit. I'm so stupid, I should've

known you didn't know. Why the hell would I have thought you'd know?"

People walking by openly stare at us as they pass, whispering to each other. "Nyah, you're scaring me. Just tell me, please."

Nyah chews on her lip some more like she's trying to figure out how to break the news to me. Tyler joins us, throwing his arm around his girlfriend.

"Hey Siena! Heard you got laid Saturday night. Nice." He holds his fist out to me like he's expecting me to fist bump him, and I stare at him.

What?

"Tyler!" Nyah exclaims, shoving him off her. "What the fuck?"

"What?" he asks, looking back and forth between Nyah's furious expression and my shell-shocked one. I feel like the floor just fell out beneath me. Everyone thinks I had sex with Brandon?! Brandon's *telling* people I had sex with him?

Tyler must get the hint because he mumbles, "Oh shit."

The walls of the hallway are closing in on me, and I try and fail to follow Anusha's breathing techniques. Everyone is staring at me, talking about me. "I didn't . . . we didn't . . ."

"Oh, honey." Nyah pulls me into a hug, but it's only making me feel even more confined, even more flustered, and I freeze up in her arms.

She must sense my discomfort because she pulls away. My throat works, "I didn't . . . I went there to study for the math test, and he threw himself at me and I left!"

"That's not what he and everyone else is saying. Apparently, Saturday evening you threw yourself at him and begged him for it," Tyler fills me in, earning a *"Tyler!"* and a slap on the arm from Nyah.

I need to sit down. No, I need to go outside and get air. No, I need to find Brandon and kick him in the balls. I don't know what to do. There's nothing I *can* do. The rumor is out there, and once it's out there, people are going to believe it; I proved that point to Principal Anderson myself.

Jason appears down the hall and my breath hitches. Has he heard the rumors? Does he believe them? I was *with* him Saturday. Does he think he hung out with me right after I slept with Brandon?

All these questions running through my mind cause the hallway to feel even smaller, and when Jason's eyes lock on mine and he strides toward me with a purpose, breathing becomes harder.

"There he is now," Tyler says, pointing in the opposite direction of where Jason is. I turn and see Brandon. He's walking with two of his friends, talking and laughing. Even from here, I can tell they're talking about me, about some imaginary sex move I did on Brandon that *never happened* but he's telling them did.

As they pass me, his friends smirk, and Brandon doesn't slow to acknowledge me. He does, however, fake-cough as he continues walking, and in between the fake coughs, says, *"Whore,"* in my direction, loud enough to be heard by everyone in the vicinity.

My face heats, and I do nothing except stand there, shocked, as do Nyah and Tyler, while his friends laugh.

But then Jason is there. He grabs Brandon by the back of his shirt collar as he tries to pass him and pulls him back in front of me. None of Brandon's friends intervene.

"What's that, Brandon?" Jason demands, his eyes hard. "I missed it. Should someone get you a cough drop so you can say that more clearly?"

Brandon doesn't say anything, just glowers as he tries to shake Jason's hand off him, but Jason's hold is firm and keeps him right in front of me.

"No, for real, I missed it," Jason presses. I've never seen him so angry before, except when Officer Liu arrested us. "Were you just apologizing to Siena for being a piece of shit and for starting false rumors about her? Because we all know she's a thousand times too good for you."

"Fuck off, Parker." Brandon shoves Jason, and Jason voluntarily releases him.

Jason stares Brandon down, and the ice in his gaze makes me shiver. "I've only tolerated you because for whatever reason, Tyler likes you, and I've known him since I was six. But I'm real fucking tired of your bullshit."

I only spare Tyler a quick enough glance to see the blood has drained from his face. He doesn't make a move to get in between his friends.

Brandon sneers at Jason as he fixes his shirt. "You're just

jealous I got in her pants before you did."

"That's not true!" I shout when I'm no longer able to hold the words back. "You forced yourself on me, and I pushed you off and left! We didn't do anything!"

Thinking about the night, about how he made me feel, the words he said to me, makes my eyes water. But I will not cry in front of everyone, will not let Brandon see how much he's affected me.

The entire hallway, normally so loud with chatter, is so quiet you can hear the slight chatter from the adjacent hall. Brandon looks around at the crowd, then takes a menacing step closer to me. "You're lying because your boyfriend is here."

The ball in my chest from Saturday is back and tighter than ever. I want to scream at him until my lungs can't take it anymore, want to shake him until I can knock some sense into him. "I'm not lying!"

He tries to take another step toward me when Jason slides between us. His back is to me, and he reaches back a protective hand to stop me from walking around him.

The five-minute warning bell goes off, but no one moves to leave. Everyone's holding their breath, watching Brandon and Jason's standoff.

Brandon's gaze moves from Jason to me, peeking around his shoulder, and the cocky smirk grows. "If you want my sloppy seconds, Parker, all you've gotta do is ask. I can tell you just how tight her hot little p—"

Jason steps forward, stopping just short of knocking

Brandon on his ass. "We're in school, but you keep talking like that then we can absolutely take this outside." Now Jason *does* sound angrier than I've ever heard him. His fists are clenched, and I can tell that the muscles in his back are tensed even through his shirt.

Brandon's comment makes my face burn, and while I appreciate Jason stepping between the two of us—even more than he knows considering the last time Brandon forced himself on me—I feel ridiculous cowering behind Jason. I force myself to step beside him, where the tension between the two guys is even more palpable. It sucks the air out of the entire hallway. I lay my hand on Jason's bicep.

"Jason," I say softly.

Brandon's eyes move to the hand I have on Jason's arm, and the smirk melts off his face, leaving a hardened scowl in its place.

"No need to go outside," Brandon says. "Right here's good." Then he swings at Jason.

Jason could've blocked it, he saw it coming and he's more than capable, but he doesn't bother saving himself because he uses both arms to move *me* out of the way. The punch is hard and connects with Jason's cheekbone. I swear I hear a crunch that makes me want to throw up.

The rest happens fast. Once Jason decides I'm far enough away to escape any damage, he turns to Brandon and, in one smooth motion, punches him right in the face.

Brandon stumbles a bit, then throws himself at Jason.

"Oh shit," Nyah and Tyler exclaim at the same time,

jumping out of the way. The previously quiet hall is now filled with noise, people shouting over each other or at the guys.

It's so hectic, I can't even tell what's happening or hear what Jason and Brandon are saying to each other.

I stand there, staring at them, for maybe a full ten seconds, before something in me snaps. This is the second time Jason is getting hurt because of me, even though I think he's winning, and I'm not going to stupidly stand here and let Brandon say filthy shit about me.

Before I know what I'm doing, I'm rushing forward, ignoring the way Jason orders me to stay back.

"Stop," I plead with them. "Please! Stop fighting."

Jason's jaw clenches, hard, but he releases the front of Brandon's shirt that was bunched in his fist and steps back. It looks like it physically pains him to do it, but he does it, for me.

In the split second it takes for Jason to step back from Brandon and look at me, Brandon growls, "Fuck that."

Jason moves, but it's at the last second because *again*, he's moving *me* away, and Brandon's fist connects with the corner of Jason's eye. I feel the hit in my bones, feel it break my heart because it's my fault Jason keeps getting hurt, and when Brandon winds up his arm again, I grab it, trying to get him to stop.

"Get off me, you fucking whore!" Brandon shoves me off him, hard, and my back slams into the locker as I gasp in pain.

If I thought Jason was pissed off before? He was a teddy

bear compared to the way his face twists up with murderous rage now. He pounces on Brandon, swearing and cursing his name up and down, and I think Jason breaks Brandon's nose. There's a crunch and blood and Brandon howls with pain.

Nyah says something to me, but I can't make out her words because I'm too focused on Jason and Brandon. I don't want them to fight, I'm not worth all of *this*. Brandon looks like he's attempting to choke Jason, so I grab his arm, but he shoves me off, which pisses Jason off more. It's only been a minute since Brandon took that first swing, but it feels like forever. Jason doesn't need my help, but when he reaches his hand out to me to tell me to stay back, Brandon gets both hands around Jason's neck again. Without thinking, I jump right onto Brandon's back, piggyback style.

"Stop this! Get off!" I order, wrapping my arms and legs around Brandon and trying to get him to pull back. Jason was willing to stop, at least before Brandon shoved me, so it's up to Brandon to calm down. "Quit it!"

"Siena!" Jason's not paying attention to Brandon trying to hit him anymore, instead stopping him from slamming his back, and therefore me, into the locker. Jason could've won this fight in three seconds if he wasn't so concerned about me.

"You . . . fucking . . . bitch . . ." Brandon grunts as he tries to shake me off him. Jason doesn't need my help, I know that, everyone in the hall knows that, but I still cling to Brandon anyway.

There's a loud, authoritative whistle, and all three of us freeze exactly how we are. Only then do I realize how quiet the hallway is, so quiet you can hear our ragged breathing and the neat click of heels on linoleum, walking toward us.

"Siena?" Gia exclaims, standing there with Brianna. They both have incredulous looks on their faces. But they're not the ones who whistled—that came from the other direction.

The crowd parts, revealing Principal Anderson, glowering from the end of the hall. She stalks toward us as kids jump out of her way, like she's telekinetically moving them herself.

I slide off Brandon's back, landing on my feet with as much grace as I can muster, and Jason and Brandon release each other, both breathing hard.

They're pissed. I can feel them practically vibrating beside me; the testosterone and adrenaline are so thick in the air it's almost suffocating. It's clear they were just in some kind of fight, even if the whole thing from start to finish was under two minutes. Brandon's nose is bleeding, and his lip is split. He spits on the floor like a caveman, leaving a tiny pool of blood there. Jason's hair is ruffled and there's a shiny bruise already starting to form around his eye. My stomach tightens with guilt when he shoots me a look—the one that says *don't say shit about shit*—and I get a better view of it. It must hurt, and it's definitely going to be a black eye in the morning.

"What is going on?" Principal Anderson screeches,

looking from us to the crowd. "Get to class! All of you!" She turns her steely gaze on us. "You three. My office. Now."

People begin scattering, and the sound of their chatter follows them. No doubt what just happened is going to be the hot topic of conversation for weeks to come. I can't even imagine what kind of rumors this is going to start, or how skewed the story will become by the end of the day. For all I know, this little tiff in the hallway is going to become a full-out war with swords drawn and limbs ripped off.

I spare a glance at Gia, who's clearly pissed, and hear Brianna hiss accusingly at her, "Your sister and her boyfriend gave my brother a bloody nose!" as they clear out too. Gia shoots me a *what the fuck* glare as she passes, but I have no answer for her.

On my other side, Nyah and Tyler stand frozen, like they're unsure whether to jump in and help or if that will only make things worse. I give Nyah a subtle head jerk in the opposite direction and an intense look that I hope says, *Get the hell out of here now.* She picks up on it, because she grabs Tyler's hand and pulls him away from us. Jason just shakes his head at Tyler when he calls his name, telling him to go too. After that, Tyler lets Nyah lead him down the hall with the rest of the crowd, even though they both shoot us regretful looks.

I appreciate that they feel like they need to help, but there's really nothing they *can* do, at least nothing that wouldn't get them in trouble too. I don't want anyone getting in trouble if I can help it. It's bad enough that Jason's in trouble. Even worse that it started because of some stupid shit Brandon's been saying about me.

Jason, Brandon, and I don't move until everyone has left the hallway and Principal Anderson shifts, gesturing down the hall as if to say, *After you.*

Jason and Brandon don't stop scowling at each other as they walk, and I follow, feeling defeated. I just wanted to be a normal kid, to not be the center of all the gossip for once, and now here I am. And I can't even blame it on what happened in LA or on Mom. This one is all me, completely my fault, and now I've got to sit in the seat of shame in the office all day while they try to get hold of Dario, who's *not* going to drop whatever it is he's doing to be told what a delinquent I am. That's not going to help ease the tension every time we're in the same room, and it's definitely not going to help convince him I'm not like Mom and to give me a chance.

As I pass Principal Anderson, her icy eyes meet mine. "I warned you what would happen if you didn't get along with Brandon, Siena," she scolds. She doesn't seem particularly happy, but she's one step closer to winning whatever imaginary chess game we have going on. "Zero tolerance," she reminds me ominously, and I hang my head as I pass her, trailing after Jason, who waits for me to catch up.

"You okay?" he asks, voice low, as his eyes scan me for any injuries.

I don't feel any physical pain, except when I look at his beautiful face and see what's the beginning of an ugly black eye, and I feel like throwing up. Other than that, physically I'm fine. Mostly I'm pissed. Pissed and annoyed. At Brandon, for being a fucking nuisance, at Jason being injured because he had to fight my fight for me, at the student body for the inevitable gossip about me, and at myself for getting tangled in this bullshit with Brandon in the first place.

"I'm fine," I tell Jason, not looking at him because I can't stand to see the bruise he got protecting me. "Are you?"

I can still sense the tension he's holding when he answers, "I'm fine."

I don't know if that's true or not, but he's glaring a hole in the back of Brandon's shirt instead of looking at me, and I can't make direct eye contact with him right now anyway.

Just as we reach the office, the bell rings to signal the start of class. Five minutes. The warning bell rang and then the fight started and now we're here, five minutes later. That's how long it took for my whole day to turn upside down, to ruin Jason's, and possibly change everything at home too.

fourteen

We're suspended for a week. Principal Anderson was not happy about it. I can tell she wanted to push for expulsion due to the whole zero-tolerance thing, but she couldn't. She hadn't actually seen anyone throw a punch, and Brandon and Jason claimed they were horsing around having fun, and not actually fighting. Brandon even said he was giving me a piggyback ride to class, and I snorted back a laugh when he said it.

When pushed about his bloody nose, he said, "It's the dry fall weather; happens all the time." He had the same answer about his split lip. When Jason was asked about the bruise that was growing darker and angrier the longer we sat there, he said he walked into a door. Imagine that. *Jason*. Walked into a door. It was just as laughable as Brandon giving me a friendly piggyback ride to class, but if that was all he was willing to say, Principal Anderson couldn't argue it. For the most part I sat there quietly, keeping my mouth shut like I knew I probably should.

I could tell both Jason and Brandon hated having to work together to make their story believable, but it was for the best if they wanted to avoid expulsion. Principal Anderson tried, but she couldn't even nail us for being late to class, because we *weren't* late. So, she settled for suspension on grounds of horseplay, acting irresponsibly, and causing a disruptive scene. I wasn't happy about it, but it was better than being expelled, and at least this time Brandon was getting interrogated too, not just me.

When Principal Anderson called Dario, he replied, "I don't have time to come in and deal with Florence's daughter's stupid bullshit." I heard him say those exact words, so when Zia Stella arrived in his place, I was shoved out of Principal Anderson's office and forced to the seat of shame in front of my friend Sergeant Secretary. Jason was placed a few seats away from me, so we couldn't talk even if Sergeant Secretary wasn't shushing us and shooting us angry looks. I couldn't look at him anyway. I felt so guilty I kept my head down even when Jason was so clearly trying to get my attention. I couldn't look even when he was moved to the *opposite* side of the office after he got in trouble for his efforts to get my attention.

I stood when Zia Stella exited the office, a grim look on her face, and she didn't say a single word to me. The silent treatment hurt more than if she actually yelled at me. I didn't look at anyone as I left, even when Jason called out my name. Zia Stella dropped me off and went back to work, all without saying anything. If it's this bad with Zia Stella, the *nice* one, I can't imagine what Dario's going to say, or *not* say about it all.

Alone in the house, I check my phone to find a What the fuck? message from Gia, but I don't feel like dealing with it. I don't have the energy to be upset that she's pissed at me again. It feels like ever since LA, there's nothing I can do to make her not pissed at me. I know she's going through her own shit, but I just can't deal with her being mad about everything right now. I'm more concerned about what Dario will do, or with Jason getting in trouble with his parents for defending me, or worse still, Jason being upset with me.

So, I turn off my phone. Maybe it's the cowardly way out, but I don't want to read Gia's *what the fuck* message or the *are you okay* messages from Nyah, Tyler, and even Warren, who wasn't there but must know all about it by now.

I kill time by showering and attempting to look nice for work, when Dario comes back home early. It's only 2:00 p.m. when his Mercedes pulls into the driveway, and I watch from my open window as he marches up the driveway and into the house. I sit at the desk in my room, not doing any homework, just staring at the corkboard above it that should be filled with pictures like Gia's but instead is glaringly empty.

Dario roots around downstairs, the heavy thump of the bottle meaning he's poured himself a whiskey. He doesn't want me here, that much is clear, he's *never* wanted anything to do with me, and now I'm making it harder for him to ignore my existence.

I should be used to this feeling of aloneness, but as I sit here in my room with no one to talk to, even if it *is* my choice to turn my phone off, the feeling is suffocating. I reach into my drawer and dig way underneath, moving spare pens and highlighters and notebooks, and find the covered pencil sharpener in the back. I unscrew it and pull out the note Mom left me.

I'm so proud of you, sweetheart. Everything will be okay now.

I read the words over and over, wishing they were true, wishing *she* was here to say them to me, and not some stupid note she left under my pillow instead of coming to talk to me. Because the truth is, nothing feels okay. Lily is still missing, Officer Liu is still eyeing me, Principal Anderson hates me, Jason's probably pissed at me too, Gia's perpetually upset with me, and Dario is likely trying to figure out how to be rid of me before I turn eighteen when he can legally kick me out.

Dario comes up the stairs, so I stash the note from Mom back in the pencil sharpener and put it away in the desk drawer as he enters my room.

I turn in my chair, facing him, and he stands at the entrance of my room for a few moments, his mouth opening and closing, as if trying to figure out how to start.

After a few moments of us staring at each other awkwardly, he says, "You look *just* like her. I swear if I tilt my head this way, you're her, and I feel like I'm seventeen again, especially with how you act." He takes a sip of his whiskey. "It's fucking me up how much you're like her. If she didn't do that paternity test when you were born, I'd never believe you were my daughter."

His words sting, but still I say nothing to the man I used to cry over at night, wishing he'd come back and be my daddy.

"At least Gia got my eyes, my hair, my tan skin, my dimples. We can go out in public, and people would know that she's my daughter. But you . . . you're all Florence."

"I'm . . . sorry?" Is that what he wants me to say? I can't help how my genes lined up.

He laughs and turns to leave, like he's done with this conversation, but at the last minute changes his mind. "You know, it wouldn't be so bad if you just looked like her. You *are* her, Siena. She was fifteen when she was arrested for the first time—stole a pair of sunglasses; I was there. But you, when you get arrested you go big, huh? Straight for the kill—ha!" He takes another gulp of whiskey, and I suddenly wonder how much he's had to drink. He's not slurring, not acting drunk, but this is the longest conversation we've had, barring the first one when he told me to stay out of his way.

"Dario . . ." I start, but he cuts me off.

"Dario," he repeats with a sneer. "You don't even call me *Dad*. Gia does."

I've had it. There's only so much I can handle, and the absolute absurdity of that statement is the last straw.

"I'm not going to call you *dad* because you're not my dad!" I stand up, storming toward him. "You haven't been my dad for the last fourteen years! Just because we have the same DNA and you put a roof over my head because of some legal obligation doesn't mean I'm going to forget about all the years you spent pretending we didn't exist!" I'm saying things I shouldn't. I can tell by the way his eyes darken that all I'm doing is pissing him off, but it feels good to say what's been weighing on my chest since I was old enough to understand that he left us and was never coming back. "And just because I *am* here doesn't mean you're suddenly my dad. You don't even know me. What's my favorite color? What am I allergic to? When is my *birthday?*"

"That's enough, Siena!" he shouts, and I snap my mouth shut. "I've had enough of your attitude and behavior over the last few weeks."

Attitude? Behavior? Other than going to school and work, I'm not causing him any trouble; I don't even ask for rides.

At my blank look, he continues, "You're never home, and you're out until midnight on school nights. When you're supposed to be home on weekends you sneak out to go to parties, even roping your innocent sister into coming.

You smell like alcohol or cigarettes, and you're always with boys. Especially the wrong kinds of boys, like the two that were in a fight today over you. Your principal has called me twice about you, and now you're suspended. And not to mention that you tried to derail the investigation into a missing girl over some petty vendetta!"

There is so much wrong with that statement I don't even know where to start. I want to argue all his points, but the first thing I say is, "Jason isn't a bad guy."

"That's all you have to say? Really? After all that, the first thing you do is defend the boy who illegally drag races? And yes, I know about that, I heard Gia talking about it to Brianna, and heard about how you took your fifteen-year-old sister there! Do you not even see how reckless you're being? How bad of an influence you're being on Gia?"

I can't even process his words properly enough to find an explanation. I *did* do all of that. Everything he's saying is true, but it isn't. However, the only way I can defend myself is if I throw Gia under the bus, and I'd never do that. So instead, I stare at him with wide eyes and say nothing.

He sneers and says to the ceiling, "God, you're literally Florence 2.0. I can't even stand to look at you."

Mom 2.0? It's bad enough I'm the spitting image of her when she was my age, but to be told I'm just like Mom from the man who knew her best? I clench my fists. Aunt Julie said I was just like Mom. Officer Liu too. When will I just be *Siena* and not Florence Bowen's daughter?

Dario gestures at me with the hand holding the heavy

glass. "It started out this way with Florence, and I saw how she spiraled. I thought she'd grow out of it when you were born, but she was still always out partying, this time for her supposed career when we moved to LA. Even after we had Gia and she made that one movie that made her famous, she was still out of control. I couldn't take it anymore, Siena; couldn't deal with her or stand by and watch her throw everything away, and now you're here doing the same thing. I've seen how this story ends, seen where people like you end up, what happens when you put your own selfish need to have fun above everyone and everything else, and I can't do it again." He points at me, mind already made up. "People like you and your mother hurt the people closest to you by doing whatever you want and acting impulsively. You drag others down, and you don't even care."

He doesn't like me, fine. I don't care—he barely even knows me. But to call me selfish? To say I don't care about the people closest to me? That's complete bullshit. All I care about are the people closest to me.

He downs the rest of his drink. "Maybe bringing you here to King was a bad decision."

All the emotions whirling around inside me come to a sudden halt. The quiet left in the wake of his statement is such a stark contrast from the back-and-forth aggression of the last few minutes. "What?"

Dario thinks his words through. "I've been talking to Anusha, and we feel that maybe moving you here was too much of a shock, after everything, and you'd be . . .

better adjusted . . . if you were in a more . . . supportive environment."

A more supportive environment? What does that even mean? He's going to put me in a support group for kids who murdered grown-ass perverts? But what does that have to do with me being uprooted to King? He's going to send me away? And Anusha agreed? She's supposed to be on my side! Instead, she's giving Dario the permission he needs to get rid of me? I already knew he wanted nothing to do with me, but hearing him actually say it hurts a lot more than just suspecting it.

"And where would a more supportive environment be, if not my own father's house?" I can't help but take that extra dig.

He looks like he doesn't appreciate the comment but keeps that to himself as he shifts from foot to foot. "I have a cousin in New York who has daughters and is a registered therapist with a specialty in at-risk youth. She's agreed to let you live with her for the year if we decide this is the best route to go. She'd be more equipped to help you, since you're not adjusting here and that's only harming Gia."

I blink at him. He's thinking about sending me across the country to New York? To live with a woman I've never met who's going to psychoanalyze every move I make? Will she realize I'm not at-risk or will she confirm everyone's apparent suspicions of me?

"We all agree that might be best," he says.

He agrees that's best. I see what he's doing here. He gets to say he tried, he did his duty as a father, but his daughter was too rebellious, too bad of an influence, *too much like her mother* for him to handle. He was at wit's end and didn't know what else to do, so he sent her to someone who could help. He gets bonus points for looking like he cares; meanwhile he wipes his hands of me.

None of that is surprising to me. Shipping off his daughters and claiming it's for their own good is such a Dario Amato move. But *everyone* agrees?

"Even Zia Stella?" I ask.

"Yes."

I try not to let the pain show on my face, but the truth hurts me. Was today the last straw? Does she see Florence 2.0 when she sees me too? She was kind of cool. Up until now, I thought that she was at least *trying* to get to know me. She was the one adult who didn't treat me like I was a criminal, but she wants to ship me off too, and that's worse than Dario wanting it.

It hurts me to say, but I force out, "All right. When are Gia and I going?"

He crosses his arms and doesn't look at me. "Siena, if you go to New York, Gia's staying here."

What? His words are like a physical blow that force me to take a step back. "What do you mean?"

Dario's stiff in the doorway, like he'd rather be anywhere than here having this conversation. "Gia's adjusted perfectly. She's on top of her homework, she's made friends, she's even thinking about joining after-school programs. The only problem I have with Gia is when she smells like alcohol from helping sneak *you* back in every weekend, or when you drag her along to parties. She'd be a perfect daughter if you weren't around."

My mouth drops open. I haven't touched a single drop of alcohol in months. I don't even *want* to go to any parties. It's me bailing Gia out of parties or helping sneak her back in while she's puking her guts out. "Is that what she told you?"

"She doesn't have to tell me; I know what goes on in my house."

I stare at him incredulously. That's ironic since he's rarely even in his house. He really doesn't want me here, and he's willing to believe anything that justifies sending me away.

I thought this was my chance at having a life separate from Florence Bowen and Stan Roven and Aunt Julie. I thought I would be able to get ahead, focus on good grades and college and being *normal*. But I can't do that if all Dario sees when he looks at me is Florence, not Siena, and he still holds hate for her in his heart.

My throat is dry when I say, "So you're going to split me and Gia up?"

"I'm in charge of you and Gia. It's my responsibility to do what's best for the both of you." He pauses for a moment. "Gia is a great kid, and I don't want her going down the wrong path because of your bad influence."

I can't be separated from Gia! I need to be here to take

care of her! Sure, Dario puts a roof over her head, buys her the necessities, but he'll never know Gia like I do, never know how to take care of her like I do. I cannot be separated from her. We stay together, always, like Mom would want. She's my baby sister.

"I'm not going anywhere without Gia," I state, standing my ground.

"Nothing is final yet, it's just something I'm thinking about."

"I'm not an at-risk youth! It was self-defense!" I screech as a last-ditch effort.

Dario backs away from me, his body still stiff, and I wonder if he's scared of me. "As I said, nothing is final yet. But if you want to stay here, you're going to need to turn your behavior around. If not for yourself, then think of Gia."

I am thinking of Gia. All I ever do is think of Gia, about what's best for her. It's so frustrating that no one is seeing that, not even Gia.

"And you're grounded for the week. You're suspended from school, so there's no reason for you to leave the house."

"I have to go to work. You know, the place I go until midnight on school nights?"

His eyes widen in surprise, like he conveniently forgot an honest job was the reason I'm always out, because it fits his narrative of me better. Or maybe he legitimately didn't know.

"Work and nothing else," he declares with finality, then turns and leaves.

And I'm left staring after him, processing his words.

No one ever just sees me. *Siena*. Dario, Aunt Julie, and Officer Liu see Florence. Principal Anderson, and maybe even Zia Stella, sees a troublemaker who's a bad influence on other kids. Gia sees an annoying big sister who's bossing her around. Brandon and his friends apparently see a stuck-up tease who walks around like she's too good for anyone.

Jason sees you. A voice nudges at the back of my head, but I ignore it, because Jason's probably pissed at me for getting him suspended, and I can't even blame him.

I spend the rest of the day sitting in my room, avoiding going downstairs until it's time to leave for work. I don't talk to Dario, don't say anything to Gia when she gets home, don't call Anusha, and don't turn my phone back on. I don't even acknowledge Officer Liu, who's standing on his porch when I leave the house and calls out that he heard I was suspended. I just keep walking and don't stop until I get to work, where I plaster on a big smile and serve happy families all night.

fifteen

The universe must really want me to suffer today, because after a slow night which leaves me way too much time to wallow in my own despair, all my tables clear out early, meaning I get to leave over an hour early. Normally I wouldn't mind, because that means I get to go home and sleep, but I don't *want* to go home, even if Gia and Dario will probably already be in bed, and I won't run into them. Besides wanting to avoid my father and sister, I won't be able to fall asleep with my mind racing like this anyway. If there was one day when I needed work to be crazy busy and leave me mentally and physically exhausted, it would've been today.

I take my time cleaning my sections and cashing out in order to stall, until Hannah, who I'm still slightly terrified of, practically shoves me out the door because she wants to go home too.

I've just slipped Jason's King City High hoodie over my head in the parking lot when my steps falter. There, in the middle of the practically empty lot, is Jason, leaning on the hood of his car. He pushes off and tucks his phone into his back pocket when he sees me. I look around as if checking that he's actually here for me and not someone else whose path I'm in.

When it's clear that he is here for me, I slowly make my way over to him.

His deep, teasing voice greets me. "I see you're still wearing the hoodie you said you didn't steal from me."

I pull the sleeves over my hands and wrap my arms around myself. I washed the hoodie and was planning on returning it but grabbed it without thinking when I left. I'm not sure why. I have plenty of sweaters, but maybe this one brings me comfort, even if it doesn't smell like him anymore. A fleeting thought running through my mind tells me to give the hoodie back to Jason to make it smell like him *then* steal it back again, but I push that thought away because it's weird and creepy.

"I didn't steal it," I say, stopping in front of him. "I'll give it back eventually."

He looks so handsome in the moonlight and soft street-lights around the parking lot, it reminds me of our night dancing in the rain. Even the purple black eye does nothing to detract from his good looks. In fact, it only makes his already sharp features sharper, makes him more intense, more intimidating. I wrap my arms tighter around myself, suddenly feeling self-conscious.

He smirks like he doesn't believe me but doesn't push it. Instead, he says, "You haven't been answering your phone."

"Yeah, I turned it off."

"Why?"

I shrug instead of telling him I didn't feel like facing everyone, like facing *him*. But here he is. "What are you doing here?" I ask instead.

"Well, you weren't answering your phone, so I figured I'd catch you after work."

I frown. "It's not even eleven, and you know I normally get off at twelve."

"I know. I was bored, and it's a nice night. Figured I'd wait." He shrugs like it's no big deal, and I stare at him. He was going to wait for an hour until I got off just because he wanted to talk to me?

"And since you are off work early," he says, "let me drive you home. Hopefully your dad hasn't left to pick you up yet."

The wind picks up, and I snuggle into Jason's hoodie. "No, I was actually going to walk home."

He stiffens, and his voice lowers. "You were going to walk home?"

"I always walk to and from work."

He stares at me for a moment and a muscle in his jaw jumps. "I can't believe I didn't think about that. Fuck, Siena. If I knew you were walking, I would've fucking driven you. You've been walking home at midnight every day? For like, what? Half an hour?"

I shrug again. "It isn't your responsibility to drive me around."

He runs a frustrated hand through his hair, and he mutters another curse. "Well, I'm driving you home today." He holds the passenger-side door open for me. "Get in."

I hesitate, which he mistakes as me not wanting to go with him. "Really, Siena? I'm not letting you walk home, so your butt is getting in this car."

The demand is so much like the first time we met, when I walked off and he came with me, that I almost smile. Instead, I say, "No, not that. I just . . . don't want to go home yet."

He nods slowly, processing my words, and says, "Then we won't go home yet."

I hold his eyes for a moment before it becomes too intense for me, and finally slide into the car. It's warmer in here, now that I'm out of the wind, and the passenger-side window is already open a tad. I smile at the gesture as Jason gets in and starts the car.

After putting my seat belt on, I can't ignore the question burning in the back of my mind anymore. "Aren't you mad at me?" I blurt.

He pauses from shifting into gear. "Mad at you?" he repeats.

"Yeah. For getting you suspended."

Jason puts the parking brake back on and gives me his full attention, making me squirm in my seat.

"You didn't get me suspended, Siena. In fact, I thought you were mad at me and dodging my calls."

"Why would I be mad at you?"

"Because I couldn't control myself around that fucker Brandon and got in a fight that got *you* suspended."

Jason thinks I'm mad at him for what happened at school? Some of the tension in my chest loosens, tension I didn't even realize was there because of my fear of losing him.

"No," I say, "I'm not mad at you. It wasn't your fault. It wasn't anyone's fault. Or I guess it was mine, for going to Brandon's house in the first place, but nothing happened! I swear! Or something did happen, but I pushed him away the second he instigated, or I tried to, I—"

"Siena." Jason interrupts my rambling. He puts his hands on both my shoulders and the weight of them is comforting. "It's okay, I believe you." He looks deep in my eyes as he says it, and my stomach tightens. "It wasn't your fault. You don't deserve any of what Brandon did. I'm sorry you had to go through that Saturday, and this morning."

My voice is weak when I say, "Thank you for standing up to him."

His jaw clenches again. "Don't thank me for that."

"How is your eye?" I ask, my finger gently skimming the edge of the bruise before I can think through whether

I should be touching him or not. He doesn't flinch or pull away, but he drops his hands from my shoulders, and I miss their weight immediately.

"It's fine," he answers briskly.

I drop my fingers from his soft skin. "Does it hurt?"

"Not at all."

He's lying for me, I realize, and the thought makes me warm.

"Did you get in trouble?" I ask as he shifts into gear and pulls out of the dark parking lot.

"For what?"

I stare at him incredulously. "You know, for getting in a fight in the middle of the hall and getting suspended?"

"Oh, no. Natalia's really chill, especially since her son, Mason, has done way worse. The only scolding I got was from Aiden who said, and I quote, 'Next time make sure the principal isn't coming first.'"

He doesn't laugh, which means he's being completely serious, but then I feel like that's to be expected of an older brother who taught you how to hotwire cars and drag race before you were even old enough to legally drive.

"Well, I mean, he isn't wrong." I give a nervous laugh, wondering what my own mother would've said about it. She probably wouldn't have reacted the way Dario did, that's for sure.

"Did you get in trouble?" he asks, sparing me a glance as he changes lanes.

"Yeah, Dario was pretty mad, I'm grounded for a week."

He knows I'm not telling the whole truth, that there's more to it, but he doesn't push me. "That bad, huh?"

"Yeah. And Gia hates me."

"She's on Brandon's side?"

"No. She's on Brianna's side, and *she's* on Brandon's side. Plus, apparently I embarrassed her. All day people were going up to her asking her if I would have a threesome with them like I supposedly did with you and Brandon." That had been in one of the texts she sent before I turned my phone off.

Jason curses, and his face morphs with disgust. "Kids are so screwed up. I'll find out who's saying those things and threaten them until they shut the fuck up about it. And I don't make idle threats, if I tell them to stop, they'll do it, even if I have to get suspended again."

"No, you won't, Jason," I tell him, not because I don't believe him—something tells me he would—but because I don't want him to get in more trouble for me.

"I can, and I will."

"I don't want you to," I amend, adding, "Thank you, but it's not your fault. Kids will grow tired of it and move on to the next thing eventually."

He scowls. "Doesn't mean I can't be pissed about it."

And it's clear that he is pissed . . . pissed on my behalf. Butterflies erupt in my stomach.

After a few moments of us sitting in silence, or rather, me trying to push away the butterflies and Jason stewing as he makes random turns on the road, he softly says, "I'm sorry Gia's upset with you. I'm sure she'll come around eventually."

Will she? It seems like she's all too happy to be upset with me, whereas before we were best friends, always.

"You don't think so?" he asks, his eyes scanning my face.

"I don't know. Our relationship feels so strained since LA, since I was, you know . . . arrested."

He nods attentively, like he really doesn't care that I killed a guy. *I killed a guy too. You're not that special.* He had joked about it when I told him. In fact, since I told him, he hasn't treated me any differently than before. He's probably been *nicer* to me since then, but that's only because we've gotten to know each other more.

"Well, why do you think that is?"

"I don't know," I tell him honestly. "I think she's just trying to process everything." I tread carefully, walking that line between keeping my secrets with Gia and being honest with Jason. "I was basically her mother when we lived in LA. After what happened with Stan, when she needed me the most, I couldn't be there. I think she's turned to other things, to partying, her friends, keeping busy, to help her cope. And now that I'm back, resuming the mothering, I'm cramping her new coping style."

"Do you think maybe she's still processing and doesn't know how to tell you what she needs?"

"Maybe," I concede, as Jason pulls into a parking lot. "But the way it's been going with me showing up and ruining the fun at her parties and now apparently embarrassing her at school, I'm not sure she'll open up to me anytime soon."

Jason puts the car in park and turns in his seat to look at me. "You're doing your best to take care of your little sister, it's really admirable."

I blush and look down at my hands in my lap. "I don't think she sees it that way."

Jason's quiet for a moment, and I can feel the searing heat of his gaze on my face before he finally says, "I may look like I have my shit together now, but I had a really rocky childhood."

Surprised by the words, I look at him, shifting my whole body in the seat to properly face him as he continues. "Our mom died when we were young, leaving us with a stepfather who used to throw Aiden around. Aiden thought he was hiding it from me and Jackson, taking the abuse all by himself, but we knew what was happening, even if we were too small to really understand."

"Oh, Jason," I say softly, and instinctively reach out to take his hands in mine. He lets me, wrapping his warm fingers around mine.

"It's not all bad. Greg went to jail, we lived with Aiden, albeit illegally since he technically wasn't our guardian. He wasn't even eighteen yet, but the three of us were happy. He did a lot to keep us safe. He was the only thing standing between me and a shitty life, and he always protected me and Jackson and tried to make our life as good as he could. He protected us from Greg, from his ex-wife, who technically had custody, and from our real father, when he came crawling out of whatever hole he was in and tried to have us killed when Aiden caused too many problems for him."

I gasp, squeezing his hands tighter. His biological father tried to have them *killed*? "What happened?"

"That's a story for another day. But Aiden saved us, or rather, he and his now-fiancé, Thea, saved us. Andrew, my biological father, is in jail, and Greg is dead. Aiden's graduated from law school and Natalia legally adopted us, so yeah, happy ending I guess."

I don't even know what to say, just stare at Jason with a lump in my throat and force my eyes not to water.

Jason quickly adds, "I'm not saying all this because I want you to feel bad for me, really, I'm lucky everything happened the way it did." He squeezes my hand and gives me a small smile, one that makes him too handsome for his own good. "I'm telling you because Aiden did everything he could to protect me and Jackson. We never realized it at the time, but looking back now that I'm older, I understand what he did for us. I know it's hard now and Gia's mad, but one day she'll look back and realize how lucky she is to have a big sister who loves her and protects her."

Now my eyes really do water, but I take a deep breath before I start crying and freak Jason out. "I try," I whisper.

He scans my face, and even though *he's* the one who just opened up, I feel vulnerable.

"Hold on," he says, releasing my hand then exiting the

car. I sit there, confused and emotional for some reason, when my door pops open. "Come on," he orders, reaching out a hand for me to take. I do, and then I'm out of the car and wrapped in his embrace.

I've been in Jason's arms before, when we were dancing in the rain, but that felt different. I hold him close to me, feeling tiny in his embrace, completely engulfed by him, and burrow my face in his thick sweater. He smells amazing, like cedarwood and something spicy and something entirely him. He's warm and solid and comforting, and every part of him pressed up against me fits perfectly, making me feel right at home in his arms. I don't think I'll ever want to let go. In fact, I think I'm going to make up an excuse to hug him at every opportunity possible from now on.

"You're doing your best," Jason assures me, holding me tighter. "Gia will see that eventually. Don't be so hard on yourself, and don't forget to put *yourself* first sometimes."

I shift to look up at him, my chin resting against his hard chest. His face is so close to mine, and my breath hitches. "How do you know I don't put myself first?"

He smirks and pushes a piece of my hair away from my face. His touch leaves tingles in its wake. "Call it an educated hunch."

"Do you mean an educated guess?"

"No." He smiles, returning his hand to my back, and my hands bunch in his sweater, holding him close to me. I don't care that we're just standing here, holding each other, in a random deserted parking lot. I never feel *good* like I do when I'm with Jason, like I can just be myself and not worry about him thinking badly of me or scaring him away. None of my problems matter if he's here with me.

His smile drops and his face turns serious, his intense eyes commanding my attention. "You really need to stop staring at me," he says, his voice deep and low.

I didn't realize I was doing that. "Why?"

His gaze is unwavering when he says, "Because I might get the wrong idea about what you're thinking about me."

My heart beats hard in my chest, and I'm worried he can feel it. Since we're being honest tonight, I decide to continue the trend, even though it terrifies me. "I think you're the best thing that's happened to me since moving here," I whisper, and Jason's smile is so beautiful it hurts.

"Even though I kidnapped you and got you involved in a high-speed police chase?" he teases, using the words I said to him that first time.

"Especially because you did that." I laugh, and so does he, and the sound is glorious. I can listen to Jason laugh all day as long as he's looking at me like that, like I'm the only thing that matters.

I draw my arms in and move them over his, so I can wrap them around his neck. He shifts too, lowering his arms slightly and pulling me even closer, if that was possible, so now I'm flush with him as I tilt my head up to look at him. His lips are so close to mine, all he'd have to do is lower his head and they'd be touching, and I suddenly realize just how much I want him to do that, how much I want him to kiss me.

His eyelids are heavy as he leans in, and so much anticipation builds in my stomach it might burst. My eyes flutter closed as his lips graze mine, gently, just barely touching me, and just when I think I can't take it anymore, he grips my hips and yanks me to him, pressing his lips to mine. I melt into him, and when our lips part he deepens the kiss with an urgent fervor. His touch ignites me all the way to my core, and my fingers grip his short hair, holding him just as possessively as he's holding me. This is everything I would have imagined a kiss from Jason Parker to be: intense, deep, and utterly addicting. I never want to stop. In fact, as he groans and intensifies the kiss, I'm struck with the thought that I'm upset we haven't been doing this already.

A car alarm near us goes off, making me jump and ending the kiss. There are a bunch of kids across the parking lot from us, and they laugh as they turn the alarm off and get into the car, completely oblivious to the fact that my world is tilting on its axis after that kiss.

I look back at Jason, but he's already gazing down at me. I'm still in his embrace, and I could snuggle up against his hard chest and stay here forever.

Once my brain clears and I'm able to find my voice, I ask, "What are we doing here, anyway?"

He blinks a few times and glances around, like he's confused even though he's the one that brought us here. He tucks my hair behind my ear again, an action I'll never get sick of, and sheepishly drops his arms. I immediately feel cold even though the wind isn't too bad.

"Right, um, you said you didn't want to go home, so I figured I'd take you for ice cream. They close in about . . . ten minutes though, so we should really head in."

He gestures to a building that I never even noticed. There's a sign outside that reads "Sweetie's Ice Cream Parlor," and it looks like the place has a retro vibe to it.

When I just stare at it, he asks, "You do like ice cream, right?"

"Yes, I like ice cream." I laugh. "It's just very thoughtful of you. Thank you, Jason."

He smiles at me, and I bask in its brilliance. He's been doing that more freely lately, and I'm getting used to it.

"Well, come on then, before they lock the doors on us." He grabs my hand, twining his fingers with mine, and even though we just had a mini make-out session, the way he holds my hand like it's the most natural thing in the world makes me blush.

To distract myself from thinking about exactly where else I'd like to feel his steady hands, I say, "We're those people who come in at the last minute while the workers are trying to close, aren't we?"

He laughs as he leads me to the door. From here, I can see that there are still a few people lingering inside, so I feel a bit better about going in at the last second before closing.

"Hey, after the day we had," he says, "I think we deserve some ice cream."

I laugh with him, because he's not wrong. But, now that I'm here, with Jason, I don't necessarily feel the heavy weight on my shoulders that's been sitting there all day. I was suspended and basically told I would be shipped away from Gia, but the worry I was feeling before isn't as prominent anymore. Is that all I need to clear my mind for a bit? Jason and ice cream?

He holds the door open for me with his free hand, but I tug him to a stop.

"Hey Jason," I say, heat creeping up my neck. I'm not used to being this vulnerable, but it's important for me to tell him. "Thank you for today, and for always . . . being there for me. It means a lot."

His eyes soften as he takes me in. "Well, someone has to make sure you're wearing shoes and not lying in the middle of the road."

I laugh and playfully shove him. "I'm being serious!"

"I am too," he agrees, and the weirdness I was feeling at being open with him disappears. I don't know how he knows how and when to do that, to joke and put me at ease, but he does, and it works every time.

But before he derails me too much, I squeeze his hand and add, "And thank you for opening up to me about your family and childhood." I feel like that's not something he tells a lot of people, and for me to be someone he finds worthy enough to tell, means everything to me.

Jason nods and gestures with his head into the ice cream parlor. "Let's get some ice cream before the clock strikes twelve and they kick us out."

We hold hands the entire time we order, only dropping

them when he pays for both of us and when we go back to his car to enjoy the ice cream. Apparently, it's a big deal that he's letting me eat in here—no one gets that special treatment, not even his twin. But as we talk about nothing and everything and enjoy our ice creams in his car with the windows open, I decide I like getting special treatment from Jason Parker. Even if I have to go home and endure a week of boredom, Zia Stella's silent judgment, Gia's attitude, and Dario's disgust, I know it won't be bad because I have Jason, and he has me. He'll always be there, I know that's true, just as I now know what his kisses are like, and know there's no way I'm letting him drop me off at home without tasting his lips one more time.

sixteen

The only good part about being suspended is that I don't have to hear all the rumors at school about me and Brandon and Jason. There are apparently no limits to a teenager's imagination when it comes to gossip, because Nyah's told me many, many different iterations of what happened Monday and why. At first it bothered me, but as the days went on and the rumors got more and more ridiculous, I stopped caring as much. People are going to talk, and I guess stupid rumors about boys go hand in hand with living a normal teenage life, which is what I've been hoping for since I moved to King. In some twisted way, I guess I really *am* living a normal life here, which is all I've asked for.

Jason doesn't care either. He said no one would be brave enough to say anything to his face on Monday, so not to worry about it. We've been texting and talking over the phone throughout the week, and he drives me to work and back home, even though I always protest. I tell him I can walk and not to worry about driving me around, but he always shows up in my driveway right before I'm ready to leave, and he's always waiting in the parking lot for me at the end of my shift, sometimes with an ice cream in his hand if he knows it was a crazy busy day. I can really get used to this, especially when he walks me to the front door when he drops me off and kisses me. In fact, despite feeling bad that he waits outside for me to finish my shift every night, sometimes I don't protest *too* hard, and not just for the good-night kiss I fantasize about all day. One time, we were out there for so long, Dario flashed the lights at us. Like flicked the porch lights on and off a bunch of times like parents do in the *movies*. I don't know how long he waited for us, and he did nothing but give me a grimace when I came in, but I definitely didn't win any brownie points with him that day.

Gia has been . . . Gia. It's hard to really tell how she feels, because when she's at school I'm at home, and when she's at home, I'm at work. Besides, I'm upset that she didn't take my side, didn't bother trying to hear me out about what happened, and I'm still hurt by her saying she wished it was me who disappeared instead of Lily. Neither of us is ready to forgive the other.

Now that it's Friday, I can hear Gia fluttering around in her room through the wall, getting ready for homecoming. I'm not allowed to go, because I'm suspended, and as much as I would've enjoyed the experience, Jason can't go either, so I don't really care. Nyah is bummed I'm not going with her, though, and since there's going to be a little tribute to Lily, who would've been on the planning committee, I know Nyah could've used the extra support. She messages me throughout the day, asking for my opinion on outfit choices.

These earrings or the gold ones?

The heels with the straps or the closed toe ones?

And even, The panties with the lace or the red skimpy ones?

I don't know how much help I am or if she even takes my suggestions, but it's fun to be part of the process anyway. I've never gotten ready for an event with friends before, and this was a mini taste of it.

She and Warren have been trying to convince me to come to the afterparty all week, but I've been using the "I'm grounded" excuse. I *am* grounded, but I also don't want to go. Warren throws a party every week—apparently he's bored in that mansion without his parents home and they don't care how much money he spends throwing them—so I don't think it'll matter if I skip out on this one, especially because it's a motel party. All the seniors rented out the rooms in a small middle-of-nowhere motel on the edge of King City. Nyah explained that they've rented out the entire motel, and that everyone runs room to room drinking and hanging out, then has a place to crash afterward. That does *not* sound like fun to me, but they do it every year.

Jason asked me if I wanted to go, and I said I didn't. I don't want Dario even more upset with me than he already is. Sneaking out to a party while I'm grounded and coming back smelling like alcohol and cigarettes like he criticized me for doing, even when I didn't do any of that, would not help things. Or if I ended up crashing in Nyah's room like she offered and *didn't* come home at all. *That* would definitely be worse. Very Florence-like, and while I don't think there's much I can do to make him change his opinion of me when his mind is set, I don't want to give him any more reasons to ship me to New York.

As I walk down the hall to get some water, Gia's door opens. She's holding her heels in her hand, along with a pretty clutch Zia Stella must have lent her. She's in a purple dress that hugs her body with some shimmery material, and she looks beautiful in it. In fact, she looks beautiful, period. Her thick, short brown hair is styled to fall perfectly over her forehead, and her eyes are smoked out with dark shadow, making them seem deep and soulful. It's sad, in a way, to see Gia all grown up like this, but at the same time she's still my little sister who I taught to ride a bike and cut the crusts off sandwiches for and built pillow forts with.

"Hey," I greet when we stand there staring at each other. We're both still pissed, but I can't help adding, "You look beautiful."

"Thanks," she says, her voice softening a bit when she asks, "Are you sad you're not coming?"

A little, but I wave her off. "Nah. I've got a lot of homework to catch up on anyway."

Her phone pings, and she glances at the screen. "It's Chris. They're outside."

"Okay, have fun," I tell her, meaning it. Gia deserves to have this normal teenage experience with her friends. "Are you going to an afterparty before the sleepover?"

Her back stiffens. Dario somehow still doesn't know that Gia's the one who's been going out to parties and coming home drunk, and I'd rather keep it that way. Gia has it good here, and I want her to stay here as long as possible, even . . . even if that means it's without me.

"Why? You gonna show up covered in mud and embarrass me?" She scowls and rushes down the stairs, eager to get away from me, I guess.

I sigh and return to my room. Through my open window, I can hear Gia squealing with her friends over the loud music pumping from the car. Then a car door slams, and the music recedes, and she's gone.

If Gia wants to go to an afterparty, there's really nothing I can do to stop her short of showing up covered in mud and embarrassing her like she said. I only hope she's not going to the motel party. Nyah said it's mostly seniors, but they can't exactly stop people who aren't seniors from showing up or from booking rooms.

I spend the rest of the evening in my room, trying to do math homework because I wasn't lying to Gia when I said I had a lot to catch up on. I already didn't really understand what was going on, and it doesn't help that now I'm behind everyone. I check my phone every once in a while and see the pictures that people are posting. Nyah looks beautiful in the dress I helped her pick, and even has little gold accessories in her box braids that pair perfectly with her outfit. She sends me pictures of her and Tyler, whose tie matches Nyah's deep-red dress, and it makes me smile. Jackson looks so handsome in his dress pants and dress shirt, and I can just imagine what Jason would've looked like, all dressed up.

Everyone looks like they're having fun, and I try not to be bitter about it. Jason took an extra shift at the shop today and will be getting off sometime soon, so I can't even talk to him to distract myself. As I'm looking at the photos people have started posting from the motel party, my phone rings.

It's Anusha.

I've been avoiding her all week. Our scheduled call is tomorrow morning, but I guess since I'm trying to distract myself, now is as good of a time as ever to talk to her. Maybe I'll even feel a little better.

"Hello?"

"Siena." She sounds almost surprised, or at least, as surprised as she can with her neutral tone. She must've thought

I wouldn't pick up again. "I've been trying to reach you."

"I know, I'm sorry. I've been busy trying to catch up on schoolwork." Kind of a lie, but not too much of a stretch.

She ponders this for a moment before she asks, "Because you've been suspended?"

The way she says it makes my defenses rise instantly. "Yes. You already know I have been. You've been talking to Dario."

Anusha is quiet again, and I don't volunteer to fill in the silence. Finally, she says, "Siena, I want you to know that what we talk about in these sessions is completely confidential."

I say nothing, still stewing.

"But," she continues, "you're a minor, and I'm obligated to speak to concerned parents and guardians."

"You told Dario to get rid of me!" I accuse, the anger I've been holding toward her all week bubbling to the surface. I know I'm just another kid on Anusha's long roster of clients, but for her to even suggest I should move away from Gia, knowing how much I value my relationship with her, is a complete betrayal.

"I didn't tell him to do that," she says calmly. "We've just been discussing how you've been adjusting in King City. It must be hard to go from LA to a new town after everything you've been through. How do you feel you're adjusting?"

"Don't goad me into giving you more ammunition to justify shipping me away!" I jump up from my seat, anger pumping through me. That's how it works. She asks me questions to get me to say things I'd never normally admit. That's therapy, sure, but not when she's pushing me into answering specific questions when she already has the answer in mind.

"That's not what I'm doing, Siena." Anusha doesn't yell or get upset or do anything other than use her calm, neutral therapist tone, and the lack of emotion only pisses me off more. Does she not care that this is my *life*? Does she not care that she's the one standing between me and losing Gia? She's the one who's supposed to reassure Dario that I'm fit to stay here, that I'll adjust eventually, not tell him the easiest thing to do is throw me away and forget about me. "We're not making any decisions without you, Siena. We're just thinking about what would be best for you, and for Gia."

I can't stop pacing. I'm so angry I can't even bite my nails because my hands are shaking. "Don't you dare tell me that going away is the best thing for Gia!"

"We're just discussing options, Siena," she repeats for what seems like the hundredth time, but it doesn't seem true. From where I'm sitting, it seems like she and Dario have already made up their minds and are just waiting to see how it plays out.

I don't know why I thought answering Anusha would make me feel better. It hasn't. I feel worse. I feel sad and angry and upset and just so fucking frustrated.

Arguing with her isn't going to change anything, so I say, "I've got to go, goodbye, Anusha."

I hang up on her before she has the chance to say

anything and continue pacing in my room. As annoying as my calls with Anusha are, I enjoyed talking with her. I enjoyed talking to someone who would listen to me, who would *understand* me, even if she was being paid to do so. But it's not even that she's suggesting moving me from King—she could suggest I move to Alaska for all I care—it's that she's suggesting I be separated from Gia. Sure, we're pissed at each other right now, but that doesn't mean she's not my little sister, and that's something that will never change.

My phone rings again. This time it's Jason.

I take a few deep breaths to try to calm myself down before answering. "Hey."

"Is everything okay?" he asks, and I wonder how he knew right away with that one word.

"Yes. No. I don't know."

"Okay, well . . . I just showered from work, and I know you're grounded but I'm not really doing anything if you want to—"

"Let's go to the motel party."

He's silent for a moment. "The motel party? I thought you didn't want to go to that?"

I don't really, but I don't want to be home anymore, and I don't want to think about all the emotions coursing through me. A motel party sounds like a perfect distraction. Plus, if Dario and Anusha are going to nail me for going to parties, then I might as well *attend* one.

"I do now. Do you?"

"Sure," he answers. "Jackson's going to be happy. I'll be there in ten."

We hang up and I change out of my pajamas and into jeans and a cute, fitted sweater. I don't know if Jason wasn't going to the party because I couldn't. It's not like we're boyfriend and girlfriend and he felt like he *couldn't* go without me, but I did wonder if he wasn't going because he felt bad. At least now, Jason will get to go if that's what he really wanted, and I get to be surrounded by people and not think about everything going on in my life.

Dario's in his den with some game blasting on the TV, so I close my bedroom door and tiptoe down the stairs, slipping out the door with my shoes in my hand. I get my shoes on before Jason can scold me, and walk down the street, texting Jason to meet me in front of a neighbor's house so his car doesn't alert Dario. He'll probably find out eventually, but I'll deal with that later.

Jason pulls up to the house a few doors down from mine in record time, and I hop in. The window's already open for me. It's a nice night, still warm even though it's almost October, and the sky is clear, giving me a clear view for stars.

Jason looks handsome, like always, and his hair is still damp from his shower. He doesn't push me to open up about what's wrong, and I always appreciate that. He knows that what I need most is for him to just be here with me, and I'm so grateful to him for that it makes my chest hurt.

He tells me about work and about his adoptive brother,

Mason, and Mason's half sister, Mia, who's only six and already cursing, because she heard Mason and his friend Noah one time and now can't stop telling everyone to fuck off, which got her in trouble in kindergarten the other day. I laugh and listen to him talk, already feeling better just losing myself in his deep voice and stories, and after forty minutes, we're pulling up to the motel.

It really is in the middle of nowhere. There's a dirt road leading to the parking lot, which isn't paved either. It's two stories high, and at least it doesn't look like a complete dump. All the doors to the rooms are located outside, and most of them are open. Kids are *everywhere*—leaning on the railings outside, hanging out, coming in and out of rooms, sitting in soccer chairs in the parking lot or in front of the room doors. There's even an empty field behind the motel where it looks like people have set up chairs and are hanging out in small social circles. It really does seem like every senior at King City is here, and even some people who aren't seniors.

Jason parks in a free spot, and I follow him out. There's music blaring from somewhere, and it seems that there are different songs blasting in every room, making the outside a jumbled medley of sounds, only overpowered by the speakers of the kids sitting in circles in the parking lot. It's a little overwhelming for the senses.

I hadn't told Nyah or Warren that I changed my mind and decided to come, but Jason said he told Jackson, who'd probably tell Tyler, who'd definitely tell his girlfriend.

Jason takes my hand like it's the most natural thing in the world and leads me through the crowds. People greet us, holding up whatever alcoholic beverage they have in their hands, asking us to join them, but Jason says some placating thing about finding them later and leads me to the second floor. We enter one of the rooms where Jackson's sitting on the floor in a circle with a bunch of other people. They're holding cards and there are poker chips in front of them, as well as beer bottles.

"Jason!" Jackson jumps up, enveloping his twin in a hug, then me. "Great timing. *Thompson* is cheating at Hold'em, and I'm the only one calling him out on it."

"That's because I'm not cheating," Thompson replies from where he's sitting on the floor between two girls, his own cards in his hands.

"He totally is," Jackson tells me before shifting his attention to his brother. "There are a lot of people here," he starts warily. "If you're going to fight, can you at least let me know this time so I can join in? I can't have your back if I can't see it."

Jason shoves his brother, but it's playful. "Don't worry, no fights. But on a separate note, is Brandon here?"

Jackson groans. "What did I just say?"

"And I just said it's on a *separate* note."

Jackson's not amused. "I haven't seen him, but Warren said he heard Brandon got a room to crash in after, so he'll be around eventually. *Text me* if you're feeling an itch to fight, and I'll come find you."

Jason rolls his eyes, but he's not really annoyed. He loves his brother—it's obvious. "I don't need your help in a fight."

"Well, *duh*. Doesn't mean I'm going to let you have all the fun." Jackson's smile is wide and only slightly drunk.

Jason claps his twin on the back. "Relax, brother. We're here for fun, right, Siena?"

"Mmm-hmm," I nod, trying to appear innocent. We didn't come here with any intentions to fight, but I'm not sure what would happen if I did see Brandon, if he did make another comment about me. There's no principal around this time, and that was Aiden's one requirement for his brother regarding fighting.

"Jackson," one of the girls calls from the floor. She has the biggest pile of poker chips. "We have a *game* going here."

"Right, right," he answers, sending Jason one last warning look. "I'm serious. I've got your back, always."

His words hit me hard. He means them, and I know Jason would do the same for his brother. They really, unconditionally have each other's backs, and it's touching to see. I'd do the same for Gia. I bet if I told Jason and Jackson that Dario was thinking of splitting me and Gia up, they'd get why I'm so enraged.

Jackson sits back down and exclaims, "Thompson, you fucker, I *know* you skimmed some chips off my pile."

"What? Did you count them or something?"

"You didn't have any blues before, and now my blue pile is *gone*."

They go back and forth while Jason guides me out of the

room. We sidestep a group of people who've set up a beer pong table right outside Jackson's door and continue down the outdoor hall. Even though it's dark out, there's plenty of light from all the open doors, plus some car headlights and the glow from the motel sign itself.

I don't know where Jason's leading me, but I don't really care. I'm just happy not to be home. He occasionally checks his phone as we weave through the crowds of people on the upper-level balcony. As we pass, some people whisper about us. They're either wondering who I am holding hands with the hottest guy in school, or they're still talking about the incident on Monday. No one says anything loud enough for us to really know what they're saying, but when it's clear they're talking about us, Jason glares at them until they duck away.

It's a lot calmer at the ends of the motel where the stairs are. It seems like most of the party is converged on both floors in the middle of the long rectangular building. Some of the last room doors are closed, and people are smoking on the dark staircase.

We pause in the hall before going down the stairs, and Jason strikes up a conversation with some people. They look familiar—I think they were at Jason's race, and one of the girls is in my history class.

They talk, and I even contribute once in a while. The whole time, Jason's hand is in mine, and no one asks us about the fight Monday or any of the rumors. It's kind of fun, being at a party, holding hands with Jason, having a conversation with people I just met. It seems . . . normal.

A voice calls, "Jason! Siena! When the hell did you get here?"

It's Warren, and his arms are spread wide, just like the smile on his face. He engulfs Jason in a bro hug. To me he says, "Nyah's around here somewhere. She said she's saving you all the pomegranate vodka sodas. But between me and you, you better get there quick because once the guys run out of beers to shotgun, they always go for the vodka sodas."

My nose wrinkles just imagining how much the bubbles would sting from chugging a vodka soda through a hole at the bottom of the can.

"Let me find out where she is then," I tell him, pulling out my phone and sending Nyah a quick text. My phone rings right away, but it's not Nyah, it's Gia.

I frown at my phone. Gia hasn't called me since I moved here, and she's currently pissed at me.

I answer the call. "Hello?"

"Siena, oh thank God!" Her urgency and frantic tone immediately puts me on alert.

"What's wrong?"

"Siena—I—I didn't mean to," she cries, mumbling something that I can't make out through the sobs.

"Gia? What's going on?" I've never heard Gia like this, at least not since Stan, and I'm starting to panic. She sounds terrified.

"Can you come here? Right now? Alone."

"Where are you? I'll order an Uber right now."

She sniffles, trying to calm down. "I'm . . . I'm at the motel party."

I freeze. The group around me carries on their conversation, but Jason catches my eye.

Gia's *here*? She told Dario she was having a sleepover at Brianna's house; her parents even confirmed it with him! I want to get mad, but I force myself to remain calm since Gia sounds so freaked out.

"I'm here too. Where are you?"

Jason raises an eyebrow at me, probably wondering what's going on.

"Room 114," Gia says. "Please hurry."

"Okay, I'm coming."

"ALONE!" she shouts quickly, then lowers her tone and repeats, "Alone."

"Okay, okay. I'll be right there."

She hangs up on me, and I shove my phone back into my pocket.

Jason moves around the group and asks, "Is everything okay?"

"I don't know," I tell him honestly. "Gia just called me freaking out and telling me to come to room 114."

The concern in his eyes makes my heart beat even faster. "Okay, let's go."

"No." I put a hand on his arm to stop him. "She told me to come alone." He frowns at me, and I add, "It's probably a girl emergency. I'll come back and find you."

I can tell he's going to want to walk me to the room,

because he's a gentleman, but Gia said to come alone, and she trusted me enough to call me. "I'll text you when I'm there, okay?" I say, rushing away before he can protest.

"Fine, text me!" he calls after me, and I shoot him a small smile before I'm charging to the stairs.

My mind runs through the different scenarios of what I'll find when I get to the room. Did she and Brianna get in a fight? Did she get drunk and throw up everywhere? No, she didn't sound drunk, so that can't be it. Did she see Mom? I rush faster, reading the room numbers.

Room 114 is at the end of the motel in a dark, quiet section. There aren't any kids here, and that gives me the creeps. I text Jason as soon as the door comes into view, then try the door. It's locked, so I knock and call, "Gia? Gia, it's m—"

The door swings open, and I'm pulled into the room.

"Siena!" Gia cries, throwing her arms around me. She buries her face in my neck and sobs as the door slams shut behind me.

I'm taken off guard for a moment before slowly wrapping my arms around her.

"I—didn't mean it, Siena, I swear! It was an accident, I just wanted him off me," she says through her tears. I don't know what she's saying, but it's clear she's in shock.

"It's okay," I comfort, pulling back a little to see her. She's changed from her homecoming dress to a fitted green sweater and ripped jeans. Her makeup is the same, except now it's all smudged from crying. "Just take a breath and tell me what you're talking about."

Gia sniffles, trying to calm down, then releases me and steps aside.

I turn, following her gaze, and look down. My heart stops.

There, lying on the floor beside the window in a pool of blood, is Brandon.

Dead.

seventeen

I look from the body, Brandon's body, surrounded by blood and towels on the floor, to Gia, who's fidgeting with the sleeves of her sweater.

I want to panic. I *really* want to panic, but Gia's so freaked out I force myself to ask as calmly as I can, "What happened?"

She rubs a hand down her face, smearing her makeup even more. "I—I wanted a fake ID to get into Limelight this week. Brandon told me he could get me one and to meet him here, but we were all alone in this room and he grabbed me and tried to . . ." She cuts herself off with a half sob, like she wants to cry but she's trying to hold it together. "He tried to . . ."

"It's okay, Gia," I say, putting the pieces together. I've been alone in a bedroom with Brandon before—I know exactly how this story ends. "I believe you."

"It just . . . it reminded me so much of Stan, and I . . . I just wanted Brandon *off* so I grabbed the vase and swung it at him but it shattered and shards went into his head and now he's . . ." She crouches on the floor, leaning her elbows on her knees and her head in her hands. "I didn't mean to kill Brandon, I promise, just like I didn't mean to kill Stan. I didn't mean it, Siena, I swear . . ." She starts crying again and I pace the room, feeling useless that I can't undo this for her, upset that Brandon tried something with her, and panicked because my little sister just killed another person within a two-month time frame.

When I walked into our shared room after work that day in LA just in time to see Gia plunge a knife into Stan Roven's neck, I didn't know what to do. I wanted to protect her, but Stan was already dead, and I couldn't undo that. So, I protected her the only way I knew how, by wiping her prints off the knife and taking the blame. I thought I was helping her, thought she'd be able to live a normal life, but here we are again, in the same predicament, with another dead man. It's not her fault Brandon forced himself on her, just like it wasn't her fault Stan did the same, but now another man is dead, and I don't know how to fix it.

"Okay, okay, let me think. Did you call the police?"

"No!" she exclaims, standing up. "I can't go to jail! I couldn't the first time and I can't now. I'm not strong like you, Siena, and even you just barely survived it. You're still all fucked up about being inside without a window open."

Her words are a surprise to me; I didn't think Gia paid that much attention to me, but I force myself to really take in the scene in front of me. There's a trail of blood, and it's clear that where Brandon's lying now isn't where he first fell. "Did you move the body?" I ask.

Her lip quivers as she nods. "I tried to clean it up and, I don't know, roll him up in the rug or something like they do in the movies, but I was crying and couldn't see anything, and I don't want to be arrested!"

Shit. I need to think, but it's hard when it feels like I'm underwater and my brain feels fuzzy. "Okay. Okay, okay."

"Stop saying okay!"

I stop pacing, my flitting eyes landing on the flimsy curtains in front of the window, which Brandon's body is lying right under.

"Okay, maybe let's just . . . let's move him away from the door and window at least, to give me more time to think. Those curtains look way too thin."

She nods, seeming to calm down now that she has a task to focus on. I have no idea if this is the right call, but Gia's freaking out, and she needs to feel like I have this under control while I think about how to handle this in the way that fucks us the least.

Gia moves to the body, then looks at me as if awaiting more instructions.

"Um, grab a leg, I guess."

I force myself closer to the body, but I refuse to look closely at Brandon's face. I don't want to see what expression he's making, don't want to see the pale color of his skin. I have enough nightmares about Stan already, and I didn't even know him. I don't want to add Brandon to the list.

We each pick up a leg. He's a large guy, and even a leg is heavy.

"On three," I instruct, gripping the leg tighter. "One, two—"

"Siena?" a voice calls out along with a knock on the door, and then the door swings open.

Jason's there, standing on the threshold, stock-still with his hand on the doorknob, taking in the scene of Gia and me, frozen over a dead body, holding a leg each.

His eyes grow wide, and Gia and I both drop Brandon's legs and take a step back. I slide in front of Gia, as if I can shield Jason from the scene, and declare, "I did it."

Jason takes everything in, from the body to the mess and towels on the floor, to Gia and me standing there looking incredibly guilty. His jaw ticks as he looks over our terrified faces, and for a moment we just stare at each other.

This is it. It's over. Not only will Jason never look at me the same again, but he's about to run out of here and get my little sister arrested.

Just when I'm sure he's going to hightail it out of here,

Jason groans and runs his hands through his hair, clenching his fingers to pull at his roots. "Shit, SHIT! Not again."

Again?

Gia and I exchange a panicked look before Jason drops his hands, and an authoritative demeanor comes over him. It's a visible shift as he fully enters the room and locks the door behind him.

"Okay, let me think . . ." His eyes bounce around the room, taking in the details. "How long ago?"

Gia and I exchange another look, because we both don't know what's going on. He's not running and calling the cops? He's not calling us murderers and proclaiming that he wants nothing to do with us?

"Come on, we have to act fast," he prompts, looking directly at Gia. Even though I said I did it, he knows. "How long ago?"

Gia's voice is small when she says, "Maybe five minutes ago? Less? Everything happened so fast."

"All right." Jason nods slowly, his eyes calculating. "And in that time, you moved the body, tried to clean it up, and called Siena, right?"

Instead of calling an ambulance. That's what he's not saying, and Gia hears it too. Her lips tremble as she tries to hold in a sob, and Jason takes that as confirmation.

"Fuck. Okay." He pulls out his phone and puts his finger over his lips to signal to us to be quiet, putting the phone on Speaker.

It rings a few times before a deep voice answers. "Hello?"

"Hey, Aiden," Jason greets, sounding completely normal. Like everything is fine, and he's not helping us try to figure out how to hide a crime scene. "Settle a bet for me. I said you'd know this because, you know, you're a criminal lawyer."

"Well, I've only just taken the bar but—"

"Yeah, yeah, whatever." Jason cuts his older brother off. "Anyway, if you killed someone but then called other people before the ambulance, that ruins your case for self-defense, right?"

"Well, it doesn't help. Especially if you tried to clean up or moved the body."

Gia inhales sharply beside me and clutches my hand, squeezing tight, while I survey the crime scene that we very clearly tried to hide.

Jason nods, more to himself since his brother can't see him, as he processes. "Okay, okay. What about bleach? Does that kill all the DNA? Is there a certain kind you're supposed to use or just any old household bleach?"

Aiden's quiet for a moment before asking in a low voice, "Is there something you want to tell me? Should I come down there?"

"What? No," Jason says, only slightly too quickly. "Don't be ridiculous, just settling a bet."

"Jason, please—"

"Oh, got another call! Thanks Aiden, talk later! Bye!" Jason ends the call and stuffs his phone in his pocket. "Well, fuck."

Gia, who's managed to contain herself through the whole call, finally lets loose her cry. "I'm going to jail!"

She drops my hand, pulling me in for a hug instead.

"Did anyone know you were here?" Jason asks, crossing the room and kneeling beside Brandon.

"No. He told me to meet him here and not to tell anyone since fake IDs are illegal. I gave Brianna some stupid excuse and got a ride with Chris, so I guess Chris knows I'm here."

"So that—wait, did you see that?" Jason's not looking at us; he's crouched near Brandon's head, with two fingers on his neck.

I look at Brandon's face properly for the first time since I first walked in here. He's pale, but not as pale as I remember Stan being, and I stare hard, noticing the small movement of his chest rising and falling.

"Holy shit, he's alive!" I exclaim as Jason withdraws his hand.

"He has a pulse. It's weak, but it's there."

I sag in relief as Gia bursts into tears.

Jason presses one of the towels around the wound, but there's still glass sticking out of his head.

"Was I supposed to pull that out?" Gia asks weakly.

"No. It's good that you left it in. If you pulled it, he would've bled out," he tells her, trying to carefully arrange the towels around the glass without bumping it.

I'm still in shock. Brandon's *alive*, and I didn't even check! That should've been the first thing I did when I saw the body. Thank goodness Jason is here; we have more options now.

"I'm going to call an ambulance," I tell Gia, pulling my phone out, when she grabs my arm to stop me.

"But . . . but I'm not ready! They're going to arrest me for assaulting him, or if he doesn't make it . . . Oh God, if he doesn't make it . . . I'm not ready, Siena, I can't do it like you! I wasn't ready then, and I'm not ready n—"

"Gia!" I interrupt, grabbing her shoulders. She feels so small, so fragile, so *scared*. At this moment, she doesn't look fifteen. She looks like my baby sister, the one I taught to read and fought off bullies for and walked home from school with every day. She trembles as I hold her shoulders.

"Listen to me," I tell her, forcing myself to be calm, because one of us has to be in control here. "You were *never* in this room. I smashed the vase over his head, okay? Self-defense. If he survives, he might not remember who it was anyway, and even if he does remember it was you, I'm the one who called 911, and I'm the one who admitted to it and was here when the ambulance came."

She opens and closes her mouth. "You'd do that for me? Again?"

I pull her into a bone-crushing hug. Her heart is beating just as fast as mine. "Go get cleaned up, then join the party. Mingle, talk to everybody, especially people who know your name already. Be memorable, just in case." I hold her for only a few more moments, then push her away. "Go!"

Gia nods and runs out of the room without looking

back, closing the door behind her. I have no idea if I'm doing the right thing or not, but Brandon needs an ambulance, and I can't bear to force Gia to make that call. I'm her big sister, and I'll protect her to the very end, even if the thought of being arrested makes me feel like dry heaving and passing out.

Just as my shaking fingers start to dial 911, Jason's voice makes me freeze. "Hi, I need an ambulance at Moss View Motel immediately. Room 114. There's been a fight, and my friend has glass in his head."

I stare at him with my hand frozen mid-dial.

Jason continues, "No, I left the glass in . . . Me? Jason Parker. No, I'm here alone."

I gasp and run over to Jason. What is he *doing*? I grab his arm to shake him, but he doesn't budge as he listens to whatever the 911 operator is saying on the other end of the line.

"Ja—"

He covers my mouth with his free hand, cutting my panicked cries short. He looks straight into my eyes with this intense look that's filled with so many emotions I can't even begin to uncover them all and gives his head a small shake.

He's really going to do this; he's really going to take the fall for my sister, for *me*. I want to strangle him, I want to kiss him, I want to cry until time is rewound, and we're dancing in the rain again, worrying about nothing but living in the moment.

I don't hear the rest of what Jason says, just stand there with his hand over my mouth while static plays in my ears. I must be in shock, because I have no idea how much time passes until he hangs up. He must say something to me, because I hear my name, but I don't process it, don't process anything until he removes his hand, and it's like that action snaps me back into reality.

"Are you insane?" I yell at him. "What did you just do?"

Jason calmly replies, "I'm fixing the problem. Go with Gia. Do the same thing you told her to do. Be memorable. Get in some videos. I'll be fine."

"I'll be fine? *I'll be fine?*" I repeat, louder and more hysterical each time. "What the hell is wrong with you? You can't cover for me!"

"I can and I just did." He's still so calm and collected under all this pressure, it's a little irritating, but also weirdly reassuring. It makes me start to believe that he really does have this under control.

"But Jas—"

"You were already arrested and acquitted for killing a man in self-defense, Siena. If Brandon doesn't make it, what do you think is going to happen to you? You think a jury is going to think there were two self-defense accidents, even though there technically were?"

"I was acquitted, those documents are sealed . . ." I start but hesitate. I hadn't thought about that, and I don't know what would happen to those sealed documents if I were to be charged.

"Officer Liu found out; other people can find out. I don't know how it would work in court if you were charged, but what about after? What do you think is going to happen to you when people find out about this incident, what they'll say about you after *both* incidents, both of which you didn't even do. Are you prepared for that, Siena? About what people will say about you, think about you? What a future college or employer might think when they look you up? How it will impact everything you do moving forward?"

I say nothing because I *can't* say anything. I hate that he's probably right, but I hate that he's so willing to fall on the grenade for me.

"But if he dies they're going to charge you with *murder*, Jason! I don't want that for you!"

"Hit me," he demands, completely serious.

"What?"

"Hit me," he repeats, grabbing my hand and making it a fist. "Try to give me another black eye or a split lip."

"Are you *drunk*?" He didn't drink a single drop of alcohol the entire time we were together, so I have no idea what he's going on about.

"This is the best I can think of right now. Despite hating his guts, hopefully he lives and it'll be easier. When the medics or whoever comes, I'll tell them some kids came in from the party, jumped us. I didn't get a good look at them since I came in just as they were leaving. Wait, Brandon is a righty, right? Use your left hand."

I stare at him incredulously. He can't be serious, and yet he is. He bends down a bit to give me easier access to his face and points at himself. "Come on, Siena, we've only got a few minutes here."

"I can't hit you!"

"Do it!"

"I can't!"

"Do it!"

"But Jason—"

"Hit me now!"

I do it. I swing my left hand with all my might, aiming for his face, and my bones vibrate all the way down my arm when my fist connects with his cheek.

"Ow!" I exclaim, cradling my hand to my chest. My hand stings, but Jason only blinks at me. He didn't even move when I hit him.

"Fuck, you're not going to leave a big enough bruise, it won't be believable."

Brandon groans from where he is on the floor, but he doesn't get up or move. It's another sign that he's going to pull through.

Jason looks back at me and is going to say something when his phone rings. He pulls it out, and shows me the caller ID.

The hotter twin.

"You can't," I tell Jason when I read his mind.

"I trust him with my life," Jason says, and when I don't stop him again, he answers the phone.

"Come to room 114. Right now. Alone. Tell no one. Hurry."

He hangs up without waiting for confirmation and goes back to check on Brandon. I'm assuming the 911 operator didn't give him any special instructions other than to not pull the glass and to wait, because he's not doing anything differently.

Not even a full minute after Jason hung up the phone, the door swings open, and Jackson freezes in the doorway, looking at Jason bent over Brandon's body.

Jackson's eyes pop out of his head. He checks the empty outdoor hall behind him before entering the room, closing and locking the door behind him.

"Fucking *fuck*! Not again!"

What does he mean *again*? Jason said the same thing.

"Well," Jackson says, calmer this time as Jason stands up. "At least you technically called me this time, if a little late."

Jason strides over to his twin. "He's alive. We don't have a lot of time. Hit me. With your left."

Before I can blink, Jackson punches his brother right in the face. I gasp, not expecting the lack of hesitation on Jackson's part at all.

Jason stumbles and straightens himself. "Again. Harder."

"It's my left, cut me some slack," Jackson mumbles, and this time I close my eyes so as to not see it, but I hear it a few times, and it sounds terrible.

"Okay, that's good," Jason orders, and I open my eyes

to see him stumble a bit but straighten up. Jason's other eye, the one that wasn't already healing, is now swelling up, and his lip is split. He rips the side of his shirt from the collar a couple inches and walks into the bathroom, while Jackson starts knocking stuff around in the room.

"What are you doing?" I ask, still in shock.

He pauses for a moment. "I'm assuming there was a fight, and we didn't see whoever it was until the tail end when Jason walked in, right?"

I blink at him. Twin connection is scary.

When I don't say anything to disagree with his theory, he resumes messing up the room.

Before I can decide one way or another what to do, Jason returns to the room. His knuckles are red, like Jackson's.

"What happened?"

"I punched the sink, not hard though. It's gotta be believable. I would've got one or two punches in."

I don't even say anything. Everything's happening so fast I swear the room is spinning. It hasn't even been a full five minutes since I arrived here, and it feels like so much has happened.

"Where's his phone?" Jason asks. I find it on the nightstand and grab it as Jason approaches me, looking into my eyes meaningfully. "Go get cleaned up. You saw nothing here, okay? Try to act normal."

"But I don't want to leave you," I whisper.

"I'll be fine, I promise," he says, but it's a lie because he can't guarantee that. No one can.

He plucks the phone from my shaking hands and turns it off, then gives it back to me. "This was stolen in the fight. Get rid of it. Now go."

I clutch the phone, wishing it was his hand. This was a lot easier when it was just me taking the fall for Gia, but now that it's Jason doing it for me, it feels impossible. I can't leave him here. I don't want to.

"We can say I walked in . . . I saw the people who attacked him . . ." I try weakly, but he shakes his head at me, his eyes softening.

"I want you as far away from here as possible. Let me handle it, okay?"

No. No, it's not okay. A tear races down my cheek, and I quickly wipe it away.

Jason's voice is a hoarse whisper when he says, "Let me do this for you. Go, please."

"I'll stay," Jackson declares from behind me. "Hit me."

"Don't be stupid," Jason says. "Me and Brandon not being able to take out some kids trying to jump us is already sketchy, but me and you losing a fight? That's downright implausible. Get out of here. Take Siena."

Jackson sighs. "If Brandon dies, Aiden is going to be pissed."

Jason gives him a stern look. "Aiden doesn't need to know anything until he absolutely has to know."

Jackson raises his hands. "Fine. Fine. Text me updates if you can, okay?"

Jason nods, and I stand there, frozen to the spot, staring

at Jason in awe as he goes back to check on Brandon. He's really going to do this for me, for Gia.

"Come on, Siena." Jackson gently grabs my arm, and I allow him to pull me from the room.

I can't say anything over the lump in my throat, but I stare at Jason, hoping my eyes can say everything I'm not able to. He knew I was terrified, knew I didn't want to take the blame for this but would for Gia, and he's taking that burden from me. I'd never ask him to do that, never expect him to and never want him to, but here he is, doing exactly that.

Jason catches my eye, and the emotion in the room is too thick for me to decipher, but he nods once at me just before I'm pulled from his line of sight.

"Let's go, Siena," Jackson orders, closing the door behind him and grabbing my hand. The fresh night air hits me as soon as we're outside, but for once, I don't want to be outside in the fresh air, I want to be back in that room, with Jason. But I don't get a chance to make that choice, because Jackson pulls me down the hall and toward the main part of the party, where people are still hanging out, drinking and smoking. I allow Jackson to pull me, unable to really see anything clearly. I can't even hear the music over the rushing in my ears, but I swear I hear sirens.

eighteen

Jackson pulls me into some random room in the middle of the party where people are lounging around, drinking, and they've even set up a game of flip cup on the TV stand. They look over at us for intruding, even though the door was wide open, welcoming anyone in.

"Hey Jackson!" some people yell, calling him over to join whatever drinking game they're playing.

"Yeah, hi," he greets briskly, pulling me through the room as my numb legs try to keep up with him. "Using the washroom."

There's a chorus of *ooohhh*s and some catcalls as they

realize he's bringing me into the washroom with him, but we ignore them. He closes the door, shutting us off from the curious drunk eyes and the loud EDM music pumping through this room.

He turns on the faucet and gestures at the running water. "You have some blood on your hands, so get cleaned up."

I hold my hands up and stare at them. I didn't realize there was a streak of blood on my fingertips; I didn't think I'd gotten that close to Brandon.

I shove my hands under the water and scrub my fingers with soap, splashing the cold water on my face too.

I move out of the way so Jackson can wash his hands too, and stare at his profile. He's Jason's identical twin; he should look just like him, but he doesn't. Jackson's hair is a bit longer, a bit more sun-streaked. His blue eyes are less intense, his smile doesn't hold the same weight as Jason's, and I don't feel that same spark and butterflies as I do when I'm with Jason. His presence doesn't calm me, doesn't make me feel at ease when everything around me is falling apart. And it hits me that most importantly, I'm in here with Jackson, when I should be there with Jason.

"Holy shit," I breathe. "What have we done? I can't let Jason do this for Gia!"

Jackson stops me from leaving the bathroom. I try moving around him, but he blocks the door with his large body. "Stop, Siena. He's not doing this for Gia; he's doing it for you."

"That's worse! What's wrong with me? If they don't buy his story, he could be charged with assault! And if Brandon dies, murder!"

"Well, technically it would be manslaughter since it was an accident. But then again, he did very publicly get in a fight with Brandon on Monday, so a motivated prosecutor could probably connect the two for a second-degree murder charge and—"

"Jackson! That's not helping!"

He raises his hands. "Sorry, just being practical."

I pace the small bathroom, his eyes tracking me as I take two steps in either direction. "No, I can't do this. I shouldn't have put Jason in this situation. It should be me."

I try to sidestep Jackson, but he blocks me again. "Siena, it's too late, what's done is done."

I stare at him incredulously. He loves his brother, I know that, and he's completely cool with letting him cover for me? A girl Jackson barely even knows?

"Why aren't you more concerned?"

Jackson shrugs. "Jason will be all right. He's a very convincing liar, and he's good at keeping his cool, especially when it comes to murder."

I eye him. "Why does it seem like you guys have done this before?"

Jackson's about to say something, then snaps his mouth shut. "That's a story for another day, when Jason's ready to tell you. The point is, you didn't ask him to do this. Jason *wanted* to do this for you. So let him. Let him worry about

Brandon instead of worrying about you, and you worry about Gia."

I don't know what that means, but Jackson's confidence makes me feel more reassured that this entire thing isn't going to go to shit. And *Gia*. She's here somewhere, freaking out. Jackson's right—I need to find her.

"He has it under control," Jackson repeats, as if trying to drive the point home.

I nod, trying to calm my breathing. If there was ever a time I wished I could talk to Anusha, it would be now, at least, if I was able to be completely honest with her and if she wasn't conspiring to send me away.

After a few deep breaths, my heart rate is somewhat under control, and my vision feels less hazy.

"Okay?" Jackson asks, scanning my face.

"Yeah, I'm fine."

He doesn't move for a moment, like he's deciding whether or not to believe that I'm not going to bolt back to Jason, then opens the door.

"Follow my lead," he whispers before exiting the bathroom, and I trail after him.

"Hey guys." Jackson joins the group of kids in the room. He points at the open door, with a direct view of the parking lot. "Did you see that group of kids in sweaters running out of here like there was a fire ten minutes ago? What the hell was that about?"

The group of mostly drunk people, some of whom I recognize from various classes, glance at each other.

Jackson subtly elbows me in the arm, and I get the hint. "Yeah. Black sweaters, right?"

One guy, I think he's in my social studies class, says, "Oh, yeah, I think I saw that! Like ten minutes ago. One guy was wearing camo."

"Yeah! That group!" Jackson exclaims, taking a beer someone offers him, I guess trying to blend in.

The guy who offered him the beer says, "Oh yeah! They ran out of here so fast!"

The group of kids nod at each other, saying things in agreement.

Jackson takes a sip of his beer. "So weird. I didn't recognize any of them from school. I wonder where they were going. They looked like they were trouble."

One of the girls shrugs. "Who knows, probably crashed the party and got caught. Probably from Commack Silver, jealous they lost the big game today and starting problems."

"Yeah, probably," Jackson agrees, and the group starts talking among themselves about how much they hate that kids from Commack crashed the party. They tell other kids about it too when they enter the room.

Jackson grabs my arm and discreetly pulls me from the room.

Once we're outside, I turn to Jackson. "How did you do that?"

He shrugs. "You know how fast rumors start and get embellished. Plus, it's easy to convince people they saw something they didn't. Easier when they're drunk. Let's do it one more time to one more group. One guy in camo, others in black sweaters, probably from Commack, maybe pissed because they lost the game. Brandon's the quarterback, maybe we can spin something about that too."

I blink at him. He thought of that so quickly, and casually manipulated an entire room of people into believing something that didn't happen with no problem. "Who are you?"

"I thought you could tell the difference between me and Jason." At my glare, he adds, "I'm joking! I know what you meant. Come on, let's go."

Until now, my back was to the parking lot, and when I turn, I spot an ambulance pulling out. They must already have Brandon in there and are going to the hospital. They pass a police car, which pulls into the lot, and two officers get out.

I suck in a breath, watching them walk to the end of the hotel. Other kids notice them, hiding alcohol and beer bottles or ducking into rooms, but the officers don't pay any attention to them. Jackson puts his hand on my back. "It's okay, the sirens aren't on, so I don't think they're arresting Jason."

"Is that a real thing?"

"Probably. Come on, let's plant those memories once more, then find Gia."

He guides me away and into another even more crowded room, upstairs this time, but I keep looking back, trying to see if they'll pull Jason out of the room in handcuffs.

I lose sight once I'm fully in the room, and Jackson works his magic again, even better than in the first room, because people leave and tell others about those asshole Silvers who hate football players and came here looking for a fight. It's almost scary how easily those rumors spread, how easily this becomes a fact.

But then someone says something that makes my blood run cold. "I wonder if anyone's looked into those Silvers for Lily's disappearance."

I tune out the rest of what they're saying, because I know that Brandon was involved someway, somehow, and if something happens to him, we'll never know.

I tug Jackson out of the room and into a quieter section of the outdoor hall. The music is still blaring from everywhere, even though there's a cop car in the parking lot. Most people don't seem to care, or they just haven't noticed, as the party goes on like normal.

"Brandon attacked Gia. He forced himself on me. I'm seeing a pattern here that must prove he's involved in Lily's disappearance!"

Jackson's eyes widen, and he pulls me over into the shadows between rooms for more privacy. I realize Jason must not have told him anything about my theory on Brandon, or what had happened to me at his house.

"He was saying horrible stuff about Lily when I went through his phone!"

"What? When did you go through his phone?"

"It doesn't matter, but last time we didn't get to go

through everything to find the proof we need. But he did it. I know he did. This just proves it." I pull out the phone Jason gave me, and Jackson frantically checks around us.

"Put that away before someone sees!"

I lower it so it's less visible. "I'm holding actual evidence about what happened to Lily!"

I can't question Brandon, but I have the next best thing, right here in my hands, with uninterrupted time to go through it.

When I turn it on, Jackson hisses, "It's also *actual* evidence of the crime we just committed! I don't think you're supposed to turn that on."

Maybe, maybe not. But I can't have this phone and *not* try to look through it for answers. "Just for a second to find what we're looking for."

The phone lights up and asks for a passcode. I type in the one from the Tracks—6, 2, 6, 4—but it says incorrect. I try a few more times because I'm certain I remembered the passcode right, but it doesn't open. He must have changed it.

"Jackson!" a voice calls, and I shove the phone into my pocket as Tyler approaches us. He seems out of breath, like he ran all the way here. "Jason's being led away by some cops!"

"What?" Jackson and I exclaim together, and Tyler points to the parking lot.

We run over to the railing overlooking the parking lot, nudging our way through the crowd of people who are already watching. A small part of me was holding on to the hope that Tyler was mistaken and it wasn't Jason being arrested, but it is. He really is handcuffed, and like the last time he was handcuffed and led to the back of a police car for me, I feel like I've been punched in the gut. Hard.

Somehow, his eyes find mine in the crowd, and he pins me with a look. I have no idea what it means, but I freeze on the spot, watching helplessly as he's guided into the car.

Gia appears at my side, squeezing through the crowd of people to get to me. "What's going on?" She's cleaned up her makeup pretty well, you can't tell she was crying not even twenty minutes ago.

"I don't know," I say honestly, watching as the officer closes the door on Jason. His eyes shift from me to Jackson beside me, and Jason shakes his head at him just once.

Jackson seems to understand what it means through their twin telepathy or something, because he nods at him. The officers get in the car, and Jason's eyes meet mine once more. I wish I could say something to him, which I could hold him, wish I knew what was going on.

Like he senses my inner turmoil and wants to reassure me, he gives me a small smile that doesn't reassure me at all, and then the car pulls away and he's gone.

nineteen

I didn't want to stay at the party anymore. We hung around for a bit, because there was another officer poking around, asking generic questions like, "Did you see anything suspicious?"

Jackson told me to do what Jason said, and say I didn't see anything, so that's what I did when it was my turn to be questioned. I'm not sure what Jackson said, because I was too busy trying to look innocent and hide Gia so she wasn't asked any questions. Not everyone was questioned, only some people, and once the officer left, Jackson drove me and Gia home. He told us he'd send Aiden's friends Julian and Chase to pick up Jason's car with the spare key at home, since they were in town, while he went to the station to figure out what was going on. I wanted to come, obviously, but he said Jason would want me to go home and make sure Gia's okay and to act normal, and after some coaxing, that's what I do.

Dario's waiting for us when we walk inside, welcoming us with his arms crossed over his chest and a disapproving frown.

"You were grounded until Monday," he tells me.

"I know."

He glances at Gia, who's quiet behind me, then says to me, "You dragged her to another party?"

I open my mouth to lie, but Gia speaks up. "I needed help . . . girl problems! So I called her to come, but she doesn't drive, so she asked Jackson . . ."

Dario's silent, eyes shifting between the two of us before he shakes his head and mumbles, "Now she's got her to take the blame for her too, just like Florence would," then turns and goes up the stairs to bed.

Gia and I stand there for a few moments before she heads up the stairs without looking at me and gently locks herself in the hall bathroom. I hear the shower run shortly after from my place in the front hall. There's no way I can go upstairs and lie in bed and pretend everything is fine. Instead, I go outside, not even stopping to put on shoes, just wanting the fresh air.

I sit on the front steps, looking out at the quiet street

with my phone in my hand, waiting for an update. I'm not used to being on this side of things, sitting and waiting for answers about someone you care about and not knowing what's happening or how to help them. Is this how Gia felt when I was first arrested?

A police car pulls onto the street, and my heart hammers in my chest. Are they coming for Gia?

But then the car pulls into the neighbor's driveway and the engine shuts off. Officer Liu steps out of the car, somehow seeing me sitting in the dark on my porch on the opposite side of the house from him.

"Heard your boyfriend was dragged through the station in handcuffs tonight," he says in greeting. "You sure do work quickly to drag down everyone around you. Just like you did to my Lily."

I don't acknowledge him, and when it's clear I'm not giving him the reaction he's looking for, he locks the car and goes inside. I hear his front door slam, and my shoulders sag.

You're going to be my undoing, Siena Amato, I already know it, Jason had said so long ago. I thought getting him arrested the first time was the worst it would get, but clearly not.

I shiver as the wind picks up. It's not warm enough to be sitting out here in the dark, but I can't go inside; it would feel like a betrayal if I did. Jason's stuck inside a police station so I can enjoy the fresh air, and I'm not going to let that act be in vain. So I'll sit out here all night and day if I have to, in the cold, listening to the cicadas, waiting for an update.

I'm not sure how much time passes, but eventually the door behind me opens, and Gia drops down beside me on the porch step.

She looks straight ahead. "Have you heard anything from Jason?"

I unlock my phone and stare at the message app for the millionth time tonight, and it shows no new notifications. "No."

We sit in silence for a moment, neither of us looking at each other, when she whispers, "That could've been you in the back of the cop car."

"Yeah," I say, my voice feeling raw.

"It should've been me."

"Gia . . ."

"Before Jason did what he did, you were going to sacrifice yourself for me. Again." She looks at me now, her eyes red rimmed. "Even after all the shitty things I said and did to you since you got here, you didn't even hesitate."

"You're my sister, Gia."

She shakes her head. "I'm a shitty sister—no, Siena, let me finish." I close my mouth and listen as she says, "I was terrified. I meant it when I begged you to do something, and some part of me knew that you'd take the blame for me, I *knew* it, and I still asked you anyway. I'm selfish enough to let you take the fall for me, again, then be angry at you for not wanting me to do illegal shit."

She rubs her eye, though she's not crying. I want to say something to comfort her, but there's a thickness in my throat that makes it impossible to talk.

"I felt bad that I made you take the blame the first time," she continues, "but I hated that I didn't regret it, hated that I wouldn't do it any differently. That makes me a terrible person, doesn't it?"

"It makes you human, Gia," I say softly.

She wraps her arms around herself. "I've been causing nothing but trouble since I got here, and Dad's blaming it on you."

I fall silent. I never told her what Dario said to me about my behavior, never told her he threatened to send me away.

"I heard him talking to Zia Stella that night you were suspended, heard what he said about you and Mom. She told him he was a dick."

I'm surprised that Zia Stella said that. We've both been working a lot, and we haven't had a chance to talk since that day. I thought she had written me off.

Gia's jaw works. "I used to be jealous of you, because you look so much like Mom. You have that connection with her that I'll never have, and I was jealous that you're the one that gets to be most like her. But since LA, I've known that's not true. *I'm* the one that's like Mom, and I hate it."

"Gia . . . what happened tonight . . . it's not your fault. You were protecting yourself."

"I shouldn't have been there. You were right."

My molars grind together. I've always hated Brandon,

and even though I hope he recovers, I especially hate him right now. "Just because you were at a party doesn't give him the right to force himself on you. You did nothing wrong, Gia, and I'm sorry this happened to you."

"But you've been telling me not to go to parties."

I search for the words, trying to figure out how to balance the facts and advice. "You're still young, Gia, just enjoy being young. Get good grades. Join extracurriculars. Figure out what you want with your future now that we have a real shot at succeeding here. You'll have plenty of time to go to parties. Will they always be the safest places? No. That's just the shitty reality of being a girl. It sucks and I hate it but it's true. We'll always have to watch our backs, and I just want you to enjoy doing things you really want before you grow up and every invite becomes one party or another. You have lots of time to party, and there's a time and a place for it. But the illegal shit and stupid shit like drinking and driving is really dangerous, Gia. You're better than that."

As Gia absorbs my words, we sit in comfortable silence. Then she says softly, "I'm sorry for being such a bitch."

I shift closer to her and put my arm around her tiny shoulders. She leans into me, resting her head on my inner shoulder.

"I'm sorry for being so tough on you."

I was upset that Gia was acting rudely toward me, but never upset *at her*. I know she's processing everything in her own way, and maybe it would've been better if I hadn't taken the blame for her with Stan. Maybe then she'd have

Anusha and she'd be able to work through her feelings and emotions about what happened. Maybe that would've helped her, but my covering for her took that chance away. But then again, I know Gia, and she would've crumpled in jail. I saw girls like Gia, girls who were so young and full of life, and by the time I left, they were completely changed, just a shell of their former selves. I never want that for Gia, and she just admitted to me that she doesn't want that either. So, would it help her to talk honestly with her therapist about what happened? Maybe. But would I be arrested in her place again? Absolutely. Besides, we can't take back what's already happened, and no good will come from admitting to it now; all we can do is move forward, and I'll have to do the same with what happened tonight with Jason.

"I—I know I don't always act like it," Gia starts, sniffling, "but I need you, Siena. If I didn't have you . . ."

"I know, Gia," I finish for her when she gets choked up. "I feel the same way."

She snuggles closer to me, and I hold her. Gia's always larger than life; it's easy to forget that she's only fifteen, that she's still trying to figure out who she is and what she wants in life, and she's doing all that without any parents.

We sit like that for a while, until I'm sure she's fallen asleep, but then she murmurs, "I love you, Siena."

My heart cracks wide open. "I love you too, Gia. Go in and get some sleep."

She sits up. Her hair is sticking up all over the place, but she still looks beautiful. She rubs her eyes and stands up, pouting at me. "How long are you going to sit out here?"

"I don't know," I tell her honestly, checking my phone again. Still nothing.

"Okay," she says, seeming to know I'll sit out here as long as it takes. "Let me know what happens. And . . . thank Jason for me, when you see him."

"Sure, Gia. Good night."

She disappears inside, and comes back with a blanket, wrapping it around my shoulders before kissing my cheek and heading inside again. The gesture is touching and warms me just as much as the furry blanket does.

It's almost 2:00 a.m., and I check my phone again. Nothing. I click on my conversation with Jason and read the last text I sent him, from when we got home. I'll be waiting up for as long as it takes.

I want to message him again, but I know he'll be in contact with me as soon as he can.

So instead, I just sit and wait, thinking about nothing and everything. I wonder what my mom would do if she were here, what she would say to Gia, what she would say to me.

Eventually, a loud engine echoes up the street, and I stand, the blanket slipping off my shoulders. Jason's car pulls into the driveway, and I've never been happier to see it in my life. It shuts off and Jason steps out of it, his eyes finding me immediately.

"Jason!" I don't wait for him to finish rounding the car,

instead launching myself at him. I wrap my arms and legs around him, and he catches me easily, holding me close.

He's here! He's really here, and not in a jail cell or an interrogation room! I feel like laughing or crying or hitting him for not texting me, but instead, I kiss him.

He urgently presses his lips to mine, possessively, and deepens the kiss, turning it almost frantic, and I match his fervor. I clutch him to me, needing him closer, feeling like he'll never be close enough. Jason's touch, his kiss, is all-consuming, and I lose myself to him, to his touch, to his taste, to the sparks lighting up my body.

We pull apart for air, panting, as I try to get my brain working and my head to stop spinning.

"You're here," I breathe against his lips, running a hand through the back of his hair and touching his face as if to reassure myself he really is here.

Jason kisses me again, quick and passionate, leaving me breathless, then pulls back just far enough to whisper, "I'll always be here."

I shiver against him, and he holds me tighter to him, holding my weight up like it's no problem. Once I've calmed my breathing and my heart no longer feels like it's going to explode, I slide my legs down and Jason releases me to stand on my own.

"You stupid, stupid, wonderful boy!" I shove him, then hug him again. It's hard to process everything I'm feeling. "Are you okay? What happened? And why didn't you call me?"

"I'm fine," he says, brushing my hair behind my ear, and I almost cry, because I thought about that tender action so much when it was a possibility he'd never do it again. "My phone died, and when I got home, I reassured Natalia, got in my car, and came straight here."

Well, that makes me slightly less upset with him.

"What happened? Are you in trouble? Why were you arrested?"

"I wasn't arrested, I was taken to the station for questioning. Apparently, they had to handcuff me as part of procedure." He runs his hands up and down my arms, comforting me as much as keeping me warm. But now that Jason's here, I don't even feel the chill in the air. "I told them that I went to the room to find Brandon when a bunch of kids ran out and took a few swings at me, so I didn't really see much before they ran off."

"Did they believe it?"

"I'm not sure. I'm not under arrest, but I'm pretty sure they can arrest you whenever they want. It doesn't have to be the same day."

They can arrest him whenever? I don't like the sound of that.

Jason gently runs his finger over my bottom lip, pulling it out from where I was worrying it with my teeth. "But apparently they interviewed some kids who didn't run away when the cops came, and some corroborated my story of a group of kids running out around the same time as when I called the ambulance. Someone even said one of them was in camo?"

I can't believe all that worked. "Yeah, your brother orchestrated that. He's either brilliant or a psychopath."

Jason laughs, his hands on my back now. He hasn't stopped touching me in some way since he got here, and I'm loving it. "What did he do?"

I tell him how Jackson planted fake memories, and how people added their own details until everyone shared the story among themselves.

He shakes his head, amazed and amused. "He didn't tell me he did that."

"Well, hopefully it worked . . ." I steel myself to ask the question I've been dreading. "Do you know how Brandon is?"

"I don't. He's in the hospital, that's all I know."

I want him to be okay, though I don't know what's going to happen if he is. Is he going to tell everyone Gia tried to kill him? Get her charged with attempted murder? Get Jason charged with aiding and abetting? Interfering with a crime? And if he doesn't make it, that makes everything ten times worse . . .

"You didn't have to do that for me, Jason."

"I wanted to."

His words go straight to my heart, and I feel the warmth of them all the way to my toes. "But you shouldn't have," I whisper.

Jason lowers his head, pinning me with the intensity in his eyes. "But I did."

I force myself to look away from him before I go and

blurt out something stupid that I'm not sure either of us is ready to hear yet.

"So, what now?" I say instead.

"Now? We act normal, and for continuity's sake, you didn't see anything at the party. Act like you normally would at school on Monday."

I frown, and Jason holds me closer, continuing, "I don't know what's going to happen tomorrow, or even next week, but we'll deal with it, together."

I've never had that before, never had another person to lean on, to solve problems with. I already knew I could trust Jason, and tonight has only reaffirmed that. Jason is here, with me, through the good and the bad, and he's the only person who's really made me feel like I'm not alone.

"I like the sound of that," I tell him, and he kisses me again, like he'll never get tired of it. I know that I never will.

epilogue

I try to do what Jason says and act normal Saturday and Sunday. Gia and I occupy ourselves with movie marathons and mani-pedis, and we even follow a workout video—anything to distract ourselves and kill time. Dario has a work conference, so we're left to our own devices, which suits us perfectly.

Before I know it, it's Monday morning, and I'm sitting in my regular seat in homeroom English, staring at the empty seat in front of me, the one normally occupied by Brandon.

I don't know how he is. Gia didn't want to text Brianna

to ask, and I think it's because she was too scared to find out the answer herself. So now I sit in class, alternating between looking at his seat longingly and at the door, as if he'll waltz through at any moment, make some stupid comment to his friends, then pointedly ignore me as he takes his seat, as we've been doing for weeks now. But when the bell rings and there's still no sign of Brandon, it's clear he's not coming. I wonder how he is, if he's woken up, if he's okay, if he remembers anything.

"All right, class," Mr. Lewis says from his desk. "Let's open—"

The door dramatically swings open, causing the whole class to look over at it. My heart stops.

Brandon's there, looking as large and imposing as ever. He doesn't look like he just spent the weekend in a hospital. The only signs that something happened are the traces of bruising from his fight with Jason last week. His head isn't even wrapped in gauze.

I stare at him with wide eyes as he walks to the front of the class. He looks angry and menacing, and even though he's not doing anything specifically threatening, I still feel uneasy.

"What's up, assholes?" he announces to the class from the front of the room. "You miss me?" His eyes land on mine, and his tone changes when he says, "Because I've missed you."

Acknowledgments

As always, thank you to you, the reader. You've made this dream possible. Thank you to everyone who's promoted, reviewed, read, and shared this story. It means the world to me.

Thank you to everyone on the Wattpad Books team, from marketing to production to everyone in between. I super appreciate all the work you do.

Thank you to Deanna McFadden for believing in me and my stories and being awesome in general. Thank you to Fiona Simpson for being the absolute best in more ways than one. Thank you for fighting for my stories, being an editor extraordinaire, and being my go-to for pretty much everything. And thank you to Dana for copyediting.

Thanks to Austin and I-Yana for being the best talent managers out there.

Thank you to my parents, Bruno and Carmela, for being the most supportive parents I could ever wish for. You're the best proofreader there is, Mom. Thank you to all my zias, zios, grandparents, cousins, neighbors, and friends for supporting me and my stories.

Thank you to my boyfriend Mario, who's definitely won the boyfriend/number one fan of the year award. And thank you to his family for being so incredibly supportive and encouraging.

To my friends Jordan, SJ, Ken, Sydni, and Lauren—you guys are awesome. And to my friends Rodney, Deb, Mason, Ava, Van, Andi, and Ami—thanks for not only being amazing friends, but for keeping me sane and sprinting with me. I wouldn't have finished this book without all those long nights.

I'm also going to be that person and thank my dog, Leo. He sat on my lap from sunup to bedtime as I wrote this story. You're a good boy.

about the author

Jessica Cunsolo's young adult series, With Me, has amassed over 140 million reads on Wattpad since she posted her first story, *She's With Me*, on the platform in 2015. It has won a Watty award, been published in multiple languages, and is in development with Wattpad WEBTOON Studios. Jessica lives just outside of Toronto, where she enjoys the outdoors and transforming her real-life awkward situations into plotlines for her viral stories. You can find her on Instagram @jesscunsolo, on Twitter @avaviolet17, or on Wattpad @avaviolet.

Meet the original Parker brother, Aiden,
in Jessica Cunsolo's debut novel,

She's With Me

Available now, wherever books are sold.

1

I've always suffered from this horribly disadvantageous condition—it's called being directionally challenged. It's self-diagnosed of course, but I'm almost positive it's an actual thing, so it's not really my fault that I'm having trouble navigating this maze known as King City High School.

The warning bell rings and animal-like students scramble from their assembled groups and lockers and head to class. Shit. I'm going to be late and I still have no idea where my first class is. It doesn't help that I can only walk so fast since I hurt myself a few weeks back, and that injury is still healing.

When I got here this morning, the curt secretary sent me off with no more than a map and dismissive "Good luck." Starting a new school a month and a half into first semester is hard enough—having my face planted in a map would just scream *New girl, eat me alive!*, not to mention trash my plan to get through senior year without drawing too much attention to myself. Not that I'd be able to read the map anyway. As I said: directionally challenged.

Pulling out my schedule again, I see that the name printed at the top reads *Amelia Collins*. It's a pretty name this time, but it'll still take some getting used to.

I reread the room number that I've already committed to memory, as if reading it again might magically transport me to it. Glancing at my brand new cell phone, I huff out an aggravated breath as I realize I only have five minutes to get to class before I'm late.

"Screw it," I mutter as I rush aimlessly down the hall while searching my shoulder bag for the school map—I really hate being late.

Not really paying attention to where I'm going, I'm blindsided by a group of giant walking trees slash teenage boys. They're talking and joking among themselves—walking through the halls as if they own the whole school. Without slowing down, I hug close to one wall, and reach into my bag to grab my map. Instantly, I'm thrown back as I collide with an outcrop of bricks, stopping just short of falling on my butt. Who designs a stupid wall to stick out like that?

My belongings have poured out everywhere, and I grab them hastily before quickly turning around, only to come face to face with something both hard and human, if the colorful curses are any indication. My stuff crashes onto the floor again as the pain in my ribs intensifies.

Great. Just freaking great.

"Are you blind? Can't you see I was walking here?" a voice growls.

My eyes meet the agitated gray ones of the most breathtakingly gorgeous guy I have ever seen. He's a member of the walking trees I saw before—tall with broad shoulders, a scowl plastered on his face.

His attitude sucks. He was equally at fault, if not more, since the skyscrapers had to walk in a horizontal line in the hall, but I seriously don't want to draw any more attention to myself.

"I am so sorry." I apologize as we bend down to retrieve our belongings.

"Is your brain not able to communicate to your legs where you can and can't walk? If you didn't notice, there was someone in front of you, which means you move out of their way," he shoots back as he stands up with his binder.

A small crowd is gathered around us, clearly interested in seeing the poor girl stupid enough to incur the wrath of this intolerant jerk.

Think first, Amelia. Don't say something stupid. You're supposed to keep your head down and get through the year unnoticed.

"Sorry. I'm new and really don't know where I'm going." I stand up with my now-collected belongings and push my strawberry blond hair out of my face. "You wouldn't happen to know where room 341 is, would you?"

"You're new, not blind. Don't use excuses to cover up your stupidity. Get out of my sight while I'm still being nice," he scoffs, and runs a hand through his blond hair.

This is him being nice? Bemused faces of the other walking trees and the larger assembling crowd surround me, and I'm doing the exact opposite of blending in. Not wanting to stand out any more, I contain my anger and don't even glance at him as I stride by.

"Oh look, she does have some good ideas in that otherwise useless brain of hers," I hear him say to his friends, like being a jerk is part of his genetic build.

That's it. I turn and walk back to him, looking straight up and into his gray eyes with my narrowed hazel ones.

"Oh, I guess her brain is a hundred percent useless after all," he says to his friends.

He bends down to match my full height, three inches taller than usual thanks to my gorgeous tan wedges, and looks me straight in the eyes, talking as though he was speaking to a toddler.

"Do you need me to draw you a map of how to get the *fuck* out of my face?" he slowly asks, putting emphasis on the curse.

"No, thank you," I say evenly and calmly. "But I can draw you a map, so when I tell you to go to hell, you'll know exactly where to go."

Everyone standing in the now-crowded hall takes an audible

inhale and stops breathing as they absorb the scene. By the looks of this stunned blond asshole and his friends, it seems like no one has ever said anything that daring to him before.

He gets up really close to my face and growls, "Now you listen to me, you little—"

"No, you listen to me asshole," I say calmly. "First of all, get out of my face, your breath stinks from all the crap that spews out of your mouth. Second, your dick belongs to your body, not in your personality,"—I push him out of my personal space— "so I suggest you pull your head out of your ass and realize that you're not the only person in the damn school. Maybe if you and your walking skyscrapers didn't bulldoze down the hall in a straight line people wouldn't have to dive out of your path to avoid destruction. I'm sorry if someone pissed in your Froot Loops this morning, but please do us all a favor and check your issues at the door. Finding a hobby or going to group therapy could really help you with your social problems. So thanks for the friendly welcome to your school, but I'd like to get to class now."

The hallway is hushed still and quiet. Blondie looks completely stupefied.

His friends are laughing—like, out-of-breath-gasping-for-air cackling. These other mountains are all just as breathtakingly gorgeous as asshole number one. The late bell rings. Great. I'm late for class.

Confident that my point was made and this jerk face was properly put in his place, I spin on my heel so my hair hits him on the shoulder and walk through the parting crowd, leaving him steaming.

"Oh my God, she so told you, Aiden! That was *hilarious!*" one of his gorgeous friends says through bursts of laughter.

So, the jerk's name is Aiden. It's a shame really that such a pretty name and face is wasted on such an ugly personality. So much for going unnoticed; I have a feeling everyone is going to have something to say about me after this. Well, at least I look cute in my skirt and heels.

Now that the entertainment is over, the crowd departs. As I strut down the hallway and turn a corner, I realize that I still have no idea where the hell I'm going. Taking a minute to collect myself, I check to see if maybe there's someone left who might know where to find my classroom.

Anxious at the best of times, hearing rather large and determined footsteps stomping behind me catches me off guard, and then I'm suddenly turned around and hoisted up and over Aiden's shoulder. With my face planted firmly against his back, my butt in the air over his shoulder, and my bag hooked through his arm, he takes off down the hallway.

"What the hell are you doing? Put me down right now!" I yell.

Aiden's stride doesn't slow, and he chuckles beneath me, the bastard. I strain my neck to see the bemused faces of two of the three gorgeous tree friends who were with him in the hall.

"Can't you two talk some sense into him?!"

"Sorry, babe," the one with short brown hair and chocolate-colored eyes yells back at me with a grin of thorough amusement. "Skyscrapers aren't much for talking."

I can't help but see that Aiden really does have a very nice back. His muscles are noticeable under his tight, but not too tight, plain black T-shirt. We round a corner and I'm met by the curious gazes of some people still in the halls—they clearly have no desire to help me either.

Pain shoots through the left side of my chest. Shit. Running into the wall, followed by the very muscular Aiden hoisting me up, coupled with this uncomfortable position is not good. The pain spreads. I have to get down before I make things worse.

"Listen, bud. I'm sorry about what I said before," I lie. "But kidnapping people is not the way to deal with your problems."

He adjusts my body, causing a burst of pain in my ribs. Without even slowing his pace, he runs up a flight of stairs. Man, this guy is like the Energizer Bunny, not even tiring once. I'm having trouble breathing. "Please," I gasp. "Put me down and we can talk this out."

He ignores me and continues his unwavering stride.

"Can you just let me go gentl—"

Aiden abruptly stops moving and deposits me on the floor.

I look up at him, the wind knocked out of me. The left side of my ribs are on fire—yup, I hurt them again.

"Room 341," he says, dropping my bag beside me and turning to leave the now-deserted hallway.

Dazed, I try to get up but pain shoots up my left side, forcing me back down to the floor. This isn't going to end well. Determined not to lie on this gross floor a second longer, I try again, but the pain spreads through my chest. Sprawled on the floor, I'm incapable of moving. Damn it. Looks like this isn't going to be my first day after all.

I've hurt my ribs three times now, which is less than ideal. Reaching into my bag beside me, I fish around for my phone and pull it out. My mom ignores my first call. Typical. The second time she answers on the third ring. "Hello? Haile—I mean Amelia?"

"Hey. I think I hurt my ribs again. I'm going to drive myself to the hospital. I'm only letting you know so you don't freak out and think the worst when the school calls saying I didn't show up for class even though I was here today," I say from my position on the floor.

She sighs as if she's wondering how I managed to screw up on my first day of school. "How did that happen? You need to be more careful. He's still out there and this isn't ove—"

"I know. It doesn't matter. I'm just letting you know." Even talking hurts. "I'll call you when I get the—" My voice cuts off when the pain becomes too much.

"Amelia? You can't drive yourself." I try to ignore the hint of annoyance creeping into her tone. "I'll come pick you up from school—I'll be there soon. In the meantime, try not to draw even more attention to yourself."

"Okay, I'll meet you in the parking lot."

Hanging up the phone, I shove it back into my bag. Staring up at the ceiling, I think of the most logical way of getting up.

"Okay, Amelia. You have three broken and two bruised ribs healing—you got through it the first time, you can do it again." I psych myself up.

Bending my legs at the knees, I pull off my heels and shove them into my bag. Before I can change my mind, I quickly roll from my right side onto my stomach, careful to avoid making my left side touch anything.

With my arm through the strap of my shoulder bag so I can avoid having to bend down and get it later, I place my arms near my head in push-up position and use my knees at the same time. Getting my feet underneath me, I stand up carefully and lean against the lockers.

"Great, you're up. Now you have to find the damn exit from this maze-school," I say to myself.

I'm trying to get my bearings when my eyes lock with a pair of familiar chocolate-brown ones. Shit. How long has he been here? Aiden's brown-haired friend who remembered my skyscraper line is standing beside an open locker, staring at me. The dirty blond-haired member of the walking trees is beside him, eyes wide and unblinking. Swallowing my pride and refusing to show weakness, I break my gaze and walk in the opposite direction.

"The exit's the other way." A hesitant voice calls from behind me—it's the dirty blond.

Damn broken internal compass.

"How much did you see?" I ask as I make my way toward them.

"Well, pretty much everything since Aiden turned and left you," he answers hesitantly.

Great, so all of it.

"And it didn't occur to either of you to *help the girl lying on the floor in pain?*"

That snaps them out of their stupor. The brown-eyed one quickly closes his locker, and they rush toward me.

"I don't need your help now!" I exclaim, wincing from the pain and causing them to freeze in their tracks.

"Are you sure you don't need our help?" asks the brown-haired one with a smirk.

Cocky bastard, way to kick a girl while she's down. It didn't help that they both look like male models, and now I look like I was dragged through a restaurant's dumpster. I'm about to tell him where to go, but my breathing starts to get worse, and I realize I still didn't even know how to get to the parking lot to meet my mom.

I take a deep breath. "Can you point the way to the parking lot, please?"

"We'll help you there," says the blond.

"Shouldn't you be in class?"

"Nah," he says. "We're in this class with you. It's the most boring thing ever, and this is much more interesting."

"Glad my misery can break up the dull monotony of your day," I say dryly.

"Damn, I didn't mean it like that," he says sheepishly, moving to my left to put my arm over his shoulder as the brunet does the same on my right side.

"*Ow!*" I exclaim to blondie as the pain pulses through my side. "That's the side that hurts, just leave it."

"Shit, sorry," he says as we make our way down the hall painfully slowly, blondie in front and my right arm around the brown-haired model, who is helping me walk.

"Screw this," the guy my arm is slung over mutters. He stops walking and scoops me up bridal style into his tanned, muscled arms, and starts walking again.

"Noah, get her bag and open the doors for us," he says, clearly tired of our slow descent.

Grateful for not being on my feet anymore, I hold my tongue uncharacteristically, too tired and in too much pain to argue. We get to a pair of heavy-looking doors that lead outside to the parking lot. Noah holds them open as we walk through, and I shield my eyes from the sudden blinding sunlight as I look for my mom.

"You can put me down now; my mother should be here soon." He sets me on my feet but keeps an arm around me, making no move to leave. "You don't have to wait with me."

"We can't leave you standing here alone, right?" Noah says, taking a seat on the concrete steps and looking at his friend, who nods in agreement.

"Aren't you guys going to get in trouble for ditching school?" I ask curiously.

"Nah. I'm Mason, by the way." He smiles and helps me sit down on the step. "And you've met Noah. You are?"

"Amelia," I reply.

The ache in my chest hasn't let up, and although I don't want to admit it, I'm kind of glad they're keeping me company.

"You know," Noah starts hesitantly, glancing at me with pale-green eyes, "Aiden's really not a bad guy. He didn't know he'd hurt you."

"If he knew you were healing from broken ribs already, he wouldn't have picked you up. It's just guys fooling around, you know? He'd never intentionally hurt anyone, especially not someone smaller than him."

I really wish they hadn't heard me talking to myself in the hall.

"He seemed perfectly fine tearing an innocent girl to shreds verbally. And from what I can tell, it seems like it's not the first time," I reply.

"He doesn't do it often—he's easily aggravated and having a rough time right now. Plus, he was in a really bad mood this morning, so naturally he snapped at the first thing that gave him a reason—you," Noah says, as if this is a perfectly acceptable excuse.

"Besides, you handled yourself amazingly. Watching you tell him off was by far the best thing I've ever seen." Mason smiles.

"Really?" I ask cautiously.

"Seriously. The drawing him a map to hell? Priceless! And did you see his face when you told him how to fix his problems?" Noah laughs.

"My personal favorite part was when she told him where his dick belongs." Mason winks at me.

"You guys aren't mad at me for what I said?"

"What? The comment about how we're walking skyscrapers that bulldoze down the halls and destroy everything in our path?" Noah asks with a cute smirk.

"Something like that," I murmur.

"Nah, it was funny, plus totally worth seeing someone other than us rip on Aiden. Especially a teensy little girl like you," Mason replies with a chuckle.

"I was getting sick of listening to his bullshit," I say.

"He isn't a bad guy, really." Noah chuckles. "And he'd feel horrible if he knew he's the reason you're going to the hospital right now."

"It's not his fault, I'm not mad at him. Annoyed by his attitude, sure, but I get that he didn't mean to hurt me," I confess. "If my ribs were normal, I would've just gotten up, gone to class, and called him a slew of bad words the next time I saw him in the hall.

"Plus, I'd rather this stay between us," I tell the two gorgeous boys beside me. "No one needs to know about my injuries, okay?"

The boys share a look, and Noah studies me. "How did you break, what was it, three ribs? And bruise another three?"

"Broke three, bruised two," I say, purposely not answering his question.

"Right, so how'd it happen? The classic singing in the shower and then slipping?" Mason jokes.

Memories of that dreadful night make me shiver, and I think about the dead, brown eyes that still haunt me—he's the reason I had to move states, *again*.

"No, honestly, I'm just accident-prone," I say, trying to get them to drop it.

"That must have been a pretty bad klutz moment," Noah chuckles.

My mom pulls up in front of us, sparing me from having to respond. The disapproving look on her face makes me immediately tense. Crap, I should've fought harder to make these boys go to class. I'm going to get a lecture from my mother now. All five foot four of her gets out of the car, and she lifts her sunglasses to the top of her head, pushing back her shoulder-length brown hair as she glares at Mason and Noah. "Thanks for helping her, boys, but I can take it from here. Get back to class."

They look at each other hesitantly, but I reassure them that I'm fine, and thank them for keeping me company.

"Really, Amelia?" my mom says as she tears out of the school parking lot, her fingers tight on the steering wheel.

"It's not what it looks like."

"It better not be. Do you really want to move again?"

I grind my teeth to stop myself from shouting at her. I know. I know all of this. I don't need her to remind me.

"No."

"Then remember what you promised. No boyfriends. No social media. No teams or clubs. You're allowed to go to the gym and practice your jujitsu. I can't stop you from making friends, but you need to be responsible."

We're silent for the rest of the ride to the hospital. I *know* what needs to be done. I have to keep my head down, at all costs.